Rough Prairie Passion

"I think I should be getting back," I said. I stood up and brushed the grass from my buckskins. He stood beside me, a little too close, and I made for the horses. I was surprised he hadn't argued with me or said anything insulting, but when I reached for Thunder, I felt Donnelly take my arm and pull me around to face him. His other arm slid about my waist and tightened to bring me close against his chest. Even as my hands pushed against him, he bowed his head and pressed his lips on mine, catching me off guard and flooding me with a sudden heat. His tongue entered my mouth easily and seemed to touch nerve endings with every move and set off tingling sensations that made my head buzz. I felt the warmth creeping throughout my body and it made me weak.

"Please," I said weakly, "please don't. I wasn't raised this way. I was taught that love was expressed through mutual sharing, not through the rutting of hot-blooded animals. If it can't be beautiful and honorable, I won't have it at all."

He watched me closely as I spoke, his ice-blue eyes giving me no indication of his thoughts. Slowly he wound his fingers in my long black hair and tugged slightly, just enough to tip my face up to his. I began another protest, but he silenced me with a finger over my mouth.

"Think about something," he said. "Even if you find your honorable love, how beautifully can it be expressed without physical desire?" He raked his fingers through my hair, letting the black strands fall slowly away. Then he released me and stepped to his horse.

Love's Savage Destiny

Melissa Bowersock

LEISURE BOOKS **NEW YORK CITY**

A LEISURE BOOK

Published by

Dorchester Publishing Co., Inc.
6 East 39th Street
New York, NY 10016

Printed in the United States of America

Prologue

EARLY ON a beautifully spring day in 1845, Jack Boudry and his fifteen-year-old daughter Jeanette waved good-bye to Mrs. Boudry and their comfortable New York brownstone home. The industrious and adventurous Mr. Boudry had fixed a gleaming eye upon the West—that profitable new frontier brimming with people searching for a marketplace for newfound wealth. As a modest importer, Jack Boudry intended to extend his holdings to include a port on the west coast and be on hand to receive the spoils of the new land.

Mrs. Boudry had declared herself vehemently against the adventure at first, objecting vehemently to her husband's explanations. It wasn't until he made her realize how much their income would be boosted that she relented. But once she learned of his intention to take Jeanette with him she flatly refused to budge. Like a feisty old bird, she sat puffed up and closed-mouthed on the divan while her husband argued and cajoled, pacing in a worried circle around her. Secure in her own territory, she let her silence speak.

This was a new tactic to Jack, who had always been able to gain his wife's acquiescence one way or another. At her stubborn silence, he felt unaccountably at a loss as to how to deal with her on this issue. Finally, though, he resolved to be as stubborn and immovable as she, and went about planning the adventure—including Jeanette—without consulting her further. He wasn't sure in the end if she had thought better of it or had merely been worn down by his relentless planning, but when the day came, she stood sobbing in the doorway while Jeanette took her place on the wagon beside her father.

Jack made the parting as brief as he could. He knew his wife's tears were infectious and resolved to be away before they spread to Jeanette. With waves and assurances and optimistic promises, he slapped his grays into a trot and left his weeping wife on the doorstep.

Father and daughter traveled with several other families west as far as Independence, Missouri. There the wagons regrouped, some going on to Oregon or California, some hanging back to await late comers. Boudry attached himself to a

6

California train that proposed to take the Spanish Trail and together they rumbled westward to Fort Leavenworth. There the daring and danger of the trip seemed to come home to Jeanette and she widened her eyes at the alien territory.

Two days out of Fort Leavenworth the train prepared to stop for the night, but before they could properly organize their defenses, the travelers were aghast to see Indians riding hard upon them. In the dimming twilight they came like ghostly devils from hell, loosing death with every arrow, surrounding the wagons in a fiendish shrieking circle. One quarter of the people lay dead before a single Indian was killed.

Being a shrewd man of action, Jack plunged quickly into the fray, throwing his daughter under a wagon and grabbing a gun in the same motion. While he fired shot after shot, missing every time, his daughter stared dumbstruck at the savages that rode endlessly around them. Hearing her father curse yet another missed shot, she jumped up and ran to his side, wanting to help but not quite sure how.

"Damn!" Jack bellowed. At first Jeanette thought he was cursing her but quickly realized he was out of ammunition. Casting about, she spotted a dangerous looking rifle beside one of the first casualties, a grizzled old scout. Thinking only to help her father, she rushed blindly across the open space to the rifle, her heart thudding so loudly in her ears that she never heard the hoofbeats behind her.

There were so many screams and cries that Jack missed his daughter's. He had found a few more bullets in a forgotten pocket, fired them, then looked about for another weapon. His eyes fell on the rifle, then raised to sight an Indian riding hell bent away from him, apparently struggling with someone. Jack wondered if the brave's horse were not used to so much noise, then saw a small white hand flail out and a flurry of white petticoats. It was then that he realized Jeanette was gone. Forgetting the danger around him, he stood up, frantically looking about for his daughter, calling for her hysterically. The Indian had ridden safely away and had turned his horse about, still grappling with the girl in front of him. An intense rage overcame the importer, blocking out everything around him as he ran crazily after the Indian. Laughing at the ridiculous white man, the Indian reined his horse toward the distant hills. Jack was still running when the savages regrouped and disappeared into the scrub-covered hills, towing their newly stolen horses behind them.

Jack Boudry hung back at Fort Leavenworth for almost two months. He met every returning company at the horseshoe shaped outpost and plied every man with questions, but no one had seen his daughter or her captors since that day. To his face they made optimistic remarks but he knew they shook their heads when they thought he couldn't see. Finally Captain Lewis himself suggested Boudry go on ahead to California before the last wagon passed. Any word would be quickly sent ahead to him.

Jack received no word during the time he was in California and none awaited him at Fort Leavenworth on his return trip the next year. On his return to New York he was able to boast proudly to his wife of the warehouse he had bought in Yerba Buena, but only after they had both cried long and hard over the loss of their daughter. They pushed hope to the back of their minds, waited patiently for any word and went about the business of living their lives and making their fortune.

In 1859 there occurred a gold rush along the Platte River. Any man who had found his fortune in California or any man not willing to travel as far as the west coast hurried eagerly to the Platte. A sudden population boom rocked the area. The outposts became towns and the limit of the frontier was pushed inward again and again. Periodically, inevitably, the gold rushers rallied against the Indians.

It was the misfortune of one small band of Cheyenne to be surprised by one such group of men. The fact that the band was almost entirely made up of women and children did not afford them any saving grace. Most were killed unceremoniously by volleys of gunfire, their lodges burned and their possessions destroyed. The only thing that saved Jeanette Boudry, for she was part of the band, was her tongue. She told her story as quickly as the slaughter around her would allow. Luckily, she was believed. The men came back

9

from their raid triumphant, having killed twenty or more savages and at the same time rescuing a captured white woman and her thirteen-year-old-daughter.

Chapter One

I suppose my room in the New York brownstone hasn't changed much since 1845, at least it didn't in the years I spent there. Before my mother and I were bought back from the wilderness it was only a guest room, not subject to much change, just maintenance. But in 1866, it seemed to me very static and hypnotically boring. The ivory carpets, china blue drapes, luxurious bed and French furniture were all imposing to me, blocking out my view and locking in my senses. I was rapidly beginning to hate it all.

 That particular spring had about it a crispness and a newness that seemed to act as a catalyst on my boredom, making it almost unbearable. Since my graduation from Mrs. Pettit's Finishing School I had little to occupy my time, so I paced or stared out my window. Grandpere and Grandmere had hoped my graduation and subsequent coming out would convert me to the ways of New York society. I'm sure they were disappointed that it hadn't. But I did not belong there and the sense of disorder I felt at being there was growing.

It was not simply my own feelings. My grandparents sensed my anxiety and had anxieties of their own. When they entertained, I did not make small talk. I answered when spoken to, befitting a lady from Mrs. Pettit's school, but I found no use for the chitchat that flowed so freely around me. It upset Grandmere terribly that I could not deign to compliment or flatter any of her guests as she seemed so prone to do. My French blood had not blessed me with a gift for false flattery. I imagine many of the older women thought me a cold child with little empathy or gratitude, but I cared very little what they thought.

Men reacted strangely to me. My grandfather's wealth was well known, so I was duly inspected by the proper suitors, usually at parties or other large affairs. Grandmere was careful to sweep my black hair high up on my head and apply makeup artfully to tone down the bronze hue of my skin, my heritage from my Cheyenne father. She could do nothing about my high cheekbones or ebony eyes, except hope no one took close notice. Few men did. There weren't many who called on me a second time, most of them unnerved by my calm and steady gaze. Some would look closer—even uncomfortably close to my way of thinking—but none ever suggested I was anything but French. Most of them, I found, were as boring as my rooms upstairs, so I did not encourage them.

My grandparents insisted I play a role in these encounters and from the age of thirteen I was schooled in it. The story was that my mother had impulsively wed a cavalry officer and chosen to remain in the wilderness. When we reappeared, the explanation was that the officer—my father, supposedly—had died and my mother had brought her only child back to civilization. I was never very good at answering questions about my false past, always afraid I'd turn things around and say them wrong. But I let it be told and I nodded when it was repeated back to me, afraid I would see that look of horror in people's eyes if they knew the truth. I frequently saw that look in my grandparents' eyes.

So, alone in my experience since my mother died, analytical and therefore irritating to members of society, and finally fearful of revealing my true self, I held myself apart and was a misfit. I felt more of a misfit every passing day.

"Catherine," Grandmere said with a light knock on my door. "Don't forget Mr. Slater is coming to dinner tonight."

"No, Grandmere, I won't," I answered. She knew I would not open my door unless asked and I knew she no longer expected it.

"Why don't you wear your blue taffeta? That

looks so nice on you."

"Yes, Grandmere."

The inevitable pause came as she searched for a new way to phrase her words. Ultimately they were said, although with more hopelessness lately.

"Catherine, do try to be gracious, won't you?"

"Yes, Grandmere."

Gracious. Such a civilized way of asking me to act normal. It was not only a ritual for her to ask because we both knew I would not be gracious, I would not be what she considered normal, and yet she still asked. I turned to my wardrobe and began to dress for dinner.

I often wondered if Grandmere preferred taffeta because of the rustle it made. When she wore it, anyone could hear her all about the house, upstairs or down. I, however, had retained a habit of walking silently, one foot in front of the other, and even taffeta could not betray my movements. Mrs. Pettit had done all in her power to correct this horrible fault, had vowed that she would do so or have a nervous breakdown trying. She came dangerously close to having the breakdown and I still walk silently. I never cared to rustle like wheat in the wind and I suppose taffeta was the only remedy Grandmere could think of.

Feeling like a belled cat, I went downstairs to dinner. At exactly seven o'clock I stood in the doorway and waited for my three companions to realize I was there.

This time it was Grandpere who noticed first,

and he gulped in surprise to see me where I had not been a moment before. Grandmere was equally surprised and threw her head up, one hand clutching dramatically at her throat. Mr. Slater started, then immediately smiled. While my grandparents caught their breath he held my chair for me.

Had we not had company I would have asked to be "a little more noisesome" by Grandpere. I would have consented with downcast eyes and the game would go on. Since Mr. Slater was present I was saved that much at least. Dinner hadn't even been served and I had already been ungracious.

I ate quietly, listening halfheartedly to the table conversation. Grandpere and Mr. Slater discussed the business of trading and the wagon trains as they always did. Mr. Slater came for dinner twice a year, once in late summer on his arrival and once in early spring before he left again for Leavenworth. I paid little attention to his visits until this one.

"It's gettin' so there's almost no open territory between here and Leavenworth," the trailmaster was saying. "What with the riverboats going up and down the Missouri all the time, people just come flocking west. Leavenworth's regular civilization now."

"I'm sure of it," Grandpere said. "The last time I saw it, it was no more than a fort with a few tents thrown up."

"You ever think on goin' back there?" Slater asked.

"No, not now. If I were younger, I might, but not at my age. We'll just stay here in New York and leave the adventuring to you."

But *I* won't, I wanted to say. I had often thought of how I might make my way to the prairie but I had almost no idea of how to do it. Perhaps, though, if the way were not so dangerous or rigorous anymore I could go. I'd get no help from my grandparents—of that I was sure.

I listened to the rest of the conversation as I never had before. I made notes to myself of the cities Mr. Slater mentioned, of the meeting places of the wagon trains. Before dinner was over I had made up my mind that I would go.

For almost a week I planned. I got an old carpetbag from my mother's old room and began to pack carefully. I was limited on space so I took only essentials. Two changes of clothes and a few toilet articles would have to be sufficient until I was in a position to buy more. I made sure I had my brush and enough pins to keep my hair back in a knot at the back of my neck. I would necessarily have to keep up my charade of being a well-bred young white woman or find my way blocked by prejudice and possible harm. I sneaked chunks of cheese up from the kitchen and some apples and salt. With any luck I wouldn't be forced to survive on these things only, as I planned to have plenty of money, but I wanted to have every alternative covered.

I considered writing a note to my grandparents, then decided against it. I wanted to leave no clues because I knew they would have me tracked down and brought back if possible. As much as they verbalized their love for me, I saw the guarded look in their eyes when they thought I wasn't looking. They pictured me as a pet dog that might turn viciously on them at any moment and they considered that only my constant immersion in civilization would keep me tame. I had lived more years as a savage than as a civilized being, and so could never be completely trusted.

On the night I chose to leave, I waited patiently in my darkened room. I let the big clock downstairs chime two before I moved. Wearing a split-skirted traveling costume and carrying my carpetbag, I crept downstairs.

In Grandpere's office I went directly to his large roll-top desk. I knew of the money he kept there for emergencies, since most of his wealth was tied up in investments and large amounts of cash could not always be easily come by. I found the back pigeon hole in the top right side of the desk and pulled out the roll of bills. I glanced through and thought there was perhaps two thousand dollars—enough to see me to Leavenworth comfortably. I jammed the money inside the bodice of my blouse and left by a little-used side door. I walked several blocks before I hired a hansom to take me to the railroad office.

In the early hours of the morning I boarded a train bound for St. Joseph. I had considered trying to buy a place on a wagon train but was too afraid I might bump into Mr. Slater. Anyway, the train afforded me more anonymity as passengers came and went, and I stayed as much to myself as possible.

The train trip was boring, although I had thought it would be interesting. I kept a window seat and watched the countryside slide by, but it was all very much the same after the first day. We pulled into and out of small towns, past farms and over rivers. None of it looked as I remembered, but that did not surprise me. I had not been in a frame of mind to remember clearly the last time I had passed this way.

Occasionally another passenger would try to claim my attention but most discouraged easily. One man sat boldly beside me and drew me into conversation until I confessed I was on my way to Leavenworth to marry a lieutenant colonel there. After that he talked for a moment longer, then excused himself and never came back.

I was extremely grateful when the train pulled into St. Joseph. I had become impatient and eager to begin the next leg of my journey. I went directly from the train depot to the waterfront and booked passage for Leavenworth on a big riverboat. Since it wasn't to leave until the following day, I rented a room in a hotel and stayed there until time to depart.

The riverboat was more interesting than the train and I relaxed enough to enjoy it. I decided I should invent and practice a story credible enough to answer questioners without arousing interest. Since the passengers all ate in a common dining room, I joined in quietly and allowed myself to be led into conversation. We sat eight to a table and it seemed that everyone was intent on finding out everything about everyone else. It was still not easy for me to initiate conversation but I answered most questions put to me until I had woven a simple history.

My father, I said, being widowed, had gone last year to California to make a new start there. I had just recently finished school—which was true—so he had sent for me. I was to be met by my father in Leavenworth sometime later in the summer and together we would go to California.

Since I did not appear to have a vast amount of money, was not related to anyone famous and had no exciting stories to tell, I was not pressed further for details. The women passengers would speak to me and then turn their attention elsewhere while the men might look fleetingly, then turn away from my own averted gaze. There were no incidents while I was on board the ship.

One morning when I awoke early and went out to stand at the rail, I saw Leavenworth come into view. It was much larger than I remembered, but I knew it must have grown quickly since Kansas had won statehood. The fort stood south of town, unassuming in its open, three-sided arrangement. I had heard people criticize the absence of walls and battlements, especially since the fort was the last bastion between the civilized east and the savage west, but still the fort had no stockade. Except for the flags flying briskly in the morning breeze, it might not even be taken as a government installation. An unknowing stranger might mistake it for the low buildings of squatters, like on the south side of town.

As we neared the wharf, the big Planter's Hotel reared above the other buildings like a beacon. It sat on a low hill and its sign could be read above all others. The rest of town fell into orderly sections, none of which looked familiar to me. Although apprehensive, I was anxious to get off the ship and see the town.

We docked shortly and after much commotion on both the wharf and the ship, the passengers were allowed off. I took my carpetbag and allowed a steward to help me down to the dock. Then I wasted no time heading toward Leavenworth.

I suppose the Planter's Hotel was the most obvious place to go first. I became part of an irregular stream of people going in the same direction, and when I entered the lobby there were already five or six people at the desk ahead of me. I waited patiently, for a feeling of giddy excitement was filling me as I looked around. I was closer to my homeland than I had been in seven years and I had escaped New York and all its constrictions with hardly a problem. I was alone and independent and self-sufficient, and I loved it!

My room was on the third floor and looked south over the biggest part of town. It was comfortable, with a dark patterned carpet and flowered walls, a single soft bed and a dresser and night stand. I unpacked my carpetbag and washed at the basin provided. Although it was not yet noon, I thought about lunch. I had been too excited to eat breakfast.

The dining room was on the main floor and I was seated at a table by myself. I ordered lunch and opened a copy of the paper I had picked up while waiting to register. The hotel was fine for a few days but I was afraid I would spend too much money if I stayed there for very long. I had no idea how long I would be in Leavenworth but until I could find some thread of information about my band of Cheyenne, I might as well be comfortable. I opened the newspaper to the ads and searched for something about rooms to rent.

"Miss Lance?" a familiar voice called. At first I didn't even look up, my assumed name not registering. I had been afraid to use my real name in case I should be recognized as Jack's granddaughter, so I had used Lance since I booked passage on the train. Now I remembered my identity and looked up to see who had called me.

A young woman I remembered from the steamboat was coming my way between the tables. She was younger than I and much prettier, I thought, with auburn hair and bright blue eyes. She was probably no more than eighteen and had been traveling with her parents. We had spoken a few times on the ship so I knew her name and that she was betrothed to a corporal in the 8th regiment.

"Melly!" I said. I had not sought her company on the ship but neither had I discouraged her. She was a vibrant girl and so caught up in her love that she was no threat to me. "Come join me," I said.

She took a chair opposite me and asked a waiter for a menu. "What are you having?" she asked.

"The fish. I heard on the ship that it was very good."

"I'll have that, too," she told the waiter. When he left she peered over at my newspaper. "What are you looking for?"

"A room to rent."

"You're not staying at the Planter's?" she asked. I had guessed from her clothes and attitude of naive assurance that she came from a well-to-do family. Her question only confirmed that for me.

"Only for a short while," I said. "I have no idea how long I'll be in town so I've decided to go ahead and get a room. It could be weeks or possibly months before my father arrives from California."

"Oh," she said. She accepted my inference that my funds were limited, which was what I wanted. I hoped to camouflage myself with mediocrity, seeming neither rich nor poor, grand nor pitiful. I would just as soon people forget my face as soon as their eyes left it. If any inquiries should make their way to Leavenworth concerning a runaway heiress, I wanted no one to be able to make any connection to me.

"When will you see your soldier?" I asked to lead the conversation away from myself.

"Oh, he's on campaign now, scouting northwest toward Fort Kearney. He wrote that he'd probably be gone two months or more, so I don't expect him until the end of April or later. We've tentatively planned the wedding for June, just to be safe." She smiled happily as she talked.

"That's good," I said. "You can always change your plans if he comes in earlier."

"Yes," she agreed. "His campaigns are the only reason my parents agreed to let me come west and marry here. If Frank could get any furlough in the east, they'd have made me wait until then. I'm glad it turned out like this. I've never been this far west, have you?"

"No," I lied. "It's all pretty new to me, too."

"It's exciting, though," she said looking about. "Who would have thought there could be this much civilization so close to Indian Territory? At first I was glad my parents came with me, but now I think I could have probably managed quite well here on my own. You're traveling alone, aren't you?"

"Yes," I said, "but only because I have no close family other than my father."

"Oh, I'm sorry," she said quickly.

"That's all right. I have relations, but not where I can reach them quickly. My father is my family and I'll be with him again soon enough."

"I'm glad," Melly said. "Everyone needs family, even if it's only one person."

"Exactly," I agreed. And grandparents tied by blood but without understanding did not comprise a family, at least not to me. I let the thought remain unspoken, especially since our lunch was being served.

"Where are your parents?" I asked, still following our thread of conversation.

"Upstairs. Mother's resting and Daddy said he would have lunch sent up. I told him I was too excited to sit in my room now that I'm here. I want to see Leavenworth!"

I laughed at her excitement. Although I was normally much more cynical than she, arriving in Leavenworth had made me optimistic also and I shared her rosy outlook. It was refreshing to let myself be caught up in her carefree mood.

"Would you like to go with me when I go room hunting?" I invited. "If your parents wouldn't mind, it would be a good way to see the town, and with two of us keeping our eyes open we'd be less apt to get lost."

"Oh, I'd love to!" she said quickly. "I think that would be fun!"

"Good. As soon as we're finished with lunch we'll go up and ask them if it's all right."

It was, but only after some thought and a piercing examination of me. Melly's father, Jason Crutchfield, eyed me coldly, as if I might be plotting to abduct his daughter and sell her to white slavers downriver. He showered me with brisk, forthright questions to which I gave equally brisk answers, sticking to my story without wavering. When he seemed satisfied, I realized that he had been noting my appearance and that my understated, tailored outfit and proud carriage might have been a deciding factor. As much as I attempted to play down my wealthy appearance, I knew a keen eye could see it if one knew where to look. Mr. Crutchfield did.

"Don't be gone more than two or three hours," he said, checking his pocket watch. He waved a cigar and used it to punctuate his words. He was a fairly short man, but burly and barrel-chested and had a look about him of one who brooked no disobedience. Melly quickly assured him we would not be late.

"And don't go gawking over on that southwest quarter. You remember what Frank said about that in his last letter."

"Yes, Daddy," she said. "We'll stick to this side of town."

Mr. Crutchfield chewed on his cigar and surveyed us one last time. "When you get back," he said, "you'll have dinner with us." When I realized this last order was an invitation to me, I accepted graciously and we left. In another instant Mr. Crutchfield might have annoyed me with his authoritarian businesslike manner, but on that day I only nodded to his dictates and smiled inwardly. In a way he reminded me of Grandpere, a man who had made his own way up the ladder of success and still retained the push and drive that had got him there.

Melly and I began our outing by walking south along the main street, looking in store windows and noting what businesses thrived there. Hardware stores, dry goods, general goods, leather and yardage stores made up the bulk of them, along with the federal offices—claims, assays and the jail. Banks and churches stood with tall steeples, signaling Leavenworth's wealth and piety, and there were restaurants and an opera house. It was all larger than I had expected and quite different from what I remembered.

After we had walked a bit and read what street signs we could find, we began to sort out the ads in my paper. A couple of them ended by directing the reader to this or that saloon, so we eliminated those right away.

"Frank says the saloons are awfully rough and no decent lady would even walk down the same street where one is," Melly told me. "Old trappers and buffalo hunters come in and spend hundreds of dollars on drink before they head out again. Can you imagine?"

No, I could not. I had a taste for wine, developed by my grandparents, and had occasionally sipped Grandpere's brandy, but getting drunk disgusted me.

"And Frank says some of those old Indian fighters and even some soldiers don't have a lick of care when they're drunk—might even accost a lady were she to wander down that way."

We stayed near the main street. Leavenworth was not so big that we'd ever get lost, but narrow, lonely streets were unappealing to us. There was a boarding house very close to the center of town and I knocked on the door there. An elderly woman almost bent double from arthritis answered.

"I'm sorry," she said when I inquired about a room. "We're all full up. Try Mrs. Reedy's down behind the church."

I thanked her and we moved on down the street.

"Which church do you think she means?" Melly asked, looking about.

"She pointed toward the hotel. Let's try a couple more around here before we go back that way."

We stopped at the dry goods store that had a ROOM TO RENT sign in the window, but one look at the dirty, unkempt room and the unkempt man who ownd it turned us away.

"How awful!" Melly said. "And that man was the worst. Imagine sleeping there on that lumpy bed and staying in the same building as him."

"No wonder he's not married," I agreed. "Any woman would have to be desperate to stay with him."

We stopped at a house located one block east off the main street, but the room it offered was small and cramped and I suspected I would have little privacy. I thanked the couple who showed it to us and went on. Finally we worked our way up to the big white church and saw the boarding house behind it. A small shingle on the front porch said MRS. REEDY'S in narrow stick letters.

"That looks like a nice place," Melly said. "It must have been a private home before."

It was a large two-story building with a raised porch running the entire length of it. Painted stark white, it was imposing in its structural simplicity and I guessed it had once been a very fine house.

We knocked and the door was opened by a tall older woman with graying hair swept back in a knot. Her gray eyes examined us curiously.

"Mrs. Reedy?" I asked.

"No," she said, "No, I'm Margaret Henkins. Mrs. Reedy is in the kitchen. May I say who's calling?"

"Yes, my name is Catherine Lance. I'd like to inquire about a room to rent."

"Oh, well, come in. Won't you wait here in the parlor? I'll get her."

Mrs. Henkins led us to a large drably furnished parlor. The overstuffed divan and chairs were of an old faded flower pattern, with crocheted doilies on the arms. There was a large dark piano to one side and stairs leading up to the second floor. It was clean but almost oppressive in its lack of bright color.

We waited standing, just looking about, until Mrs. Reedy came in. She was taller than Mrs. Henkins and much thinner, with piled white hair. Although I guessed her age to be in the late sixties, she looked hard, as if she might have had more bad times than good in those years. Her face was shrunken and wrinkled and her eyes peered out of deep sockets. She was somewhat overbearing and had an arrogant manner.

"I'm Mrs. Reedy," she said, not offering her hand. "You've come about a room?"

"Yes," I said.

"Both of you?" she asked a little suspiciously.

"No," I said, not liking her manner. "I want the room. My friend is lodging elsewhere. May I see it?"

Mrs. Reedy drew herself up a bit as if affronted

by my question and I assured she was used to doing all the asking. I decided then that, if I took the room, I would not succumb to her dominance.

"This way," she said, starting for the stairs. Melly looked questioningly at me behind the older woman's back, but I just shrugged. We followed her upstairs.

The room was small but neat and clean with a single bed, a washstand and a large highboy. The window looked north, toward some low hills. Mrs. Reedy offered no comment about the room and I gathered it would not dismay her if I chose not to take it. Still, I liked the idea of being upstairs and away from the communal rooms below, and the room was decent and sufficient for my needs. Anyway I didn't want Mrs. Reedy to think she had cowed me.

"I should like to take it," I said finally.

She looked at me steadily for a moment and I met her steely gaze. "Very well," she said. "Come downstairs and we'll make the arrangements."

Over tea served by Mrs. Henkins, the rules of the house were explained to me.

"Breakfast is at seven and dinner is at six. Anyone later than half past the hour will not be served. The front door is locked at eleven every night. I do not permit ladies to entertain gentleman guests in their rooms and if I decide a boarder is . . . unsuitable, I give twenty-four-hours notice."

"That sounds satisfactory to me," I said. I drew out my purse and counted out enough money for two weeks' rent. "Will this be enough to secure the room?" I asked.

Mrs. Reedy counted the money carefully. "You may move in any time," she said.

Melly could hardly contain herself until we left Mrs. Reedy's and started back toward the hotel. "Wasn't she awful?" she said in a high voice. "She reminded me of a witch with her staring eyes and bony hands. Do you think you'll like it there?"

"It'll do," I said. "I don't plan on associating with Mrs. Reedy unless I have to, so I shouldn't have any problems."

"Oh, I don't think I could bear it there," she insisted. "She's awful."

When we reached the hotel, we went up to the Crutchfields' suite and I met Melly's mother. She was a willowy woman, softspoken and frail and I guessed Melly must be a handful for her. Mrs. Crutchfield immediately assumed the role of hostess and we three women sat in the large front room of the suite while dinner was being set for us.

"Have you any idea when your father will arrive?" she asked me. Mr. Crutchfield had apparently explained to her about me.

"None," I said, "except sometime before winter. It's even possible we may have to spend the cold months here and start for California again next spring, although I hope not. I've heard the trip from Los Angeles to Leavenworth is still very rough."

"Yes, they say it is," Mrs. Crutchfield agreed.

30

"Will you be all right by yourself? We have plenty of room here, if you'd care to stay with us. We'll be here at least until Melly and Frank get married."

"Thank you," I said, "But I'll be fine. I'm used to living alone."

"She has no one except her father," Melly explained in a pitying voice.

"Oh, I'm sorry," her mother said.

"That's all right. I can manage quite well. I've thought I'll probably take a position in town somewhere, at least until my father arrives."

"What sort of position?"

"Oh, I'm not sure yet. I've had very little work experience—none in fact—but I'm sure I can find something."

"You poor girl," Mrs. Crutchfield said.

"No, it's all right. I've got to keep busy somehow."

"But surely you're not used to working?" she asked. I noticed Mr. Crutchfield's quiet interest and I was afraid my schooling was showing.

"No," I said finally, "but it can't be too bad. I'm sure I can find something useful to do."

When dinner was over I found I had to bear both Mrs. Crutchfield's mothering sympathy and her husband's sharp eyes. He was not completely sure of me yet, and I decided I would stay out of his way from then on. I wanted no one trying to piece together my true story while I was in Leavenworth.

The next day I removed my few belongings to

Mrs. Reedy's. Being a weekday, there were no other boarders about besides Mrs. Henkins and I was grateful not to have prying eyes on me as I settled in. I hung up my extra clothing in the wardrobe, hoping Mrs. Reedy was not a snooper and would wonder why I traveled so light. Then I examined my room. The bed was comfortable if a bit lumpy, but with clean sheets and a neatly mended bedspread. The room was even cleaner than I had realized at first, and there was fresh water in a pitcher on the dry sink. I remembered Mrs. Henkins saying there was a large tub for bathing in the service porch off the kitchen, and I could wash my clothes down there as well. All in all, it looked to be a satisfactory place. I even had a view of the north end of town and the prairie falling away in green and brown waves.

Standing at my window, it seemed odd to see Leavenworth through adult eyes. When I was dragged to the fort as a half wild thirteen-year-old my eyes had rested on nothing for very long, but darted about wildly in the way of a panicked animal. Even knowing that my mother had come willingly and that these were the white people she told me of so often didn't help. I can remember feeling that I was about to die. Perhaps I did. I was certainly not that same person now.

I wondered how the good people of Leavenworth would react to me if they knew I was a half-breed. So far I had been treated with deference and respect but that would quickly turn to hate and contempt, I was sure, if I were found out. In order to find my lost land, I would have to play my charade well or I would get no cooperation from anyone. If I had my way, I would take a horse and ride straight out of town, out onto the prairie, but that was impossible. I would have to bide my time and find the best way to proceed.

As I stood at my window gazing down on Leavenworth, I felt almost as if I stood in the wings of a theater and that very shortly the important drama of my life would begin. I watched the shadows elongate and stretch eastward and it seemed that there was a hush in the air. Everything was in readiness—but for what? I wondered.

At breakfast the next morning I had the feeling that I was an insect stuck in a pin and displayed for all to see. My fellow boarders greeted me with interminable questions, only part of which I had time to answer. I had had ample experience in telling my fabricated story and luckily they chattered so that if I chose to ignore a very pointed or prying question, no one seemed to notice.

There was only one other woman boarder beside myself. Della—she insisted I call her by her first name—was about thirty-five or forty and a very friendly woman. She asked most of the questions of me but either didn't wait for an answer or surmised out loud, so she did not threaten my privacy. She had been a mail-order bride years before but had stayed on when her man had traveled westward. Now she took in sewing and did some cooking and cleaning occasionally for a widower in town.

The male boarders, I knew, would require more time to get to know, so I tried not to form opinions right away. Sometimes that was difficult, though.

Charles Lafferty was the youngest, no more than five years my senior and as out of place in Leavenworth as I had been in New York. His conservative gray suits looked incongruous next to the rough frontier garb of everyone else, but I suppose it was in keeping with being a young lawyer. He was very well mannered and listened rather than talked at breakfast. I decided to reserve judgment of him much as he seemed to be doing of me.

Jacob Greene was older, probably fifty or so, and rough as a cob. I wondered why he even chose to board in town, since he struck me as a diehard mule-skinner type, complete with full beard and rather distastefully smelling clothes. Later I found out he had been a scout years ago, as well as a prospector, buffalo hunter and trapper. During his younger years he had received numerous wounds from white men's guns, red men's arrows, and wild animals, and he was arthritic besides. Although his advice was still elicited from the fort on occasion, he was no longer content to sleep in the dirt and eat half raw meat by a smokeless fire. Rather than admit to his weakness, he ignored it, as if it were normal for an aged scout to board in town. Rough as he was, I rather liked Mr. Greene.

I was thankful that breakfast was a brief affair and the other boarders ate quickly before going off on their daily business. I offered to help Margaret with the dishes but she insisted that I must have other things to do. Mrs. Reedy appeared to watch me carefully, as if verifying for herself that I would occupy my time properly. It was enough for me to decide that I would look for a job right away.

Walking downtown, I was again amazed at the hundreds of buildings and the extent of the town. In no way did it resemble the Leavenworth of seven years ago. I assumed the gold rush, the Civil War issue of State's Rights and the westward growth of civilization were responsible. Even in New York we had heard of Bleeding Kansas and the migrations from Missouri to tip the voters' scales. Clearly the town had just grown up and over itself.

There were any number of stores in which I could inquire. Since Mrs. Pettit's school taught only basic education—and only as much as it was considered proper for a lady to know—I decided I'd best look for a general position. A seamstress would have little use for someone who only knew needlepoint and embroidery, and a newspaperman would have no use at all for a girl who had studied Shakespeare. No, best to lose myself in the obscurity of a general store.

I chose the largest of the dry-good stores on the main street to start with. There were barrels of goods almost blocking the doorway, with brooms and dusters threatening anyone intent on leaving. I pushed past the choked doorway into the most amazing assembly of things I'd ever seen. There were long tables piled high with all sorts of objects, much of which I had no idea what their use could be, and spaced so that only narrow aisles divided them. I saw kitchen utensils, wooden and metal bowls, pots, spoons and knives; all sorts of lanterns and candles; washtubs and washboards, barrels of grains, salts and meals, hand tools, hardware, and finally millinery. And there were at least a hundred things I didn't recognize or wasn't sure of.

"Can I help you?" a voice boomed behind me. I was so caught up in the conglomeration of things around me that I was startled by the sudden question.

"Yes, I think so," I said, turning to face the proprietor. He was a big man, tall as well as wide, with short cropped black hair and blue eyes. He smiled at me.

"I was wondering if you might have a position open here? I'm looking for work for a few months or so, and I thought, well . . ." My voice trailed away, my eyes running over the strange objects. It must be obvious that I knew nothing whatsoever about this kind of store.

"Where are you from?" he asked. I looked back at him and could tell he found me amusing.

"New York," I confessed. "I don't have much knowledge of the things you sell here. I'm—I'm more used to specialty shops." I decided I would have to do a little more researching before I could find a job easily. "I'm sorry to have bothered you,"

I said, turning to go.

"No, wait," he said. His bulk blocked my way anyway. "New York, huh?"

I nodded.

"Hmmm," he mused, looking about. "Do you know anything about millinery, yard goods?"

"Some," I lied.

"I've been thinking about hiring someone to manage that back corner for me. There's so many women about these days that I can't keep up with all they ask for. Half the time I don't know what they want, anyway." He began to walk toward the back as he talked, and I followed him to where bolts of cloth lay haphazardly on a table. "It's pretty much a mess," he said.

"Yes, I see," I agreed. Notions were spilling out of boxes under the counter and lace and trim snaked around the half unrolled bolts of cloth.

"Where are you staying?" he asked suddenly.

"Mrs. Reedy's boarding house."

"What's your name?"

"Catherine Lance."

"Catherine," he repeated. "I'm Harry Altvater. I couldn't pay much, and you'd only be working on trial at first, to see how it would go. If there isn't enough to keep you busy or you can't handle it, I won't keep you," he warned.

"I understand," I said. The suddenness of his offer, and the conditions, surprised me.

"Fine. Can you start tomorrow?"

"Oh, well, yes, I guess so."

"Good. Be here at eight." Mr. Altvater was

beaming at me, obviously very pleased with the arrangement. The man's abruptness was something I would have to get used to, although I preferred that to the insincerity typical of most people. Feeling bewildered but happy, I left the store.

I took the liberty in my free time to inspect the town. South of the store I proceeded on down the main street. I passed more stores and trade booths, noticing how the status of the businesses seemed to diminish the farther south I went. Passing blacksmiths and leather workers, liveries and stockyards, I saw the men eyeing me as if I were up for sale. Finally I crossed the street and went back up town. I could see now how the town was divided and where decent women were expected to stay.

East of the main street, down a few blocks at every cross street I could see the garishly painted false fronts of the saloons. There were also established businesses, but most of them male oriented, as if women had no need to even wander down that way. That was fine with me. I wanted no part of the drunk and gold hungry sorts that stayed there.

Finally back uptown, I stopped in a small home-cooking establishment for lunch. The family-run business catered to the passengers on the stage, which had its depot just across the way and I relaxed in the anonymity of the place. One nice thing, I realized—Leavenworth was not so small that everyone kept track of everyone else. That sort of small-town awareness was exactly what I did not want. I decided to spend the rest of the day acquainting myself further with the town and perhaps see about having some new clothes made, ones that would suit my new identity.

Chapter Two

THE NEXT day I was apprehensive about beginning work. I had never worked a day before, especially not serving the public, and I was not looking forward to it. I decided to show up early so I'd have some time to familiarize myself with the store.

"Good morning," Mr. Altvater rumbled. "I'm glad you're here early. Here, I'll show you where to put your bag." He led me to a room behind the front counter where there was a desk covered with papers and an overstuffed chair. I put my bag in the bottom drawer of the desk as directed by Mr. Altvater and followed him back to the front.

He apologized for what he was about to do, then

proceeded to show me everything in the store and tell me so much about it that I couldn't possibly remember it all. I followed as much as I could and asked a few pertinent questions, but quickly felt lost.

"I'm sorry, Mr. Altvater," I said. "But I've already forgotten at least three-quarters of what you've told me. I'm not so sure I can do this after all."

"Oh, sure," he insisted. "Where is the salt?"

Thinking, trying to remember, I pointed to a sack behind the front counter.

"Yeah, right!" he said. "Where are the twitches?"

I glanced around, trying to find a clue to that one. Finally I saw a bucket of horseshoe nails and I pointed to the jumble of articles next to the bucket.

"Yes! See, you'll do fine. Anyway, I'll be handling most of the customers. This is your part back here."

Back in the millinery, he showed me where everything was kept—the thread, buttons, needles, scissors and tapes—and explained the types of cloth he stocked. He also had some yellowed newspapers, tucked preciously in a drawer that showed drawings of New York fashion. The dates on most of the papers were years old but still the only vestiges of civilized fashion in Leavenworth. I was allowed to show them to anyone who asked, but they were not to leave the store.

"Any questions?" he asked.

"Hundreds," I said, "but there's no point in asking them all now. I'd just forget again. I'll just have to wait until the customers come in and take them one by one."

"Sure," he said, "You'll do fine, don't worry. Oh, there's someone now."

I looked around and saw my first customer heading toward me. Suddenly I was panic stricken. I could already feel my tongue balling up in my mouth. Mr. Altvater stood expectantly just a few steps away so he could watch.

"May I help you?" I managed to blurt out. The woman glanced at me curiously, then proceeded on to my boss.

"Mr. Altvater, that thread I bought yesterday is the wrong color." The woman held up a swatch of cloth and the thread as an example. The cloth was a dark indigo blue while the thread tended more toward a purple.

"Oh, that's okay, Mrs. Rollins. Here, this is Catherine. She's in charge of yard goods now. She'll find you the right color."

Mr. Altvater turned toward me, grinning pleasantly, while Mrs. Rollins looked at me stupidly. Finally she stepped up to my counter.

"Here," she said. "It's the wrong color," again waving the cloth.

"Yes, I see," I managed. I stooped down and found a box of thread and brought it up for Mrs. Rollins to look through. While she was doing that, I found two more boxes. The two of us rummaged through the countless spools, occasionally holding a color to the cloth. None were close enough for her taste.

"Is this all you have?" she asked finally. I looked to Mr. Altvater and he just smiled.

"Well, let me look." I bent down again and tore through the jumbled boxes and bags of notions. I found lace, buttons, needles and pins but I could see no more thread.

"I'm afraid that's all we have," I said.

"Oh, but none of these are the right color," Mrs. Rollins said disappointedly.

I considered. Since we couldn't match the color exactly the only other alternative was to contrast.

"We don't have the same shade, but we do have that color, only lighter." I held up a blue neither too purple nor too green, but some shades lighter than Mrs. Rollins's cloth. "That might look very nice," I offered.

Mrs. Rollins looked at the thread I held, then looked at her material and back again. "Let me see," she said. She took the spool and held it against the cloth. I wasn't sure what Mr. Altvater was thinking of the whole affair, but I hoped he was bearing with me.

"You know," Mrs. Rollins said finally, "That might look all right after all." She studied it for another minute. "Yes, I think I like that. I'll take it."

"Fine," I said. I breathed a sigh of relief. While Mrs. Rollins made her way out of the store, I glanced at Mr. Altvater. He was smiling.

"Very good," he said. "Mrs. Rollins is a persnickety old bird, and not usually pleased with anything you do for her. You handled it just fine."

With no help from you, I thought grimly. I was glad Mr. Altvater was pleased with me, but I resolved to put some sort of order to the yardage goods. I didn't want to have to scramble through boxes and bags like that for every customer.

Since there was no one else in the store, Mr. Altvater returned to the front and I plunged into my new job. I began by pulling everything out from under the counter and making piles of like objects. When I had that done, I arranged the bolts of cloth by type and surveyed how much room I had left to work with. It wasn't much, but somehow I would get it all in order.

After the first customer the rest weren't quite so bad, although Mr. Altvater still had to refer them back to me. Most people expressed surprise that he had hired a helper, especially a woman and most surprisingly someone new in town. Most of the women seemed happy enough to talk to another woman about fashion, though, and I found myself being asked all sorts of questions about fabrics and colors. By the end of the day my terror had vanished and I felt much more at ease.

Other than Mrs. Rollins, there was only one other customer who struck me as unique and therefore memorable. I could not remember ever seeing a man like him before although it seemed to me that I must have seen mountain men sometime in my first thirteen years. This man was probably

45

ten years my senior and tall and broad shouldered. When he came in the store I was speaking with two other women but I noticed him just because of his size. He greeted Mr. Altvater and then deliberately looked back at me. By then I knew word must have gotten out about the girl working at the general store, so it really didn't surprise me that people were curious. I was rather taken aback by the man's good looks, though, and the rough, stony features of his face. His hair was a dark auburn and blue eyes added startling color to his face. He caused me more discomfort than anyone else I'd seen.

I met his gaze briefly then managed to return to my customers' conversation. The man spoke with my boss for a moment or two, glanced back at me and then left.

Had I been any other girl I might have asked Mr. Altvater about him, but I kept my curiosity to myself. My stoic ways were stamped deep upon me and not overridden easily. Instead I wondered to myself and idly hoped I had not seen the last of the mountain man.

Toward closing time I realized how tired I was, then felt instantly ashamed because I actually had sold very little. Mr. Altvater seemed not to mind, if he noticed at all.

"Don't worry about that," he said when I mentioned it. "Just get used to the store first and you can work on your sales later. Go on home and rest up. Tomorrow will be just like today, only worse."

Nodding, I went to get my purse. When I turned around from the desk drawer I was surprised to see a boy of about ten years old staring at me. I hadn't heard him come in and as I met his gaze he still made no sound. I knew instantly by his black hair and copper skin that he was an Indian and my heart began to pound furiously. I was almost afraid I would reveal myself to him somehow, project my excitement at seeing a Cheyenne face, but he seemed unaware of what I was feeling inside.

Mr. Altvater broke into the tableaux and luckily misinterpreted my shock.

"Red Cloud! How many times have I told you it's not polite to stare? Quit scaring the lady and be about your work." He turned to me as the boy took a broom and went out into the store. "Sorry, Catherine. I forgot to tell you I had a little Indian kid help me clean up after hours. It must have been quite a shock for you to have an Indian sneak up behind you like that."

"Just—unexpected," I said. I wanted to know more about the boy but kept myself from asking. Instead I clutched my bag and left.

I thought about not going to dinner that night. So much had happened today and I had so much to think about that I would rather have stayed upstairs and just thought about it all, but at the same time I was afraid to cloister myself in too much mystery. If I kept myself too distant from the others, that would arouse more speculation than if I allowed myself to be seen. Knowing it was best for my facade, I forced myself to go down to the table.

Della cross-examined me about my first day on the job and I tried to give her answers before she supplied her own. The others listened or added an occasional comment while Mrs. Reedy sat in regal silence. When Della had asked every question she could think of, the others were allowed to tell about their day. It was almost like a family coming together at the end of the day to a mutual sharing. By the time dinner was over, I was feeling less isolated and almost glad I hadn't stayed in my room.

I excused myself after dinner and went upstairs. After the constant association all day in the store I felt I needed some solitude. I washed my face and neck and stood at my window watching the distant hills fading to purple. While clouds had gathered all along the horizon beyond them and the beauty of it touched me. I suddenly wished very much that I could be out walking those hills instead of here in this room.

A knock at my door brought me out of my day-dreams and I opened it to admit Della.

"Why don't you come down for a bit? Mrs. Reedy likes to play her spinet in the evenings and we usually listen. She plays pretty well." I hesitated, not wanting to join the group again. Della seemed to realize I needed more persuasion. "Mr. Lafferty asked me to ask you. I think he fancies you."

I blushed immediately, which only made Della

laugh. She refused to listen to my objections and took my hand.

"Come on, just for a bit. Then you can say you're tired from being on your feet all day and come back upstairs."

I followed, hoping my terror didn't show. No man in New York had "fancied" me for long, which was exactly how I preferred it. I had never cultivated flattery to attract men and could usually drive them off with my silence. Knowing that Mr. Lafferty had taken notice of me and that we shared the same roof made it difficult. I had too many other things to think about to worry about parrying a romantic interest.

The boarders were all arranged about the parlor, Mrs. Reedy having already begun playing. I took a seat near a window so I could still see the distant hills, although I watched Mrs. Reedy as much as I thought was necessary to be polite. I had to admit, she really did play well and occasionally her birdlike voice escaped to accompany the music. It was more pleasant than I expected.

Between pieces, the others would comment or request favorites. At those times I sat quietly and kept my eyes directed away from Mr. Lafferty.

"Do you have a preference in music, Miss Lance?" he asked me suddenly. His tone was casually curious but he watched me steadily. To make it worse, his questions turned everyone's attention to me.

"Nothing that Mrs. Reedy could play more

admirably than she has been. Please don't stop, Mrs. Reedy," I said.

She glanced at me curiously. "Thank you," she said, and began a new piece. I felt pleased that I had turned the attention away from myself so easily. Feeling a bit smug, I returned to my window and the hills beyond.

When Mrs. Reedy stopped playing and straightened the lace coverlet on top of the spinet everyone changed attitudes. I realized later that was the lady's way of ending the performance and by doing so she threw the decision of what to do next on the boarders.

"Mr. Greene," Della said quickly. "Won't you tell us some of your stories? You tell them so well." She looked at me. "You wouldn't be offended by stories about Indian wars, would you? Mr. Greene used to scout for the cavalry and he took part in several raids."

At first I had the horrible feeling that everyone knew of my cross blood and they were all mocking me with their deference. Panic almost choked me until I made myself think sensibly. No one knew— if they did, they would not ridicule me but would harrass me and drive me from town.

"Actually," I said addressing Mr. Greene, "I would be most interested to hear your stories but I am feeling a bit tired. I thought I would just take in a little fresh air and then retire. May I reserve a time in the near future to hear your stories, Mr. Greene?"

"Surely," he said with a nod. Before anyone

could protest I got up and made my way to the front door. As I walked out I heard Mr. Greene clear his throat and begin.

The cool night air was like a balm to me. I breathed deeply of it and willed myself again to the far hills that had now turned indigo. Darkness was only a matter of minutes away and I was sorry I wouldn't be able to see them very well. A few stars glimmered weakly but I knew there would soon be more.

While I was taking in the beauty of the plains night the front door opened and Mr. Lafferty stepped out onto the porch. He smiled tentatively at me.

"You don't mind, do you?" he asked quickly after he closed the door.

"Of course not," I said, although I did. The last thing I wanted was anyone fancying me or showing any interest in me at all. I stayed where I was at the rail and he joined me there.

"What are you looking at?" he asked after a moment.

"The hills, the stars—just everything. It's very beautiful here."

"Quite different from anything back east," he agreed obliquely.

"You don't care for it here?" I asked. I glanced sideways at him and was relieved to see he was looking about and not fixing his attentions on me as I feared.

"Not really," he admitted. "But it's hard starting a law practice in New York where there are already so many lawyers. Here, there are almost none, but so many people who need them."

"Then you don't think you'll stay here in Leavenworth?"

"No. As soon as I have enough years in—and some sort of reputation—I'll go back east. My father has agreed to help me set up a practice once I prove myself."

So that was it. Leavenworth was to be his proving ground. And that was why he seemed so incongruous here, I realized. He was as out of place here as I was in my grandparents' parlor.

"Do you think you'll like it here?" he asked.

"Oh, well enough, for the time I'll be here," I said.

"And then California?"

"Yes."

He said nothing for several minutes, as if not sure what to ask next. I was about to go inside, becoming uncomfortable with him on the porch.

"How long do you think you'll be staying?" he asked finally.

"I really have no way of knowing. It could be weeks or months. I've heard the trip from Los Angeles to Leavenworth is quite extensive."

"Yes, I guess so," he said. He cleared his throat nervously. "While you're here, if you would care to, uh, have an escort, I would be more than glad to take you anywhere you'd like to go. There isn't much to do—there's the opera house or occasional social things at the fort—but I'd be pleased to escort you."

"Thank you, Mr. Lafferty," I said. "I'm grateful, but I doubt that I'll be going out much socially. I usually tend to stay by myself."

"Oh," he said. "Well, if you should . . ."

"Yes, thank you."

"It's just that there is an element of undesirables in Leavenworth and I would hate to see you run into that sort of thing on your own."

"Undesirables?" I asked. "Do you mean the saloons?"

"Yes. There are some Indian fighters and buffalo hunters who hang around, and since they've run off the Indians and buffalo, they seem to have nothing to do other than drink and fight and cause disturbances. And they don't always stay close to the saloons."

"Are there no Indians here, then?" I asked. I spoke evenly, hoping my voice wouldn't betray my sudden alertness.

"Oh, not to be alarmed about. There are still some diehard renegades, but they mostly sulk about the borders of the remote farms and steal horses and such. They never venture close to town."

I wondered if my father was one of those "diehard renegades."

"There was an Indian boy at the store . . ."

"Red Cloud? He's tame. He was captured in a raid some years back and brought in wounded. Mr. Altvater took it upon himself to care for the boy so now he works there. He disappears for a few days every now and then, but he always comes

53

back. He probably realizes how fortunate he is to live in a white man's town."

"Probably," I said, gritting my teeth. "Were there any other survivors from the raid?"

"I don't think so; at least I never saw any. Our men have been pretty thorough in that respect. You can't trust any of them, really, even the young ones. You just can't seem to break them of their savage ways."

I could have laughed. I imagined Mr. Lafferty's face falling from an easy smile into a look of shock if he knew he was speaking to one of those savages. He probably would not fancy me much then.

"It's getting late," I said, turning to go in.

"Of course," he said, and jumped to get the door for me. "You must be tired after working all day."

"Yes," I agreed. "I should sleep very well." I said good night to the people still in the parlor and made my way upstairs.

But I did not sleep well. I had too many things all running through my mind, too many new ideas and cautions to think about. I would have to make my inquiries discreetly if I wanted to avoid the anti-Indian feelings I had encountered so far. It was not going to be easy.

Saturday was as Mr. Altvater had promised—busier than Friday. I met many more people and was even able to remember a few names from the day before. I sold more yard goods, as if women were pleased to buy from another female, and I found myself pointing out this or that article elsewhere in the store. The work was tiring but I felt that I was doing well and making a fairly good impression. At least Mr. Altvater seemed pleased.

In the afternoon Melly and her mother came in.

"We went to the boarding house and that Mrs. Henkins said you were working here," Melly explained. "Do you really think you'll like doing this?"

"Oh, it's not bad," I said. "It will keep me busy and I won't have to watch my pennies so closely."

"You know, we really could make room for you," Mrs. Crutchfield offered again. "Melly's father found a little house down the street that we're going to rent while we stay here and you're more than welcome to stay with us."

"Thank you, really, but I need to be on my own. I don't like to have to depend on others to provide for me, especially friends."

"It just seems so odd that someone with your grooming should have to work," she said. "We know you must have had good schooling."

"Yes," I admitted slowly. I must have been betraying myself more than I realized. Mrs. Pettit would have been proud. "I did go to a young ladies' academy, but still I don't mind it here at all. In a way it's almost fun."

Melly and her mother cast strange glances at each other as if they didn't believe me. I just laughed.

"Is there anything I can do for you as long as you're here?"

"No, dear," Mrs. Crutchfield said. "We were

just strolling about and thought we'd drop in for a minute. We won't keep you any longer."

"Our house is that tiny white one right next door to that first boarding house you asked at," Melly said.

"On the other side of the street?"

"Yes. You know which one?"

"I think so," I said. "I'll have to come down on my day off and see it."

"Yes, do," Melly said. "It isn't much, but it's only for a while. After we're married, Frank and I will live in the married men's quarters at the fort."

Mrs. Crutchfield smiled at her jubilant daughter and I thought I could see the painful realization that she would soon lose the girl she had raised. It was touching to me, more so because the Crutchfields were releasing their daughter even though it hurt them to do so. I felt a genuine affection for the two women, more than I had felt for anyone for a long time. Even after they left the store I went about my work feeling glad that they had stopped in.

Red Cloud came in before closing and I watched him out of the corner of my eye while he swept around the front counter. It was then that I noticed his slight limp—probably a souvenir of the white raider's bullet. The women that chatted to me about fashion and cloth seemed not even to notice his presence, but it affected me like an electrical charge. I determined I would speak to him.

When I heard Mr. Altvater close the front door

56

my palms began to sweat. I was more nervous than I had ever been meeting any of Grandmere's high society friends. I put the last bolt of cloth away and picked lint and bits of thread from the counter, then turned to find Red Cloud.

He was sweeping my way, his head down almost religiously. I wondered if he had been watching me as I had watched him, and was now trying to look engrossed in his work.

"Hello, Red Cloud," I said quietly.

He stopped and looked up at me slowly, his face and eyes blank. It was much the same sort of look I had used in New York to discourage others from conversation. Seeing it on his face now was a great disappointment to me, but I knew I had expected too much.

"Hello," he said, and returned to his sweeping.

So, I thought, it was not going to be easy for me to find my kinsmen. I had so desperately hoped that Red Cloud would recognize the Cheyenne in me and tell me about my people, but that was painfully unrealistic. Whatever searching I did would have to be on my own. But I was determined to do it.

"Catherine, are you almost done back there?" Mr. Altvater called. "I know how Mrs. Reedy is and it's going on six now. You shouldn't miss your dinner after a day like this."

"I'm coming," I called, and went to get my bag. As I walked toward the door I looked again at Red Cloud. I saw his black eyes on me briefly before he put his head down and disappeared behind a table.

Mr. Lafferty was absent from the dinner table which relaxed me considerably. I noticed Della raising her eyebrows at me but I made no comment. Instead I began planning how I would go about finding my Cheyenne.

"Mr. Greene," I said half way through dinner, "Would it be presumptuous of me to ask to hear some of your Indian stories this evening? I was very tired last night but I really am interested."

"Sure," he said in his unemotional way. "I was affeared my tales might scare you, but you know they happened a long time ago. Haven't had any real trouble for years."

"That's very comforting," I said. "Which brings another point to my mind. Would it be safe for me to ride alone on the outskirts of town?"

Several pairs of eyes swiveled toward me and I was afraid I had overstepped my bounds. I hastened to explain, weaving a story quickly.

"It's just that I am used to riding almost every day at the riding academy," I lied, "and it's my favorite exercise. It is unsafe, then?"

"No'm," Mr. Greene said. "It's not unsafe, just—odd. Out here we don't ride for exercise. More like have to. But I don't see no reason you couldn't if'n you wanted to."

"I understand," I said. "I suppose it does sound strange, but of course we don't have the open spaces in New York that you have here. Could you direct me to where I might purchase a horse?"

"You want to buy a horse of your own?" he asked.

"Well, yes, I would like to. I have enough money, I think."

I could see my cultivated, citified ways were confounding to Mr. Greene, but that was all right. So long as my inquiries and practices seemed eccentric to them they would have no suspicions of my real motives.

"The liv'ry," Mr. Greene said.

"The livery down the street in town?"

"Yes'm. Hank Weller owns it. Tell him I said to give you a good one, else he'll probably sell you a bag of bones."

"I will," I promised. "Would he still be there this evening? I thought I would walk over quickly after dinner, unless he goes home early."

Mr. Greene snorted so I knew I had said something silly again.

"He don't go home—he is home."

"Oh, he lives at the stables?"

"Yes'm. Has a place in the back, so if he ain't in front, well—I'll take you down there. My wagon's still hitched up and I'll run you over. That way I know he won't sell you no bag of bones."

"Thank you, Mr. Greene. That's very kind of you." It pleased me to have him think he must look after me, as if I were an addle-brained woman. And if my encounter with Red Cloud was disappointing my plans this evening were going extremely well.

The livery was dark inside and I was glad Mr. Greene had offered to come with me. I probably would not have gone in at all if I had been alone.

He pulled the buckboard up and handed me down, then led the way inside. We passed stall after stall of munching, nickering horses, but none that I could see clearly. At the very back a light shone through a doorway and Mr. Greene routed Hank Weller from his dinner.

"What you got to sell, you old geezer?" Mr. Greene demanded. "Miss Lance here from New York wants a ridin' horse. You got anything that ain't foundered or gone loco?"

"How do, ma'am," Mr. Weller said to me. He wiped his mouth on his sleeve and glared at Mr. Greene. He was probably a few years younger than the aging scout but accepted the elder's slanderous tongue with friendly derision.

"I got the best horseflesh—pardon me, ma'am—in the country and you know it, Jake. You say you need a ridin' horse, ma'am?"

"Please," I said.

He retreated to the back and got a lantern, then led us back down the row. I saw several horses I would have liked to take a better look at, but if they had been for sale I was sure Mr. Weller would have stopped. Finally he stood in front of a stall and held the light high.

"Here's a mare I got. She's mostly quarter, but some mustang in her, too. Good little mare. Got small feet, good mouth."

"May I take her out?" I asked. Mr. Weller nodded and unlatched the door for me and I led the little mare out of the stall. She was probably just fifteen hands, I guessed, and was not deep in the chest. I walked her out into the evening air where I could see better by the setting sun.

"She's a real nice little mare," Mr. Weller continued. "Gentle and all. She's a lady's horse."

I walked her around a bit more and glanced at Mr. Greene. His forehead was creased and I thought he either was doubtful of the mare or perhaps of my ability.

"Do you have anything else?" I asked. "Something perhaps a little taller?"

"Taller?" Mr. Weller repeated. I could see he had been very certain I would take the mare. "Well, yeah, I have one, a gelding." He sounded less sure of this one and I almost decided then to take the mare.

"I'll put this one up," Mr. Greene offered quickly. So I would see the gelding.

"He's a mite tall," Mr. Weller said, leading the way up a second row of stalls. "And he's mucked up pretty bad right now. I was using him down by the river today."

He held the light up and a black head with a startling white blaze bobbed at the door.

"May I?" I asked, motioning to the door. He unlatched the stall and I led the gelding outside. In the fading light I could see that he was a pinto, but almost sixteen hands. Mud was caked on him clear up to his belly but the outlines of his white patches showed through. His eyes were keen and he had good conformation. He was much more to my liking that the quiet little buckskin.

"May I ride him?" I asked.

Mr. Weller looked doubtful but I would not back down. Finally he handed the lantern to Mr. Greene and went to get me a sidesaddle.

"You sure you want to ride him?" Mr. Greene asked. "He's awfully dirty."

"It's dry, though," I said, feeling the hard mud. "And it'll only be for a moment."

Mr. Weller returned and threw the saddle on the gelding, clinching it and adjusting the stirrup. With a hand up from him I settled myself in the obnoxious saddle and vowed I would be rid of it as soon as was feasible. Taking the reins, I guided the pinto up and back in front of the livery, then kicked him into a trot. His gait was a little rough from his long leggedness but not unpleasant. As the two men watched I galloped him up and back and backed him a little. Satisfied with that, I jumped down and looked more carefully at his feet. They were trimmed and good sized, with no signs of scars or thrush. His chest was deep and his flanks well fleshed.

"I'd like to buy him," I said finally.

The two men glanced at each other, and Mr. Weller cleared his throat.

"All right," he said.

"And of course I'll need the saddle and blanket, and the bridle. Will you figure it all up for me?"

Mr. Weller calculated in his head.

"Oh, and I'll need to board him here. Mrs. Reddy has no room for horses."

Taking it all in account, Mr. Weller gave me a price and I counted it out of my bag. Then, having stuffed the money in a pocket, he unsaddled the horse and I led him back to his stall.

"I think I should like to go riding tomorrow," I said. "Could someone brush him down for me?"

"Yes'm," Mr. Weller said. He latched the stall door as I held the lantern. I raised the light high so I could see my horse better.

"What's his name?"

"Patch," Mr. Weller said. I disliked it and decided I would give him my own name later. I patted his soft muzzle and made to go when a nicker sounded from the next stall. Holding the lantern over, I saw a mule unlike any I'd seen.

"What a beautiful mule!" I said. She had the conformation of a horse with gleaming chestnut skin and large clear eyes. Even her face was not so comical with its huge ears and long nose.

"Ain't she a beaut?" Mr. Weller agreed.

"Yes," I admitted. "Who does she belong to?" I patted her nose.

"Jory Donnelly."

The name meant nothing to me. I wondered if she was as good an animal as she looked.

"He bred her," Mr. Weller continued. "Matter of fact, that's her sire right there next to her."

I moved down to the next stall, one with a high door and heavily bolstered sides. A large, finely shaped head peered out. He was a large dun with a hint of Arabian in his dished face. I reached to pet him but he nipped at me.

"He don't hanker to pettin' much," Mr. Weller said. "Jory don't treat his stock like that."

"What does Mr. Donnelly do?" I asked.

"He's a trapper. Stays in the mountains all winter long and comes to town to sell his skins in spring. You probably seen him. He's a big Irishman, don't talk much."

Something clicked in my mind. "Does he have reddish-brown hair and blue eyes?" I asked, watching the stallion bob his head.

"That's him. Big fella. He sure knows his horseflesh—pardon me, ma'am."

"Yes, I see that," I said. I handed the lantern back to Mr. Weller. "Thank you, Mr. Weller. You've been very kind, and I'm sorry I interrupted your dinner."

"That's okay, ma'am," he said quickly. "I'll have Patch ready for you tomorrow."

"Good." Feeling pleased over my purchase, I left with Mr. Greene and we drove back to the boarding house.

When we arrived the boarders were all assembled in the parlor. Della asked me if I had actually bought a horse and I had to describe him. She thought that was a great joke and Mr. Lafferty who had rejoined the group listened intently.

"Surely you don't intend to ride alone?" he asked finally.

"Yes, I do," I answered sweetly. "Mr. Greene has assured me there's no harm in it." I turned to the older man. "And you said you would tell some of your stories."

Mr. Greene settled into a chair and lit a pipe before beginning. I took my seat by the window but tonight did not turn my attention to the hills. Tonight I wanted to hear about the Cheyenne.

"I was captured by the Cheyenne once," he began. "This was some years ago. I'd been out alone, riding the Platte and not paying as much mind as I should have. A she-bear with cubs spooked my horse before I even knew she was there and I went a-flying. I just about figured I was dead when that she-bear charged me, but I fought her. I had a heck of a time getting my knife out and trying to keep her off my face, but finally I did. She'd clawed my chest and tore half the skin off my arm, just about had me scalped. I don't know how I did it, but I got my knife and killed her. By the time she was dead I didn't even have the strength left to push her off me. I just lay there in the blood—hers and mine—and finally passed out.

"When I came to, there was a fire going and the she-bear was gone off me. I hurt so bad I couldn't hardly move, but I looked around careful like and saw the Indians. Well, I thought, if it ain't a bear it's Indians and I was as good as dead anyway. I pretended I was still asleep 'cause I figured they wouldn't kill me when I was asleep.

"Pretty soon this Indian starts talking English at me, broken English, but I could understand.

" 'You fight bear well,' he said to me.

" 'No,' I said, 'I fight bear, but not well.' I tried to touch my arm but it hurt too bad.

" 'You will live,' the Indian told me. 'We have medicine.' And he walked away.

"Well, I laid there a couple of days and watched them smoking that bear meat and going about their business. They left me be mostly but that one, he come and talk to me ever so often. He told me they had been watching me when the bear attacked and they saw the whole thing. He said they admired the way I fought back and killed her even though I was sorely wounded. They admired that in any man, white or red, and that's why they healed my wounds.

"After about a week they insisted I travel with them to their camp and not knowing what else to do, I did. We rode two days to a small camp, about thirty Indians in all. They showed me a teepee I was to sleep in and gave me food. They even had my horse—the darn fool thing.

"Well, I stayed with them two weeks. The one who spoke English explained things to me, talked to me about hunting and fighting. He said they would have killed me if I hadn't met the bear. They were getting ready to move west, away from the white man, but they killed any white man they saw. They were still feuding over the raids on their camps and he asked me if I'd ever killed a Cheyenne. Well, right there I was about as scared as I'd been, but I looked him in the eye and I said, yes, I had killed Cheyenne. But I told him that I wasn't ever going to lay a hand to another one, not after they saved me. I made that Indian a promise right then and there.

"Next day, they said I could go. The one that spoke English, he brought me my horse and gave me a blanket, then he said he had a present for me. He gave me a necklace of that bear's teeth. And I thought, that bear almost killed me, but I'll never forget it. I said goodbye to them Indians and rode out of camp and home. Never heard about 'em again. Guess they moved west like they said they was."

Mr. Greene bit his pipe and sucked on it thoughtfully. It seemed that everyone else had been as engrossed as I was and there was a short silence.

"And did you?" Della asked finally.

"Did I what?"

"Did you keep your promise? Did you ever kill another Indian?"

"Oh, I've killed Indians, but never another Cheyenne. No, not since then. I made that promise and I'll keep it."

Mr. Lafferty snorted. "What's the difference? They're all alike anyway. Probably the only reason they didn't kill you was to let you bring back stories of how noble they are. If you came face to face with another Cheyenne, he wouldn't hesitate to kill you."

"Probably not," Mr. Greene said coolly. "But I'm not concerned with what the Cheyenne would do. I gave my word and I'll keep it. That's enough for me."

I was enjoying the conversation and was disappointed when everyone suddenly began to say their goodnights. I supposed there was some regulation about the length of Mr. Greene's stories and I had failed to see it, but I made my way up-stairs beside Della.

"Ain't he fascinatin'?" she asked. "I've lived here quite a while and I've heard lots of stories, but not like he tells 'em."

"Yes, he's very interesting," I agreed. "I hope he'll tell more."

"Oh, he will, don't worry. As long as anyone will listen, he'll tell."

Alone in my room, I felt I had accomplished a good amount that day. Besides working a full shift I had bought myself a horse and discovered a probable ally in Mr. Greene. At least I knew he woudn't condemn me for my Cheyenne blood. And lastly, I had found out the name of the big mountain man.

Chapter Three

I AWOKE Sunday morning to the clatter of footsteps on the stairs. It was breakfast time, but I lay abed. I wanted no questions, no encouragements about going to church. When Della tapped lightly on the door, I remained silent and she went away. I slept another hour before I forced myself out of bed.

I dressed carefully for what I had planned for the day. I would ride, but not in the fashion of a New York lady. Beneath my skirt I wore no petticoats. Outwardly I would look no different, except perhaps a little less billowy, but outside of town a transformation would take place. I wore leather boots that laced up to my knees and my black stockings would cover the rest of my leg if my skirt became unruly. I secured my hair in a knot low on my head and left.

I headed for the livery, then had to change direction. I couldn't walk past the church in front of Mrs. Reedy's, so instead I made my way behind the main street. It seemed no one else was about. I even avoided the wood sidewalks so my boots would not sound on the boards.

At the livery I went directly to my horse's stall. He was just nosing the last of his feed from the bin and then turned toward me. Munching contentedly, he permitted me to pet his shiny neck. All the mud had been curried from his fur and he shone starkly black and white. I thought him the most gorgeous horse I had ever seen.

"Shall we ride?" I asked him quietly. He swallowed his last bit of grain and blew through his nose. "A fine answer," I said.

"The only answer you're liable to get," a voice said behind me. I spun around and had to look up to see the trapper's face.

"And the only answer I was expecting," I said embarrassed.

"Oh," he said, his eyes crinkling at the corners. "Sorry, I didn't mean to intrude." He walked past me to his mule and went into her stall.

I stood at my horse's head for a moment, wanting to talk more with Mr. Donnelly but still feeling embarrassed. I watched him as he ran his large hands down the mule's legs. Up close he was even more imposing. He wore Indian fashion buckskins that only seemed to accentuate the bulk of his body. I had seldom seen a man that broad of chest. I imagined him well at home on a mountain trail.

"That's a very unusual mule," I said finally.

He looked up at me and seemed to consider what I'd said.

"Yes, she is. Valuable, too. I've been offered a lot of money for her, but I won't sell her. She's too good on the trail." One hand on the jenny's hock, he stared at me until I became uncomfortable.

"Is Mr. Weller in? I haven't seen him." I glanced down toward the back but saw no movement.

"Yeah, Hank's there. I'll go get him for you."

"No," I said quickly, "that's all right." Before he could rise I turned and walked down the length of the stable.

I found Mr. Weller in his back room, soaping the saddle I had ordered with my horse.

"Why, Mr. Weller, that's very thoughtful of you," I said sincerely. "You really didn't need to go to all that trouble. And Patch looks wonderful. You must have spent hours cleaning him up."

"Oh, that's okay, ma'am. I wouldn't let you ride a mucked up horse, nor a dusty saddle, neither." He winked at me. "That'd be bad advertising."

"True, Mr. Weller," I agreed. "And I'll be pleased to tell anyone who asks where I bought my beautiful horse and saddle."

While Mr. Weller saddled the gelding for me, I noticed the mountain man saddling his stallion. I chanced to look at him when I thought he wasn't watching but he caught me staring. After that I turned my back and waited patiently for Mr. Weller.

"He's all set, ma'am," the livery man said finally. "Come on outside and I'll give you a foot up."

In the saddle, I adjusted my skirt modestly and took the reins. Mr. Weller watched me as I trotted off northward. I wondered if Mr. Donnelly watched also.

I cut through town, keeping clear of the churches, and headed my horse toward the hills. He picked up his feet nicely and I patted his neck.

"I think we shall get along very well," I told him, "and I don't care if you don't answer me at all."

Once away from the town, I kicked him to a loping canter that carried us quickly across the level ground. I was in a hurry to be rid of the obnoxious sidesaddle but I had to make sure I wasn't seen.

Finally we reached the seclusion of the hills and I guided him among the trees. I searched for a landmark, a place I would find easily later on. Before I had gone very far I found an outcropping of rock with a shallow, low-ridged cave. I slid off my horse and removed the saddle, placing it back in the hollow where it couldn't be seen. Then I stood back and looked at my horse.

Patch, I thought sourly. It sounded like a dog's name. I loved my horse's coloring and the vivid etching of white against black on his side. It reminded me of thunderheads and rain.

"Thunder," I said. He showed no response at all.

I came closer and stroked his neck. "You are like thunder and lightning," I said, "and I will call you Thunder whether you like it or not." He reached for some tall grass at his feet but the reins caught him short and he snorted. "Be that way, then," I said. I untied him and threw myself up on his back, my skirt riding up almost to my waist. I tucked it beneath my legs so only my boots showed black against the white of Thunder's side and we rode off.

I gloried in riding in the forest. Having Thunder beneath me picking out a way up the narrow deer trails seemed to transport me back more than seven years. Suddenly I was a child again, riding carelessly through the woods on my barebacked pony. The jays squawked at me from overhead and I urged Thunder to a gallop. The wind in my face fanned a fire in me and I drove Thunder madly up the hill, up to the crest where I could look out over the countryside.

I realized then how much I had missed it all. In New York I had been more concerned about my ailing mother and hadn't pined for my homeland as much as for her. When the lung sickness had finally killed her, I had been too miserable to be homesick, too frightened to miss the land. Now that it was all before me again it was almost a physical pain in my chest and I think I could have cried.

Breathing in the scented air, I kicked Thunder down the back side of the hill and along the narrow trails. He flicked his ears forward and back, his eyes alert to the stirrings in the forest. At the base of the hill was a tiny stream and Thunder leaped it easily. I laid low on his neck and allowed him to make his own way through the trees.

I rode for hours that day. It would not have been possible for me to have ridden too long. In the early afternoon I stopped and tethered Thunder to a tree beside another, larger stream and I relaxed in the grass. I had brought some cheese with me and I nibbled at it while I sat and listened to the bubbling water. I decided if there were a heaven like Grandmere spoke of, it would have to be like this.

When the shadows began to grow long, I climbed aboard Thunder and started back. I was not as disoriented in the forest as I thought I would be and found my way with only a little trouble. Feeling contented and quiet, I laid along Thunder's neck and spoke softly to him as he walked.

We crested one hill after another and finally crossed the stream that marked the final leg. Feeling saddened that we must return to town, I let Thunder pick his way slowly up the hill. As we crested it, I froze. A lone figure on horseback sat not a hundred yards up the ridge from me.

I did not think the rider had seen me so I guided Thunder cautiously behind a group of large trees, hoping their wide trunks would hide us. Then I sat and waited. Unfortunately the rider began to urge his horse my way.

Thunder stamped his foot nervously at the tight

rein I kept on him but I could not allow myself to be seen. Now I almost wished I had chosen the buckskin mare, for her coloring would melt into the background and her small frame could be hidden easily. But I hadn't chosen her and the rider came on. Very shortly I recognized him.

I sat Thunder quietly behind the trees until I met the blue eyes of the trapper staring at me. Then it seemed a little ridiculous to stay hidden so I walked my horse forward to meet Mr. Donnelly. He quickly assessed me, noting my barebacked straddle and my skirt tucked immodestly under my legs. I lifted my chin and stared at him expectantly.

"I had heard you took riding lessons in New York," he said. Well, I thought, news travels fast. About the lessons was true, although they were more to acquaint me with the hated sidesaddle than to teach me to sit a horse. When I said nothing he continued. "You didn't learn to ride like that back there."

"Where I learned to ride is no concern of yours, Mr. Donnelly," I said. "And I do not appreciate being followed and spied upon."

"How was I to know you were so well versed in riding the wilderness? Had you been merely a city woman like you claim, you never would have found your way out."

"Again, what I do is no concern of yours. Now I must be getting back." I turned Thunder and started down the hillside but the dun stallion fell into step alongside. I refused to look over. How was I to explain to anyone why Mr. Donnelly had seen me ride in such an unladylike fashion?

"Is it really so important that no know of your, uh, riding habits?" Mr. Donnelly asked. I turned toward him and found him studying my face, which I was sure must be mirroring my dismay.

"Important enough," I said. "I do not wish to be regarded as a freak or pressed for explanations."

"But you already are a freak," he said smiling, "but a nice one."

"How dare you?" I bristled, pulling Thunder to a stop.

"You are a fine, well-mannered lady from New York, practically royalty to hear it about town. That's odd enough, yet you seem to want that much known." He gestured at my boots. "This seems more in keeping with a rugged way of life. You ride as if it's second nature to you. How would that make you a freak? Because it's not keeping to your image?"

"Are all mountain men as nosy and speculative as you?" I asked, kicking Thunder into a walk.

"I don't think so," he laughed. "But you see, there is very seldom anyone about as interesting as you seem to be."

The last thing I wanted to be was interesting. When word got around of my wild excursions, questions would be raised and speculations would be voiced and I imagined it wouldn't be long before my high cheekbones became noticeable, or my raven-black hair. In New York exotic looks were not associated with Indians; it would be different in Leavenworth. I was afraid I might be forced to leave and strike out on my own, ready or not.

"Well, you may not have me around to study much anymore," I said, thinking of my choices.

"Even if I say nothing about what I've seen?"

I couldn't help staring over at him in disbelief. "Why should you keep any secrets for me?" I asked. I noticed how his blue eyes sparkled.

"Strictly personal reasons." He grinned. "If you get scared away, I'll never know the reason behind your double image. Curiosity is a terrible trait of the Irish."

"How can I be sure you'll keep your word?"

"You can't," he said simply. "You'll just have to trust me, although I get the feeling you don't trust anyone. But it's either that or take your strangeness someplace else, and I don't think you're ready to do that. It'd be much simpler to trust me."

"If you're expecting me to feel obligated to you, Mr. Donnelly, you will be extremely disappointed."

"I doubt that you'll disappoint me, Cathy," he said smugly.

"That's not my name," I flared.

"What is your name?"

"Catherine."

"Cathy will do fine."

I didn't say anything to that. Mr. Donnelly was far too curious and interested and I was afraid that anything I said would only interest him more. Anyway, having him so close to me and staring at me with those eyes made me nervous. I found I couldn't think rationally and I was sweating. Better to ride in silence than to have him play his cat-and-mouse games with me.

When we neared the rocks that hid my side-saddle, I stopped well back. He knew too much already to add my hiding place to his store of knowledge.

"I can find my way back by myself now," I said. "You needn't feel you must escort me."

"I don't," he said easily. When I didn't move, he looked to the rocks and back to me. "If you're worried about my finding your hiding place, I already know. As a matter of fact, I put some rocks and brush over the entrance so it couldn't be seen so easily. You ought to do that from now on."

"What makes you think I'm going to do this again?" I asked, sending Thunder toward the rocks. I tried to keep some semblance of dignity, even as Donnelly cut down all my defenses.

"You enjoy it too much to quit after one ride," he said.

Ignoring him, I stopped at the rocks. He dismounted and walked toward me but I slid from Thunder's back before he could help me down. Instead he took my rein and held both horses while I got my saddle.

I thought he would offer to cinch it for me, but he just watched without comment. When I was ready to mount he made no move to hand me up and I climbed into the uncomfortable contraption as modestly as I could. He seemed to enjoy my discomfort. When I had arranged my skirt over my ankles, he stepped aboard his dun and we headed for town.

"You stay at Mrs. Reedy's, don't you?" he asked.

"Yes, if it's any of your business," I said. "But she's very strict about visitors."

"That doesn't bother me," he said lightly. "I don't plan on visiting. I'll know where I can find you." He tipped his battered hat to me, and said, "Goodbye Cathy." Then he suddenly spurred his dun away. I had to rein Thunder in to keep him back and I watched as Mr. Donnelly rode westward through the prairie grass.

As far as I was concerned the exhilaration had gone out of my ride. Mr. Donnelly's knowledge of my secret was a nagging worry and his behavior toward me assumed too much for comfort. I wondered if he was as familiar with all women. No doubt he was one of those foul-tempered mountain men who held no respect for anyone.

I loped Thunder back to town and put him up with Mr. Weller's help. He offered to brush the gelding down for me so I hurried back to Mrs. Reedy's to get out of my dirty clothes. Luckily no one was downstairs and I went up quietly and bathed. I barely had enough time to dress and pin my hair back before dinner.

I entered the dining room demurely, as silently as I could. As I slid into my chair I noticed eyes swiveling toward me.

"Were you riding all this time?" Della asked.

"Yes. I rather lost track of time, I'm afraid.

There's so much country out there."

"How do you like it?" Mr. Greene asked.

"I think it's beautiful," I said, avoiding Mr. Lafferty's eyes. He regarded me curiously and I decided I would stay clear of him if I could. The talk centered around the interesting places within riding distance and I was glad to be out of the limelight.

After dinner there seemed to be no hurry to the parlor so I assumed Sunday evening was a free evening without planning. Della had some knitting she was doing and asked me to sit with her but Charles was the only other person in the parlor with us.

"Riding must be good exercise," Della remarked. "At least it seems to do *you* good. Maybe I should try it."

I laughed. "It is definitely exercise," I said, "I feel the muscles in my back aching already, and tomorrow it will probably be worse." It was true. My thighs ached a little, although I couldn't admit that in mixed company.

"Well, then I think I'll stay on my own two feet," Della said. "That's safer for me."

"There's a lot I want to see while I'm here and on horseback will be the best way for me. Anyway, I might as well get used to riding the plains before my father comes."

"You don't have to ride alone, though," Mr. Lafferty broke in.

"Thank you," I said, "but I just wanted to sort of wander around today by myself. It takes me awhile to get used to new places and I like to do it my own way." I was more nervous discussing this than I should have been, but I thought of Mr. Donnelly and the flurry that would result if people knew we'd been together. I was sure common knowledge of our rendezvous would do nothing at all to help me in my search, aside from my own confused feelings in the matter.

"Would you help me wind this yarn?" Della asked.

"Of course." She put one strand around my outstretched hands and began to straighten the yarn around them.

"Do you knit?" she asked.

"No. I do some needlework and embroidery, but I'm not very good at it. What are you making?"

"A shawl. When I'm done with this one, I'll make one for you. Would you like me to teach you how?"

"I could try it," I said. Knitting didn't appeal to me at all, but I hated to hurt Della's feelings.

"When I'm done winding this, I'll show you a little bit."

Charles seemed bored by our discussion and finally excused himself. I was glad. I had too much to think about this evening to worry about him. I was still sorting out my feelings for the disrespectful, handsome mountain man.

My working days went quickly. It seemed all my time was caught up in challenging situations and I had little time for boredom or even introspection.

I learned a lot every day, about the store and Leavenworth and the people in it. If I had realized it then, I could have learned a lot about myself, too. But there was no time.

In a week I grew comfortable in my back corner of the store. I knew where almost everything was or could find without asking what I didn't know. I could direct customers to most anything they needed or at least to the general area. Mr. Altvater praised my retention and allowed me to make change by myself. One day of watching over my shoulder seemed to convince him of my money sense and honesty.

I saw Red Cloud every day and made it a point to speak to him. So many times I thought of speaking Cheyenne to him, just one word, but I held back. It had been years since I had spoken a Cheyenne word aloud, but I often ran them through my mind or deliberately made myself think in that language so I wouldn't forget. The image of my own mother practicing her native tongue drove me to practice mine. But I could not say a word to Red Cloud.

He remained uncommunicative. I felt him watching me from time to time but I could not fathom the reason. If he noticed the similarity between his dark eyes and mine or the blackness of our hair, he gave no sign.

Mr. Donnelly came into the store once that week, and that I think more in spite of me than because of me. He purchased some small item from Mr. Altvater, seemed to remember me and touched his hat brim to me solicitously. I only nodded and he left. That silent exchange seemed almost conspiratorial to me and it embarrassed me to think that I had agreed to or acknowledged any relationship with the mountain man.

Melly made it a habit to drop by the store every other day or so, usually accompanied by her mother. I came to look forward to her visits. She was so full of love and life that she offered me a temporary relief from all my concerns, far more serious in comparison. When she spoke about Frank, her eyes lit up and she smiled unwittingly, as if just the thought of him was enough to send her soaring. I began to feel envious of her.

"Have you ever been in love?" she asked me one day when she and I stood alone in my back corner. Mr. Altvater, I found, didn't mind at all that she visited with me during my work hours, so long as it didn't interfere.

"Once," I said, thinking back.

"Was he very handsome?" Even as she spoke I knew she was imagining her soldier.

"Yes," I said.

"Isn't it funny how it makes you feel? Daddy gets so annoyed at me when I talk about Frank, but Mother understands. I wonder if men never feel that way?"

"Surely Frank loves you, though," I said.

"Oh, I know he does, but it just doesn't seem to affect men the same way. You never see them just sitting and daydreaming, but that's all I seem to be able to do." Melly laughed at herself. "Isn't it odd?"

"Yes," I agreed, laughing with her. She was so funny I couldn't help it. I even found myself wishing I could be as lucky and as happy as she.

"I've heard there are lots of men in California—rich and poor and in between. You'll probably meet so many of them, you can choose out of the lot who you'll marry."

"I'm not even thinking about marriage yet," I said, dusting my shelves of notions.

"But you will be," Melly insisted. "I'm so excited about marrying Frank—but I'm scared, too."

"Scared?" I asked.

"Yes, terrified. We're going to be married at the fort, and all those officers will be there. I can't even imagine what it'll be like."

"You'll get through it all right," I assured her.

"Yes, I suppose I will," she laughed. "It's just fun to think about. You're going to have to come by the house and see my wedding gown."

"I'd like that," I said. I was sure she would look beautiful even if the gown were a rag.

"How about tonight?" she asked suddenly. "Come for dinner. You haven't even been down to see the house yet. It's a tiny thing, but it's kind of cute."

"But it's such short notice," I said.

"So? Mother won't mind. Really, it's all right. I'll go tell Mother right now. Can you be there by seven? Or even earlier. We can talk."

"All right," I laughed. I knew I couldn't argue with her. Excited by the idea, Melly rushed out of the store.

As soon as Mr. Altvater locked up that evening—and I said hello to Red Cloud—I rushed to Mrs. Reedy's and told Margaret not to set a place for me at dinner. I cleaned up quickly in my room, touching up my hair, and left for the Crutchfields.

Even though I'd never been to the house, I knew where it was. It was located just across the street and a little north of the livery, right next to the first boardinghouse I'd inquired at. Melly was right—it was tiny—but well cared for and clean. Lights glowed from inside and I knocked at the rough wooden door.

"Catherine, come in," Melly said as soon as she jerked the door open. She was still as excited as she had been at the store. "See what I mean about the house? Isn't it funny?"

She closed the door behind me and I looked about. The living room took up most of the floor plan, having a large stone fireplace and a bare wooden floor. To the right of the door was the dining area, and beyond that the kitchen, all an open, elongated dogleg. I couldn't imagine the Crutchfields taking such a frontier style house, even for the short time they'd be in Leavenworth.

"I'm so glad you could come," said Mrs. Crutchfield suddenly. She had just come out of the bedroom, to the left off the living room.

"Thank you," I said.

"Melly's been chasing me about all afternoon, saying we must have this for dinner and that for dessert. She never got this excited over any dinner guests back east."

"This is different, Mother," she said. Then to me, "Come and see my dress."

I followed Melly into the bedroom and she pulled open the doors of a wardrobe. I noticed that all the furnishings, from the used couch in the living room to the plain bed and wardrobe, looked second hand.

"Isn't it beautiful?" she asked.

The gown was lovely. It was long and white, with a high lace collar and long, lace sleeves, cut in a point at the wrist. The train fell away in yards of lace, and Melly held up the matching veil.

"It's gorgeous," I said, sincerely. "You didn't get that here."

"No," she laughed. "We brought it with us. I just love it." She held it up to her and whirled around. "Do you think Frank will like it?"

"He'd have to be blind not to," I said.

Melly laughed and put the gown away. As she did, she almost caught it on a splinter on the wardrobe.

"Isn't this furniture awful? Daddy said it was all the owners could get on such short notice. There aren't any houses for rent here—only hotels for overnighters and places to buy for settlers. Mother hates it here."

"It is a little rough," I agreed. "But at least it won't be for long."

"No, that's what else I was going to tell you. After I left you at the store a messenger came from the fort. They said Frank's campaign was cut short and he'll be home any day!"

"Wonderful!" I said. "Will you be setting the wedding date then?"

"I'll have to check with Frank as soon as he gets back, but I think so. Mother and Daddy need to get back as soon as they can."

"That's wonderful. I'm really happy for you, Melly."

In a burst of enthusiasm, she came and hugged me. It was the first time I'd been touched in an affectionate way since my mother died and it filled me with happiness for her. I began to feel that I at last had a real friend.

We sat down to dinner shortly after and Melly kept up an almost running chatter through the meal. Mrs. Crutchfield and I occasionally answered a question or a thought put to us, and Mr. Crutchfield seemed satisfied—or perhaps used to—letting his daughter go on. I supposed he was forced into a silent role whenever Melly was so excited. I doubted there was anything that could subdue her at times like that and I also doubted either of the Crutchfields would do or say anything to dampen her enthusiasm. It was a very warm and pleasant evening for me. If Melly's happiness hadn't been so infectious it would have made me pine for the family I never had.

After dinner Melly and I helped her mother with the dishes and cleared off the table. Mr. Crutchfield excused himself to walk uptown to get a cigar so we three women continued our girl talk. Melly and her mother told me as many details about the wedding as they had worked out and Melly insisted I come. It began to sound very complicated and exciting, even for a military wedding. I was glad it was not up to me to plan.

Finally I had to leave. As much as I enjoyed the Crutchfields, I was not used to such intimacy and I craved the privacy of my own room. It was hard for me to be receptive to customers all day and have no time to myself as I was so used to. I made my excuses and began to leave.

"Wait until Daddy comes back," Melly said. "He should be back any time and he'll walk you home."

"No, that's all right. It's just five blocks or so and it's all on the main street. I don't want to bother Mr. Crutchfield."

"It's no bother," Melly's mother said.

"No, really," I said, my hand on the door. "It won't take me five minutes to walk it. I'll be all right." I thanked them again for the dinner and left.

As long as I was so close to the livery, I decided to walk over for a minute and see Thunder. It was dark inside, but I knew where his stall was and walked down to it. When I stood at the door, I heard his soft nicker and held my hand out. He pushed his blazed muzzle into my palm.

"How are you, boy?" I asked quietly. He blew into my hand, probably disappointed that I didn't offer a tidbit, but stood beside the door where I could pet him.

"You like me, don't you?" I said. "You like to go riding in the hills, huh?" I ruffed the sleek fur on his neck with my fingers and toyed with his forlock. I would have liked to take him out for a midnight ride but knew it was impossible. I would be glad when I was free of the restrictions Leavenworth imposed on me and I could ride across the plains anytime I chose.

Just then I felt a prickle of fear and I froze. At the very edge of my field of vision I realized a hulking figure was standing silently in the darkness. The man's purposeful quiet and the fact that he blocked my way out of the livery caused a shiver of panic to run down my back. My mind instantly touched all points of action—running, screaming, fighting. I wished I had a weapon. After what seemed like endless minutes of indecision, I simply turned my head.

It was Donnelly.

"Do you enjoy scaring women to death or do you just have a natural talent for it?" I asked. My fear melted into relief at seeing someone I knew, but I was angry at his method of approach. I reasoned that he could have attacked me much more easily in the hills than here in town, so I didn't fear that, but I was infuriated that he skulked about in the dark without me being aware he was there.

"Sorry," he said with a grin. "Didn't mean to scare you." He walked toward me, his boots making no sound on the hard dirt floor.

"Is there some reason why you keep following me?"

"I didn't intend to follow you," he said, leaning against the stalls. "I just saw you and wondered what you were doing. You seem to do such interesting things."

Anger was welling up inside me at the joking tone of voice he used. I studied his face in the dimness and wondered how he could be so handsome and so infuriating at the same time. In another place or time I might have welcomed the way his eyes felt on me, but in Leavenworth he was a threat to my search. And besides that, he took far too many liberties and made me feel uncomfortably sensual.

"I won't be doing anything interesting tonight," I managed and turned to pass him. He stood in my way just a second longer then he needed to, then let me by. I thought I had handled that very well until he fell into step beside me.

"I can walk home by myself," I said, feeling like a supervised child.

"You ever heard of Quantrill's Raiders?"

"I, uh, yes, I think so."

"The war hasn't been over that long and there's still a lot of high feelings and blood letting. Just because we've got a jail doesn't mean all the criminals are locked up."

I didn't see any point in answering him so we walked in silence for a bit. I was aware of the trapper's size and strength and thought that if anyone would make a good bodyguard, he would. If he weren't so damned smug.

"You raised on a farm or something before you went to school?" he asked.

"What are you, the official investigator of new

people in town?"

"No, I stay by myself unless I know someone interesting enough to be with. I wouldn't give you a wooden nickel for most people. But I figure you must have been on a farm or a ranch, maybe raised poor."

"Why?" I demanded, piqued by the inference.

"Because of what you said about Beauty."

"Who's Beauty?"

"My mule," he said, still sounding thoughtful. "There's no city-bred woman alive who would find a single good thing to say about a mule, no matter what it looked like. So you can't be from New York, even if you were schooled there." I remained quiet. In Cheyenne camps mules were rare and greatly prized but I doubted the trapper knew that.

Suddenly I realized he was watching me. I hoped he hadn't read the dismay I was feeling. I composed my features into a blank wall that I knew was unreadable. Luckily we were almost to the church and soon I could escape into the boardinghouse.

"When are you going riding again?" he asked.

"Do you really think I'd arrange to meet you?" I asked testily. "You must be insane."

"Could be," he said grinning. I almost thought he was going to escort me up the boardinghouse steps, but he stopped there. I decided the only way to discourage him was to ignore him and I walked up the steps and went inside without a word or backward glance. I went directly to my room and, much as I hated myself for it, went to my window and looked out. Donnelly stood below until he saw me, smiled and turned away.

Chapter Four

THAT SUNDAY I was still undecided about going riding. I was afraid if I did I would somehow bump into the mountain man and I didn't want him gathering any more clues about me. On the other hand, I felt stifled in my room and wanted to get out. Finally I couldn't stand it at my window a second more and I left for the stable.

Hank saddled Thunder for me and I rode out toward the river. I had thought of investigating south of town but didn't want to ride too near the fort, so I went east instead. I rode along the river, watching the sun sparkle on the water. It was a beautiful May day, clear and bright. Thunder's legs swished through the tall grass along the river bank and a light breeze played over us. It did a lot to ease my tension.

I realized I had become sidetracked. My intent was to use Leavenworth only as a jumping off point, but so far I had done nothing to find my Cheyenne. I couldn't strike out on my own and just start looking; I had to have something to go on. But how was I going to find that something?

There were only three people I could think of who might know. Red Cloud would probably be my best bet, but he seemed afraid of me or at least distrustful. I wasn't sure if he was that way with everyone or if he just wasn't sure what to make of me yet. And then I wondered if he was aware of band movements. It was possible he had entirely lost touch in the years he had spent here.

Mr. Greene might know. Being an ex-scout, he probably kept his ear to the ground and would know as much about Indian movement as anyone in Fort Leavenworth. Although I knew from his storytelling the other night that he was respectful of the Cheyenne, that didn't mean he would help me. Men sometimes turned funny when faced with a squaw, be it full-blooded Indian woman, a mixed breed or even a white woman who had lived among Indians. I remembered sneering remarks about my mother and me at the fort, although at thirteen I didn't understand the words, just the tones. So I couldn't be sure of Mr. Greene, not yet.

That left Donnelly. Since he traveled the plains regularly every year he would have a lot of working knowledge, but there was no way I could ask him. He was too curious, too perceptive and too masculine. Around him my emotions swayed between excitement and annoyance and I had trouble doing anything except reacting to him. He was far too upsetting to me to even consider telling confidences to. I would have to find another way.

During my musings Thunder had walked lazily along the riverbank and we were some distance from town. Since I still rode with my sidesaddle I didn't bother to avoid the farm houses here and there along the shore and even answered a wave from a farmer or two along the way. It was much too nice a day to hide in the trees and skulk about like an outlaw.

Eventually I found a quiet, shaded place where the cottonwoods grew thick and I tied Thunder there to graze. I made a seat for myself in the lush grass and threw sticks and leaves in the water and watched them float lazily downstream. I reflected that I had come a long way from my grandparents' brownstone, but I still had almost as long a way to go. Still, there had been times when I wondered if I would ever see the plains again, much as I dreamed about it. Now the buffalo grass spread out behind me as far as I could see, and somewhere out there was my father. I wished I could simply get on Thunder and ride directly to camp. If I could to that, I'd leave without a backward glance.

I don't know how long I sat there, but the sun warmed my back and Thunder grew restless.

Returning to town didn't appeal to me but I felt tranquil after the time by myself. I could manage to spend the rest of the evening among people again.

Thunder trotted into town, probably barn sour and anxious to be fed. I unsaddled him and let Hank put him up, since we hadn't ridden hard enough for him to need brushing. I noticed the stallion two stalls down was gone and wondered where Donnelly was. If he had gone out intending to find me in the hills he would be disappointed.

As I walked up town I noticed the number of soldiers riding or walking about. I wasn't sure, but it seemed like there were quite a bit more than I had seen before on a Sunday. Idly I wondered why that was, but went on to the boardinghouse.

Charles Lafferty was there.

"Good afternoon," he said. "You've been riding?"

"Yes. I rode along the river; it's such a beautiful day."

"I looked for you this morning," he said. "I was hoping I could accompany you to church."

"Oh," I hedged. "I prefer to worship alone. It's a habit I developed from being on my own a lot."

Charles watched me closely as if he doubted the truth of my words. I was afraid not going to church would cast suspicion on me, but I still would not go. I refused to accept the white man's god who called for wholesale slaughter of nonwhites. That was one point I would not budge on, so I would just have to endure the sidelong glances.

'I hope you won't think me presumptuous," Charlies said finally, "but I'd like to invite you to dinner next Sunday evening. Tom Evans, the newspaper publisher, owns the building I work out of and I go to dinner there occasionally. I happened to mention you to him the other day and he insisted I ask you along. Tom's always eager to hear about events back east. They're wonderful people, really. Would you come?"

A newspaper publisher? That might be someone worth knowing, I thought. Perhaps he might have access to Indian movements and I could learn about them without revealing myself.

"Yes, I'd like that," I said.

Charles's face lit up. "You would? Oh, good. They generally have dinner at six on Sunday so we ought to leave here about five-thirty. They live just two blocks west of the Planters'."

"That's fine," I said. "Now I really need to go upstairs. I'm a mess from riding and I need to wash my hair."

"Of course," Charles said. "I'll see you at dinner."

Perhaps this was just what I needed, I thought as I washed my hair in a basin. Any large migrations of the Indians, any raids or skirmishes with cavalry troops would be newsworthy and so acceptable topics of conversation. It was possible this was the best lead I had so far. I sat at my window and thought about it as I combed my long hair dry.

That evening Charles was more attentive than he had been and I took another look at him. He took life very seriously for twenty-four and was very mature. I imagined he would make a thoughtful husband and an excellent provider—for someone else. If I were to choose to go back east and live my life there, he would be a good man to do it with. But the only direction I was going was west.

I almost laughed at the predicament I was in. Where before I had never had a problem with men, I now had two of them interfering with my search. I wondered if I had lost my ability to freeze men out of my life like I could in New York. Certainly I had not suddenly become so beautiful that they couldn't help themselves. Or maybe I was dropping my guard as I got closer to my homeland. I wasn't sure what it was, but it was bothersome. I couldn't let anyone stop me now.

When I climbed the stairs that night, I looked back and saw Charles's eyes on me. They were steady and dark, as if they would bore into me. I thought about him, and myself, until I fell asleep.

My work at the store was comfortably routine now. When it was slow I had taken to dusting, not only by back corner but the rest of the store as well. Mr. Altvater seemed pleased. At other times I would replenish the stock or straighten the shelves, pulling items forward in full view. The menial jobs kept me busy so I wouldn't think of the obstacles I was running into. I enjoyed my work and Mr. Altvater. We had a good arrangement at the store.

I had become a good customer as well. Since I had so few clothes, I began to buy material for Della to sew for me. I had her keep to a basic style, simple long skirts and tailored blouses. I certainly didn't need much in the way of fancy clothes, not with my destination in mind.

That Monday afternoon, Melly came into the store. I could tell by the wide grin on her face that she was fairly bursting with good news. She hurried back to my counter.

"Catherine!" she said. "Frank's home! His unit got back yesterday."

"I knew there was some reason your face was lit up like that." I laughed. "Have you been able to spend any time with him yet?"

"A little, last night," she said. "But he's coming to dinner Wednesday night. Will you come, too? I told him about you and I want you to meet him. I know you'll like him."

"But you'll want to be alone," I said. "You have a lot to talk about."

"No, I want you to come. Please? You're my best friend, at least in Leavenworth, and I want you to come. I want you to meet Frank."

"All right, you've talked me into it. What time?"

"Just come over right after you get off work. We'll have time to talk before dinner."

"Okay, Wednesday after work."

"Yes, don't forget." She laughed at herself. "I may not be back in before then to remind you."

Lucky Melly, I thought. So young and sure of her

future. I wondered if she knew how lucky she was to have a niche, a place where she unrefutably belonged. It was probably something she never thought of. Whose fault was it that I had no place and she did? I dismissed the thought that the white man's god had thrown his lot against me again. If I had no help from anyone else, I would find my way. There had to be a place for me and I would search until I found it.

Tuesday afternoon Jory Donnelly came in. He leaned against the front counter and talked to Mr. Altvater for a time. At first I was afraid he had come to see me, but the longer he spoke with my boss the more I thought otherwise, so I went about my work. He hadn't even looked back, so I ignored him. I was stooped down behind my counter when he towered over me.

"Can I help you with something?" I asked coolly. I stood up and smoothed my skirt.

"Maybe," he said. He grinned in his infuriatingly charming way and his eyes seemed to play over me as if he were seeing me for the first time. He deliberately looked me over in a way that excited even as it insulted. I refused to shrink away from him, though.

"I have work to do," I said when he remained silent. "I can't stand here playing games with you."

"You were avoiding me on Sunday," he said.

"I was doing nothing of the kind. I didn't even see you Sunday."

"That's what I mean. You rode someplace else."

"I'll ride wherever I please. Now if you'll excuse me, I have work to do." I turned away from him and began to arrange the items on the shelves behind me.

"It's too bad you can't wear your skirt up around your knees in town like you do out there."

I spun around, a shocked look on my face. "How dare you say a thing like that to me here?" I demanded in a hushed voice. "If you had any decency at all you wouldn't mention that."

He smiled. "It's true, though, and I don't have any decency. At least that's what I've heard."

I didn't realize I had leaned across the counter toward him until I saw Charles at the front of the store from the corner of my eye. I straightened up and looked down at Charles. At the same time, Donnelly turned and looked also, although he stayed leaning on the counter the way he had been.

Charles's face was anything but friendly. He met Donnelly's eyes, then mine, and left as quickly as he'd come.

"Friend of yours?" Donnelly asked cheerfully.

I was seething. What must Charles think now? "Will you go away and leave me alone? You've caused me enough problems!"

"Oh, I see," he said slowly. "Well, I wouldn't want to cause you any problems, especially with your lawyer friend." He stood up and shoved his hands into his pockets. "Does he know about your Sunday outings? He doesn't seem very tolerant; maybe he wouldn't want his woman out riding bareback like an Indian squaw. You'll have to watch that." He nodded once for emphasis and left.

If there had been a sack of flour close by I would have kicked it. As it was I had nothing to vent my anger on, so I merely walked jauntily past the store window. I would have liked to pick up a cast-iron skillet and thrown it through the window right at his head.

Then I thought about what he had said—like an Indian squaw. Did he know? Was that his way of implying he had a hold over me? As if I would let myself be blackmailed! And that remark about me being Charles's woman. God, he was infuriating!

It took me some time to compose myself again, but luckily the afternoon was slow and no customers came in right then. Trying to set aside the disturbing feelings I had, I threw myself into my work and cleaned and dusted like never before.

I was apprehensive about dinner that night. I hoped Charles would let the incident slide without a comment, but that look on his face had not been passive. Still, I couldn't very well avoid him.

In my time at the boardinghouse I had become used to sitting at the corner of the long table next to Della. I took my place there and said my hellos, trying to sound normal when I spoke to Charles. His eyes flicked to me once, then went down and stayed there. I wasn't sure if he was more angry or hurt, but I hoped no one else noticed.

As usual, Della did most of the talking. She was a warm, scatterbrained woman who might have been annoying if she weren't so genuine. Sometimes her talking got on my nerves but more than once I had been thankful for the distraction. This was one of those times.

"Catherine," she said. "With a jolt I realized she'd been talking to me. "I've almost got that dark brown skirt finished and I need you to try it on for me again."

"Of course," I said. "I'll do it right after dinner. As fast as you've been sewing for me, I hope you're not neglecting your other customers."

"Don't worry about that," she assured me. "I sew almost as fast as I talk."

As soon as Margaret began to clear the table, Della and I went upstairs. In her room I put on the skirt inside out and stood while she examined the seams and put a pin here and there.

"It's none of my business," she said, "but have you and Charles had words? He looked like he'd lost his last friend in the world."

"There's nothing for us to have words about," I began. "He came by the store today and I was talking to a man who'd come in. As soon as Charles saw us, he acted like a jealous lover and stormed off." I hoped my casualness sounded convincing. "I don't know why he should be so upset about it. There was nothing to it."

"Huh," said Della. "Ain't that something? Men and their big heads, gets 'em into trouble every time. When I was married, my husband was always spoutin' off at me what a good provider he was, and how good he was taking care of me. You should've seen his face when I told him I wasn't goin' to California with him. You'd think I'd emptied a load of buckshot in his drawers.''

Della laughed at her own joke and I smiled. She was right—whatever Charles thought or felt was his own problem. I could probably explain to him how harmless my conversation with Donnelly was, or even tell him I was rebuffing the trapper, but I owed him nothing. If there was a rift between us now, it would be up to him to bridge it.

"That's all I need," Della said. "Just a bit more here at the waist and straighten this seam so it'll hang right and it'll be done." I stepped out of the skirt gingerly, watching the pins. "I think Mrs. Reedy's going to play tonight. I saw Margaret waxing the piano today. You going to come down?''

"For a bit, I think. You know, as sullen as she is, she does play well." I pulled on my own skirt and fastened it.

"That she does," Della agreed grudgingly. " That must be her silver lining because the rest of her's dark as an old black cloud."

We had just stepped out of Della's room when I saw Charles. He was standing at the top of the stairs, waiting, apparently, for me. Della cast one curious glance back at me and went on downstairs.

"Catherine," he began, then with more determination, "Catherine, I'd like to have a word with you."

"Yes?" I said calmly. "About what?"

104

"Today at the store . . . I, uh, you . . . do you know anything about that man you were talking to?"

"Mr. Donnelly? I know he's a trapper but I really don't see what that has to do with anything."

Charles seemed perplexed. "He's not . . . of good character. He's a rough man, not used to women of your caliber. I wouldn't trust him if I were you."

"What makes you think I trust him?" I asked. "I know what he is, I can see. Just because he came into the store doesn't mean there is anything between us, and I don't care to have it inferred that there is."

"I wasn't!" Charles said. "It's just that I wouldn't want you to . . . to . . ."

"To what?" I asked, growing irritated.

"Nothing," he said. "I'm sorry. It's just that he looked so compromising. I'm sure you're much too intelligent to fall for his line, but he makes a questionable appearance out of nothing. Really," he said, his voice suddenly lower, "I'm only thinking of you. A character like that can ruin your reputation without you even knowing it. Just his hanging around."

"I assure you, Mr. Lafferty, he is not hanging around. Now, I'd like to go downstairs."

I let him know I was still annoyed by his assumption and took a seat by myself in the parlor. Mrs. Reedy was already beginning to play but I was sure no one had missed the fact that Charles and I came downstairs together. I didn't look at him the rest of the evening.

Wednesday morning I remembered to tell Margaret I wouldn't be to dinner. I dressed in one of my better outfits so I wouldn't have to come back and change after work. Charles watched me intently at breakfast but I pretended as if nothing had happened.

The day passed slowly. Mr. Altvater even came back and commented on how slow it was. Finally he said there was some cleaning and rearranging that could be done in the next room, so I attended to that while he watched the front. Most of the mess in back was half-empty boxes and haphazard dumping of stock, so I straightened and cleaned and found more than enough to keep me busy. After that, I noticed the time went by more quickly.

I was caught by surprise when Red Cloud came into the back room for his broom. He started when he saw me, then looked around anxiously.

"It's much neater now, isn't it?" I asked. "You won't have to look for your broom in all the mess anymore."

Red Cloud watched me as I spoke and I noticed his eyes touching my face and hair. I felt I wanted to reach out and touch him, tell him we were of the same blood, but I couldn't. I still didn't know how he felt about me or even his own people. It would be ironic if I put my trust in him and he betrayed me to the whites.

He still didn't speak. Finally he took the broom

and left, that blank look on his face. I sighed heavily and got ready to go to Melly's.

As I walked down the street I began to feel apprehensive about meeting Frank. He was a soldier, employed by the government to fight and defend against Indians. After seeing so many on a campaign, wouldn't he be apt to recognize the Cheyenne in me? If in his mind's eye he pictured me with my straight black hair in braids and buffalo robe around me, wouldn't he know? The thought of it made me slow my steps and I found when I stood on the wooden porch that I couldn't touch the door.

"Come in!" Melly said as she pulled the door open. "What are you just standing out there for? I saw you through the window. What are you doing?"

"Oh," I said, swallowing, "I was just daydreaming. Am I too early?"

"No, you're fine. Come on, don't stand out there all night. Frank should be here any minute."

I followed Melly inside and answered Mrs. Crutchfield's greeting. Melly's father had apparently walked uptown for a newspaper. Melly insisted I sample her mother's bread pudding and we set the table while Mrs. Crutchfield tended to the roast. I was just beginning to relax when a knock sounded at the door.

"Oh, that's Frank," Melly said excitedly. I froze. I tried to think of something I could do, something very un-Indian, but instead I just sat dumbly at the table. Melly opened the door and took Frank's hand as he walked in.

He wasn't what I expected. I pictured him about twenty-five with dark hair and a muscular build. Instead Melly introduced me to a tall, thin, blond boy not much older than me with shy, darting blue eyes.

"How do?" he said awkwardly. I shook hands with him and almost laughed. He was more nervous than I was! Melly was beaming with pride and I grinned at my own foolish fears. Finally Frank smiled. I thought, compared to Jory Donnelly, he's just a boy! Much relieved, I followed them into the living room.

"Frank, tell Catherine about your campaign," Melly said when we sat on the couch. "Tell her all the things you did."

"Oh," he said shyly. "It wasn't very interesting."

"Not very interesting?" Melly said. "If you don't call fighting Indians and seeing great herds of buffalo and hunting mountain lions interesting, I don't know what is!"

Frank colored and looked to me to see if I really wanted to hear.

"I'd love to hear about it, but I'm sure you've already told it several times since you've been back. If you don't want to, I can hear it some other time."

"Okay," Frank said agreeably. Melly was disappointed, but nothing could keep her down for long.

"Well at least show her the scars from that awful lion," she insisted.

108

"Melly!" her mother's shocked voice came. "That is not the kind of thing . . ."

"Catherine doesn't mind, do you?" she said quickly. "It's healed, but you can see where the lion scratched him. Things like that don't bother you, do they?"

"No, I said.

"Show her, Frank," she hissed so her mother wouldn't hear.

Embarrassed, Frank pulled the collar of his shirt away from his neck and showed me several red scars that slashed around his neck and into his hairline.

"Aren't they awful?" Melly asked.

"They must have been," I agreed. "How did it happen?"

"We were riding through some rimrock on a scouting foray, just four of us, and found some cat tracks—big ones. They were leading the same way we were going so we followed along. The tracks went up a way, then disappeared on the rock, so one of the guys took his gun and went up after it. Stupid thing, I know. I was sitting my horse at the bottom there, waiting, and suddenly that cat just came out of nowhere and wrapped himself around my head. Almost took a chunk out of my arm, too, then skittered off as fast as he'd come. I hardly knew what hit me before he was gone."

"They didn't catch him," Melly said to finish.

"Not with Frank bleeding to death," I surmised.

"Oh, it wasn't that bad," he said. "It looked a lot

worse than it was, but I was lucky. That cat could've torn my head off if it had a mind to."

Suddenly the door swung open and Mr. Crutchfield came in. Frank immediately went to offer his hand.

"Sir," he said.

"Hello, Frank," Mr. Crutchfield said. He shook Frank's hand and saw me over the boy's shoulder. "Catherine," he said, nodding.

"Hello, Mr. Crutchfield," I answered.

"Well, nothing like a dinner party here in our frontier home," Mr. Crutchfield said amicably. "How soon will we be eating?"

"In about ten minutes if I can get some help in here," Mrs. Crutchfield said.

Melly and I took our cue and went to help in the kitchen, leaving the men to talk in the living room.

"Isn't he wonderful?" Melly whispered to me.

"He's very nice," I said. "You two should get along fine."

"I think so too," she laughed.

"All right, girls," Mrs. Crutchfield said. "Let's get dinner on the table."

The dinner was good and with so many people, I didn't have to worry about keeping up the conversation. The Crutchfields were much more interested in Frank than in me and I was content to sit and listen to the table talk. I realized that they were all genuinely fond of Frank, as I knew they would have to be to let Melly stay in Leavenworth with him. Melly had told me they met back east after Frank had already joined the cavalry. He must have passed the Crutchfieldses' standards then or they would never have come west. Now they all engaged in friendly banter like one family.

"Have you heard anything from your father?" Mr. Crutchfield asked me suddenly during a lull. For a moment it caught me off guard and I almost choked on my wine. Then I realized what he was asking and regained my composure.

"No," I said, "I probably won't. He should be traveling almost as fast as any post, so I'll just have to wait and see him when he gets here."

"What part of California does he live in?" Frank asked.

"The southern part, near Los Angeles. I'm not exactly clear on where it is from there. He just said the land is good for growing things and the country is beautiful."

"What does he grow?" Mr. Crutchfield asked.

"I-I'm not sure. I don't think he told me in his letter. He didn't say much except to give me directions to meet him."

Mr. Crutchfield nodded thoughtfully and I had the express feeling he didn't believe me. It was almost as if he had set out to trap me with his questions. I was glad when the conversation veered back to Frank, but I decided I would not accept many more dinner invitations. Mr. Crutchfield wouldn't have any more opportunities to question me.

After dinner Melly and I helped her mother in the kitchen and the men got comfortable in the living room. I didn't relish the idea of any more

111

conversation so I decided to excuse myself early. As close as Melly and I had become, I was not part of the family and never would be.

"But it's early," Melly argued when I said I was leaving.

"It's not so early," I said, "and besides, you and Frank have a lot to talk about." I went into the living room and said my thanks and goodbyes.

"It was nice meeting you," Frank said politely. "Will we see you at the wedding?"

"Of course," Melly said, smiling to me. "I won't let her out of that one."

"I'll be there," I agreed.

With summer coming on, it was staying light longer and twilight was barely decending when I stepped off the porch. I saw the livery stable across the way but thought better about going in there. Tonight I would walk straight home.

I hadn't gone a block before I heard footsteps on the wooden sidewalk behind me. I didn't turn around but I could hear the footfalls coming faster than my own and closing on me.

"Nice evening, isn't it, Cathy?" Donnelly asked as he fell into step beside me.

"I've asked you not to call me that," I said.

"I don't like Catherine. It's too formal."

"If my mother had known that, I'm sure she would have picked another name for me," I said sarcastically.

"Still sore, huh?" he asked cheerfully.

"I'm not sore, Mr. Donnelly, I'm just trying every way I can to let you know that I do not want your company. Normally a man asks a lady if he may accompany her."

"But you're not a lady," he laughed.

I stopped, spinning to face him. "Then I guess that makes us even because you're not exactly a model man, either," I said.

"Depends by whose standards. Now if you're comparing me to Lafferty, I—"

"Mr. Donnelly," I interrupted, "I don't care to discuss this sort of thing with you." I began to walk again, my back stiff.

"I like the way you call me Mr. Donnelly," he said. "Hardly anyone calls me that, and none with as much enthusiasm as you."

"I could think of other names," I offered.

"I'm sure you could," he agreed. I glared at him. "Now don't go getting mad about that. You said it first." We walked on, me trying to ignore him and he apparently thinking of new topics. "You know that nag of yours is getting barn sour?"

"Thunder's not a nag," I replied cooly, not rising to the bait.

"Thunder, huh? Funny name. But he is barn sour."

"I'm aware of that."

"If you'd ride him more, you could knock the edge off him."

"When am I supposed to ride? During my work hours at the store?"

"Evenings are getting longer. And there's always Sunday."

"I suppose you want to set up an itinerary for

me," I suggested, hoping he didn't know what he word meant.

"No, I'm just saying he won't be any good if you don't ride him. Shaman gets that way every summer while I'm in town, but I can't ride him all the time. I've got Beauty, too."

"Well, don't worry about me. I know how to take care of a horse."

"Yeah, it seems like you do. Hank was saying how you passed up the little buckskin of his. He can't give it away; it's got feet like a pony."

"You don't miss a thing, do you?" I asked. "Don't you have anything better to do than hang around town asking about women's riding habits and waiting in the shadows when they walk alone? You ought to be a sheriff—you'd make a wonderful one-man posse."

"Naw," he said. "I don't want any part of the law. I live by my own rules and let everyone else live by theirs."

"Then why are you imposing yourself on me?" We had almost reached the church by then.

"Just curiosity." He grinned.

"Such flattery," I said sarcastically.

"Would flattery improve your opinion of me?" he asked.

"No."

"Didn't think so. Well, looks like you've got people waiting up for you."

I looked up and saw lights on in the boarding-house and—was that someone in the window? I couldn't be sure but I thought I saw a head silhouetted for a moment; then it was gone. I wondered who it was.

"He sure keeps close tabs on you, doesn't he?" Donnelly asked.

"No one keeps tabs on me," I said, "not even you." With that, I marched up the steps and went inside.

Everyone was in the parlor, all seated, but none of them stopped me from going upstairs after their evening greetings. I was glad for that. Whoever had been in the window wasn't going to press me for an explanation.

The rest of the week I was jumpy and nervous. I half expected Donnelly to appear without warning. He didn't. Then at the boardinghouse I watched for signs in the other boarders, but none behaved differently except Charles. He was still quiet since the time he saw me with Donnelly at the store. Melly was busy being with and thinking about Frank so I didn't even have her constant chatter to distract me.

Sunday I left for the livery as soon as I thought everyone else was safely in church. Hank saddled Thunder for me and I rode away quickly. Both Donnelly's mounts were still in their stalls.

I rode almost directly to the rocks I had found on my first ride and hid my saddle there, grudgingly covering the hollow with brush as Donnelly had suggested. Riding bareback and astraddle I felt much better and loped Thunder along deer trails and walked him across streams. It was a beautiful early summer day and just being part of it raised my spirits.

Toward noon I rode Thunder up the spine of the hills and looked west. I don't know what I expected to see, but all that fell away before me was the prairie in its rolling swells of buffalo grass. In the far distance I could follow the path of a stream by the cottonwoods that sprouted in an irregular line. It looked like an awful lot of ground to cover without help.

Feeling thoughtful, I turned Thunder back east and took a long way around to my cache. I was still probably a half mile from it when I saw Donnelly urging his mule down a ridge toward me. Seeing no sense in running from him, I let Thunder walk at his own pace until Donnelly fell into step beside us.

"You got out of your cage early," he observed.

"I thought I was supposed to," I said.

"Yeah, but I didn't think you would. Most women don't take suggestions, even if it's for their own good."

"Is that a compliment?" I asked. "I thought you weren't going to use flattery."

He laughed almost as if I had said something pleasing to him. "No flattery," he said. "I'm not too good at that sort of thing."

"No, I think you must just wear women down."

"Am I wearing you down?" he asked.

I hesitated, lifting my chin. "No. I just don't feel like letting you ruin my day today."

He chuckled. "Okay. What can we talk about that won't ruin your day? You've been blazing these hills pretty well, haven't you?"

"Fairly," I admitted.

"Let's go east at the top of this ridge and I'll show you something I'll bet you haven't seen."

"I have to go back to town."

He eyed me closely. "What's the matter? Are you afraid of me? Or afraid of what I want to show you?"

"I'm not the least bit afraid of you," I retorted, "and anything you want to show me is probably just as well overlooked." I kicked Thunder into a trot up the hill, Donnelly trotting alongside.

"How do you know until you've seen?" He grinned.

"Mr. Donnelly, I do not appreciate crude humor at my expense. You're free to ride wherever you want, but I have an engagement in town."

"An engagement, huh?" he asked. "Sounds fancy. I could show you a fancy time right here in the trees."

I rammed my heels into Thunder's sides and he lunged forward. We topped the ridge and vaulted over, his hooves sending rocks clattering ahead. I didn't look back but galloped through the trees to my cache and only reined up when I had guided Thunder behind the rocks. Donnelly loped up shortly.

"Hey, Cathy," he said, "what are you trying to do, kill yourself?"

"I'm trying to get away from you as fast as I can," I said, cinching up my saddle. "If you're looking for relief, go find a cathouse or a crib

117

somewhere. Just stay away from me."

"Oh, touchy!" he said. "You're too good to need relief, is that it?"

"I don't see any point in discussing this any further," I said.

"Does that mean I've ruined your day again?" he asked with a smug grin.

"Mr. Donnelly, you have ruined the last half hour but you're not important enough for me to fume over for the rest of the day. I have better things to do."

"I see. Well, give my regards to Lafferty. Tell him I've been taking good care of you for him."

I threw myself up on Thunder and kicked him into a lope almost before I was settled in the saddle. As soon as we hit the open plain I slapped his neck with the rein and he leveled out. We left a plume of dust all the way back to town.

When I came downstairs, Charles was waiting at the bottom and smiled up at me.

"You look lovely," he said, taking my hand. I had worn the one good dress I had, a rust colored satin with black trim. It fit me perfectly and I saw Charles's eyes slip shyly over my figure. "I hope you don't mind if we walk. It's just a few blocks."

"No, I don't mind."

"I think you'll like the Evanses," he said as we crossed the main street. "They're very warm people."

"I'm sure I will," I said. "I've met very few people in Leavenworth so far that haven't been very nice."

Instead of taking that the way I intended, Charles frowned.

"I've been meaning to talk to you about that," he said. I glanced at him curiously. "That evening Donnelly walked you home—I'm not trying to tell you who you should or shouldn't associate with, Catherine, but I worry about you being with him. He's a terrible liar and he has no respect for women at all. If he acts like he does, it's probably only to make you trust him. I'd be afraid to think of what might happen if he were to take you alone someplace."

"Really, Charles, I think you're being overly cautious. I can see Mr. Donnelly for what he is and I have no intention of allowing him any liberties." I couldn't very well say I wouldn't go anyplace alone with him—it seemed we ended up alone every weekend now. "I've tried to discourage him, but it isn't taken well. Lately I've just been ignoring him."

"If you like, I could talk to him, maybe explain . . ."

"No!" I almost shouted. Quickly I regained my control and tried to even out my voice. "I don't want you confronting him over me. It would only cause more notice. I think it best to just ignore him." I could just imagine Donnelly advising Charles of our meeting in the hills and my bareback rides. Not that he might not do it anyway, but there was no point in rushing things.

"Well, all right," Charles said. "Here, this is the

house."

The Evanses were in their early forties and both very genial. Mrs. Evans, or Mae, as she insisted I call her, took me away from the men and showed me the front rooms of the house. I was glad to get away from Charles for a moment and noted with interest the tasteful underplay of quality in the furnishings around me. The Evanses, I decided, had more money than anyone in Leavenworth dreamed.

When the men finally joined us in the front room, Mr. Evans seemed cheerfully disposed toward me. I wondered what Charles had said to him. The older couple plied me with questions about New York and my future journey, but they seemed more polite questions and not the keenly prying kind that I had been met with elsewhere.

"Are you enjoying your stay?" Mr. Evans asked finally.

"Oh, yes," I said. "I like Leavenworth. It's a very personable town, so much more than New York."

"Yes, I think so, too. I hope you'll stay awhile. As nice as Leavenworth is, it will benefit greatly by your presence, I think."

I blushed at the older man's compliment and Charles looked as if someone had just praised his favorite horse. Ignoring him, I decided I liked Mr. Evans and his wife and would like to continue this friendship.

"Do you read much?" he asked.

"Some," I admitted, "although I haven't had much of a chance to since I've been here. Or were you speaking of newspapers? I have picked up yours a time or two, but haven't done it justice. I will have to read it more carefully from now on."

"I'd be curious to have your opinion of it," Evans said. "I'm always interested in how my paper strikes a stranger."

"Now we're talking business," Mae said, "and I won't have it. Why don't we start dinner?"

Following her lead, we all went into the dining room to the huge oak table placed back beneath an ornate lantern. I was seated across from Charles and had a clear view of his happy face. He was obviously very pleased with the way the evening was progressing.

The Evanses had a girl help out with the kitchen and she served us as properly, I thought, as Mae could train someone to do so. It almost reminded me of being at my grandparents' again. The china and silver gleamed with the look of daily care and the food was delicious. We talked about every topic Mr. Evans seemed able to think of and I was delighted to find a man so keenly intelligent and so conversational. I warmed to him as I did to the red wine we drank. At the same time I found Mae to be equally articulate and the most interesting woman I had spoken to in months. It struck me as odd that I must have missed some of the intellectual stimulation I had been used to in New York. Mae and I talked as easily as old friends and time flew much too quickly to suit me. I began to feel that, if the time came when everyone else in Leavenworth turned against me for my Indian blood, these people would stand by me. They seemed much too intelligent to be narrow-minded.

When Charles signaled it was time to leave, I had no choice but to go along. If I could have, I would have stayed and talked far into the night. They seemed equally pleased with me and when we left, Mae insisted we plan on returning the following Sunday. I was more than happy to agree. Charles and I walked back to Mrs. Reedy's both extremely pleased.

"They're wonderful people," Charles said. He cradled my hand on his arm like a child.

"Yes," I agreed. "I suppose it sounds snobbish, but I hadn't expected to meet any people quite like that in Leavenworth."

"I know what you mean. The rest of the people around here are so backwoods, it's quite refreshing to find someone as learned as Mr. Evans."

That wasn't what I had meant but I saw no point in correcting him and perhaps starting an argument. It was just that I seemed to feel an affinity for the Evanses that I didn't feel toward the townspeople. But I hardly considered the rest of my friends backwoods.

"I would think Mr. Evans's being as liberal as he is would come under a lot of fire from the goings on he reports about here and in Missouri. Aren't there still a lot of people who think the other way about slavery and slave rights?" Steering the conversation into another direction, I remembered some of the topics we'd covered, and Mr. Evans's foresighted opinions.

"Oh, yes, there's still a lot of feeling, even bloodshed now and then. But I think Tom is pretty well respected by all. He doesn't particularly like having it talked around, but I've seen him with a gun, and he's good. There was a time some years back when some drunken cowboys from Missouri, came to town, intending to burn down the newspaper office. Tom killed one and wounded two more before they changed their minds. No one's bothered him since."

"I would think not," I said. The more I heard about Mr. Evans the more I liked him. I had no way of knowing, but I was sure he would back me should my secret be known. He was the type who would always help the underdog and, if it came to that, I would definitely be the underdog.

"Well," Charles said as we stepped up the boardinghouse steps, "I hope you had as nice an evening as I did."

"Yes, I did," I said. "Thank you very much for asking me." The way Charles stopped on the porch, I was afraid he might try to kiss me. Before he could do anything I pulled the door open. "I'm so tired I think I'll go straight upstairs. Thank you again, Charles. I'll see you tomorrow." And I almost ran upstairs.

Chapter Five

THE NEXT week went quickly. Melly was in on Monday to tell me the wedding would be the following Sunday. Frank had been badgering his captain and had finally been given the okay. Now she was all in a dither over the plans and it seemed like every day that week she rushed in to the store with new bits of news to tell me. I had never seen anyone so excited in my life.

As soon as I learned of that, I told Charles I would have to skip dinner Sunday with the Evanses. He seemed disappointed but understanding but was very cheerful. Sometimes at the table at the boardinghouse I felt his eyes on me and if I looked up, he smiled secretly at me. I felt like telling him we shared no secrets.

Mr. Donnelly was conspicuously absent for days. I expected to see his bulk filling the doorway or an aisle in the store, or possibly bearing down on me walking home after work, but I did not. As curious as I was—and I'm ashamed to myself for being that—I refused to ask anyone about him. I didn't care to admit, even to myself, that I was disappointed in not seeing him.

By Saturday I was restless and the thought of waiting another week to ride was more than I could bear. Deciding quickly at quitting time, I hurried to the livery and entreated Hank to saddle Thunder for me.

"You sure you want to go ridin' now, Miss?" he asked. "It'll be dark in an hour or so."

"Yes, I'm sure, Hank," I said. "Please hurry. I'm sorry if I'm interrupting your dinner again but it's important to me, especially after being on my feet all week."

Hank shrugged and checked Thunder's cinch for me, then handed me up. Feeling instantly free as soon as I hit the saddle, I loped out of town and headed for my rocky cache.

My saddle hidden, I turned east instead of northwest as before, and decided to explore more along the river. I avoided the farms dotting the banks and rode through the graying trees like a fugitive. The idea of being close to homes and slinking by undetected thrilled me. It had been long since I had needed to rely upon my Indian training, and I resolved from then on I would not be seen unless I wished to be. Feeling like a giddy child, I practiced guiding Thunder soundlessly through the trees.

The twilight came on quickly and I did not cover as much ground as I had wanted. I rejected the thought of staying out past dark although it was very tempting to me. That would be calling undue attention to myself though, and I did not need that. Instead I reined Thunder around and tried to pick a different way back than I had come, being as silent as I could.

As I approached the rocky outcropping I motioned Thunder to a stop with a hand on his neck. In the increasing dimness I could see an unfamiliar shape but had trouble making it out. The silhouette of the rocks was not right and I sat quietly trying to discern what the difference was.

Then a horse snorted and a long-eared head bobbed up above the rocks. At the same time the odd silhouette turned and I barely made out Jory Donnelly's surprised face.

"Where'd you learn that trick?" he asked, coming to stand beside me.

"Proper young ladies are taught not to make excessive noise," I said smoothly. I moved Thunder closer to the rocks and slid off. Leaving his reins free while he touched noses with Beauty, I went to retrieve my saddle. Instead I found a soft leather bundle.

"What's this?" I asked.

"Open it," was all he would say.

I unwrapped the leather and found myself staring at a pair of roughout leather breeches, much like the ones Mr. Donnelly himself wore.

"And just what am I supposed to do with these?" I asked shortly.

"They're a damn sight more practical than riding with your skirt bunched up around your legs," he said.

"Mr. Donnelly," I sputtered, "you are far from a gentleman."

"That's okay, Cathy," he said easily, "you're far from a lady and we both know it."

Angry and insulted, I wadded the breeches up and threw them into the hollow. I dragged my saddle out and threw it up onto Thunder, tightening the cinch with merciless jerks.

"If you think I'm going to stand here and be insulted by you and have you make such ridiculous, intimate suggestions as wearing men's pants, you're mistaken, Mr. Donnelly. I ride to get away from bothersome people like you, not to rendezvous with them." The cinch tight, I climbed up in the saddle and turned Thunder away from the mule. "Neither you nor your gifts are appreciated, so you can take your misguided thoughtfulness elsewhere."

I kicked Thunder down out of the trees and toward the lights of Leavenworth, confident my scathing remarks had left Mr. Donnelly behind. Instead his mule clattered alongside in short time and the two animals walked head to head.

"I am quite capable of finding my way back to town," I said after a minute of silence.

"It's not safe for a woman to ride alone after

dark," he answered simply.

"I wish you would make up your mind whether or not I'm a woman," I said.

"Oh, you're definitely a woman, but you're not a lady."

"Thank you very much."

"You're welcome."

We rode on and I wondered why he was being protective of me after I railed at him the way I had. It seemed that everyone was trying to protect me against something. Without realizing it, I must have smiled.

"What are you chuckling about?" he asked.

I straightened my features and my back. "I was just thinking how odd that you should offer me your protection when I have been adamantly warned against you."

"By who?" he asked.

"I'm not at liberty to say. But so far I have found my informant to be correct in that you are foul-mouthed, ill-mannered and lacking in respect for women."

"I can guess at the rest," he said. I felt rather than saw him studying me. "Would you care to have me prove my greatest vice?"

Even in the dark my face flamed. "I'm sure I have no idea what you're talking about," I said hotly.

"Except for thirdhand knowledge, no, you probably don't. A pity." We rode on. "It's best on a bed of pine needles or out in the middle of a moonlit meadow. I like to have the wind blowing just a little, so you can feel it on your . . ."

"Mr. Donnelly!" I gasped, outraged. "You are by far the most vulgar, shameless and despicable man I've ever met and if you think a flowery description will drive me to present to you like a bitch in heat, you had better think again. I don't see how you've survived this long when you seem to be able to think only with the lower half of your body."

My tirade over, I drove my heel into Thunder's side and he lurched forward in a lunging gallop. In a few seconds Donnelly was loping alongside, a smile on his face.

"I knew if I stuck enough pins in you I'd find out what color blood you had," he called, "and it's not blue!" The rocking motion of his mule caused no hinderance to his actions and he tipped his hat to me. "Good night, Cathy. Sleep well!" His smile flashing at me in the dark, he spurred off and left me loping alone toward the livery.

My anger and indignation flaming hot within me, I unsaddled and brushed Thunder down myself, being quiet so as not to waken Hank. Thunder had probably never been brushed so vigorously and in a short time all trace of dirt and foam was gone from his coat. Still fuming, I strode back to Mrs. Reedy's and hurried upstairs.

"Catherine!" I heard when I was almost to my door. I wanted desperately to walk on, to close my door against what I was sure was coming. Drawing on my New York propriety, I turned to face Charles.

"I felt the need to be alone," I said levelly, "and I didn't judge the time well. It became dark before I could get back and so I galloped." Period, I felt like saying.

"But Catherine," Charles said, his eyes taking in my wind-whipped hair and dirty dress. "We were all so worried about you. You really shouldn't go out like that with no chaperone and leaving no message. It's not . . ."

"Charles," I interrupted, "I am not a child or a fool. I am capable of taking care of myself and would rather not feel that I must report everything I do to you. Now if you'll excuse me, I would like to clean up."

"Of course," he said in a bewildered tone. "But before you do, I wanted to ask you if you would care to accompany me to church tomorrow morning."

"No, thank you, Charles. I have a lot to do tomorrow to prepare for my friend's wedding and I plan to spend what little time I'll have on my own." I spun on my heel and closed my door firmly between us.

I was beginning to think it was too much for me. Between the two men I was mad half the time and exasperated the other half. It was getting harder and harder to retain my singlemindedness. I had either overestimated my own acting ability or underestimated the people around me. I wished that at least I had some indication of where all this agitation was taking me so I could know if it was all worthwhile. Instead I had visions of Donnelly's moonlit meadow and Charles standing frowning to one side.

Melly's wedding was a whirlwind for me. I'm sure if I could have driven out to the fort like a regular guest I could have relaxed and enjoyed it but Melly was adamant that I come with them and attend to her dressing. I really didn't mind; it took my mind off other things, but I felt as rushed and anxious as the rest of the wedding party.

Mrs. Crutchfield and I helped Melly dress in a room off the fort's chapel and the poor girl was so excited she was almost in tears before she left the room. Over and over she peered at herself in a full-length mirror, concerned about the lace laying correctly or the train fanning out just right behind her. Mrs. Crutchfield and I attended her diligently, smoothing out wrinkles and assuring her she was beautiful. And she was. I envied her, although I doubt I would have traded places with her.

When Mr. Crutchfield finally came for Melly, Mrs. Crutchfield and I went into the tiny chapel and took our seats. It seemed deserted although there were some of Frank's friends on his side of the chapel, all in full uniform. I was sure Melly wouldn't notice the lack of guests.

The ceremony was quick and unimaginative but the words were nothing next to the faces of the two people. Melly fairly beamed, so radiant was she, and Frank's eyes shone proudly. When the words were said and he slipped the ring on her finger, she burst into tears. That was too much for Mrs. Crutchfield, who had been sniffling anyway, and almost too much for me. Luckily we left shortly after that for the room rented by Mr. Crutchfield for dinner.

I found the dinner slightly boring since all attention was focused on the newly wedded pair. Not that I minded, I was just as glad to remain obscure, but I could have been doing other things much more interesting.

Unbidden, my thoughts strayed to the trapper. I wondered if he were riding the hills looking for me, or if his peculiar sources of information told him I was attending the wedding. He seemed to know all of my other movements about town, and I was sure he knew this one, too. That thought bothered me. I realized I did not so much dislike Mr. Donnelly as fear him, or fear what he might do to my search. Now that I thought about it, he was hard to dislike, although he was arrogant and crude and tactless. Still, he had backbone and principles and he was as individual a a man as I'd known. Heavens, I thought, I'm letting this wedding get to me! Shaking my head I tried to pick up the thread of conversation around me.

Melly would not be going home with us tonight, I learned. The fort had married officer's quarters, such as they were, and that would be Melly's home from now on. I imagined the quarters—and Mrs. Crutchfield's horrified reaction to them—as something far removed from the luxury in which Melly was raised. But she was in love and would accept a hole in the ground if Frank had offered it to her. I felt a twinge of pity for her parents, having to release their daughter to the bare practicality of military life. But they would learn to let go and go on without her—grudgingly.

When the dinner and its rituals finally came to a close I drove back to town with the Crutchfields in the wagon he had rented. Mrs. Crutchfield cried silently into her handkerchief while her husband drove, stony faced, beside her. It was a depressing end to the day, but Melly was probably happier than she had ever been in her life.

In my room that night I couldn't help but wonder what Melly was experiencing. My mind flicked over the thought of me and Charles, but that was a little too ridiculous even to think about. I could have thought about Donnelly, but his words about the moonlit meadow came back to me. Feeling my cheeks flame in the darkness, I made my mind a blank so I could sleep.

The following week, the Crutchfields made ready to leave. Mrs. Crutchfield came in the store two or three times on the pretense of needing some small thing, but I recognized a need in her to talk to another female, so I listened. She talked of Melly, of her childhood, her years in school, her accomplishments and virtues. In proud tones she told me how lucky she was to have such a daughter, to be able to raise her up and see her properly wed, but I knew she could not say what she truly felt—that her heart was aching to leave

Melly, and that she felt terribly sad and bereft. I felt sorry for her, that she had so much and now felt so alone. Perhaps it was a mark of how much she had that she felt so deprived now, for there was little in my life I couldn't give up without a care. Even in her sadness, Mrs. Crutchfield was very lucky.

They were slated to leave on a riverboat that Thursday afternoon. I asked Mr. Altvater for a couple of hours off to go to the wharf and he granted it generously. I had already arranged through Mrs. Crutchfield to have Melly and Frank pick me up at the store so we could all drive down to the dock together.

I was just putting things into order when Donnelly walked into the store. Mr. Altvater was busy in the back room so he walked directly back to my corner. Luckily the rest of the store was vacant.

"Hello," he said amiably. He watched me while I neatened up my counter, his eyes crinkling with a knowing smile.

"Good afternoon," I said cooly. "You look like the cat that ate the canary."

"Could be," he said. "You're getting off work early tonight?"

"Sounds like you already know the answer to that. Why bother asking?"

"You going riding?"

"I doubt it. Mr. Altvater has only given me time off until the riverboat leaves; if there's time after that, I plan on coming back to work. It wouldn't be fair of me to take more than he's allowed me."

"He wouldn't mind," Donnelly said.

I looked at him. It almost sounded like he'd already discussed the matter with Mr. Altvater. Knowing him, I wouldn't put it past him.

"Like I said, it depends on how soon the riverboat leaves." Then I noticed Frank's cavalry wagon pulling up outside. "There's my ride, now." Ignoring Donnelly, I finished putting my things away and went to get my bag. I told Mr. Altvater I was leaving and started out the door.

"Have a nice time," Donnelly called. I threw him a glance over my shoulder and went outside.

Melly and her mother were already tearing. We drove to the dock in a confused jumble, some moments engaging in falsely light banter, some in morbid silence. Melly sat between her mother and me holding both our hands in a death grip.

At the dock the men wrestled with the Crutchfieldes' luggage while we women watched and then went to inspect the room. This was a different boat than the one we had come on, larger and more elaborate. Their room was exquisitely done in purple velvet and, although small, looked comfortable enough for the trip. Melly and her mother kept clutching each other's hands and sobbing.

When the men had seen to the luggage we all went to the dining room for the last drink of wine. We found out there was almost thirty minutes until departure time and we sat and talked of the future in quiet tones.

"We'll be back from time to time to visit," Mrs. Crutchfield said positively. "But probably not before you go to California."

"Probably not," I said. "But we can write. You've both been very thoughtful of me and I appreciate that."

"Nonsense," she said. "It was nice of you to help us out with all the plans and everything. And if Melly hadn't had someone else to talk to I don't know what I would have done. I think she would have talked my ears off." We all laughed at that.

"And I won't be so alone with you gone," Melly told her parents, "Not while Catherine's here."

"I don't think you'll be alone much at all," Mrs. Crutchfield said, nodding to Frank. Then, to him, said, "But you take good care of her."

"I will," Frank said earnestly. "Don't worry. If she gets the least bit lonesome, I promise I'll put her on the first riverboat for a visit."

"That sounds fair," Mr. Crutchfield said. "Well, it's about that time. How about one last toast to the happy couple?"

We all raised our glasses and drank to Frank and Melly. Then it was time for the three of us to leave.

Standing on the dock, Melly cried hoarsely into a handkerchief beside me. She alternately clutched the shred of lace to her mouth and worried it frantically in her hands, waving to her parents up at the boat's rail. I could see Mrs. Crutchfield crying just as hard into her own hand-kerchief and Mr. Crutchfield waving with the stony face I now recognized as his defense against tears. I thought I hadn't seen so much crying since Grandmere tried to talk Grandpere out of his last wild scheme. And even I was feeling a lump in my throat. I felt guiltily relieved when the boat finally began to move slowly down the river. We watched it around the bend just south of town until it became just a small shape drifting farther and farther away.

"Oh, I don't think I could have stood it another minute!" Melly sobbed. "I wish it was a month from now so I wouldn't miss them so much!"

"But they've hardly even gone," Frank said. "How can you miss them already?"

"What do you mean?" Melly said. "I've missed them for the last couple of days and they hadn't even *left* yet." She began to cry again but this time there was less enthusiasm and I thought she was probably tired. If Frank was lucky, she would sleep very soundly tonight.

"Well, let's go. We have to get Catherine back to the store." We climbed into the wagon and drove back to town, Melly's eyes still drifting back to the river.

They dropped me at the store and I noticed I had less than an hour till closing. I glanced about to see if Donnelly were anywhere around. He wasn't. Smiling to myself, I finished out my shift and walked home alone.

Sunday dawned clear and glorious. I laid in bed until the house cleared and then made my way stealthily to the livery. To my surprise Thunder was already saddled and waiting for me.

"All ready for you, Miss Lance," Hank said. "And don't go brushing him down yourself anymore like you did last week. That's my job."

"Thank you, Hank. You're a dear man."

"Oh," he blushed. "No, no I'm not. But have a good ride."

I loped easily toward the foothills, an idea barely conscious in my head. I knew it was there and yet I didn't want to acknowledge it. But I had deliberately worn a white tailored blouse and a long skirt instead of a dress. I refused to admit the reason, even to myself—at least not yet.

At the rocks I stripped Thunder's saddle off and shoved it into the hollow. I arranged the bushes over the opening but stayed on my knees. Still not allowing myself to think about what I was doing, I pulled the wad of leather out.

Standing up, I held the buckskins up to my waist. They looked big and saggy, but I had already planned for that. I went to Thunder and climbed up, stuffing the breeches beneath me along with my skirt.

The ride to the large stream took longer than I remembered and I was glad when I finally reached it. Looking about cautiously, I walked Thunder along the edge and watched for a deep pool. When I had traveled a half mile or more, I found it. I slid off Thunder and tied him to a bush, then ran behind a screen of brush.

At first I was tempted to leave on my stockings but finally took off everything below the waist except my imported French panties. I slipped the buckskins on and they were so big I had to hold them up to walk at all. Still checking around, I went to the pool and eased in. The water was cold and seemed to wrap the leather around me like ice. I clenched my teeth and waded in to my waist, completely soaking the soft leather. When I thought it was wet enough, I waded heavily out and lay down on the grass in the sun.

The late morning sun quickly dried the water from my skin but the leather clung like a wet blanket to my legs. It seemed so odd to lay in full view with breeches on. I felt clothed and yet half naked. Even as a child I wore the ankle-length buckskin dress, complete with knee-high leather moccasins in winter. I had never had my legs outlined in the sensuous fitting mode of these pants and I felt both embarrassed and wonderfully sexual. Letting my mind wander with these unfamiliar thoughts and feelings, I relaxed and soon fell asleep.

A minute noise somewhere behind me snapped me awake. I lay as I was, my eyes closed, but my ears were keen to every sound. There was no repeat of the noise that woke me, yet a terrible feeling crept over me. I had to fight to keep my breathing even and I lay still until I thought I would go crazy.

Finally, carefully, I opened my eyes. Jory Donnelly's upside-down face towered over me.

"What in hell do you think you're doing?" I demanded. Embarrassment and indignation boiled up inside me. I jumped up as fast as the still soaking pants would allow and ran to stand behind Thunder.

"'Just trying to get a better look at your legs," he answered. "I think the buckskins will shrink just right, don't you?"

"You, you . . ."

"I think you've called me every name already, if I remember right. You'd be hard pressed to find any worse names for me today. Pretty soon we should be past this name-calling stage."

"You keep away from me!" I shouted as he walked toward Thunder. Using my hands on the horse's back and neck, I kept him safely between the trapper and myself. Donnelly stood looking over Thunder's back at me, then suddenly feinted toward the gelding's rump. As I moved the opposite way, he snaked one arm under Thunder's neck and grabbed my wrist. Twisting and fighting, I was dragged under my horse's head and into the open.

"Let go of me!" I demanded. I let go a sound slap on Donnelly's face and jammed a bare heel down on his booted toes as hard as I could but it seemed to hardly phase him. Instead he caught my free hand and held my arms crossed in front of me. His boot pressed warningly on one bare foot and I stopped struggling. I desperately wished for a knife. I was not as proficient with one as a Cheyenne warrior, but I could make myself dangerous. I determined to get one for future use.

"So now the wildcat behind the genteel face

comes out," Donnelly said lightly. "Now we know that all that ritzy business is just a mask."

"Let go of me, you bastard!" I cried.

"First tell me where a New York born and bred debutante learns to talk like you do when you're mad."

"Being raised in New York doesn't mean I don't have ears."

"True, but someone with the background you boast wouldn't have picked up on it."

Tired of his insults, I heaved forward and slammed my shoulder into his chest. I caught him enough off guard to escape from his grip and I ran for the bushes. Thunder would do me no good now. I dove through the brush and turned up along the creek. I was hoping I could outdistance him, but the heavy leather dragged on me like an anchor. Suddenly I felt Donnelly slam into my back, throwing me down on the hard ground beneath his own weight.

He held my wrists and his body on top of mine pinned me down. My struggles did absolutely no good so I turned back to verbal abuse.

"Let me go, you beast! Don't you have anything better to do than ambush women? If you were a real man you'd use your manners instead of your muscles. Let me go!"

"How would you know a real man?" he asked lightly. "You wouldn't even recognize one after spending time with Charles Lafferty."

"You conceited horse's ass!" I cried. "Leave me alone. What do you want from me?"

Instead of saying anything, he bent down and kissed me, the last thing I expected at that moment. In panic I tried to squirm away but he held my head pressed against the ground and I had nowhere to go. To make matters worse, he forced my lips apart with his tongue, something I had never experienced before. No man had ever kissed me and surprise laced with excitement coursed through me.

"I want to know all of you," he said when he drew back.

"Never!" I cried. "You'll never know me, not in any way." Before I could say more, he kissed me again, longer and more leisurely, more insistently than before. I was terrified I wouldn't be able to stop him and my anger began to be replaced by fear. I didn't want this, not here, not now, like this. Even as his mouth and tongue revealed pleasantries I had never imagined, my mind was screaming.

"No," I moaned when he finally lifted his head. "Please no."

He must have seen the fear in my eyes for I was sure I must have looked like a terrified rabbit. He watched me closely for a moment and seemed to consider. Then he pushed himself up and was standing, pulling me along with him.

"Let's go riding," he said shortly. "Those buckskins will never dry this way." He tugged at my wrist and started for the horses.

"Why should I go anywhere with you?" I blazed. The threat of seduction past, I regained my wits and tongue.

He turned and circled my waist with one easy motion, pulling me hard against his chest.

"I didn't think you wanted to stay here," he said huskily. "But if you want, it's nice and quiet, very isolated. No one would see us—or hear us."

"We'll ride," I said, refusing to shrink from him. He laughed.

"Okay. Haul yourself aboard that nag of yours and we'll go." As I walked past him, he slapped me squarely on the rump, his hand stinging on the still damp leather. I jumped and spun around to dress him down properly, but all I met was his laughing blue eyes and flashing smile. Ignoring the sting, I threw myself up on Thunder.

Donnelly was beside me on his stallion before I could even think of escaping. He came around the stream side of me, cutting off my way to town.

"I'll keep these," he said, holding up my skirt and underthings. He rolled them all up in the material of the skirt and tied the bundle along with my boots to his saddle.

"I really don't think it's your style," I said sourly.

"No more than it is yours, Cathy," he replied.

"You're impossible, Mr. Donnelly," I said.

"Not quite. You can call me Jory if you like. You've called me everything else."

"No thank you. I hardly feel we know each other well enough."

"That's not my fault. I was trying to get to know you back there." He chuckled.

"You really are an arrogant bastard," I said. "I suppose just because you're not terribly ugly you think I will fall over my face for you. Actually, I had many suitors back in New York that were much more impressive than you. Better mannered, too."

"Is that why you left New York?" he asked. "To get away from your mannered, impressive suitors?"

"My reasons for leaving are none of your business," I said ignoring the jibe.

"And I don't believe meeting your father is one of them," Donnelly continued.

"What makes you say that?"

"Because you've never once mentioned him, even to threaten me with his vengence if I should sully your pearly white reputation. Also, you've been on your own a long time. You don't mix well and you're used to depending on yourself. As far as why you left New York, maybe to find a husband?"

"That's the least of my concerns."

"Then what are your concerns?"

"None of your affair."

We rode in silence for a while. After a bit he guided his stallion across the stream at a shallow spot and led us west along the northern side of the foothills. Grasslands spread out to our right.

"Where are we going?" I asked finally.

"Nowhere in particular," he said. "How are the buckskins?"

"Drying," I answered grudgingly. I had forgotten about my improper outfit and now was embarrassed all over again. He grinned at my flaming face.

"I'll get you a buckskin shirt, too. Then you won't look so God-awful when you come back to town. You don't want to look like you've been to hell and back every Sunday."

"I want nothing from you," I said.

"And you probably ought to have some different boots before you ruin your New York ones or your horse steps on your bare foot."

"I am quite capable of outfitting myself. I'll accept nothing else from you."

"How's that nag doing, anyway?"

"He's not a nag!" I flared. "He's got good lines and I'll bet he's faster than that short-coupled stallion of yours."

"What will you bet?" he asked, grinning at me.

"What?" I asked. I suddenly realized he was serious.

"You want to put something on it?"

"I'll bet a week's pay at the store," I said confidently.

"Hell, I don't need money. Bet me something worthwhile."

"And just what do you consider worthwhile? I suppose you'd like me to bet myself or something equally as ridiculous."

"Now that's an idea," he said. When I shot him a murderous glance he feined thoughtfulness. "Actually, I was thinking more along the lines of betting your secret."

"What secret?"

"Why you're here; who you are. There's a story behind you that I want to know."

"Why should you care?" I asked, dismissing the subject.

"I didn't say I did," he replied. "But I'd like to know. Is it a bet?"

I considered. I was positive Thunder's long legs would carry him faster than the stud, but was I *that* positive?

"What would you put up?" I asked.

"What do you want?"

"Possibly a guide."

"A guide?" he asked loudly. "What the hell do you want a guide for? To go where?"

"I'm not sure yet," I answered truthfully. I didn't see any point in pretending that I was waiting for my make-believe father now. Donnelly was too clever for that. "I may want to head into the higher country." I looked at him, fixing my eyes on him steadily so he'd know I was serious. "If I did, and I won, would you take me?"

Now it was his turn to give it some thought. I was sure he was weighing the odds, wondering how much I could take—if we set out in the wilderness, would I quit in two days' time or would I be plucky enough to go on, maybe getting us lost or stranded or worse? He had no way of knowing, but would be agreeing to a blind trek.

"You're on," he said finally. "Whoa up."

We drew rein and stood in a wide, deep bay of grass curled against the hillside. On the far side of the bowl, probably five hundred feet away, was a single burned and blackened tree stump.

"To the tree," he said, "from right here."

I judged the distance. Thunder would need it all to get his speed to where his long legs could carry him easily while the Arabian would have early speed with his short back. But I thought it distance enough.

"Good," I said.

"On the count of three," Donnelly said. I wound my legs around Thunder's sides and lay low on his neck. He began to quiver. "One," Donnelly said. "Two . . . three!"

I jammed my heels into Thunder's belly and held on to his mane as he lunged forward. He stretched magnificently, taking a full first stride. The dun had gathered and was plunging away beside and just a little ahead of us, his powerful feet whipping the grass. Crouching even lower on Thunder, I gave him his head and rammed my heels into his sides again. His mane lashed my face, but I could see the tree and I urged him on.

"Come on!" I said under my breath. "Come on, Thunder!" He swiveled his ears backward and bowed his head in new effort. I glanced over and saw the straining head of the dun and kicked Thunder again. The tree was looming up on my left and we didn't have far to go. I heard Donnelly yell at his horse and I felt Thunder double, then I looked over to see the tree slide by and the dun's head at my knee.

I rode Thunder around and back to where

Donnelly waited, letting the horse catch his breath. I found it difficult to get the smile off my face, and Donnelly was grinning wryly to me.

"Jory Donnelly, guide and trapper at your service, ma'am," he said, sweeping his hat low to me. I laughed.

"That'll teach you to bet," I said.

"No it won't," he answered. "But it will teach me to win." Reining our tired horses around, we began to walk back up into the hills.

I was exhilarated. I had won the race, the bet and, I thought, a little bit of respect as well. At the same time I had ridden faster and harder than I had for years and that alone was enough to send my spirits soaring. Feeling the wind around me and the power of Thunder's muscles beneath me was stimulating. I felt alive and good for the first time in seven years.

"Did you know there was a lake up here?" Donnelly asked.

"No." I didn't remember any lake, but this close to Leavenworth most of the country was unfamiliar to me.

"Well, it's not really a lake, more like a large beaver pond. Depends on what you're used to. I'll show you."

We rode southwest along the deer trails until we crested a hill and stared down a gully. A stream ran splashing down alongside us. I minded Thunder so he wouldn't put one of his large hooves down on a loose rock and go down on the grade. We rode downward for a bit, then leveled out toward the west again.

When we came to the lake I saw what he meant. It was not huge, but larger than most beaver ponds. We rode around one edge of it and stopped on a clear stretch of ground. We tied the horses to some saplings and they both began to graze contentedly.

"Hardly anyone comes here," Donnelly said as we sat on the grass. "Most of the townfolk have too much to do to get out riding like this, and it's too close in for hunting or trapping. Not much game left around here, anyway."

Since he seemed in a talkative mood I would have liked to ask him about the Indians, but I didn't dare. I knew his mind was turning constantly and he would pick up anything I asked about and figure it in with what he already knew. Better to keep him as ignorant as possible, although that was getting more and more difficult.

"Where do you trap?" I asked. That was a safe enough question.

"I go west, to the high mountains. I built a cabin there some years ago and there's still good trapping. I run into Indians every now and then, but they know me by now and pretty much leave me alone. I don't usually have any trouble with them."

"What brings you back to Leavenworth every year?"

"Habit, mostly. When I started trapping, this was the most likely place to trade. Now it's just the natural place to come and I get good prices for my skins since it's right on the wagon route back east. Farther west they pay less. I think when I've trapped this area out, though, I'll go farther west. Too many people coming now, more than I like."

My sentiments exactly, I thought. Even though Leavenworth was so much smaller than New York, there were still too many people to suit me. I wondered what the high mountains were like. All I knew were the plains and the city. I had heard of the Rockies but could not imagine them as big as I had heard. I asked Donnelly about them.

"They're fantastic," he said. "Nothing can compare with them. They're so high, the trees only grow half way up the sides and they're as sharp and jagged as a razorback."

The way he described them sounded strangely beautiful. I thought someday I would like to see them for myself. Perhaps when I finally found my Cheyenne we would travel to the mountains. I knew they were not too distant from the mouth of the Platte.

Lost in my thoughts, I hadn't realized Donnelly had stopped talking and was watching me.

"How old are you?" he asked.

"Twenty," I said. I glanced at him defiantly as if he would twist that around somehow in an insult.

"Almost an old maid by civilized standards, aren't you?" he asked. "I thought back east a girl was generally married off by eighteen or so."

"That's normally true," I said, although I hated to admit he was right. "If a girl is not engaged or betrothed by seventeen or eighteen people usually start looking askance at her."

"Is that why you left? You had no prospects?"

"Mr. Donnelly," I said, drawing myself up defensively, "I'll have you know I was betrothed at one time and your snide questions will not help you at all."

"Betrothed? You mean bartered off for your dowry?"

I felt like slapping him. His tone was so innocent and yet his words were so barbed.

"He wanted it as much as I did," I said through clenched teeth. "It was arranged in that it would have been good for our families to be tied together, but neither of us would have had it any other way."

"Then why didn't you get married?"

"We were—separated," I answered haltingly, "by outside circumstances." It seemed so long ago and so far away now. "He's probably married someone else by now." The words slipped out unbidden, more a spoken thought than anything I had meant for the trapper's ears.

He watched me for a moment, then a funny look crossed his face. "Cathy, you aren't—pregnant, are you?" he asked hesitantly.

I should have been outraged at his insolence and familiarity but the expression on his face sent me into gales of laughter. His look had changed from inspiration to wonder to almost fear and I thought he would be of no use to a midwife at all.

"No," I said, still laughing. "I'm not pregnant. Is that why you think I came out here? To have a fatherless baby?"

He smiled, obviously relieved. "You've got to admit, it's what a lot of girls would do."

"Not me," I said.

"No, I suppose not." He looked at me seriously and I began to feel uncomfortable. The conversation was too much about me and I had revealed more than I intended. Somehow I had let my guard down and I forced myself to put it back up again.

"I think I should be getting back," I said. I stood up and brushed the grass from my buckskins. He stood beside me, a little too close, and I made for the horses. I was surprised he hadn't argued with me or said anything insulting, but when I reached for Thunder I felt Donnelly take my arm and pull me around to face him. His other arm slid about my waist and tightened to bring me close against his chest. Even as my hands pushed against him, he bowed his head and pressed his lips on mine, catching me off guard and flooding me with a sudden heat. His tongue entered my mouth easily and seemed to touch nerve endings with every move and set off tingling sensations that made my head buzz. I felt the warmth creeping throughout my body and it made me weak.

"Please," I said weakly, "please don't."

"Who are you saving it for?" he asked, still holding me. "The man who's already married someone else?"

"No," I answered. Without his kiss driving all rational thought from my mind I was able to reason. "I wasn't raised this way," I said truthfully. "I was taught that love was expressed through mutual sharing, not through the rutting of hot blooded animals. If it can't be beautiful and honorable, I won't have it at all."

He watched me closely as I spoke, his ice-blue eyes giving me no indication of his thoughts. I was afraid he would find my little speech as laughable as he found the rest of my refined behavior and force himself on me. But I would not be used or act as an animal in heat. Physical love would come to me my way or not at all.

Slowly he wound his fingers in my long black hair and tugged slightly, just enough to tip my face up to his. I began another protest but he silenced me with a finger over my mouth.

"Think about something," he said. "Even if you find your honorable love, how beautifully can it be expressed without desire?" He raked his fingers through my hair, letting the black strands fall slowly away. Then he released me and stepped to his horse.

We rode on down the lake side, taking a circular route back to my cache. Donnelly rode in front of me and I languidly allowed Thunder to walk at his own pace across the moist ground. I let my mind wander, not wanting to think about what the trapper had said.

Suddenly Thunder stopped and I looked up to see Donnelly bending over sideways to study something on the ground. I kicked Thunder up alongside and tried to see what it was.

"Hoofprints," Donnelly said. "Unshod."

I looked carefully and separated the markings.

They were fresh, maybe as fresh as a few minutes. I walked Thunder on, examining the prints.

"This horse—or pony—the prints are so small, is lame," I said.

"Where?" he asked, and I pointed to one set in particular. One hoofprint was noticeably deeper, showing where the pony had borne most of its weight while the corresponding one was much lighter. And the pattern held.

Donnelly looked at me curiously. "Yes," he said finally. "It's got to be that Indian brat. He's got a pony with one leg shorer than the other."

I felt suddenly angry and defensive. "Do you mean Red Cloud?" I asked.

He nodded, looking about, appparently unmindful of my irritation. He scanned the trees.

"There he is!" he said, and rammed his dun hard in the sides, sending it lunging through the brush. I whirled after him, just barely getting a glimpse of Red Cloud as he disappeared into a gully.

The boy slipped his pony through bushes and around rocks that our larger horses had difficulty passing. I heard Jory swearing angrily as he scraped his face on bushes trying to follow. The gully was narrow and steep, but somehow the pony was getting up it and we were not. I kept Thunder close behind the dun but by the time we crested the hill, Red Cloud was nowhere in sight. The rocks that ridged the hills gave no clue of his passing and the unshod hooves of his pony left no marks.

"Come on," he said curtly and turned his stallion back toward Leavenworth. I followed at a safe distance. When we regained level ground again I moved up next to him.

"Why should he watch us?" I asked.

"I don't know, but next time I see that little whelp I'm going to thump him on the head so he'll know not to do it again. I don't like anyone spying on me, especially a sneaky little savage."

"Is there a personal reason or are you prejudiced against all Indians?" I asked coldly.

He glanced at me, trying to gauge my anger. "Are you one of those libertines?" he asked. "One of those idealists who believe in the noble savage?"

"No, but it sounds like you're one of those hard-headed bastards that believes the only good Indian is a dead Indian." I sat ramrod straight, my eyes not deigning to meet his.

"If it's all that important, it's strictly personal. I tried to befriend that kid a year ago but he wouldn't have anything to do with me. Wouldn't even acknowledge that I was talking to him. So I gave up. But I'll be damned if I'll have him spying on me."

We rode in silence for a bit and I wondered how much of that was true. I had seen the prejudice in Leavenworth, felt it. It was evident in Mr. Altvater's assurances to me that Red Cloud was harmless and in Charles Lafferty's loud denoucements. Even my grandparents shook their heads when they thought I didn't see, and my own mother had tried so hard to persuade me to the white world even before I was dragged into it. I wondered if I would ever meet anyone who would not be appalled by my mixed heritage. And if not, how could I ever be fully myself except when I was totally alone?

"How did you know enough tracking to pick up on that pony's bad leg?" he asked suddenly. "You didn't learn that in New York."

I decided not to answer. I wasn't above lying but I couldn't think of anything plausible and I had already given too much of myself away. Donnelly waited for my answer for a moment, then turned his attention back to the trail.

"Why does the pony have one leg short? Was it born that way?" I asked.

"No, it was shot accidently. It should've been finished off, but Red Cloud begged them not to kill it and he got Hank to help him doctor it. It was really surprising how well it healed, except being too short like that. Red Cloud almost lived in that pony's stall until it stood again. I guess he deserved to have it after that."

We gained the rocky cache in silence and I slid off Thunder and retrieved my saddle. Donnelly tossed me my skirt and grinned when I stepped behind the rocks to change. By this time, thought, I figured if he had wanted to see me naked he could have managed it before. I adjusted my civilized clothes and twisted my hair back into a knot at the base of my neck. I was sure I didn't look fresh from my vanity, but it would have to do.

"I suppose you plan to escort me back to town

and sully my reputation all the more?" I asked briskly.

"Not today," he said as if turning down a treat I had offered. "It's still early and I think you can make it back to town before dark." I ignored his sarcasm, since it was still hours until sunset. He sat his dun idly so I kicked Thunder into a walk. I had planned to go on, walking toward town without a backward glance, or even a parting word. I guided Thunder through the trees and out onto the plains grass. When Donnelly made no sound, I bit my lip and twisted around in my saddle. He sat jauntily on his dun, one knee hooked over the saddle horn and a cheerful smile on his face. Before I could turn away he doffed his hat to me in that ingratiating way he had that infuriated me. I pressed Thunder to a canter and loped back to town without looking back again.

Hank offered to put Thunder up for me so I made my way quickly back to the boardinghouse and went upstairs to clean up. No matter how I straightened my clothes or smoothed my hair, I could not look freshly groomed after riding for hours. Luckily it was still some time until dinner and I could at least give the appearance of lounging quietly on a Sunday afternoon.

I went down to the parlor, taking some needlepoint with me, something I hadn't done since I left New York. I decided that, as well as giving me time to think, it would look properly domestic. The only other person I saw was Margaret and she was just dusting and doing some light cleaning.

She smiled to me and thankfully went about her work.

I was afraid things were getting out of hand but I had no way of regaining control. Every time I rode I placed myself in a position of meeting Mr. Donnelly, yet he knew as well as I that I could not give up my excursions. It was the only part of my life that was not a fiasco, and I would fight for it if I had to. But every meeting with him endangered my lifestyle in Leavenworth. He picked up clues that I didn't even know I was leaving and he had already pieced too much together.

And aside from that, he affected me strangely. He seemed to prick my emotions constantly, either angering me or sending tingles through my body. I attributed the paradox to the fact that no man had ever touched me before, but that did not lessen my confusion. I felt each moment spent with him brought me nearer to weakness, but I could see involvement with him as an obstruction to my plan.

I felt as if my time in Leavenworth were running out. Soon I should be forced to leave and strike out on my own. But where would I go? Would it be possible for me to set out alone across the prairie and find my band? Or, I thought, perhaps I might be forced to take the prize I had won in the bet, and have Mr. Donnelly guide me. That was disconcerting enough.

The next day I settled back into my routine at the store and I was glad for the business that kept my mind from wandering. Now that people knew me and were used to seeing me behind my counter, they came in and passed the time, bought what they wanted and left. I was glad we had gone beyond the standing and staring phase and that I was now accepted as a normal occupant of town. It gave me time to think about my job and doing it well instead of worrying about the image I was projecting.

Mr. Altvater seemed pleased with me and my work and would occasionally come to the back of the store to discuss something with me. Although I felt I had won his respect, I was taken aback when he asked me how I might do my corner over again to make it more appealing to women.

"You know more about women than I do, what they want and what they want to be. Why don't you think about it and see what you can come up with? The store could use a little fashion."

I was pleased that he put so much store in my opinion and I tried to picture how I might make the millinery more appealing. At that time I wished I had paid more attention to the frivolities of New York society, if only for this project. I pulled out the yellowed copies of eastern papers Mr. Altvater kept for reference and pored through them, trying to get ideas. With that to keep me busy, the day passed quickly.

Mr. Altvater locked the door and I went to get my bag. Then I thought of Red Cloud. Trying to look busy, I rummaged in my purse until I saw the boy out of the corner of my eye. He grabbed his broom and almost ran out of the small room.

I put my purse back in its original order and stepped out into the store. Mr. Altvater was busy behind the front counter so I walked purposefully to the back where Red Cloud swept. Walking quietly, I reached the boy and put my hand on his shoulder.

It was as if I had touched him with a branding iron. He spun to face me, then backed frantically away, his eyes wide with fear. I grabbed his wrist to keep him from bolting completely away and his expression turned to abject terror.

"Red Cloud," I said softly, "don't be afraid. I won't hurt you." My words made no difference. I couldn't understand why he should suddenly be so terrified, but then I remembered how Jory had sworn and cursed the boy yesterday in the hills. Red Cloud obviously thought I shared the trapper's opinion of him.

"Listen to me," I said. "Mr. Donnelly was very angry that you were spying on us yesterday, but he won't hurt you," I hoped. "Do you understand? Neither of us will hurt you."

His only answer was to shake his head slowly and try to twist out of my grasp. As young as he was, he was strengthened by his fear and was close to slipping away.

"You must understand," I said. His failure to comprehend was maddening and the urge to cry came over me. I grabbed his other hand and tried to hold him still for a moment. "I am like you," I said suddenly. "I am Cheyenne. I am Tsistsistas."

The word slipped out before I could stop it,

rolling off my tongue as if I stood again in my lodge, proclaiming my race. Red Cloud's eyes grew wider yet and his struggles became more violent. I rushed on in whispered tones. "Listen to me! I am Gray Feather, daughter of Painted Lance, the mighty warrior. I have come to find my people. The trapper has agreed to help me. That's how I know he will not hurt you."

Red Cloud watched me as if I were blabbing in a crazy, unintelligible tongue. In a moment's panic I wondered if he had forgotten how to speak Cheyenne. No, that was impossible.

"I appeal to you as my brother," I said softly, still in our native language. "We are of the same blood."

Much as I had hoped for a positive response to my surprising outburst, I was disappointed. Red Cloud backed out from under my hand and stared strangely at me.

"Tsistsistas?" he echoed.

"Yes," I said. "I am Cheyenne."

His eyes flicked over me one more time, as if seeing me for the first time, and then he ran out of the store.

Well, I thought, now the cat is out of the bag. Only time will tell if that had been a smart move or a mistake. I felt certain Red Cloud was not so "tame" that he would reveal my secret to any white men, but there was still the possibility that he just plain couldn't help me. I desperately hoped that wasn't true.

On Tuesday I waited around at closing to talk to

Red Cloud again. I hoped we could go walking somewhere and talk privately. I wasn't sure how we could accomplish that without drawing attention to ourselves—perhaps go riding—but I needed to talk with him more.

I puttered about in my corner working on my remodeling project for several minutes.

"Aren't you going home?" Mr. Altvater asked.

"Oh," I said, "yes, I am. I guess I was just so involved I forgot the time." I put a few final touches on my plan and walked slowly to get my purse. Still no Red Cloud. The thought crossed my mind that he was avoiding me. Was it possible I had misjudged him? Maybe he was unwilling—or unable—to help me. I waited as long as I thought I could without seeming peculiar, then went on home.

The next day was the same. Usually Red Cloud came a few minutes before closing or at the very latest a few minutes after. I'd noticed he was often out of breath, as if he had run some small doings of his own, but he always came. Just as I was about to leave I noticed Mr. Altvater staring out the window.

"Is Red Cloud late again?" I asked innocently.

"I'm afraid the little savage has disappeared on me again."

"Disappeared?"

"Yes, damn it. Excuse me." Mr. Altvater sighed. "Every once in a while he just up and takes off somewhere, out scouting in the hills or something. I've told him I don't mind so much his going as his not telling me. Can't seem to get it through his head, though."

"I see," I said noncommitally. "How long is he usually gone?"

"Anywhere from a couple days to a week."

"And you have no idea where he goes?"

"None. Maybe that's why he won't tell me ahead of time; maybe he's afraid someone will follow him."

Leaving Mr. Altvater to curse his luck, and Red Cloud, I went home. I barely dared to hope that the boy's disappearance might have something to do with my revelation the day before, but it was possible. It was also possible he just didn't want to face me again.

When he didn't reappear each day, I forced myself not to think about it. I didn't want to become jaded by imagining the worst or be falsely hopeful by thinking the best. I decided to put Red Cloud out of my mind until he showed again and I would know what to think. It would have been difficult if I didn't have so many other things to think about.

Often in the evenings now Charles would sit uncomfortably close to me in the parlor. Della, I noticed, would try to act as if nothing were going on, but her eyes would stray to Charles, then to me, and I knew what she was thinking. I began to think I had somehow trapped myself in an implied relationship I wanted no part of. At the boarding-house I could sometimes evade Charles, or the whole group if I chose, and sit alone in my room, but the Evanses had come to expect us on most Sunday nights. I would have felt badly about snubbing them just to be free of Charles and, besides, I enjoyed dinner with them. I would rather put up with Charles than not see them.

That Sunday Della asked me to help her with some sewing—her own this time—and I felt I couldn't refuse. I fairly ached with a need to go riding but she had been very considerate of me and I felt only fair in paying her back in kind. The only consolation was thinking about Jory perhaps waiting for me out in the hills. It made me smile wickedly.

"You still have no idea when your father will be arriving in town?" Della asked as I pinned a hem in a skirt she wore.

"No," I lied. It had been a while since I had even thought about my false identity, so caught up had I been in things.

"It's getting on," Della said. "Do you still think he'll make it this year?"

"It's only June," I said, although it was late in the month. "There are still good traveling months left. Turn a bit." I pinned more of the hem. "Anyway, if it's too late for us to start out again, which it looks like it will be, we'll just stay here until next spring. I'll still have my job so it shouldn't be a problem."

"That job was a lucky hunch. Good thing for it."

"Well, it keeps me busy, too. I can't see just sitting around waiting all summer."

"Hmmm, no," Della said. Her voice turned suddenly funny. "You ever think what would happen if you was to meet someone—maybe not go to California?"

I looked up at her. "What on earth are you talking about?" I asked.

"I've seen how Charles watches you," she said, smiling. "I think he'd just as soon talk you into staying around. Maybe for good."

"That's ridiculous," I said, feeing uneasy. "We're just friends. Turn again."

"You say," she chuckled, making a quarter turn. "I've known enough men to know that look when I see it. Men's looked at me like that in my day."

"I'm sure they have," I said softening. "But I'm not even thinking about marriage right now. No, no matter what Charles thinks, I won't be staying in Leavenworth."

"Too bad. It's more than him would like to see you stay."

I looked up at Della to see her smiling down at me. "Thank you, Della. I—I have made a lot of friends here, but I never intended to stay. It's just a stopping point for me."

"I know," she said. "And you'll have a whole new life in California. I hope you'll write to us, though. Some of us, we'll never get out of Leavenworth. We'd like to hear how it is in the gold country."

"Of course I'll write," I said with a steady voice that even surprised me. "I'll tell you all about California. But that's a long way off."

"Yeah, it is. You and Charles going to that newspaperman's for dinner again tonight?"

"Yes," I hated to admit. "They're wonderful people to talk to."

"Smart, huh?" Della asked.

"Yes, they are very intelligent."

"Not like most folks around here," Della laughed.

"Oh, I wouldn't say that," I argued. "It's just that they're more articulate than most. People don't have to have a lot of education to be intelligent."

"Whatever that means," Della said. "You 'bout done with this hem?"

"This is the last pin."

"Good. Then I got a dress I need you to pin for me. I didn't cut it down enough and it's way too breezy."

We spent the day sewing and talking, only stopping to steal some bread and cheese from Mrs. Reedy's kitchen for lunch. Finally at five I excused myself and went to my room to get ready for dinner.

Charles was as thoughtfully considerate as always. He held my arm as we walked to the Evanses' and spoke in the low tones he'd adopted lately. I was worried about what those low tones meant.

Mae and Tom, as I had come to think of them, were both happy to see us come. We went into the front room where Tom poured us each a glass of wine. I saw a chessboard had been set up since the last time I was there.

"Do you play?" Tom asked when he saw me looking.

"Some. I'm afraid I haven't for quite a while, but I used to."

"Would you care to play a quick one before dinner?"

"A quick one?" I asked. "Is there such a thing in chess?"

"Well, maybe not. How soon is dinner, Mae?"

"Go ahead," Mae laughed. "Dinner will wait."

Tom and I sat on either side of the marble playing board while Charles and Mae sat nearby to watch.

"Smoke or fire?" Tom said, holding out his two closed fists to me. I chose the left. "Smoke. You go first."

We talked as we played, Charles and Mae joining in during the waiting periods of the game.

"Have you ever heard of the Buffalo Soldiers?" Tom asked.

Neither Charles nor I had. "You don't mean buffalo hunters?" Charles asked.

"No. There's talk about a law that's soon to be passed in Washington outfitting two full regiments of entirely black soldiers. I have a connection in Washington who said Fort Leavenworth may be their first assignment."

"You mean coloreds?" Charles asked.

"Yes, ex-slaves mostly. I've been thinking of running a piece on it in my paper. Any suggestions?"

I was flattered to realize he was asking me. "I

think it would be good," I said. "After all, they did fight in the Civil War, on both sides. There's no reason why they shouldn't have regiments. It seems like whites are so fond of forgetting that blacks are Americans too, and just as capable and willing to defend it. It would be better than the second-class treatment they usually get."

"Yes, but it's not quite the same thing," Charles said. "I should think they'd need much more training and discipline, and be more apt to desert."

"Why should they?" I asked. "They're people, too, just like us."

Charles snorted. "So are Indians, but you won't see anyone training them for the cavalry."

"What's that supposed to mean?" I asked, my voice ringing with indignation. Too late, I realized everyone was staring at me, Tom with a pawn in his hand. "Surely you can't expect Indians to join Americans in their own slaughter," I said, trying to sound reasonable.

"Of course you can't," Tom said. "And Indians are different." I eyed him as he spoke, my belief in him shaky now. "Indians are far too disorganized to fight the white man. They get into the heat of battle and it's every man for himself, fighting his own little war. That's why our companies have beaten them so often."

I wanted to object, but it was true. How often had I heard braves explaining a plan to attack only to have it disintegrate once shots were fired. The Cheyenne, particularly, loved a battle too much to accord it any rules. Carried away by their own excitement, they often lost sight of larger goals.

"But that's more because of their methods and not their capabilities," I insisted.

"True," Tom agreed. "On their own terms, Indians are the best. Like their silent, sneak attacks. No one can do that better. But getting back to black soldiers—they're the same as whites, think the same, fight the same. I think the new regiments will work out very well."

We bandied the issue about a bit more as Tom proceeded to slaughter me in chess. I was rustier than I had thought, and I had trouble keeping my mind on the game. I kept remembering Charles's degrading remarks about Indians and Tom's knowledgable defense of them. That was one way of finding out people's inner beliefs.

"Checkmate," Tom said finally. I examined every possible move open to my king but Tom's rook and queen had me completely blocked.

"Your game," I conceded. "I told you I haven't played for a long time."

"That's all right, it was a good game."

"All right, you three," Mae said from the doorway. I hadn't even noticed when she'd left. "Come and get it."

The dinner was good and we talked of less serious things. It was a pleasant evening, warm and comfortable. As before, I was disappointed it had to end.

"Next week?" Mae asked as we were leaving.

"I don't see why not," I said looking to Charles. He nodded.

"Good. We'll see you then."

We walked home slowly, not saying much. Charles was unusually quiet and I wondered what he was thinking but I was afraid to ask. When we neared the boardinghouse I realized I was going to find out anyway.

"Catherine," he said, "are you still planning on going to California?"

"Of course I am," I said impatiently. "That's my whole purpose in being here."

"Yes, I know, but I had just wondered if there might be a chance, any chance at all that you might like it well enough to want to stay."

"Charles," I said slowly, "my opinions of Leavenworth is not the issue. I do like it, and I like the people, but I can't stay." Hadn't I just said the same thing to Della? "What would I do, greet my father after not seeing him for three years and say, 'Sorry, I'm not going with you'?"

"Of course you couldn't," Charles agreed. "I just had hoped I could . . . talk you out of leaving."

We reached the boardinghouse steps and Charles turned toward me. "You have to know that I care for you," he said. "I know you've kept your distance between us, but I still care for you, very much. I just want you to know."

"I—I'm flattered," I said, greatly embarrassed. "But it's impossible. I can't stay, and I can't permit anything . . . between us. It's just not possible."

"I understand," he said miserably. "It's all right. I won't press you about it again. But if you should ever change your mind . . ."

"I'll remember," I said. "Thank you. Now I think I should go upstairs. I'm really very tired."

Lord, I thought as I lay in bed. I didn't see how Charles could think there could be anything between us, now or ever. Our differences blared out to me like off-key notes, but apparently he was deaf to them. On the other hand, he was probably presenting a fairly accurate picture of himself to me while I was showing him a totally false image of myself. No one in Leavenworth knew my true self. Except, I thought, maybe Jory Donnelly.

Chapter Six

THAT WEEK started out badly. On Monday I tried to work on my remodeling project but every time I picked up my pencil a customer would come back and want something. It annoyed me, even though I realized my job was them, initially. To make matters worse, everyone else seemed in a foul mood as well, and I had trouble pleasing people. Monday night I was glad to go home and forget the store.

Tuesday Melly dropped a bombshell on me. She came rushing into the store, excited as usual, and began babbling almost before she reached me.

"Catherine!" she began. "You'll never guess! Frank just got the news yesterday or I would have told you sooner."

"What?" I asked. "What is it?"

"Frank's been transferred. He has to be in St. Louis in a week. Isn't it wonderful? It'll be just no distance at all for my parents to come visit now."

"Oh," I said slowly. "That's marvelous, Melly. A week—when will you leave?"

"We have to leave tomorrow, on the first boat. When Frank told me I was so shocked. I've been packing like crazy, just throwing things in. It's almost funny. Here Mother and Daddy just left and we're practically on their heels." She was so excited that she didn't notice my quietness, which was just as well. I was surprised at my own depression, myself. I hadn't realized how much I counted on Melly's friendship, and now she was leaving. Idly, I wondered if her father had had anything to do with the transfer. He was just influential enough to have the power—and concerned enough to use it.

"Well, say something!" Melly demanded happily.

"Oh, I'm sorry, it was just such a surprise. Of course I'm happy for you, Melly. It's wonderful. You'll like St. Louis much better anyway."

"Yes, I think so, too," she said. "Leavenworth is all right, but it's awfully boring. In St. Louis there'll be lots more for me to do while Frank's out soldiering. Are you all right? You don't look very well."

"No, I'm fine. It just hasn't been a very good day."

"Oh, I'm sorry," Melly said, smiling sadly. "I will miss you terribly, Catherine. You've been my best friend in Leavenworth. I almost feel like I've known you for years."

"I'll miss you too," I said, surprised because I could feel tears behind my eyes. "But you'll be so happy with Frank you won't even be thinking of anything else."

"That's probably true," she admitted. "But I will think of you, Catherine. After all, you'll be going farther west to a whole new land, while I'm only going backward. You'll have so much to think about, you'll forget all about me and my silly chatter." Even as she spoke, her smile trembled and her eyes turned moist. "Oh, dear," she said, "I'm afraid I'm doing it again. It seems like I've done nothing but cry for weeks." She took out her handkerchief and dabbed at her eyes.

"It's all right," I said, pushing back the desire to cry myself.

"I'd better go. I still have so much to do. I probably won't see you again before I leave."

"Probably not," I agreed.

Suddenly she leaned across the counter and hugged me, tears rolling down both her cheeks.

"Goodbye, Catherine," she said. "Do take care of yourself."

"I will," I promised. "And you, too, Melly. Make sure Frank keeps you happy."

"Oh, he will," she laughed, through her tears. One last hug and she started out the store. "I'll write to you."

"And I'll write back. Say goodbye to Frank for me. And good luck."

"Yes, goodbye." She waved at the door, and again at the window, childlike. I watched until she disappeared down the street, feeling as if my last friend in the world were retreating away. I reasoned with myself that it was silly to attach so much to her leaving when we'd only known each other a few months, but that didn't eradicate the way I was feeling.

She was happy. She had loving parents, a doting husband, a clear vision of her future and a definite idea of her role in life. I had none of those. Not only that, my prospects were dreary. My greatest hope for finding my family, Red Cloud, was gone, and I didn't even know if he could or would help me if he returned. I had Charles pressuring me, albeit gently, and Donnelly confusing the issues as well as my emotions. Now Melly and her family were gone and it was as if the last outlet of expression had been plugged and I was totally isolated in my problems. I felt like a steam engine with the last vent slammed shut and no one to open it for me.

Every contact with a customer after that was unbearable. I tried to smooth my face and feelings out but inquiries irritated me and my explanations only seemed to worsen things. I found myself fighting back tears more than once for no apparent reason, and I watched the hands of the clock inch by painfully. When I finally heard Mr. Altvater close the doors I could almost have cried with relief. I didn't even delude myself into waiting to see if Red Cloud would show, I just left the store and turned toward the livery.

I almost broke into a run so I could get Thunder out, and as it was I worried Hank into saddling him as quickly as possible. Feeling the tears coming as soon as I relaxed a little, I rammed my heel into Thunder's side and galloped out of town.

At first I automatically turned toward the hills, but just out of town I veered right and headed for the Missouri. I wanted to take no chances on meeting Mr. Donnelly today. Instead I wanted to find a place where no one would interrupt me, where I could cry alone. My eyes filled with tears until my vision blurred. I whipped Thunder into a run, letting the wind streak the tears back across my face.

At the river I slowed and picked a way through the bushes that grew so dense along the banks. I avoided cabins and farm houses and finally found a small clearing in an overgrown copse of trees. I tied Thunder so he could graze and settled myself in the plush grass. Knowing I was finally alone, I let my tears well up and flow freely.

I wondered how long I would have to play this charade. It was eating at me, the lies, the setbacks, the dramatics of it all. But I had few alternatives. I couldn't—no, wouldn't—go back to New York; I couldn't proclaim myself in Leavenworth. I supposed I could leave, strike out on my own. I wondered if it would be difficult to find some Cheyenne by myself. Red Cloud was obviously going to be no help. If I left Leavenworth, it wouldn't matter what opinions I left behind me, but how easy would it be for me to get supplies? It seemed that every alternative had drawbacks and I was stuck between a rock and a hard place. I watched the clouds above me turn a salmon pink and knew all my frantic thoughts would not provide a solution.

When I heard a twig snap behind me I assumed it was Thunder, but then the hair on the back of my neck rose. I turned to see the dark shape of a horse and rider behind me, except the horse had long ears.

"Go away," I said, not caring if he knew I had been crying. My voice quivered and hearing it made me start to cry all over again.

The mule's hooves moved lightly through the grass and I heard the squeak of leather as Donnelly dismounted. In a moment he sat down beside me.

"You rode out of town like a bat out of hell," he said softly. "What's wrong?"

"Everything," I said brokenly. "Please go away. I just want to be by myself." I turned away from him and began to shred leaves that I found on the grass. I heard Donnelly move and then his hand lay on my arm. I could feel the brush of his body against my back.

"Tell me, Cathy," he said.

His reassuring touch and comforting voice only added to my depression and I shook with new tears. If I allowed myself to turn to him I knew my unhappiness would devastate me. I couldn't let myself go. I tried to shake off his hand.

"Go away," I sobbed. "Can't you see I don't want you here?"

For an answer, Jory pulled me around, forcing me to face him and then held me tightly in his arms. I found I was unable to fight him. His arms felt so warm and comfortable that I surrendered myself to them and pressed my face into his chest, my tears dampening his buckskin shirt. I cried miserably, not caring how I sobbed or how I gasped for breath. I cried until I felt weak and my nose ran embarrassingly. Finally, when I seemed through, he relaxed his hold on me enough so I could lean back and look up at him.

"You ought to cry more often," he said, wiping my cheeks with a rough finger. "You keep it all inside of you and when it does come out, you've got a regular flood on your hands." He smiled at me but I couldn't join in his humor.

"Please go away," I begged quietly.

He shook his head. "Not until you tell me what's wrong. Maybe I can help."

"You can't. No one can."

"I can try." He began to pull the pins from my hair until it fell in a black curtain behind me. "You messed up your hair riding so hard. Do you have a brush with you?" I shook my head. "Well, this will have to do." He put his fingers to my temple and ran them through my hair, pulling gently on the tangles. His caresses made my skin tingle and made me feel weak. How easy it would be to give myself up and let him carry me into a dream world. It would be so nice not to think for a while, not to have to worry about anything. All I would have to do would be to succumb to the pleasurable feelings he released in me. His fingers in my hair sent small waves of sensation through me and I stared up into his lake-blue eyes.

I hadn't meant for it to be an invitation, but looking back now I suppose it was. I can still imagine my tear-streaked face staring pleadingly at him, asking for solace or any sort of peace he could give me. He met my gaze for a moment, then leaned down and pressed his lips on mine. For a moment I did nothing but let the feel of his mouth comfort me but, then, almost unwittingly, my arms went up around his neck and held him tighter to me.

It wasn't so much desire that drove me to him, but desperation. Once locked in his arms I found I didn't want to be anyplace else. His large rough hands pressed me closer to him and wound their way through my hair. When he parted my lips and I tasted his tongue in my mouth, I allowed it, then responded to it. Jory had succeeded in lighting a fire in me and I encouraged it until it threatened to engulf us both. Finally he lay back and stared at me.

"Now," he said, ignoring the fact that I had returned his kiss so willingly, "tell me."

"No," I said. I lay cradled against him and ran my fingers over the damp spot on his shirt where I had cried. He stared at me quietly, then took my hand and raised it so he could kiss my fingers. That small act sent shivers of delight down my spine. All I wanted at that moment was to be very far away in a moonlit meadow with Jory.

"You're about the unhappiest girl I've ever met," he said, "and I have the feeling you've brought a lot of it on yourself."

Instead of becoming angry as I probably should have, I considered that. I had to agree. Perhaps if I had stayed in New York I would be bored and discontent, but I had never been as miserable as I was here.

"That's partly true," I admitted finally. I released my hand from his and laid it along his cheek, letting his beard stubble tickle my palm. I had never touched a man so familiarly before, but it didn't seem unnatural.

"Why are you so unhappy?" he asked.

"Because I don't know what to do," I said. "It seems like everywhere I turn there are people and things I can't face and I don't know what to do."

"What do you want to do?"

"Be myself."

"Is that so difficult?"

"Yes," I said. "If I were to simply be myself, no self-respecting person would have anything to do with me and I don't think I could live with ridicule. It's hard to be yourself if you won't be accepted that way."

"That depends," Jory said. "I can't see why riding astraddle or swearing like a trooper should make you unacceptable. Unusual, yes, but not un-

181

acceptable."

I couldn't help but smile. It seemed so simple to him, but what little he knew was simple.

"That's just how much you know," I said aloud.

"But aren't you being yourself now, here with me? Those tears weren't fake. Neither was that kiss."

I blushed. He had skirted around the issue of the kiss so well that I had almost forgotten about it.

"I suppose I am," I said. "As much as I can be."

"And I don't ridicule you or think you're unacceptable. Just a little strange."

"Thanks."

"You're welcome." He took my hand again and studied it as if it would tell him my secrets. "Why don't you trust me? Haven't I kept your wild rides to myself?"

"Yes," I admitted.

"Then what holds you back? It would seem easier for you to surrender your virtue to me than your inner self."

I almost thought that was true. In the darkening twilight the copse seemed so remote and comforting that I almost thought I could surrender to him. It certainly couldn't make my situation any worse, I thought ironically. But I still couldn't say what Jory thought he wanted to hear.

"I just can't," I said. "I don't think I could stand to see your eyes change. I couldn't stand to see that look that everyone gets when they know."

His eyebrows edged downward and I knew he

was wondering what it was that could be so awful. But even in the land of Indians I knew how it would be. It was as if half-breed meant half-human.

"It's getting dark," I said. "I should go back."

"Not yet." He leaned down and pressed me into the grass with his lips. Again I reached for him, loving the way he felt in my arms. I hadn't remembered ever feeling so good or warm and I wanted it to last for a long time. This time I opened my mouth under his and met his tongue with mine. His hand cupped my face, then slid down to encircle my throat. His fingers kneaded my skin and flexed under the collar of my dress. I wanted him to unbutton the front of it, to spread it apart and lavish kisses all over every part of my body but I couldn't tell him so. His hand brushed my breast once, fleetingly, as he circled it around to my back again and then he drew away and pulled me up to sit beside him.

"If we keep this up, neither one of us will be going anywhere," he said throatily. He brushed a strand of black hair off my face. "You are feeling better now, aren't you? Better than when you came?"

"Yes," I answered truthfully.

"Good. Come on." He stood and pulled me to my feet, then helped me brush grass from the back of my skirt.

"I hope all this wasn't just to make me feel better," I said suddenly. I don't know why I said it out loud; it was such a shameless thing to say.

Jory looked at me curiously.

"No," he said with a funny note to his voice, "It wasn't."

Thinking I had said enough, I only nodded and walked to Thunder. He and Beauty both jerked their heads up at our approach. Jory handed me up and then mounted beside me as we walked slowly back toward the light of town.

"Your hair is still down," he said after a bit. "I think I have your pins in my pocket." He got them out and handed them to me but I put them immediately into my bag. If he thought anything about my leaving my hair down, he didn't say anything. We rode into Leavenworth silently, paying little attention to the few people who saw us. Always before Jory had left me before we entered town, for whatever reason, but this time he walked alongside all the way to the livery. Hank came out just in time to see Jory help me down and we unsaddled our own horses and put them up. He threw them each a flake of hay and we stood together by the stall doors watching them eat.

"Would you like me to walk you back to Mrs. Reedy's?" he asked when we turned to go. He placed his hand at the small of my back and guided me outside.

"I don't think so," I said. "I suppose I shall have enough explaining to do as it is. Della always asks a million questions and Charles—Mr. Lafferty— thinks he is my guardian angel and protector."

"Why don't you find another place to live?"

"I don't know. I hadn't really thought about it

184

much. Maybe I will." I smiled. "I can just imagine Charles's face if I did. I think he would probably give me up for lost then."

"Maybe he should anyway," Jory said. He looked down at me in the darkness by the livery and I wished we were alone so he could kiss me. But the main street of Leavenworth was no place for that.

"Thank you," I said.

"For what?"

"For—talking to me. For following me."

"I told you the Irish are bad for curiosity."

"Yes, I know," I said. "Good night."

"Good night, Cathy."

I didn't see him again for days. Of course I didn't go riding any other nights that week, but I looked for him to come into the store. It wasn't until Thursday that he finally did, and only then to buy boot laces. He asked me where they were and I pointed them out although I was sure he already knew. I counted his change for him, acting as businesslike as he was.

"How are you?" he asked finally.

"Better," I said. "Crying does a lot to ease a desolate mood."

"It was just a mood, then?"

"Yes. I think so. It's passed now."

"All of it?"

I didn't want to answer that. In daylight I thought how familiar I had been and allowed him to be and it worried me. How would I ever find my people if I let myself become involved with Jory? I didn't want to answer his question.

"Donnelly!" Mr. Altvater called suddenly from the front. The big German walked toward us but still I remained silent. "I hope you're not trying to steal my help away," he said jovially. "Now that she knows the job I don't want to lose her."

Jory stared at me a moment longer, then turned to my employer.

"Don't worry about that. It'd be a foolish girl who would leave a good job for me." He and Mr. Altvater walked together up the aisle talking in less bantering tones and leaving me to my yard goods. Before he left, Jory turned and touched his hat to me. I kept the image of his face in my mind for a long time.

The days following seemed uneventful for me, as if I were marking time. Even Charles didn't force the issue of our gentle bond, for which I was grateful. Since Jory and I had ridden together into town that night I was afraid Charles would rant to me about such associations. Instead I noticed a slight raise in his eyebrows but he kept his counsel to himself.

That Thursday I made my way home with no particular plans. So far I wasn't any closer to my goal of finding my Cheyenne kinsmen than when I arrived in Leavenworth. I wondered if I would ever be able to find them. I resolved to bend my efforts more toward that and less toward the goings-on in town.

After dinner that night I was the first to seat myself in the parlor and I waited anxiously for Mr. Greene. When he appeared I immediately put in a bid for Indian stories.

The others added their votes and Mr. Greene took up a purposeful position in a straight-back chair. He pushed his mustache aside and packed his pipe, deciding, apparently, which story to tell.

"Well," he began, "I don't think I've told the one about the Dog Creek Raid. That was back in '59 during the gold rush. I was going to head up toward the Platte and see how pickin's were and I fell in with some other fellas, gold diggers or what have you. They was kind of a rough bunch but I didn't pay much mind. So long as they didn't get riled up and shoot me, I didn't care.

"We'd only rode a day or two out of Leaven-worth, northwest as I remember, and we were making for Dog Creek. Happened to reach it along about dark and we were looking for a good spot to camp. One guy rode up ahead, scouting, and all of a sudden he come down on the run hollering about Indians on up the creek and if we did it right we could wipe out the lot of them. I couldn't see five men taking on a whole camp for love or money but the scout said it was a small band, not more than thirty and not many fightin' age. Well, my opinion didn't count for much in that crowd so I went along. I had a better chance that way than maybe getting bushwacked on my own.

"We tied the horses and sneaked up on the camp. Just being dark, the camp was busy settlin' in and kids were talking and crying and women were cookin.' We killed one watch without a sound and edged in closer. We was all loaded up, every pistol and rifle, and we all went in together. Never saw so much confusion in my life. Squaws and kids runnin' everywhere, young bucks going for their knives and bows. When I saw they were mostly women and kids I held off. Never hankered much for that. But those bucks, they charged us like they planned the damn raid, whooping and hollerin' and comin' at us hell bent. It wasn't pretty, but I had to kill to save my own skin. 'Course," he said with a wave of his pipe, "that was before I stayed with the Cheyenne and gave my word on killin.'

"Well, the blood was everywhere. Those gold-crazy fools I was with went Indian crazy and they wouldn't let up for nothing. I saw women pleading for their children but they all went by the gun or knife. It was awful."

I watched it in my mind. I saw the gun blasts like spitting fire in the dim twilight and saw the frenzied shadows running madly around the campfire. The air was filled with screams and wails, all unheeded. I huddled at the far side of our lodge where my mother had ordered me but then tepees began to go up in flames. She watched from behind the flap momentarily, then suddenly seemed to decide.

"Here!" she said firmly. I could tell how frightened she was because she spoke English. She only did that when she wanted me to practice

188

the white man's tongue or when she was too upset to speak Cheyenne. I went to her quickly and backed into the buffalo robe she wrapped around me. She pulled on her braids, yanking out the doeskin leather thongs and raking her hair out so it hung loose. Finally, taking a big breath of air, she herded me out of the lodge and glanced around. The confusion was almost too much. Bullets flew and people ran madly in every direction. Fire blazed all around and it terrified me. I began to cry.

"Hush," she said sternly. Before I could subdue my wails she was half pulling, half dragging me toward one of the white men. I knew he would kill us. Weren't they killing every other Indian in camp? Didn't my mother pull me screaming past the mutilated body of my best friend, Little Doe?

"Don't shoot!" my mother cried suddenly. The white man lowered his gun at her and I squeezed my eyes shut tight. "I'm white!" she screamed. "I'm a white woman, taken captive! Don't shoot! Don't shoot!"

Although the gunshot I expected didn't come, others did. My mother rushed on in the white tongue while the rest of the camp still screamed in terror. I pulled the buffalo robe closer around me and tried to block out the sight of my friends and relatives as they died. When a rough hand pushed me down by the creek, I went. I stumbled along behind my mother and wondered why we must walk to another place to be killed. I wondered why we couldn't die in camp like everyone else.

"It was a plain miracle those fools didn't kill 'em anyway," Mr. Greene was saying. "But that woman talked a blue streak explaining all about how she'd been captured and given into marriage to a warrior whose first wife had died. Said she hadn't been mistreated but nobody'd left her alone much either, so she'd just bided her time and waited to be rescued. Turned out to be fourteen long years. It was the most amazing thing I'd ever seen."

"Well," Mr. Greene said after a moment, "we brought the woman and her daughter back to the fort and reported. The captain sent out a squad to clean up the mess and they took the woman and fixed them up a place where they'd be safe until they could join a train going back east. She was mighty grateful at being back in the white man's territory, I'll tell you, but that daughter of hers was a little wildcat. Raised Indian, though, so I could understand why. It was something to see her wear a white girl's dress and glaring daggers at anyone close. You'd think she'd tear a man's heart out for saving her. I never forgot that girl. Don't think I ever will."

Mr. Greene looked about to punctuate his sentence, then his eyes fell on me. I don't know what expression I wore but it must have said something to him. Perhaps the color had drained from my face or my eyes were far away. In any event, he stopped speaking and stared at me.

"Catherine!" I heard Della say. "Have you taken a chill? You look like death warmed over!" She came to me and felt my forehead and cheeks, held my hand.

"No, I'm all right, I just feel—dizzy," I managed.

"Come on upstairs," Della ordered. "All that talk of killin' and fightin's too much for you."

"No, really, I, I . . ."

"No arguments. Here, let me help you." She pulled me up out of my chair and put an arm protectively about me. I mumbled apologies and allowed Della to help me upstairs.

"I'll speak to Mr. Greene about that," she said. "He's got no right tellin' such awful stories."

"No, please," I said. "It wasn't his fault. I asked to hear. Don't say anything to him."

"Humph," Della muttered. She led me to my room and helped me undress and slip into bed. When I insisted I was all right and only needed rest she finally relented and left me. I was tired but I didn't sleep for a long time.

It was almost as if I were remembering another incarnation, so far removed had my Indian life seemed. Now it all came painfully back to me in pieces like a tattered rag. What had been ordinary to me then was like a fantasy now. I saw myself dressed in my miniature buckskin dress, following after my mother when we went out to pick berries or gather firewood. We were rarely separated except when I was off playing with Little Doe and her baby sister, Yellow Leaf. I always helped my mother put up our lodge, tan our buffalo hides and make our clothes. If our existence was not idyllic, it was ordered and clear; I don't remember a Cheyenne who had doubts about his life or his purpose.

I remembered my father, tall and lean, with coal-black eyes that saw through any story I might consider telling. Although I never spoke to him unless he addressed me first, we would sometimes go walking and he would tell me timeworn stories of our people and their exploits. He told me of great battles and warriors who always took the first coup or great successful raids when fifty or more horses were stolen and I would swell with pride for my people. I thought there was no one as brave as my father, who had countless scalps sewn along the seams of his war shirt and gave away many horses. Even though sometimes he would go for days without speaking to me, that was befitting a mighty Cheyenne and when he would finally smile and lay his hand upon my hair, it was the greatest of praise.

And for the first time in many years I allowed myself to think of Barred Owl. I wondered what he had thought when he learned of the raid and my disappearance. He had already spoken to my father for me and had given him gifts to seal the engagement. Who would he have chosen, I wondered. I still remembered his handsome, planed face and his serious eyes. He would have made a good husband and the uniting of our families would have called for a great celebration. I desperately wished it had been that way. I wished I could go back to that day and have it pass peacefully and with no bloodshed, instead of as

Mr. Greene had told. Had that one day been different I might never have known the confusion and misery that plagued me now. Feeling self-pity well up in me like a fever, I cried myself to sleep.

Chapter Seven

THE NEXT day at work I threw myself into Mr. Altvater's remodeling project. I made sketches of ideas I had, like arranging fashion drawings on a board overhead so the women could see what features were stylish. It was my intention to keep up with east coast fashion as much as possible, even to the point of begging newspapers from the stage office. When I showed Mr. Altvater what I had in mind, he pronounced it a splendid idea and said he would build me a poster board as soon as I gave him the dimensions.

I occupied myself between customers by adding to my drawings or doing some minor rearranging. I began placing bolts of cloth by type instead of haphazardly as they were and I resolved to get Mr. Altvater to build a place for displaying notions. It would simplify my job if my customers could see what was available, and solve problems like on my first day with Mrs. Rollins.

It was while I was working on my ideas that a woman I had never seen before came in and spoke with Mr. Altvater. He apparently turned to help her with some article and I dismissed her from my mind. Then my boss's voice cut across my thoughts.

"No, Mrs. Slater, you'll have to go to the smith for that. I don't carry heavy stuff like that."

I looked up and felt panic flash across my brain. Had I heard him correctly? Was she the woman I thought she was?

"I thought you had irons here," she said.

"No, not branding irons. I've got nails and hammers but no irons."

"Oh, all right. Maybe I'd better let Hal get those anyway. Thank you."

After she left I realized I was trembling. I tried to work on my drawing but my hands shook. Finally I put it away and went up front to Mr. Altvater.

"That woman," I said as casually as I could, "has she been in before? She looks familiar." It was the only lie I could think of.

"Mrs. Slater? Maybe. She doesn't come in very often, though. They live out of town and her husband's a wagonmaster so he's gone a lot. They're pretty self-sufficient."

"Oh, I see. I guess she just reminded me of someone. Where does her husband guide wagon trains, California or Oregon?"

"No, back east. He works for an importer there, seems like it's a man with some French last name. Guess it pays all right, but he's gone a lot."

"Yes, I guess he would be." I was afraid my voice was quivering like I felt the rest of me was. "Is he here now?"

"Must be. She said he needs some branding irons. Can't be too careful around here, even if all you've got is a milk cow. Give 'em a chance and somebody'll steal it."

"Yes," I agreed, backing away. Mr. Altvater seemed already caught by another train of thought so I hurried back to my corner. I hoped no one came back there for a long time. I was sure if they did, my fear would show in my eyes.

How stupid of me! I thought. I had never once considered that I might run into Slater. The prospect hadn't even crossed my mind. And here I had prided myself on how easily I had slipped out of New York and melted into Leavenworth with the biggest stumbling block of all right in front of my eyes. The oppressive feeling of having things closing in on me weighed on me again. I decided I was going to have to do something definite, and do it quick. When I had calmed down some I realized I would have to go to Jory for help.

I realized I did not have the vaguest idea how to find Jory. I was almost on the verge of asking Mr. Altvater since he seemed to be on such friendly terms with the trapper. It was getting close to closing and I didn't want to waste another day. I had just resolved to ask Mr. Altvater when Jory himself walked in.

He stopped at the front counter and spoke to my boss about ordinary things. At first I thought he would only nod to me from the front, then leave again, but when he and Mr. Altvater had pursued their topics he turned and walked deliberately toward me. Mr. Altvater didn't even seem surprised.

I kept my pencil and papers in front of me, adding an unnecessary line here and there to my plans. Jory didn't speak but came and stood in front of me, waiting until I looked up.

"Why don't we go riding tonight?" he asked.

I thought about it for a moment, but that wasn't what I wanted. I needed to talk business and I felt it would be difficult aboard the horses.

"I think I'd better stay in town tonight," I said. His expression remained blank. "But I would like to talk to you. I need your help."

He nodded slightly, as if it were as much as he had expected.

"Is there someplace in town where we can go?"

"Not if you care about being seen," he said. "You know people are starting to talk, don't you? About the way you rode hell bent out of town that night, then came back with me. Anyplace we go in town will just be fuel for the fire."

"I don't care about that," I said. He raised his eyebrows and it irritated me. "Shouldn't I be allowed to choose whatever company I want?"

"Sure," he agreed, "except you're not keeping with your image. I thought you were worried about that."

"I was, but I've got other things to think about now. I can't afford to feel sorry for myself now."

"Oh," he said with a grin. "That's too bad. I kind of liked it when you were feeling sorry for yourself."

I could feel my face getting warm and the color creeping over it.

"All right," he said, "What about tonight?"

"Is there some place where we can talk privately?"

"That depends on how private you want to get. I have a room upstairs at the Gold Pan."

I knew enough about town to know that was not one of the better saloons. "Not that private."

"Oh, too bad. Well, there's the dining room right next door. There are some booths in the back that are kind of secluded. We could be seen but not heard."

"That sounds all right."

"In that case, may I invite you to dinner?" he asked politely. His eyes sparkled with his own game.

"Yes, thank you," I said. "I'll have to go tell Mrs. Reedy I won't be taking dinner at the boarding-house. The few times I've been absent without telling her she's been very put out."

"Let her be."

"No, I've got to go to the house anyway. But I

can meet you there, can't I?"

"Sure. That way Mr. Lafferty won't know we've been together until tomorrow."

"That wasn't the reason," I said hotly. "What I do is my own business and no more Charles's concern than it is yours."

"Oh," he said with a laugh. "All right, have it your way. Seven o'clock?"

"Fine," I said, slightly mollified.

"I'll be waiting."

Now that I had arranged the meeting with Jory I was wary of keeping it. How fast would word spread of our being seen together? Especially in a back dining-room booth? But I had no other way to get the information I needed, and I was running out of time and room. I pushed my doubts away and resolved to meet Jory with determination. I'd have to face the consequences later.

I found the Gold Pan primarily by the bright lights and loud piano music. I had never been inside but through the windows I could see men at poker tables and house girls hanging on their shoulders. I wondered if Jory's room there included any of those girls.

The dining room was more subdued, although an open archway let the music and laughter drift through. When I came in the door I noticed a head or two turn my way but not as much as I had feared. I stood and let my eyes become accustomed to the smoky dimness, then saw Jory coming toward me.

"We're back here," he said, guiding me toward

the booths with a hand at the small of my back. We passed tables of diners, most of them talking among themselves and too busy to notice us, but a few looked up or waved to Jory. He would only nod and walk on.

The booths were three steps up from the main floor and enclosed on three sides. The only open side was framed in a curtain of strung beads, so actually only a portion of our table was visible. I was surprised at the plush red carpeting and comfortable chairs. I was sure Jory had to pay especially for a booth, or else was influential enough to command one. Either way, I felt uncomfortable. It was like being put on a pedestal and it was not the mood I wanted to create.

A simple candle burned in a red glass hurricane holder and I thought it probably looked very cozy from outside. I looked to Jory and found myself embarrassed by his eyes on me. I was afraid I had compromised myself without realizing it.

"Would you care for some wine before dinner?" he asked after we were seated.

"Thank you," I said. He poured from a chilled bottle at his side, but only in one glass. I noticed a half-empty whiskey glass at his side.

"I've already ordered dinner. I hope you don't mind. There are some things on the menu that aren't worth looking at, but some are excellent."

"Fine," I allowed. I toyed with the stem of my wine glass and kept my eyes down. The situation was going in exactly the opposite direction I wanted it to. Jory seemed to act as if this were a social dinner, something that might have been his idea and I had demurely accepted. It was difficult for me to keep my mind on my original purpose with him sitting so close and our little booth so dim. I found myself unable to think of anything to say, all my prepared speeches gone completely out of my head. If Jory noticed, he said nothing of it.

Before too long a well dressed woman of about forty brought our dinner. Her gown was simple but elegant, and she had beautiful red hair that was swept up on top of her head. She smiled to Jory in a friendly manner.

"Cathy," Jory said, "this is Adele Witham. She owns the place, and the Gold Pan."

"How do you do," we each said. I tried not to behave condescendingly, but her bright hair and made-up, although pretty, face seemed to put us at odds. Our social spheres revolved in entirely different directions and we both knew were it not for Jory we never would have spoken to each other. I think it made us both uncomfortable and Adele only said she hoped we enjoyed the dinner.

The steak was excellent as Jory said it would be and we ate in silence for a while. Occasionally I would look up at Jory and find his eyes on me, staring as if he would look inside me. He ate heartily but seemed disinterested in the food itself. His plate was clean long before mine and he signaled one of the girls to refill his glass.

At last I pushed my plate away and sipped my wine. As Jory filled my glass again, the girl took the plates. Jory settled back in his chair and lit a cigar.

"Now," he said commandingly, "what kind of help do you need from me? The other night when I offered it, you wanted none of it."

"I know," I said, staring into my glass, "but I told you, I was in a very self-pitying mood that night. That's passed now."

"Yes, I remember you saying that." He looked at me pointedly but I refused to acknowledge the question he had asked that day in the store. Instead I spread a napkin on the table and took a pencil from my bag.

"Will you draw me a map?" I asked.

"Of what?"

"The country between here and the Rockies."

I hadn't realized he was tilting back in his chair until the two front legs came down hard and he leaned across the table toward me.

"What the hell are you going to do, go off exploring by yourself?"

"Perhaps," I said. "But before I do anything I need to know what's out there. I need to know where rivers are, forts, towns—and Indians."

"You're crazy," he said stubbing out his cigar in an ashtray.

"No, just determined."

"To what? Get yourself killed?"

"No. That's why I need a map. I know I can't just set out blindly. Here." I handed him the pencil. "Show me."

"You said you needed a guide," he said. "Remember our bet? You're not planning on going alone."

"I'm not sure yet. I can't plan anything without knowing what's out there. Please draw the map." I sat and stared at him, waiting. I would not be shaken from this. I could do nothing, make no decisions without knowing the territory. Then, if it looked risky, I might have to collect on my bet.

"Here's Leavenworth," Jory said, drawing a circle on one side of the napkin. "The Missouri runs down like this." He made a long wavering line. "Then there's the Arkansas, the Kansas and the Platte." More lines. "Fort Kearney's here on the Platte, and that's the way the stage goes. Matter of fact, the stage goes on along the South Platte all the way to Denver. That's just where the Rockies start."

"What about Indians?" I asked, leaning over the map.

He eyed me curiously. "The South Cheyenne are mostly down here in Colorado now, but the Northern Cheyenne and Sioux still camp around the Platte. They're close with the Arapahoe, camping together sometimes. Some have gone on to Colorado where the government's setting up a reservation for them, but there's still a lot up on the Platte."

"What's over here?" I asked pointing toward the west.

"Dakota and Crow in the north, some Ute farther south. The Ute and Cheyenne are fighting back and forth which causes a lot of problems for settlers. Seems like someone's cabin or farm house is always in the middle of a warpath."

These were all timeworn enemies and I could still visualize celebrations after successful raids or war parties. I was sure that had not changed.

"If the stage goes all along the Platte, then it's safe to assume there are settlements there, too?" I asked.

"All along," Jory affirmed. "Forts, too, and lots of raiding on both sides." He put down the pencil and stared at me. "That's why you can't be serious about going. No matter who you are or what you're doing, you're on the wrong side of somebody's camp. If Indians didn't get you, the blood-crazy cavalry would. And either side can be pretty ruthless when it comes to unprotected women."

"I know," I said bitterly.

Jory's face twitched and I immediately regretted saying that. He eyed me keenly.

"You know what?" he demanded.

"Nothing." I picked up the map and folded it to put in my bag. Jory grabbed my wrist and twisted it so I dropped the napkin on the floor.

"You know what?" he asked again, his voice cold.

"You're twisting my arm," I said in an angry whisper.

"I know. Tell me."

"There's nothing to tell. Everyone's heard about the atrocities Indians commit on white women. It's common knowledge that they take scalps and mutilate whites, even dismember them."

"I said both sides," Jory pressed.

"You think we didn't hear about Sand Creek in New York?" I said angrily.

Jory released my arm. I picked up the map and put it in my purse. He still eyed me suspiciously, but I ignored it.

"You're not going alone," he said.

"I'm not sure I'm going at all," I replied, staring back at him levely. "Right now that's just an idea."

"Tell me what you're looking for."

"Peace."

"You can't go looking for that as if it's a special color rock sticking out of the ground. It's not something you can find by searching. What makes you think you'll find it in the west when you didn't find it in New York or here on the plains?"

"I'm not sure I will, but it's one place I have to look. I have to keep looking until I find it."

Jory shook his head impatiently and I knew he was exasperated with me. I was sorry for that but it couldn't be helped. I could not allow him to persuade me from what I had to do.

"It's late," I said, looking at the watch pinned to my dress. "Thank you for dinner."

"Oh, hell, it was my pleasure," he said loudly. He leaned back in his chair and relit his cigar. At my stubbornness he had changed and no longer acted like a concerned friend. He eyed me coldly. "If you ever need anything else, just let me know. I'm good at drawing maps and covering up embarrassing habits. I can even lie if I think it might help."

"Jory, don't talk like that," I pleaded.

"How the hell do you expect me to talk?" he asked. "I'm good enough to come to for information, but not good enough to know what it's for. I had thought that we were some kind of friends or something, that we might be beginning to care about each other. I was hoping you'd realize you could trust me and tell me what this awful secret of yours is. What could be so bad? Are you a murderess? Have you committed some terrible crime? Or is there some ugly disease in your family?"

"No, it's nothing like that," I said. I was afraid people were beginning to notice our argument and I wished I could make him stop.

"Then what is it?" he demanded. His voice was hard and cold, and it unnerved me. I felt my resolve begin to crumble and I was close to tears. He seemed not to notice.

"I have to go now," I said, standing. I took my bag and started out of the booth, hoping I could keep a cool appearance until I got outside. I half expected Jory to follow, but he stayed behind puffing his cigar. As I walked out of the building I knew some heads were turned my way and speculations were rising. I must have been insane to arrange this meeting, I thought. The information I had was not worth the arguments and humiliation. As I closed the heavy door behind me and stepped out into the dark street, my eyes filled with tears.

I walked briskly to Mrs. Reedy's hoping I would

not have to pass anyone who might see me crying. Luckily there were few people about and I made my way toward the main street. As I stepped out to cross, heavy footsteps sounded behind me. I kept staring ahead but I saw from the corner of my eye that Jory fell into step beside me.

"You didn't have to bother," I said cooly. I ignored the fact that my voice wavered.

"You're about the goddamnedest women I've ever met," he said, "but you still shouldn't walk alone."

"Thank you very much," I sniffed. I walked on, not looking at him and trying not to cry. He walked beside me, his long strides matching my quick ones and his hands jammed in his pockets. Neither of us spoke as we passed the church and neared Mrs. Reedy's.

The parlor windows were lit and I knew everyone would be there. I wished there was a back door somewhere so I could sneak in without them seeing me. I could just imagine the questions if I walked in with a tear-streaked face. I hesitated before climbing the porch steps and Jory grabbed my arm.

"You don't have to go in yet," he said.

"I didn't think we had any more to say to each other," I turned and leaned against the porch, away from the lighted windows. Although I was fearful of more recriminations from Jory I didn't want to go inside. At the moment facing him seemed the least painful of the two.

"You're the one who doesn't seem to have any

more to say," he said. He came and stood close to me, so close that I could see a white hair here and there in his sideburns. His expression was still fierce but I met his gaze. "Did they teach you to be a scheming woman in New York?" he asked. "You may have been schooled there, but you weren't raised there, so where did you learn to tease a man into giving you what you want, then toss him aside?"

My jaw dropped. "What are you talking about?" I asked. "I have never . . ."

"Never what?" he asked angrily. "Never arranged to meet me? Never lain in my arms or let me kiss you? Never kissed me back as if I really mattered?"

"Jory, I didn't—I wasn't teasing."

"But you have no further use for me now, is that it?"

The tears began to come and I couldn't hold them back. I found I was sobbing as I spoke.

"Don't you see?" I cried. "It's something I have to do, and I can't let you stop me. I can't let myself become—involved."

His face was incredulous. Either I was not explaining myself or he just didn't believe it. I didn't know which.

"What's that supposed to mean?" he asked. "Were you—*are* you becoming involved?"

"Yes!" I sobbed. "If that's what you want to know, yes I am. And I can't let you stop me!" I broke into tears and turned my head away.

"What's going on out here?" an angry voice cut

in. I didn't look. I didn't have to. I knew it was Charles and no telling who else. I heard the front door slam.

"Nothing that concerns you," Jory said sharply. He moved slightly away from me as if to face Charles.

"Catherine?" Charles said. His steps echoed on the wooden porch.

"It's—it's all right, Charles," I managed. "Please go back inside. I'm all right."

For a moment no one spoke and I let my tears fall silently so he wouldn't see me brush them away. Jory stood defiantly beside me.

"Are you sure, Catherine?" Charles asked. "If this man is bothering you . . ."

"No, it's all right. Really. Please go inside."

"All right," he said finally. "But if you need me, I'll be just inside."

"Thank you," I said. I heard his steps retreat to the house and the door opened and closed. I knew he would be as good as his word and would not go far. Jory stared after him a moment, then turned back to me.

"Come on," he said taking my hand. He yanked me along so quickly I didn't have time to resist.

"Where are we going?" I cried. His grip was too strong for me to break and I had to hurry to keep up with him.

"Someplace were we can talk without some horse's ass butting in," he said.

We retraced our path across town and I realized we were headed for the Gold Pan. I was aghast. He wouldn't take me in there, would he? Not to his room? That would be more humiliation than I could stand. I was on the verge of saying so when he turned down a back street behind the saloon and dragged me into a stable.

The smells of horses and hay were thick and I heard the shuffling in mangers as the animals ate. Jory passed several stalls and finally pulled me into a corner and sat me down on a hay bale. He made no move to sit beside me, but paced in a short pattern in front of me.

"You're a goddamned crazy woman," he said in an exasperated voice. "You're so mixed up you don't know what you want or what you have to do. No wonder you're looking for peace, because you sure as hell don't have any inside you."

"Don't you think I know that?" I said miserably. "If I knew what I needed do you think I would go on playing these stupid games?" The tears came again and I buried my face in my hands. "I wish I'd never come here," I sobbed.

"Why?" he asked. "So you wouldn't have me railing at you or your beloved Charles worrying about you?"

"Charles is the last thing I'm concerned with," I said.

"Oh, really," Jory said. "And what about me? Am I the second to the last thing you're concerned with?" He stopped and grabbed my hands away from my face, pulling me to my feet in front of him. "What about me?" he demanded.

"I already told you!" I cried. "I told you how I

felt! What else do you want me to say?" The tears streamed down my face and I couldn't brush them aside while he still held my hands. I stared up at him, pleading. There was nothing else I could say.

He kissed me then. He pulled me hard against his chest and crushed my mouth with his so that he knocked the breath out of me. His arms went around me in an iron embrace and I thought he would squeeze the life from me. His mouth was demanding and insistent, his tongue invading, sending waves of heat through me that made me dizzy.

"This is what I want you to say," he said in a ragged voice. He placed my own arms around his neck and kissed my tear-streaked face. He found my mouth again and explored it as if he would claim it all for his own. His hands moved searchingly through my hair, across my back and around to my breasts.

"Jory," I said pleadingly. "Jory."

With one quick, dizzying motion he laid me down on the loose straw on the floor. I was thinking that I should stop him, that I should not let this happen but the words would not come. He raked his fingers through my hair and pulled it loose from the pins. Twining one hand in the black strands, he kissed me feverishly and began to unbutton the high collar of my dress. I let him press me into the straw and returned his kisses shamelessly. The touch of his fingers on my skin sent shock waves through me, making my breath catch in my throat. I felt the cool night air on my breast, then his warm hand closing over it, caressing and kneading it, cupping it so he could kiss my tingling flesh. He moved his mouth over every inch of skin he exposed, arousing and exciting me in a way I had not thought possible. When he pulled on my dress, I lifted slightly and let him ease it down off my shoulders, then off my hips. My undergarments posed no problem for him and he quickly pulled off everything I had on. Caring only for the touch of his hands and lips, I allowed it, then lay patiently while he removed his buckskin pants and boots.

I tried not to be afraid but I was. Jory touched me carefully, handling my body as if it were china. He caressed my breasts which now stood taut under his hand, let his fingers trail gently over my stomach and thighs. When he parted my legs and began to stroke me, I almost cried out in pleasure and surprise. Unfamiliar sensations threatened to engulf me as he explored me with gentle probings. I felt surges of pleasure unlike anything I had known before, hot pulsing feelings that drove me to cling to him as if for my life.

Kissing me almost constantly, Jory pulled himself upon me, his hand replaced by the hardness I had not seen. I let him guide me as he nestled between my legs, one hand in my hair and the other at the small of my back. He stroked and caressed me, then began to push, slowly at first, but encouraged by my response. It hurt and I hung back a little but I bit my lip so I would not cry out and he kept on. Suddenly it pained as it he probed me with a knife but before I could cry out, he had gone on and was moving slowly within me. The sharp pain died but the soreness was there, dulling the pleasant feelings he had aroused in me before. Still I clung to him, urging him on, raking my nails through his hair and across his neck. He moved in a rocking motion, holding me close and carrying me with him. Finally the soreness seemed to ease and I could feel the waves of heat washing over me again, red fires that swam before my eyes and made my mouth dry. I held onto Jory frantically, willing him to hold me and take me with him. He rocked both of us in an ever-quickening motion, filling me up until I thought I might burst, his being full and pulsing inside me. I found myself moving to my own rhythm, a timeless and mindless motion that was increasing along with his and we rocked and moved together toward the final thrust, each of us moaning as the feelings coursed through us and the climax shook us on our bed of straw.

I was embarrassed to realize I was panting, but Jory seemed not to notice. He laid his head along my cheek and his fingers traced delicate patterns on my bare shoulder. I moved my hands over his back as if feeling it for the first time, feeling his muscles beneath the buckskin. Finally he raised himself up on his hands and looked down at me.

"Are you all right?" he asked.

"I think so," I said. I wasn't sure how I was

supposed to feel but I didn't feel bad so I assumed I was all right. His eyes searched my face in the darkness, then he laid down again, satisfied.

"I tried not to hurt you," he said quietly.

"I know."

"But I did, didn't I?"

"A little. It's all right." I soothed his hair with my hand and kissed his forehead.

"You're not sorry?" he asked.

"No, I'm not sorry." I tried to think about it, put into words what had happened but it was still too new. All I knew was that I felt contented and happy. Nothing else mattered.

Jory lay still for a moment longer, then pushed himself up on his hands again.

"I can't breathe like this," he said. He eased off me, our bodies separating in a way that made me want to reach out and pull him back. Finally he lay beside me and cradled my head in the crook of his arm.

"You still have your shirt on," I said foolishly. I had barely noticed before.

"I know; I was in a hurry. It was hard enough waiting while I got all that fancy stuff off you."

We said nothing for a bit while I lay against him, then the oddest thing happened. In my mind, over and over, the words, "I love you," ran but I knew it wasn't true. It was almost as if, after loving physically, I felt the need to say it out loud. But I didn't. I was sure he didn't love me, no matter what else he felt and I wasn't even sure what feelings I had for him.

"Cathy," he said finally, "tell me what you're looking for. I won't let you go off on your own; it's too dangerous. I'll go with you and take you wherever it is you think you want to go, but you've got to tell me what you're looking for."

At first I stiffened, ready to refuse. After what had just happened, wouldn't he reject me if he knew I was a halfbreed? But for some reason I couldn't muster up enough caution to say no. I felt too restful, too contented to start another argument, and I wanted to confide in him. I just prayed he would accept me.

"It's a long story," I said. "It all started when my mother was fifteen . . ."

For the next several minutes Jory remained silent while I told him my story. He held me close and stroked my hair as I talked, his grip tightening when I told of the massacre, loosening when I said my mother died. When I was done I lay quietly and waited for him to say something.

"You're looking for your father?" he asked.

"Yes."

"Do you think you'll stay with your band if you find them?"

"I don't know. I won't know until I find them."

"And nothing I say will stop you?"

"No. It's something I have to do."

"Then I'll go with you," he said.

Suddenly loud music and raucous talking sounded outside the stable. I stiffened in Jory's arms but he kept me still. Then the music faded as a door was closed but the drunken talking continued. Two men, both well sotted, made their way into the stable. Amid loud joking and laughing they rattled stall latches and somehow managed to saddle a pair of horses. Jory slid one hand over my mouth protectively while I lay completely still and willed the men to hurry and leave. How compromising to be found like this, I thought. It wouldn't bother me so much being found with Jory, but not in a stable behind the Gold Pan. I prayed to whatever god that would listen to let us go undiscovered.

"Where's my goddamn saddlebags?" one man asked in a slurring voice.

"Over there, on that peg," the other answered. "You stupid ass, you hung 'em them yourself."

The first man grumbled as he walked down our way and I felt my skin tingle with fear. I wanted desperately to turn over or cover myself but Jory held me motionless against him.

The man walked opposite our stall, his head turned to the wall as he looked for his saddlebags. He found them on a rough peg and pulled them off, dropping them in the process. Swaying dangerously, he picked them up and examined the contents as he walked back down the stable.

"Everythin's still here, I guess," he said.

"Come on, dammit, quit fartin' around here and let's go."

"All right, all right."

The men finally managed to climb into their saddles and ride away. Jory took his hand away from my mouth and we both breathed deeply in relief.

"I guess we ought to get out of here," he said.

"Yes," I agreed. I reached for my dress and held the watch up so I could see the time. "Uh, oh," I said. "It's ten-forty-five."

"So?"

"Mrs. Reedy locks up at eleven and won't open up for anyone."

"Let her," Jory said.

"I can't do that," I said. "I've got to keep some sort of propriety, at least for the time being. I think I've got all my clothes, but where did you put my shoes?"

Jory left me at the porch steps after a quick walk. He took me once more in his arms and kissed me, bringing back the feelings he had evoked in me earlier. At that moment I wished I could have stayed with him all night, but I heard the rattle of the front door knob.

"Goodbye," I said quickly and ran up the steps. I tried the knob but it was locked. Feeling like a thwarted child, I banged loudly on the door and Mrs. Reedy's long face appeared at the window. I wondered if she would let me in. She was just ornery enough not to, I thought.

I was about to pound on the door again when the knob turned and the door was pulled open. Mrs. Reedy stood patronizingly to one side and allowed me in, her cool gaze taking in my dishevelled appearance. I only nodded briefly to her, then went upstairs. I refused to make apologies or even attempt to explain, and I could feel her eyes boring into my back as I climbed the stairs. From my bedroom window I watched Jory walk away.

Chapter Eight

THE NEXT day started out all wrong. My hair was unruly and didn't want to stay sleeked back at the nape of my neck and every dress in my wardrobe dissatisfied me. I broke a nail when I banged my brush down on the vanity and I was almost late for breakfast. I was the only one left at table when Mrs. Reedy came in and sat opposite me.

"I've been considering our agreement on your board here," she began in a superior voice, "and I have concluded that it would be best for everyone if you find room elsewhere."

I put my fork down carefully and met her gaze. I resolved I would not flinch or look away no matter what. She would not have the satisfaction of seeing me cow down.

"I had been thinking of moving out in any event," I said. After all, it was party true. I had considered it. "I'm afraid I find living here too constricting. As I recall I have twenty-four hours."

"That's true," Mrs. Reedy said.

"Fine. I'll be out by then." I pushed my plate away and left the table.

For a while at the store I was too busy to think much about what to do, but I was angry. True, I hadn't been as discreet as I might have, but what right did she have to judge me? I wished I had given my notice first, but I hadn't been quick enough. Still, I would retain my pride and dignity. Mrs. Reedy would not see me cringe.

As the day passed I kept a watch out for Jory but his big frame never appeared in the doorway. I thought he might be able to help me find a place, hopefully on the right side of town. When the afternoon drew on and I still hadn't seen him, I began to worry. I had to have some place to move my things.

A lull in business prompted me to approach Mr. Altvater. After all, he was friendly with Jory and not unduly prudish.

"Mr. Altvater," I began, "could I talk to you for a moment?"

"Sure," he said, putting down the pencil he was figuring with. "About the remodeling?"

"No, not this time. This is personal."

His eyebrows lifted slightly, then returned to their proper place.

"Mrs. Reedy and I have had a—a clash and I'm going to move out of her house. Would you have any idea where I could find another room to rent?"

I could see my question caught him off guard but he quickly recovered. He looked out the door as he thought.

"There's a house down across from the livery, but I can't recall if there's an opening or not. Since most of the wagon trains have passed already, there won't be much turnover until later in summer when wagons come back from the west. But you might try it." He thought again, but couldn't think of anything else very helpful. "There's always rooms on the west side, but I know you wouldn't want that."

"No," I said. "I don't think that would work, either."

"Well, offhand, I just don't know. Try that boardinghouse, though. If they don't have a room, maybe they can tell you who does."

"All right," I said. I was grateful to him for not asking about the problem but I hadn't thought he would. "By the way," I said, "do you know how I could get in touch with Mr. Donnelly?"

"Hard to say," he said with a smile. "Leave word at the Gold Pan or maybe try the livery. You can't ever tell where Jory'll be."

When the doors were finally closed and locked I hurried to get my purse. My twenty-four hours were going fast.

I walked down toward the livery, since the

possibilities of finding a room and Jory both lay that way. I decided to try the stable first. If Jory wasn't there, I would try the boardinghouse across the street.

When I reached the stalls, the mule and stallion were eating but I found out Hank had fed them and hadn't seen Jory. He directed me across to the boardinghouse and after petting Thunder's nose, I went over to it.

It was the same house I had asked at when I had first arrived in town. The woman inside was kind and sympathetic, but of no help. All her rooms were rented with no promise of a vacancy. I stood on the sidewalk and wondered what to do now.

I looked up toward town but could see no signs, no notices of rooms. I glanced back at the livery and thought I might be forced to sleep in a stall tonight if I didn't find something. I had already decided I would not sleep at Mrs. Reedy's no matter what.

Then I looked south and my eyes fell on the little house the Crutchfields had rented. On a hunch, I walked to it and ventured to peer in the window. It was still deserted, the only furniture in it being the couch in the living room. Everything else was gone, the curtains, the kitchen utensils, the lamps. If only I could find out who owned it.

I hurried back to the boardinghouse and knocked on the door. The old lady smiled questioningly at me and I asked if she knew about the house. Feeling my luck change, I attended to her directions and walked back across town.

Within half an hour, I had met the owners, agreed to terms and paid my first two weeks' rent.

Feeling much better, I returned to my room at Mrs. Reedy's and threw my things into my old carpetbag, unmindful of wrinkles. The new clothes and toilet articles I had acquired since coming to town I put in the bag I used for dirty clothes. Carrying my two bags of all my earthly possessions, I left Mrs. Reedy's and walked to my new home.

Inside the house I set my bags on the living-room floor and looked about. It was almost laughable. I had no furniture except the couch that came with the house and no other household items at all. As I looked about I realized I didn't even have an ax for chopping wood, although I thought I remembered some wood outside. Well, I said to myself, at least I have money to buy what I need. For the short time I would still be in Leavenworth, it shouldn't be too bad. I decided I would ask Mr. Altvater to let me into the store tomorrow so I could pick up some smaller articles. Even though it would be Sunday I thought he might be willing.

Since it was getting dark, I decided I had best be ready for it. I had no light, so I arranged my toilet on the bedroom floor and went outside to get some wood. At least the fireplace was centrally located and it would provide me with light for most of the house. I went around to the wood pile and began to pull out small pieces of kindling.

While I was around the side, I heard a knock on my front door. Wondering and hoping, I walked around to the front.

"Charles," I said. He stood expectantly, his manner and dress formal. He turned at my voice.

"Catherine!" He rushed to me. "I heard Mrs. Reedy—asked you to leave and I wanted to see if there was anything I could do. I wish I had known earlier. I went to the Evanses' for dinner and you could have come with me."

"Oh, thank you," I said, "but I'm all right."

He took the kindling from me and followed me inside. While I sat on the couch, he built a fire and soon had it going merrily. It did a lot to lighten the room.

"Did Mrs. Reedy tell all the boarders about my leaving?" I asked.

"I don't think so. Della told me, but I don't think she knew the whole story." He looked at me curiously.

"There isn't much of a story," I laughed. "I was about one minute late last night and she almost locked me out. If she hadn't asked me to leave I would have, anyway. I'm afraid I don't like being treated like a schoolgirl."

Charles stared at me intently and I remembered the near scene on the front porch. Had he seen Jory drag me toward the wrong side of town?

"No," Charles said, breaking into my thoughts, "You certainly aren't a schoolgirl."

I looked away from him, not knowing how he meant that. His unerring stare made me uncomfortable.

"Will you be all right here alone?" he asked. "I

hate to think of you unchaperoned here on the edge of town. You need someone close by to protect you."

"Charles, I am perfectly all right. Anyway, that boardinghouse is just across the way and Hank is over at the livery, so I've got people close by. Don't worry about me."

He came and sat beside me on the couch. The weight of his body depressed the old cushions and I involuntarily leaned toward him.

"I can't help but worry about you," he said. He moved suddenly and slid one arm around me to pull me closer. Before I could resist, he kissed me, unsure, yet determined. Even my hand pressing against his chest didn't seem to deter him. It was as if he could no longer hold himself to propriety. The insistent pressure of his mouth on mine surprised me and when he finally withdrew, I was sure it showed on my face.

"Don't tell me you haven't expected that," he said. "Just because I don't treat you the way Donnelly does doesn't mean I don't want you."

"Charles!" I said. As certain as I was that he cared for me, it was a shock to hear him talk so frankly.

"I've been trying to court you, to win you since you first moved into the boardinghouse, but you always evade me. You said it was impossible to think of getting involved with anyone here, that you would only be staying a short time. I believed you, Catherine. But then that rough-and-tumble mountain man comes along and you fall into his arms as if you were made for him."

"Charles!" I said. It was as uncultured as he had ever been and I didn't care for his tone.

"Maybe I should start being rough, too," he said. "Maybe I was wrong to take you at your word and try to be understanding. Maybe I should stop being a gentleman."

I was so amazed by his words that I was still registering shock when he forced himself on me again, his hands gripping me in a painful hold. His mouth was hard and unyielding on mine, his breath hot on my cheek. The insistency of his manner frightened me and I began to pound on him, pushing and hitting until he drew away. When he sat back, I slapped him as hard as I could.

"Get out," I said in a low voice. I managed to stand up, my back to the fire. I was angrier than I had been since I left New York, angrier and more outraged. I would not tolerate having Charles there another minute. "Get out," I repeated.

"All right," he said finally. "If that's the way you want it. I guess you'll find out about Donnelly after he's used you." Taking up his hat, he left.

If I had any furniture to speak of then, I think I would have kicked it. I was still fuming as I paced about the empty room, still infuriated by Charles's crass remarks. To think that he prided himself so on being civilized and then acted like an animal. Now I knew what it was about him that I disliked; it was his savage intensity, only held in check by his manners. It was almost as if he strained

228

against his proper image like a dog against its leash. I hoped this was the last time we came together. I would not permit another scene like this one.

I pulled a light blanket out of my bags in the bedroom and made up my bed on the couch, Charles's words still running through my mind. Yes, I supposed I had fallen into Jory's arms, finally. But Charles was wrong about Jory using me. He could have any of the girls at the Gold Pan or any other saloon, so why should he need me to satisfy his lust? But then, I wondered where he was. He hadn't come to the store, which wasn't unusual in itself, but I had thought after last night he would come by more often. I was sure I wasn't wrong about him, that once he possessed me he would still care about me, but what if he thought differently now? What if he had decided I was no longer worth having, being a half-breed? The thought chilled me. I pushed it to the back of my mind and huddled under my blanket on the couch. As warm as it was, I was cold, and I watched the flames until I fell asleep.

The next morning when I awoke I felt strange. The events of yesterday were almost surreal-istically clear in my mind, yet in spite of their clarity, made no sense to me. I felt disjointed and out of sorts. It didn't help matters when I realized I had no food or anything to cook it in if I did.

First things first, I decided, and took a chance that I could catch Mr. Altvater before he went to church. Luckily he went to a late service and was agreeable to letting me into the store. Knowing how his opinions went, I wasn't surprised at the grin on his face when I told him I'd moved.

In the store I picked out a few pots and pans, a couple of bowls and some wooden tableware. Mr. Altvater made suggestions that I was grateful for, since I had never kept my own house and some things escaped me. I got some material for curtains and added some things to the sewing articles I already had. Finally Mr. Altvater helped me carry the whole collection to my house.

"You have no furniture," he said as he stood looking about with his arms full.

"No," I said, "just the couch. Do you know where I could buy or borrow some second-hand furniture?"

"Hank may have something. He's got that back room of the livery so crowded I know he's got things in there he doesn't need. But I think I have a table you can have, and a chair or two. I'll go see after we get this stuff put away.

True to his word, he brought over a rough wood table and two chairs, both minus a rung here and there. I had already put away my utensils and now my pots and pans lined the plain wood shelves. It looked a little more like a kitchen at least. Mr. Altvater also brought me some foodstuffs—eggs, coffee, flour, jerky and beans. It would do until I could do some serious shopping. When I had thanked him profusely, he left me and went ahead to church.

I turned my attention to the food and tried to remember all I knew about cooking, which wasn't much. The experience I had was in the Cheyenne village making pemmican and such, but I did not have the materials for that. Mrs. Pettit had skimmed over this type of homemaking since it was assumed that her wealthy charges would always have servants. Deciding I could hardly ruin biscuits and eggs, I began.

As I moved about my kitchen I began to feel better. As hard as it would be for me to furnish a house on my own, I would be happier here away from Mrs. Reedy's sour face and Charles's recriminations. How many times had I insisted to Grandpere that I preferred to be alone? Well, now I would be, until the time came when I chose to seek out company. Perhaps the people in town would mark me for a maverick but I could live with that easier than the ridiculous charade I had played before.

Almost like a hard blow, that idea took hold. No wonder I had been so miserable. How could I have ever expected to be happy when I wasn't being myself? Suddenly the things Jory had told me came back. I had to become myself before I could find any peace. Well, I had begun and I already felt a small measure of peace. And it was worth the chance that I might be snubbed in Leavenworth. Thinking about Jory's wilderness wisdom made me wonder again where he was.

I had not wanted to think too much about that night in the stable. I was afraid it would all seem wrong in the daylight and I would feel dirty and regretful. Now that I forced myself to think about it, I felt fine, even content. No matter what Jory thought of me now, I still had no regrets about what I'd done. I had given myself to a man with no talk of love or marriage, for no reason except that the time was right and I wanted to do it, and it was all right. Even if Jory discarded me today, I would not regret it. It was part of my new being and I would be proud of what I did.

My eggs turned out fine but my biscuits were barely edible. I choked the heavy bits down anyway, figuring I was hardly in a position to waste food. Then I cleaned up, thankful that I had something to clean, and changed into a blouse and skirt so that I could go riding.

Thunder seemed as eager to ride as I was, and once out of town I let him breeze through the prairie grass. He stretched in long magnificent strides and even shook a little at his freedom. It was easy to feel happy on Thunder and let him carry me toward the trees.

I went directly to my cache and threw the sidesaddle into it. When I reached in for my buckskins, I found a soft leather shirt as well. It was slit low at the throat but with laces crisscrossing over the opening so it could be tied closed. So that was why Jory had wanted boot laces. Taking the leather, I changed behind the rocks and bundled my city clothes into the cave. Feeling wild and free, I jumped on Thunder and kicked him into a lope up the hill. As he crested it and started down the other side, I pulled the pins from my hair and shook the black mass loose behind me. I felt better than I had in weeks.

I rode Thunder hard across the creeks and through the trees. We passed the pool where I had first soaked my buckskins, then turned north, going across the spur of the hill to the plains again. When we reached the bowl where Jory and I had raced, I clung low on Thunder's back and kicked him across the grass as fast as he would go. On the other side we turned back into the hills and I promised him we would stop at the lake and he could rest.

The midsummer day was as bright as any I remembered and squirrels and birds chattered and hopped about through the trees. It seemed that the seasons were never so beautiful in New York as they were here on the plains, for all the autumn color in the east. I supposed it was just me and I enjoyed everything here more. As I crested the last ridge and started down the gully, I wondered what it would be like in the high mountains.

Before we had ever turned out of the gully, Thunder pricked his ears and snorted. I heard an answering snort and the unmistakable whinny of a mule. Rounding the last rocks, I could see Jory's long-eared prize tethered at the lake edge, with her master lying sprawled on the grass, his battered hat over his face. He remained motionless until he could hear the soft plodding sounds of Thunder's feet on the grass, then pushed his hat off and sat up.

I slid off Thunder and tied him beside Beauty, then walked over to Jory. I was suddenly unsure how to act and I could see the same uncertainty in him. Deciding honesty was better than more games, I went and sat beside him.

"It's about time you got here," he said with a grin.

"I don't recall that we had arranged a meeting," I answered with mock arrogance. I kept my face straight until he seemed to sag a little, then I laughed at him. He grabbed his hat up and pushed it down over my head.

"Every other Sunday you've been out an hour before this," he said.

I threw his hat back to him. "Every other Sunday I haven't had to cook my own breakfast. In case you haven't heard, I am no longer a boarder in Mrs. Reedy's house."

"I know," he said. "I guess I should have been a little more concerned Friday night. Was it because you were late?"

"Just general principles, I think. Mrs. Reedy apparently decided I am unsuitable as a boarder in her house." I laughed. "I think so, too."

"Good," Jory said. "I'm glad you moved. You didn't belong there."

"But where were you when I needed you?" I asked pointedly. "I could have used a strong back when I was carrying things down to my house."

Instead of answering right away he stared at me, studying my face. I didn't know what he was looking for, or if he found it, but he finally answered me.

"I wanted to give you time," he said.

"Time for what?"

"To think. To decide how you felt."

"How did you think I would feel?" I asked.

"I didn't know. But I've seen women the morning after, and I've seen some of them turn love into hate once they think about what they've done. I don't know why they always think the man is responsible, but it seems that they do. If you regretted what happened I didn't want to see it in your face."

I thought about that for a moment and thought I understood. I could think of some women I had known in New York who might react that way, complete with indignant recriminations. But that wasn't my way.

"I don't regret it," I said. "And I was as much responsible as you were." I met his gaze steadily until a slow grin spread across his face. Then I looked away.

"How does your shirt fit?" he asked.

"Fine," I said. "Thank you. Where did you get it? You don't make these things yourself, do you?"

"No. There's an old Indian woman who works at the kitchen in the Gold Pan. She's been making my clothes for years, and when I asked her to make yours, she agreed. I pay her pretty well, more than anyone else would, I think, and I give her my own skins to work with so I know they're good."

His immodest statement struck me funny, but I was sure his furs were only the best. I had no doubts that my buckskins were top quality.

"What kind of Indian is she?" I asked.

"Arapahoe." Jory watched me closely as he talked. "I'll introduce you to her. She's a funny old gal, but I think you would like her."

"Did you—when you asked her to make these things for me, did you—"

"No." He looked at me pointedly. "I told you, I'm pretty good at keeping secrets. If you want anyone else to know, I'll let you tell them."

I smiled at him. "Thank you. I didn't realize there were any other Indians in town, I mean other than me and Red Cloud."

"Oh, sure, there's some. They just aren't always visible."

"By choice or public pressure?" I asked.

"Oh, probably a little of both."

"Well," I reasoned, "at least I'm not the only social outcast in town."

"Hell, no," Jory said. "You've got lots of company."

With that, he wrapped one bearlike arm around me and pulled me over to him. I came willingly, enjoying the feel of his hard chest and big hands. He pressed me down into the grass with a forceful kiss that I responded to immediately. Being like this was as natural with Jory as it was strained with Charles, and I thought this could easily develop into a habit. The only thing that bothered me was being so visible. If Red Cloud could spy on us, couldn't anyone else?

"Jory," I said as he kissed my neck. "We can't—

do this. Not here."

"Why not?" he asked against my hair. He pulled on the boot laces at my throat and exposed the soft skin above my breasts, then pressed his lips against it.

"Because, it's too open. What if someone is watching?" I tried to pull my shirt together but he firmly pulled it open again.

"Let them," he said.

"No!" I wailed. "Jory, we can't. My God, haven't you ever heard of a bed? First in a stall and now here. That's what beds are for."

He stopped what he was doing and looked down at me. "If that's an invitation, I accept."

"No, it's not an invitation," I said. "I don't even have a bed. I slept on a couch last night."

"I've got a bed," he suggested.

"Are you offering it to me?"

"On one condition."

"What's that?"

"I go with it." He grinned devilishly.

"No," I said, and pushed him over so I could sit up. As he watched, I straightened my shirt and pulled the laces up. "You're supposed to help me. Here I am, practically homeless and all you're interested in is pulling out my boot laces."

"That's not all I'm interested in," he said. One hand snaked out and grabbed my arm and he pulled me down beside him again.

"Relax," he said when I tried to pull away. "I just want to hold you. Let's hear about your problems. You're not homeless; you've got your very own house."

"I know, but I don't have anything in it. All I have is a couch, and now a table and two chairs Mr. Altvater gave me. Do you know where I can get some furniture?"

"Maybe," he said. "I'll see what I can do. Is furniture all you need?"

"No. I need just about everything. I asked Mr. Altvater to let me in the store this morning so I could pick up some things, but I just got the necessities. I even forgot to get a lantern."

"Okay, we'll get you some more things today."

"Thank you, Jory." I smiled to him. "You're not afraid I'll take advantage of your help and then walk out?" I asked lightly.

"No, I'm not worried about that. I was wrong about you the other night. But you were so damn mysterious and kept up that double-image business. I was afraid you were one of those snotty bitches from the east who thought all mountain men were stupid apes, good only for their innate tracking ability."

I laughed. "And I was afraid that if you knew I was a halfbreed, you'd spread the word and help the townspeople tar and feather me." I looked deeply into his eyes. "I'm glad we were both wrong."

He kissed me, meeting me halfway as I came to him, and our lips and tongues mingled sweetly. Being in his arms was like being in a safe harbor, protected from all the pain and fear I had been surrounded by before. I found it hard to believe that I was still the same girl I had been a week ago, that miserable, frightened, lonely girl. My thoughts were brought back to the present by the insistence of Jory's lips, and I realized he was breathing deeply.

"Why don't we ride?" I asked. "We have a lot to do today and if we stay here, I don't think we'll get anything done. You promised you'd help me."

"All right," he growled. Letting me go, he pulled on his hat and we got on our horses.

We went west up the hills, farther than I had ever been before. I asked Jory how the territory lay to the south and north, just out of curiosity, and he told me as much as he knew. I found that he rarely traveled in this area, but did most of his exploring in the mountains. He knew the Rockies like the back of his hand, but had never been to Sante Fe or California. "Too many people," he said again.

We rode up the bare ridge of the hill and I could see over the trees to the expansive prairie on both sides. It unfolded like a golden sea in every direction, with only the cottonwoods marking the rivers and the conglomeration that was Leavenworth and the fort. Far to the west I could see clouds on the horizon, blocking any view I thought I might have had of the mountains. It was a beautiful day. Jory stopped and let me look my fill before starting down the south side of the hill.

We rode south and then turned back east along a deertrail, Jory's mule picking out the way carefully. I began to think of the time but realized that

I had no more need for clocks. I had no time schedule to keep but my own, and no explanations to make. I could stay out all day and the hell with anyone who noticed my unchristian hours. It was a good feeling.

"There's a meadow up here," Jory said, breaking into my daydreams. "You'll like it."

We jumped a small stream and started up the other side. The trees thinned and before we had topped the hill, the rounded crest gave way to lush grass, crossed here and there by deer trails.

"It's beautiful," I said when Jory reined to a stop. The meadow fell away in a bowl below us with trees standing smartly around its edges. I could imagine the deer grazing nights under a full moon. It all seemed idyllic.

"You're right," I said. "I do like it."

"I thought you would," he said. "You belong in a place like this." Without explaining, he nudged Beauty down the meadow and I loosened rein on Thunder to follow.

We walked quietly on through the trees until I realized he was leading us back to my rocky hiding place. I considered telling him I wanted to ride more, but we had things to do in town. When he pulled up by the rocks he sat his mule silently. I slid off Thunder and changed clothes out of sight, then Jory helped me saddle up. I pinned my hair back at my neck and Jory handed me up on Thunder. We rode back to town together, neither of us giving a thought to the picture we presented.

Hank was at the stable and offered to put the

animals up for us so I suggested we go to my house and Jory could see for himself the state it was in. I felt funny unlocking the door for him, almost as if dozens of eyes were watching us. I yanked the shawl off the curtain rod where I had hung it last night, as much to let anyone see in as to let the light in, and Jory took a look around.

"You sure don't have much, do you?" he said finally.

"No," I answered. "It's pretty pitiful."

He went into the bedroom with all my things arranged on the bare floor, then surveyed the living room. Finally he took in the kitchen and came back to me.

"Well," he said. "I think I can get you some things. I know Adele's got a chest of drawers she doesn't use, because it's in the hall and I always just about trip over it. I've got a small table in my room that you can have, too, and I can get a couple of lanterns. Do you want to wait here for me?"

By the way he asked I wasn't sure if the question was so much if I cared to go or if he would rather go without me. I still had no idea how binding our relationship was, if it was at all.

"Can't I go with you?" I asked.

"Why, sure," he said in a surprised voice. "Come on."

We walked uptown together. It was almost funny watching people's faces. Some folks I knew from the store stared icily at Jory even when they nodded to me. A couple of men who spoke to Jory eyed me in a bold way. It was almost as if we walked a boundary, he and his acquaintances on one side and me and mine on the other. And there was no overlapping. It might have been depressing to me at another time, but on this day it just seemed humorous.

Jory surprised me by not going to the front door of the Gold Pan. I had pretty much made up my mind to the idea that I would walk tall and proud into the saloon, no matter what happened inside, but now I didn't have to. Jory held the back door for me and I stepped up into a warm, pleasant-smelling kitchen.

The first thing I saw was a huge old Indian woman, her bulk hidden in a great red dress. She turned when we came in and grinned warmly at Jory, her teeth worn down stumps.

"Cathy," Jory said, "this is Angel. Angel, meet Cathy Lance."

"How do," Angel said. She took my hand and pressed it firmly between hers, her smiling face taking me in. "How you like buckskins?" she asked.

Before I could answer, Jory shushed the old woman with a finger over her lips. "You're not to mention that, remember?" he warned.

"Oh," she said. "I forgot. Sorry."

"I love them," I whispered quickly. She smiled at me and chuckled.

"Good," she said. Then to Jory, "Now what you want? Dinner not till seven."

"We don't want dinner," he said, "We want furniture."

"Furniture? For what?"

"For a house, of course. Where's Adele?"

"In front."

His hand possessively at the small of my back, Jory guided me through the kitchen out into the saloon itself. This time in the afternoon it wasn't very crowded, but some heads turned and Jory nodded or answered friendly calls. I tried my best to look at ease and hoped I was succeeding.

Adele was standing at a table where two cowboys sat. The three of them talked easily, as friends do, and I felt very much an outsider as Jory greeted them all. He made brief introductions, but I didn't even remember their names.

"Glad to see you again," Adele said to me. I envied her easy manner.

"Thank you," I said. "It's nice to see you again, too."

"What are you up to, Jory?" she asked, "besides no good?"

"I'm up to moving furniture," he said. "Cathy moved into the Faylor house last night and there's hardly a stick of anything in there. How about letting her have that dinged up old chest of drawers upstairs? You never use the damn thing."

"Dinged up?" she said indignantly. "That thing's in perfect condition."

"You still never use it," he said. "We'll just take it over and if you decide you've got a place for it where it's not in the way all the time, I'll bring it back. Come on, Cathy," he said to me, "I'll show it to you."

"You better be careful with that thing," Adele called as Jory led me to the stairs.

I could see why it was a hazard. The hall was dim upstairs and the dresser sat against the wall just around the corner from the stairs. It was a beautiful old piece, not at all what I expected, and I knew I must be extremely careful with it.

"What do you think?" Jory asked.

"It's perfect," I said. "Are you sure Adele won't mind my borrowing it? I'll take good care of it but I wouldn't want her to worry about it."

"She won't. She trusts my judgment." He took my hand and pulled me down the hall. I had quick glances of framed pictures on the wall, some ordinary, some definitely more risque. The plush red carpet only added to my feeling of embarrassment.

"I'll show you that table I was talking about," Jory was saying. "Actually it's more like a stand, I guess, but you can use it for whatever you want."

He stopped at a door and pushed it open for me, letting me go in first. I stood dumbly, never having been in a man's room before. The bed was unmade and the sheets wadded, clothes lay all about over a chair and on the floor and a saddlebag lay across a washstand. The place looked like a cyclone had hit it.

"Sorry about the room," Jory said. "I don't stay in it long enough to clean it, just long enough to mess it up. Angel probably hasn't had time to get to it yet."

It struck me funny somehow, but I refrained

from saying anything. The only problem was that as I looked around, my eyes always came back to rest on the big unmade bed and I could imagine lying in it with Jory. Finally I decided I had best look at something else.

"Here's the table," he said. I came to look at the small stand that had a gun, a cup and some dirty dishes on it. It was short and only about two feet square, but it had a shelf underneath and was purposeful enough that I was sure I could use it.

"You want it?" he asked.

"If you're sure you won't need it," I said.

"No, it's all right. I'll tell you what. Adele has a wagon out back. I'll go hitch it up and get some of those drunks downstairs to help me carry the dresser out. Why don't you just take this stuff and put it over there?" He pointed to the washstand that was already jammed with things.

"Okay," I said.

"I'll be right back."

When he left I looked about again in amazement. How could he spend any time in a room like this? I decided to risk upsetting his arrangement and began straightening up. I piled all the dishes so Angel could find them easily and I picked up his clothes and hung up what looked clean. The few dirty things I found I threw in a corner by the door. I cleared off the washstand and hung his saddlebags over the brass rail of his bed, then hung his gun and belt beside it. Finally there was room to transport the few things left on the table to the washstand and I blew the cigar ashes off it. When that was done and Jory still hadn't come back, I walked timidly to his bed and began to pull the sheets up.

Then the door swung open. The suddenness of it scared me and I was relieved to see Jory standing there instead of one of the men from downstairs. In a glance he had taken in what I had done and how I stood with the bed covers in my hand.

"You shouldn't do that," he said as he walked toward me.

"Well, I thought it wouldn't hurt as long as you were busy, and it's just less for Angel to . . ."

"I don't mean that," he cut in. He stood close in front of me and put his hands on my shoulders. "You just look too good standing there by the bed. I'd rather see you turning it down than making it up, though." His fingers flexed at my shoulders and I could tell he was fighting his own impulses. It was difficult for me to say anything because I was doing the same. When I stood quietly under his hands he leaned toward me and pressed his lips to mine gently. It was like a sudden surge of adrenalin in my blood and I began to tremble. Having him so close and being in the intimacy of his own room made my mind whirl and I knew it was affecting him the same way. Still holding me, he pulled me down onto the bed and began to kiss me passionately. He curled one hand around my back and with the other he cupped my breast, the touch of his fingers sending my blood racing. His warm breath tickled my skin when he kissed my face and neck and the urgency of our movements made me fear we might actually consummate the moment. Dragging myself out of the glorious sensations that washed over me, I pulled away from him.

"Jory," I said, "we—"

"I know," he said, not angrily. "But, goddamnit, you make it hard to stop. Just don't go making my bed anymore." He stood up and pulled me after him, going immediately to the small table. While I smoothed my clothes and pushed my hair into place, he picked up the table and started down the hall. I pulled the door shut behind us and started after him.

I followed Jory downstairs and out through the kitchen to the wagon. He put the table just behind the box and helped me up. While I sat demurely in the wagon, he went back inside to get the dresser. I wondered if anyone could tell by looking at me what I was thinking.

When the kitchen door opened again, Jory backed out with one end of the dresser while one of the cowboys held the other. Adele followed with a crate full of articles and Angel stood watching from the doorway.

"I can't thank you enough for this," I said to Adele while the men loaded the dresser in the wagon.

"That's okay," she said. "Here's some other things you might need, too." She put the crate in beside the furniture.

"Thank you," I said again. "I'm afraid I wasn't at all prepared for setting up on my own and I really appreciate your help."

Adele looked up at me as if considering my words. Her attitude was such that I knew she was deciding whether I was being truthful or just condescending. Finally she stepped back out of Jory's way and he climbed up next to me.

"Anytime," she said, and she smiled. "Matter of fact, why don't you see if you can talk that moose next to you into bringing you back for dinner tonight?"

I looked from Adele to Jory and they were both grinning. Suddenly the Gold Pan seemed a very friendly place and I felt warm and comfortable.

"We'll be there," I said and Jory nodded agreement. He slapped the reins over the horse's back and we drove away. I looked back once and could still see Angel standing in the doorway.

We drove to my house and Jory handed me down. At first he refused to let me help at all, but when he almost dropped the dresser trying to get it down out of the wagon, I ignored his warnings and picked up one end of the thing. Stopping every few feet to get a better grip and watching my toes when we set it down, I managed to help him wrestle it inside. We set it in the bedroom and I immediately started putting my things away.

"Where do you want the table?" Jory called from the living room.

"Oh, next to the couch, I guess," I said. "At least that's good enough for now." I managed to put everything that was on the floor up on the dresser, then went into the living room. Jory had set the table beside the couch and was unloading the crate on the kitchen table.

"What's in there?" I asked. I came to look over his shoulder but he was too tall so I had to stand beside him.

"Two lanterns, this iron pot, let's see, some tongs, some plates, a blanket, cups. Damn, she put a lot of stuff in here."

I examined what Jory had taken out. Every bit of it was good, nothing broken or old. There were two good linen napkins, a couple of towels and a bar of delicious smelling soap. I took out a coffee pot and a small tin of coffee, and at the bottom of the crate was a large hand mirror.

"How wonderful!" I said. "She thought of everything. She's really very nice, isn't she?"

"A damn sight nicer than some," Jory agreed. "Where do you want to put all this stuff?"

We put things away and then sat at the table. The place was starting to look like a home. I even made us a pot of coffee that turned out pretty well and we sat sipping out of Adele's cups and surveying my house.

"About all you need now is a bed," Jory said. I expected to see a smirk on his face, but he was serious.

"I have the couch," I said, "so I'm not without anything at all."

"Not much privacy in the living room, though."

"I know. I'm going to make some curtains, and I have my shawl until then."

"Why don't I just move the couch into the

249

bedroom? It's not cold enough at night that you have to sleep by the fire."

"All right," I said. "That's a good idea. I can do my entertaining here in the kitchen."

"Who are you planning on entertaining?" he asked.

"Oh, any bugs that manage to get in the house, I guess. And you."

"And Lafferty?"

That caught me completely off guard and for a moment I just stared at him.

"What?" I said finally.

"Lafferty," he repeated.

"I don't expect to see Mr. Lafferty," I said levely.

"Why not?"

"Because."

"Because why?"

"Because I do not chose to invite him over," I said.

"Why not?"

"You're awfully nosy," I commented.

"Why aren't you going to invite him over?"

"Because last night he—he tried to—he was getting too serious. I had to ask him to leave." It was so ridiculous not to be able to talk about it to Jory. After all, sitting across from me was the man I had given myself to in a bed of straw and yet I couldn't explain about the way Charles had kissed me. I could only stammer and get more embarrassed.

"Did he hurt you?" Jory demanded.

"No."

He sat back in his chair and sipped his coffee. I wondered if he were angrier over the idea of Charles forcing himself on me or over my seeing anyone else. I finally decided it had to be the former. I couldn't imagine Jory demanding a commitment from me when he gave none. It wasn't his way.

"If he ever touches you again, I'll kill him."

"Don't be ridiculous," I said.

"I'm not."

I looked deeply into his lake-blue eyes and decided he wasn't kidding. I had never had a man speak so possessively about me and it caused a pleasant shudder to go through me. I realized this feeling was all at Charles's expense but I didn't care. He had shown his true face and I wanted none of it. All I wanted was Jory.

"Would you like some more coffee?" I asked, willing myself up from the table.

"Maybe just a little," he said. I brought the pot over and poured a half cup for him. I could feel his eyes on me, taking in my entire appearance, and I could feel again the wave of desire rising between us. It would be so easy to go to Jory, to kneel at his side and let him kiss and caress me. Instead I poured his coffee and walked away, still very aware of his appraisal of me.

"Do you think we should start back to the Gold Pan?" I asked. "It's six-thirty."

"Yeah. Might as well."

We didn't speak as we drove back uptown. I

think both of us were thinking the same thing and it would have been awkward to try to talk around it. Instead we rode silently. When we reached the saloon, Jory handed me down and I waited while he put the wagon up and the horse away. Then we went in the back door to find Adele.

"Just in time," she said. She had changed into a green satin gown for hostessing and it went beautifully with her red hair. I was genuinely glad to see her.

"Come on in here," she directed, leading us across the saloon. "I've got a waiting booth for you."

I wondered if she had chosen the same booth on purpose. Jory and I took our seats, the conversation of last Friday night far from our minds. Adele left to check on the kitchen but then came straight back.

"Dinner will be along shortly. Did you get settled in?"

"Yes," I said. "And I can't thank you enough. The dresser adds a lot to the bedroom, since it's the only piece of furniture in there."

"You don't have a bed?" she asked.

"No. There's a couch, though, and it's really quite comfortable."

"Well," she said, "I can't think of any place offhand where you can get a bed, but I'll think on it and see if I can't come up with something."

"Thank you," I said. "You've been very kind."

I smiled at her and she smiled back. I realized that running a saloon did not mean she was a bad woman, a lesson no one could have taught me before. It made me realize that, even though there were rigid class distinctions, they did not limit people's attitudes. I felt I would have a good friend in Adele.

"I'll go get your dinner," she said, and left us.

Jory sat back and lit a cigar. He looked so incongruous with it in his trapper's buckskins and thick reddish-brown hair. I liked the way he smoked, though, and the way he watched me.

"What are you smiling about?" he asked.

"I don't know. You, I guess."

"Why?"

"Just because you're you. Everyone warned me about you, you know. Everyone told me what a crude, thoughtless man you were."

"And they were right, too," Adele said. She appeared at the table with two plates and set one in front of each of us. "Just look at this food I have fixed for him, and you can bet your bottom dollar he'll inhale it without even tasting it." She shook her head at him. "But I suppose he's just a backward trapper who doesn't know when he has it good." She looked at him pointedly and I thought I saw him nod almost imperceptibly. It was as if they exchanged some private thought.

"Well, go on," she said finally. "See if the steaks are all right."

We each tasted our dinner and the steaks were better than they had been before. I complimented Adele on whoever her cook was and she beamed. Stepping close to Jory, she bumped his leg with hers.

"At least you've got good taste in women, even if you are an uncouth lout," she said. She turned and began to walk away and I saw Jory's hand steal out and pinch her rear. Whirling on him, she was the picture of indignation.

"Even if I am an uncouth lout, this is one hell of a steak and you're a hell of a woman," he said.

I hadn't really thought Adele was capable of blushing but she did, until her face rivaled her hair in color. Swatting playfully at Jory, she walked away.

Dinner passed like that, Adele checking back every short while to find out if everything was all right and she and Jory engaging in their playful battle. She was always solicitous to me, grouping me with Jory all the while that she teased him. I wondered briefly if they had ever shared a bed but decided it was none of my concern if they had, and would have no bearing on us now. It was enough that she recognized us as a couple and that Jory seemed not to mind.

When Adele had cleared away our dishes and brought a new bottle of wine, I told her I must return the favor and cook for her once I had my kitchen outfitted. She seemed pleased with that and left us to enjoy our wine. We sipped it quietly as we let our dinner settle.

When we walked back through the saloon, Jory's hand rested lightly at the small of my back. Just before we reached the kitchen Adele burst through the door.

"Are you leaving?" she asked.

"Yeah," Jory said. "Don't look for this." He held up the half bottle of wine. "By the way, there's something else I want." He pulled Adele aside for a minute, whispering in her ear. If I had been the jealous type it probably would have worried me, but I wasn't so it didn't. Adele listened to Jory, nodded once and laughed when he turned and ran up the stairs.

"That Jory," she said with a laugh. "He's crazy." She took my arm and walked with me back through the kitchen. I thanked her again for dinner. "Don't mention it," she said. "Just seeing Jory like this makes it worthwhile."

"Seeing Jory like what?" I asked.

"Oh, he's like a kid at Christmas. I got so tired of having him hang around this place like a heartsick dog, and since he's been seeing you, he's been happier than I've seen him. It's good to know that crusty old trapper still has a heart in him."

Before I could speak again, Jory had reappeared with a cowhide bundled up under his arm.

"What's that for?" I asked.

"You'll see. Let's go."

We walked quietly back down the main street. Being Sunday there was hardly anyone else about and I imagined all Mrs. Reedy's boarders gathered in the parlor. I wondered briefly if I was a topic of their conversation. At least, I thought, there were few prying eyes about to watch me unlock my door and close it again behind Jory.

"I think I'll move the couch now," he said,

setting down the wine and cowhide. "Good for the digestion."

While he pulled and tugged at it, finally dragging it across the wooden floor, I got two coffee mugs and poured wine in each and brought them into the bedroom.

"Where do you want this?" he asked.

"Over there, I guess. Next to the dresser."

He positioned the couch and sipped at his wine. "Terrible," he said.

"The wine?"

"No, this room. It's worse than my room at the Gold Pan, not friendly at all."

He was right. The two pieces of furniture were mismatched and impersonal and even my toilet articles on the dresser didn't add much personality to it.

"There's not much I can do about it right now," I said.

"True," Jory agreed. "But we can do something about the living room."

Taking his cup, he went into the front room and checked the fireplace.

"I'll get some wood," he said and went outside. Since it was beginning to get dark, I lit one of the lamps and set it on the table. I watched Jory as he fanned a fire up. Although the place was not cold, it was somehow more cheerful to have a fire.

When he was satisfied with the fire, he came to the table and took up the cowhide.

"This is where this comes in," he said. He took it over by the fireplace and shook it out, the huge red and white pattern taking shape on the floor. He positioned it right in front of the fire and turned to me.

"Now that's friendly," he said. I had to laugh at him. His idea of furnishing a house was so simple, yet so warm. Just the cowhide rug in front of the fire was more inviting than any bed I had ever seen.

"What about that thing you had over the window?" he asked.

"My shawl?"

"Yeah. Get it and I'll put it up."

I handed it to him and he draped it over the rough curtain rod. The whole thing must have looked very compromising from outside, but I didn't care. It was just so nice being alone with Jory.

"Turn that lamp down," he said. "Now get your cup and come over here." His clipped words but gentle tone only excited me. Feeling no shame whatever, I followed him to the cowhide. We settled down on it in front of the fire, each with a coffee cup. The wine tasted better than it had in the dining room, and I was feeling the effects of it. The fire turned my face hot and my head was light. I sat close to Jory and just enjoyed his presence.

"You aren't saying much tonight," he said as he slid one arm around me. I settled against him.

"Don't have much to say." It had been such a nice easy evening that I wanted it never to end. "You talk," I said.

"About what?"

"About the mountains."

After a short pause, Jory began to talk. He told me about the way the mountains lunge up out of the plains, about the rocky faces and sharp planed sides and the treeless, snowbound tops. He described the way the seasons passed and the mountainsides turned from newborn green to gold and rust and scarlet, then finally to gray and white. He told me about the animals, the wolves and cougars and deer and bear. It all sounded wonderful to me.

Finally he put down his coffee cup and turned me toward him, his arms tight around me. I loved the feel of his hands on my back, holding me in a ring of contentment.

"What will people say when we leave town together?" he asked.

"They'll say I am a brazen, fallen woman and you are an ill-mannered, opportunistic scoundrel. And they'll probably be right."

"Will you care?"

"No."

Jory watched me for a moment, as if considering what I'd said. Then he bent close and kissed me softly. The warmth of the wine and the close flames made me feel on fire, and I willingly responded to him. I laced my arms around his neck and pressed myself against him. It was all the encouragement he needed.

Taking my cup and setting it beside his, Jory bent me back down on the rug. Curling his arms around me, he kissed me again, more slowly and passionately then ever before. I concentrated fully on the feelings he evoked in me and instinctively worked to arouse him the same way. When he kneaded my shoulders with his fingers, I raked my nails through his hair. He pressed his lips to my face, my ears and my neck, sending shivers of anticipation through me. When his wayward hand brushed across my breasts, my breath caught in my throat and I searched out his mouth with my own. He began to undress me then, slowly and patiently, each of us reveling in the slow process that was leading us on. He kissed every inch of skin as he unclothed it, covering my body with so many pleasureable impulses that I thought I couldn't wait any longer. When I was finally naked I began the same process on him, pulling off his buckskin shirt and pants, tossing his boots aside. In the golden glow of the fire we explored and caressed each other until our bodies fused together and moved as one. We coupled first as lovers, tantalizing and teasing, loving slowly so as to relish every minute; then we joined as all living things, desperately and instinctively in a way that neither of us could control. Our bodies molded together, we rocked to a higher and higher pitch, moving faster and faster until the sensations blended in a frantic wave that created over us and carried us off the earth. Then we lay quietly in each other's arms.

"Is it always like that?" I asked finally.

"Like what?"

"Like that—wonderful."

He laughed at me, the fire glinting in his eyes

and burnishing his hair. "No," he said, "it's not always. Not even close to always."

"Oh." I slid my fingers through his hair and down to his neck. There I toyed with the rawhide thong he had tied there and the leather bag dangling from it.

"Why do you wear a medicine bag?" I asked. I had noticed it earlier but hadn't been of a mind to ask about it.

"You know why a man wears a medicine bag," he said.

"Does it work for you?" I thought of my father's medicine bag with the eagle feathers tied to it. It was a well known fact that my father had very strong medicine in camp.

"Seems to. At least I'm still alive and kicking.

"What's in it?" I asked.

"You know better than to ask that," he said. It was true, I did know better. A man's medicine was his protection, his life force and his capability, and what was inside was his own secret. I always used to wonder what my father kept in his, but had never dared to ask.

"What are you going to do when you find your band?" he asked.

"I don't know. I'll have to decide that when I find them."

"Will you stay with them?"

"I don't know. Maybe. That's as far as I can see right now." His questions seemed to have an urgency to them, an apprehension I hadn't noticed before. Was he worried about me among the

Indians? Or could he possibly be worried that I would find what I was seeking and not need him anymore? I couldn't tell.

"That man—the one who's probably already married someone else—will he be there?"

"I don't know. Probably, unless he's dead by now." I faced him. "Jory, it's pointless to ask all these questions now. I won't have any of the answers until I get there. That's too far in the future to worry about. I'm not even thinking that far ahead."

I stared into his eyes, but I couldn't see that he had even heard me. "Jory, I can't tell you anything now. Can't we just enjoy being here now? We'll have time to worry about the future when we get there."

"I guess you're right," he said. For the rest of the evening he was very quiet, and when he left, I had the feeling he was somehow disappointed, but I wasn't sure why.

Chapter Nine

I DIDN'T know if it showed, but a sense of contentment glowed within me. At the store I was cheerful without having to force it and I felt genuinely interested in my customers' problems. I pursued my remodeling project with new enthusiasm and even drew up plans so Mr. Altvater could begin the carpentry. And every spare minute I had, I turned my mind to Jory.

If my gaity endeared me to some of my customers, it alienated me from others. My fall from grace was well known and some of the higher aspiring women stared at me rudely or made condescending remarks. On some days the atmosphere in my back corner became very chilly, and although I didn't care for myself, I was worried about losing business for Mr. Altvater. About Wednesday I approached him about it.

"Don't worry about that," he said with a chuckle. "There's not that much competition in town that I worry about losing customers, and anyway, everyone likes a little scandal now and then. It keeps things interesting."

"Am I causing a—a scandal, then?" I asked.

"No doubt about it," he said. "Why, a woman your age living alone and having gentlemen callers at night?" He laughed, then looked seriously at me. "It's none of my affair, of course, and I don't judge. I know Jory to be a good, true man but nine out of ten people in town would disagree with me. So long as you know what you're doing and can handle it, I wouldn't fret about it. But you have set Leavenworth on its ear."

I was glad he felt that way. I was beginning to recognize Mr. Altvater as an objective, guiding personality, almost like an uncle, and his opinion was important to me. I also knew what he said about Jory was true; most people never bothered to look under the rough exterior of the man to see what he was really like. I was glad to have an ally in Mr. Altvater. With so much town opinion against me, it was nice to have a friend.

I found one other friend, much more unexpected than Mr. Altvater. One particular day a trio of ladies came into the store, all three of some position in town. Mrs. Lewis was married to the manager of one of the banks, Mrs. Lehman was a lieutenant's wife from Fort Leavenworth and Mae Evans was, of course, the newspaperman's wife. I hadn't thought about the Evanses much since Charles had abandoned me to ruination, for I had considered their door closed to me now. Both Mrs. Lewis and Mrs. Lehman had been in earlier that week so I knew their opinion of me. When they came in, I expected cool treatment from all three.

"Catherine!" Mae said when she saw me. "I haven't seen you in weeks. Why haven't you come over?"

"I, uh, didn't think—you see, Charles and I haven't . . ."

"Posh," she said to my stammering. "You don't need Charles to come for dinner. I know he's been acting like a tail-shorn banty rooster, but that's his problem. Can you come tonight? Tom would love to get you into another chess game."

"Oh, well, I guess I could, if you're sure it's no trouble for you."

"No trouble at all. Is seven too early?"

"Seven is fine."

"Good. Now what do you have in eyelet lace?"

The other two women had been staring slightly aghast at Mae, and now stood by silently while I showed her the lace. It was funny to see the indecision on their faces. Since I was so brazen, they really shouldn't acknowledge me, but Mae had treated me like a long-lost friend and Mae was very well thought of. I knew their status-conscious brains were buzzing.

"Let me have five yards of this," she said finally.

I measured and cut the lace for her, wrapped it and gave her change. She made ready to go and her two companions started for the door. Hanging back a moment, Mae waited until they were out of earshot.

"If you'd care to bring a friend over, I'll set another place," she said.

"What?" At first I didn't understand, then it registered. "Oh, that's all right, you don't have to . . ."

"Quite all right," she said with a wave of her hand. "You know how Tom is—likes anyone with enough brains to pick. If he'll come, bring him along."

"Thank you," I said warmly. "Very much."

"See you at seven," she said, and followed her confused friends out the door.

It almost made me smile to think of Jory and me going to dinner at the Evanses. The two outcasts breaching the doors of the upper class. I had been so painfully aware of my "descent" into the lower level of society with Jory, I now wondered how he would feel about being elevated into higher circles with me. I hoped he would come in before closing.

He didn't always. Since that Sunday night, I had thought I would see him more regularly, but I was wrong. Some days he would come in and talk to me, usually only for a moment or two, but other days would pass when I wouldn't see him at all. I wasn't sure what to think—his eyes looked at me in a way that said he cared yet he often spoke impersonally. He came by the house one night but wouldn't stay long. I wasn't sure if he was protecting me or himself, but he seemed bound not to carry our affair to an extreme. It was just as well; if we were awfully blatant about it, Leavenworth would crucify us, while this way there was still room for doubt. In a way it bothered me, though, but I was secure in my feeling for Jory and confident in his for me. For right now, it was enough.

That day he did come in, just before Mr. Altvater closed the door. The two men talked for a moment as they always did, then Mr. Altvater went about closing up. I went into the back room to get my bag and met Jory at the front counter.

"I'm glad you came by," I said. "We've been invited to dinner."

"By who?" he asked suspiciously. He leaned one elbow on the counter while I talked.

"Mrs. Evans, the newspaperman's wife. I met them while I was still at Mrs. Reedy's and they're very nice. Openminded, too."

"Thanks but no thanks," he said.

"Why not?"

"I'd just rather not. You go."

"All right," I said, disappointed. "What are you going to do?"

"I thought I'd go riding. I haven't taken Shaman out for a few days and I don't want him going barn sour on me. He's been loafing too much this summer. I've got to get him back into shape for our trip."

"How soon will we be going?" I asked, making sure Mr. Altvater was out of earshot.

"This is the first week of August, so pretty soon. I've got a lot of things I have to get ready."

"All right," I said. I thought he would leave then, but he brushed my neck with his fingers, so briefly that an unmindful eye wouldn't have even caught it. It surprised me, since he rarely touched me unless we were completely alone.

"Go to dinner," he said. "I'll see you later." He tipped his hat to Mr. Altvater and left.

At that moment I would rather have gone riding with Jory than to dinner at the Evanses' but I couldn't ignore Mae's invitation. I called goodnight to Mr. Altvater and went home to change for dinner.

Tom was as glad to see me as Mae had been. It was comforting to enjoy their open friendship and we talked easily over an excellent dinner. Although Mae lifted her eyebrows questioningly when I showed up alone, no mention was made of Jory. Instead Tom lured me into another chess game which I promptly lost. We talked of several things and the Evanses began to tell me what they had done in their earlier years. Before settling in Leavenworth, Tom had traveled all the way to California and back, then had brought Mae the short way west with him. He told me about the journey and the new wilderness that was rapidly becoming civilized.

Mae had even toured Europe when she was younger and she described the sights she had seen there. It was odd, but while she talked I felt Tom's eyes on me as if he were examining me, searching for something. It was the first time I had felt uneasy in their house and I had difficulty trying to figure out why.

When I noted the time and began to say my thanks and goodnights, Tom suddenly stopped me. "Catherine," he said, "come in here for a minute, will you? I want to ask your opinion of an article I wrote."

Leaving Mae with the dishes, I followed Tom into his study. He had a large desk there, almost covered with papers. Sorting through them, he pulled one out and handed it to me.

Instead of being a rough editorial as I expected, it was a public notice. "One thousand dollars reward," it read, "for any information regarding Catherine Marie Boudry, late of Boston, New York." Almost hypnotized with terror, I read the handbill as it described me carefully, down to every detail. Grandpere had covered me neatly.

Had Tom not pulled up a chair for me, I might have slipped to the floor. He took the bill from me and regarded me seriously.

"I got this yesterday," he said. "Mae hasn't seen it. At first I thought it was just a coincidence, but now I know. It's you, isn't it?"

I nodded, unable to speak. How fast could I get away? How soon could Jory outfit us and get us out of town?

"I don't plan on answering the notice," Tom said.

"What?" I asked, not understanding.

"I'm not going to turn you in. Not unless there's

a good reason I should."

"No, there's no good reason, except my grandparents hanging onto an illusion. I didn't belong there, I didn't fit in. They thought I could, but they were wrong. I couldn't stay." How much should I tell Tom? "I can't say anymore. But if—if you should answer that, I'll be gone before anything comes of it."

"I figured as much. That's why I don't see any point in answering it. But I thought, after you leave Leavenworth, I might let them know you're all right."

"I guess that wouldn't do any harm," I said. "It'll be some comfort to them, and they'll know I'm getting along very well on my own. But I can't go back. I'll never go back."

"No one's asking you to. I just wanted to know for my own mind. I won't even tell Mae."

"Thank you, Tom," I said. "You don't know how reassuring that is for me."

That night I thought a lot about the handbill while I lay in bed. I couldn't believe my luck that it had come to Tom and Tom was my friend. Still, I was relieved that Jory and I would be leaving soon. Once I left Leavenworth, anyone would be hard pressed to keep track of me or pin me down. Perhaps I would even write my grandparents myself, and post the letter as I left town. Perhaps if they knew their notices were useless they would leave me be and go on about their lives without me. I fell asleep composing that letter in my head.

Saturday was busy but I had time between

customers to begin assembling my pictures on the poster boards Mr. Altvater had made for me. I placed them in as presentably as I could and it began to take a definite shape. I even had some comments on it from customers, which encouraged me, too. By closing it looked pretty good, and I was so pleased I decided to reward myself. Hurrying home quickly, I packed a saddle-bag with some things and went to get Thunder.

I noticed both Shaman and Beauty were in their stalls, which meant Jory was still in town some-where. Part of my reward to myself included him, so I would have to find him somehow. Once Hank saddled Thunder for me, I rode directly to the back door of the Gold Pan.

Angel was in the kitchen and greeted me enthu-siastically. She had adopted me in her way, much as she had Jory, and would even scold me if I failed to visit very often. Now that I knew Adele and was more familiar with the Gold Pan, I wasn't so skittish about coming over.

"Is Jory here?" I asked when she had sat me down and insisted I taste what she was cooking for dinner.

"No. He down at blacksmith. Having new pack harness made for mule."

"Would you tell him I was here?" I asked. "And that I've gone riding?"

"Sure," she said with a toothless grin. "You want him to follow you?"

"Oh, Angel," I said, embarrassed. "Yes, I want him to follow me. Will you tell him?"

"Sure. He come soon."

Laughing at the old woman's matchmaking, I went back outside to Thunder. I looked down the main street, then headed for the hills.

By the time I had stripped the saddle from Thunder and changed into my buckskins, I half expected to see Jory come riding up, but he still hadn't come so I rode on ahead. I took the short way to the lake and tied Thunder to a sapling by the water's edge. I sat on the grass and unpacked my saddlebag, laying out cheese, slices of ham and crackers. I also had bought a bottle of wine, which I put in the shallow water of the lake. Nibbling at the cheese, I waited for Jory to come.

I didn't have to wait long. I heard Thunder snort and he bobbed his head, then an answering snort came from Shaman. The stallion picked a careful way through the trees and took a place near Thunder to begin grazing. Jory dismounted and came to sit beside me on the grass.

"What's this?" he said about the food.

"Dinner, or a simple version of it. Are you hungry?"

"As a matter of fact," he said, and reached for a slice of ham.

I got the wine from the lake and we ate quite a bit of food. Jory piled cheese and ham and crackers up into little towers and would demolish it all with one gulp and wash it down with wine. I was genuinely happy just being with him.

"Angel said you were having a new pack harness made," I said.

"Yeah. My old one's so cracked I don't think it could make another trip."

"How will we go?" I asked.

"Up the Platte, I guess. You'll have to tell me as much as you can as we go. If we run into any Indians, maybe we can ask."

"Any Cheyenne, you mean," I corrected.

"What do you mean?"

"I don't intend to declare myself to any Pawnee or Crow. I don't think being half-white will be any saving grace for me."

"Oh, yeah. Well, if we meet any but Cheyenne, I'll do the talking. We'll be loaded with supplies, too, so we can trade if we have to."

"How do you go to your cabin?" I asked. I don't know why, it wouldn't involve me, but I was curious.

"I go to Denver, then straight up into the mountains. My place is over the divide, then southwest a little. It's not really far into the mountains, but it's rough country, so it takes a while to get there. And I have to be there before snow sets in."

I nodded, imagining him snowbound in his cabin. And where would I be when winter hit? In a lodge among my people? Or would I be someplace else by then? I looked at Jory and realized he was watching me closely. It struck me that he might be thinking the same thing, for his expression was serious and solemn and he was very quiet. We both knew our time together was running out.

"Can we go to the meadow tonight?" I asked.

His eyes scanned my face, taking in my entire

image. It was a sensual look, and I would have fallen into his arms right then if he had made a move for me. Instead he just nodded.

"Sure," he said.

Without another word he began to pack up what was left of dinner and he tied my saddlebag behind Shaman's saddle so I could ride unhindered. We rode quietly through the twilight trees, the sun ahead of us sending out failing rays. It was a very pleasant time of day and I was bound to make Jory forget our parting and enjoy our time together.

When we reached the meadow, Jory tethered the horses to saplings so they could graze, then unsaddled Shaman. I wasn't sure what he was planning until he took the blanket in one hand and me in the other. We walked to the sloping bowl of the meadow and he unfolded the blanket, laying it out carefully over the lush grass. We sat on the blanket and he began to unbutton his shirt.

This wasn't the way I wanted it at all. I wanted Jory to make love to me as he had described it to me months before. I wanted a moon over us and the gentle wind caressing us, and I wanted him to smile.

Forgetting all the gentility I had ever been taught, I moved over to him and brushed his hands away from his shirt front. I held his hands until I put them around my waist, then I put my own arms around his neck and kissed him. I knew he was surprised, as I was, but it didn't take him long to recover. I pressed myself against him wantonly and moved sensuously, until, in a few short moments, he was holding me as tightly as he could.

Using my lips and tongue as he had taught me, I kissed and caressed him until his breathing became irregular. When he would have pulled off my buckskin shirt, I put him off and instead began a slow seduction. I unbuttoned his shirt and spread it apart, letting my tongue trail down his neck to the hollow at his throat while my fingers traced gentle patterns over his chest. I slid his shirt off and stroked the smooth muscles of his back, kneading and massaging. Finally I could not deny him any longer and he pulled my own shirt off and with his medicine bag clasped between us, we fell down on the blanket together.

From then on, our lovemaking was a mutual sharing, each of us taking our turn at arousing the other. When we were both completely naked, I found myself able, for the first time, to caress Jory the way he had me, touching and stroking him openly. I learned then what things drove him to distraction, and I was able to please him and still enjoy the attention he was giving me. It was a unique experience and we climbed steadily toward our sensual heights by stages, each of us giving and accepting more than we ever had before. I think we covered every inch of each other's bodies, kissing and touching and exploring the wonder of it all. Jory showed me things I had never dreamed of which added to my pleasure. I reciprocated in everything he did. When we finally came together in the way of lovers and moved excitedly toward the climax I was already more satisfied than I had ever been, and when Jory shuddered and lay still over me, I was fully at peace.

From the ground where I lay I could look over Jory's shoulder and see the nearly full moon shining down on us, and almost on cue the light evening breeze sprang up and rippled over us. I nibbled on Jory's ear and said, "Look at the moon."

He rolled over beside me and looked up at the silver globe while I snuggled into the crook of his arm. The moonlight showed pale on our bodies, almost as bright as daylight, and the wind cooled us as it blew over. It was as perfect an evening as I could imagine.

"Have you ever been here like this before?" I asked.

"Nice girls aren't supposed to ask questions like that," he said.

"When did I ever say I was a nice girl? I just wondered because it's so beautiful. You did tell me about it once. Do you remember?"

"Yes, I remember. But I've never brought anyone here before. It just seemed like a good idea."

"You were right about that. Do you think anyone would miss us if we stayed here all night?"

Jory turned on his side so he could look down on me. He brushed my tangled hair back from my face and ran his fingers lightly over my lips.

"Would you like to stay all night?" he asked.

"Yes. Wouldn't you?"

He smiled. "You ask the damndest questions. Didn't anyone ever teach you any manners?"

"No." I laughed. "Actually I'm beginning to like doing and saying whatever I please so I guess you'll just have to get used to it. If you want a woman who will stare at you wide eyed and innocent, you'll have to find someone else."

"I don't want anyone else," he said, and covered my mouth with his. It was the most definite statement Jory had ever made to me and I fairly swelled with the thought of it. I twined my arms around his neck and pressed close to him and he ran one hand down the length of my body as if committing it to memory. While the moon slipped higher up in the sky, Jory made love to me again and the wind caressed us as we lay on the grass.

Sunday morning I stayed home and did some baking. I had bought a cookbook earlier that week and wanted to try some simple bread recipes, but by the time I was done I didn't believe there was such a thing. Still, my bread wasn't too hard and, dunked in coffee, it tasted all right. I decided I would have to start learning to cook sometime, since in the future I might have to depend on it for survival. Luckily that was still some time away; if I had to depend on this bread, I would probably starve.

After that, I walked down to the Gold Pan. As long as I was preparing for my exodus, I had to get as many things in readiness as I could. I went to the back door and let myself in. Adele was there.

"Hi, Cathy," she said. "You're just in time for lunch. Have a seat."

"Thanks," I said. "Actually I didn't come to beg food."

"Oh, I know," she laughed. "But Jory's not here so you might as well relax."

She spooned me up a heaping bowl of stew that smelled delicious. After my paltry bread for breakfast I realized I really was hungry. I waited until she brought her own bowl to the table and we ate together.

"I don't know where Jory is," she said.

"Oh, that's okay. I know he's got things to do. I just stopped by to talk to Angel. Is she here?"

"She's upstairs cleaning that mess Jory calls a room. The only chance she ever gets to clean properly is when he's gone." She sighed. "I guess if he spent more time there he'd be more careful, but as it is he just sleeps there and throws clothes around. What did you want to talk to Angel about?"

"I wanted to ask her if she'd make me some gloves. Jory said she's wonderful at leatherwork and I need gloves for riding." The lie slipped out easily enough so Adele didn't question it. She only nodded.

"She is good," she agreed. "And with cooler weather coming on, you'll need gloves. You'll have to see if she's still got some of that doeskin Jory brought back."

We talked more about the weather and the

coming of winter. Adele didn't look forward to it since it restricted business. She told me about the migration of trappers and wagon trains out in the fall and back in the spring. I wondered if she ever wanted to be a part of it instead of staying here and only watching it go by.

When we had finished lunch I helped with the dishes and then went upstairs to Jory's room. Angel was almost done, but I was in time to help her make the bed.

"Angel," I said, "could I get you to make me another outfit? Just like the one I have?"

"Sure," she said happily. "Just pants and shirt?"

"And soft boots, too, if you can manage it. Like about knee high?"

"Yes. Does Jory have leather?"

"I don't know. I haven't asked him. If he doesn't can I buy some someplace else?"

"Jory will have," she said decidedly. "How soon you want it?"

"Oh, anytime in the next couple of weeks. Will that give you enough time?"

"Sure," she said. She looked at me conspiratorially. "You going with Jory?"

I blushed at her pointed question, and that was answer enough for her. She grinned happily.

"Please," I said, "don't say anything to anyone."

"Who, me?" She laughed. "Dumb Indian don't know anything, anyway." I joined in with her joke and when Jory came into the room we were still laughing.

279

"What the hell's going on around here?" he demanded. He looked from me to Angel and back again.

"Girl talk," Angel said, and still chuckling, she left us.

"I'd sure like to know what's so damned funny around here," he said again when he closed the door behind Angel. "First I can't find you anywhere, then I come back and find Adele grinning like the cat that swallowed the canary, and now you two. What's going on?"

His gruff tone might have bothered me except that while he talked he pulled me over to the freshly made bed and drew me down on it.

"I can't say for Adele," I said as he kissed my neck, "but I just commissioned Angel to make me another set of buckskins and for some reason it made her very happy. I told her I was going with you, but I made her promise not to tell anyone."

"Good idea. You'll need another outfit," he said as he pulled pins from my hair.

"Yes, I'll have to have a change of clothes. Jory, you're messing my hair." I tried to grab my pins but he threw them on the floor.

"Yeah, you will. After all, I might end up tearing your clothes off the first day out and then what would you do?" He began pulling the sheets back.

"Jory, we just made this bed. What are you doing?"

"Unmaking it. Don't worry. I'll let you make it again pretty soon."

By the time I got home it was late afternoon so I

didn't have time to ride. Still, things were working together for our trip and it was taking shape. I just hoped it all came together smoothly and we got away from town without any fuss. I knew I was still sitting on a powderkeg.

At work Monday I put the finishing touches on my fashion display and got several compliments on it. Mr. Altvater seemed very pleased and I was glad I could at least leave that much for him when I left. I was beginning to think like that—how things would be after I left. Although I tended to feel I was letting some people down by not saying anything ahead of time, no one would be inconsolable when I was gone. I had made some genuine friends but none that I couldn't make again.

I saw Jory for at least a minute or two every day that week and on Friday he came by the store at closing and insisted I go to dinner with him. We left Mr. Altvater sweeping up and walked across town. Adele had already set up a booth for us.

"Angel said to stop in the kitchen before you leave tonight," she said. "I guess she's done with your gloves."

Jory cocked an eyebrow at me when Adele walked away. "Gloves?"

"I didn't know what else to say," I explained. "I'd just as soon not have everyone know we're both leaving soon. It would only complicate things."

"True," he agreed. "I can get everything ready without arousing curiosity. Everyone knows that

I'm planning to leave once my beard grows in good."

"Your beard?" I asked.

"Sure. Have to keep warm somehow, you know. Get's cold up there in the mountains."

I hadn't thought too much about it before but now I saw that it had been a few days since he had shaved. There was enough stubble that I could tell his beard would be red, more so than his hair, and would make him look twice as burly. I knew it would look good.

"What are you smiling about?" he asked.

"You with a beard. You already look like a grizzly bear with your shaggy hair and buckskins."

"If you stick with me this winter I'll show you how grizzly I can get."

I tried to laugh that off but I heard the unspoken question behind Jory's words. Luckily Adele brought our dinner then, and sat to talk with us for a short while.

"What are we going to do for entertainment when you're gone, Jory?" she asked. "There's no other men around here worth looking at."

"You know you'll get a whole batch of new ones off the wagons," Jory said. "What you ought to do is get a few nice-looking girls while you're at it. The ones you got now are looking a little hollow eyed."

"Will you come back next year if I do?" she asked. She winked at me so I knew what game they were playing.

"Maybe. Town's getting awfully crowded. Why don't you write me and sketch me pictures—if I like what I see, I'll come back."

"Write you? Who in blue blazes would deliver a letter way the hell up in the mountains?"

"Beats me, but you asked."

Adele left us then to attend to other tables. We ate in silence for a moment.

"Are you coming back to Leavenworth next year?" I asked.

"I don't know. I kind of doubt it. Too many people with too many problems. It gets harder and harder for me to even stick around all summer. Why? Do you know where you'll be next year?"

"No. It seems funny not knowing exactly where I'm going to be. Doesn't it ever seem strange to you?"

"No. I like it that way, at least for me. I don't like not knowing where you'll be, though."

I didn't look up. I didn't want to see how he was looking at me. "I can't help that," I said. "You know . . ."

"Yeah, I know. I'm not trying to stop you. I know I can't."

We ate dinner quietly, as if a cloud hung over our table. Adele came back now and again but she soon noticed the solemnity and didn't bother with more games. When we had finished we went out through the kitchen and Angel gave me a package wrapped in brown paper.

"You like this," she said with a grin. "It make you look like beautiful Indian princess."

I thanked her without even opening the package and Jory walked me home. It was a pleasant evening, although a slight chill in the air made shivers go up my back.

At my house I put coffee on and Jory made a fire. I was not really enthusiastic about my new buckskins but I unwrapped them and took out the shirt anyway. I held it up and Jory came to see.

It was beautiful. Angel had used a light tawny doeskin and all her talents as a seamstress. The shirt was slit low at the throat in a simple V neck but it had a strip of dark brown leather threaded along the edge. The same dark brown was sewn along the outside seams of the sleeves, along with small bright blue and orange beads that she had worked in at intervals. A short fringe of the slit doeskin hung from the same seams, giving the shirt a graceful movement, and the sleeves belled out ever so slightly at the wrist in a feminine flare.

"Put it on," Jory said.

I took the leather into my bedroom and changed into it. The pants were large, but they were fitted enough to stay on and I even pulled on the soft high moccasins. Finally I combed out my hair so it hung straight and dark. When I looked into my small mirror I was amazed. Angel was right. I looked just like an Indian maiden.

When I went back into the living room, Jory stood by the fire and turned toward me. He said nothing but his eyes took me in, from my black hair to my booted feet. I saw a sort of shock come into his eyes, as if he saw me for the first time, but then they rested on my face and softened. He came to me and put his arms around me.

"You're beautiful," he said softly. It was the first time any man had ever spoken such works to me and suddenly I found myself clinging to him and crying against his shoulder. He didn't even ask what was wrong, but just held me close and let me cry. I sobbed until I thought my own heart would break and I had thoroughly soaked Jory's shirt. When I finally weakened and fell limp against him, he picked me up and carried me to the rug in front of the fire. He sat me down and held me close, just stroking my hair and saying nothing. We both sat quietly and watched the fire.

It was almost as if we knew the end was coming near. I felt caught by destiny, as if Jory and I were being pulled apart by a mindless fate that paid no heed to our feelings. We sat huddled in front of the fire as if a blizzard howled around us, and we would soon be forced out into it. This was our sanctuary, and would only be available to us for a very short while.

Jory made love to me that night, slowly and quietly, and when we were done I cried into his chest again. We spoke very little. We had said all we could, and when he left I lay on the cowhide and slept there.

Saturday night I walked home from the store and fixed myself a quiet supper. I had thoughts of going riding, but I didn't really feel like it. Finally I ended up packing away my new buckskins and going to bed early.

I slept fitfully. No thought seemed enough to placate me or send me into a sound sleep. I found myself drifting in and out of consciousness. To alleviate the feelings that depressed me, I mentally checked over what I would need for the trip. Finally I did sleep, but not for long.

The slight rapping entered my mind unnoticed at first, but as I emerged from sleep it grew louder. When I suddenly jerked myself fully awake I still didn't know what it was, but it sounded again and I pulled a robe on and went to the door.

I lifted the curtain at the window just enough to look out and could only make out a dark shape huddled by the door. The sliver of moon didn't afford much light, but even without seeing, I knew who it was.

I unlatched the door silently, knowing how sound carried in the still of night, and as soon as I swung it halfway open, Red Cloud slipped inside.

"Gray Feather," he said in Cheyenne. "I have gone to the village on the great plain and told of your being here. Our people wait for me to bring you to them. Will you come, now?"

The words struck me like a thunderbolt. Now. Leaving Jory and the white world that had been my home for seven years. Suddenly I wanted very much to tell him to go away, I was staying, but I couldn't. I was going.

"Yes," I said. "I'll go with you."

"Get dressed and I will get your horse. Meet me behind the house as soon as you are ready."

I nodded and he was already out the door. It all happened so fast I almost thought I was dreaming, but I knew I wasn't. I ran into my room and threw on a blouse and skirt for the ride to my cache.

Running around in a frenzy, I got out my saddlebags and began to throw things into them. Besides my buckskins, I had a brush, my mirror, as much food and coffee as I could fit, and a couple of knives I had bought earlier. I tried to think what else I would need but my brain refused to function well and I couldn't think at all. Finally I tied the thongs and ran into the living room.

How could I leave like this, I thought. How could I leave Jory with no explanations, no apologies. Quickly I grabbed a piece of brown paper and a pencil and wrote to Jory.

"Dear Jory," I wrote, "I'm sorry to leave like this but I must go with Red Cloud. He will take me to my father. Adele can have any of my things because I've taken all I need. Please forgive me. I'm truly sorry to leave you like this. Don't try to follow me. Maybe someday we'll meet again. At least I would like to think so."

I read the letter over and hated it, but I had no time to write another. I prayed Jory would understand and not be angry with me. Leaving the note on the table and the door unlocked, I went around the back and found Red Cloud holding Thunder and his own horse, a bay gelding I hadn't seen before. Throwing ourselves up on our horses, we set out through the back streets of town and across the prairie.

We rode for hours. I had noticed that Red Cloud followed a trail, although one I couldn't see in the dim moonlight. He led us along the edge of low hills and then west where we crested swell after swell of buffalo grass in our flight. Since he seemed well versed in the trail, I lay low on Thunder's back and let him follow Red Cloud's bay.

The night seemed endless and unreal. I tracked the moon as it crept over us, then hung low before us on the horizon. After so many hours I ceased to think about what we were doing and sat Thunder in a mindless trance, listening to the quiet plodding of the horses' feet. I wondered how long Red Cloud would go until we stopped, but had no desire to ask. I let him lead us as long as he wanted

Shortly before dawn, he pulled his horse north toward a creek lined with cottonwoods. We found a wash backed by the bluff of the creek and sheltered by the trees and slept until the sun was well up. I was so tired I fell asleep instantly and when Red Cloud roused me it seemed that only minutes had passed.

We went on almost due west, sometimes trotting, mostly loping. The landscape rose and flattened beneath our feet, then disappeared behind us. I thought about my journey from New York to Leavenworth, when I had the leisure to watch scenery go by and even became bored by it. Now I barely saw anything around me. Every muscle in my body was aching and the sun was giving me an awful headache. I felt like the insides of my thighs were rubbed raw and my throat was dry. If Red Cloud ever thought to stop for water, he made no sign.

We made one other brief stop sometime after noon, then kept on. Finally Red Cloud turned us north again into some wooded hills and I was grateful for the shade. The pace was necessarily slower in the trees and even Thunder hung his head as if dead tired.

We rode up the hill, then across the ridge and down the other side. After an hour or so, Red Cloud crested a smaller ridge and stopped. While I sat resting he called like a bird, and in short time we heard an answering call.

Suddenly no longer tired, I urged Thunder after the bay and we made our way down the ridge. I strained to see through the trees but could make out no shapes out of the ordinary. I looked down at the path ahead of us, then up again and he was there.

Barred Owl.

I don't remember pulling Thunder to a stop, but I must have, for I sat and stared ecstatically at the man before me. He, as much as my father, was the reason I had come so far and braved so much. This was the man I had loved as a child, had prayed for, had waited impatiently for to send a spokesman to tie horses outside my father's lodge and ask for me in marriage. This was the man that, when I was not grieving for my mother and my lost life, I was wondering what he was doing, feeling and thinking.

He stepped toward me and I slid off Thunder and went forward to meet him. When only two feet separated us, I stopped.

He was more handsome than I'd remembered, and more rough hewn. I must have smoothed his features over in my worn memories, but now I saw how angular his face was, how sharp grooves lined his mouth and how his nose curved sharply from between black, bottomless eyes. His hair was parted and braided, the braids laced with rawhide strips. He was clad in a breechcloth and high moccasins, the leanly muscled wall of his chest bare to me the way no white man's had ever been —except Jory's. With a rush I realized how glad I was to be among my people again, people devoid of the pretenses and restraints I'd endured for the last seven years.

"Barred Owl," I breathed, his name in the Cheyenne language rolling off my tongue delightedly.

"Is it you, Gray Feather?" he asked in awe. I realized that while I had been drinking in the cherished sight of him, he had been taking in every aspect of my appearance, and I understood what a shock this must have been. No doubt I had been buried, emotionally, along with all those who died in Dog Creek, and now I was resurrected before him. I smiled happily.

"Yes, it is I, Barred Owl. I have come home. I have come back from the white man's land, back to my people."

Barred Owl's black eyes touched on my hair, loose and tangled, on my trail-dirty buckskins, on my begrimed yet radiant face. He smiled at me with a restraint that wounded me.

"Your father will give great thanks that you have returned. He mourned you for a long time, as he would for a son. He will be glad to see you."

"Are you glad?" I asked, stepping closer. It was a foolish question, asked by a white woman and not a Cheyenne, but I was tired and nervous and I wanted Barred Owl to reassure me. After traveling so far, I couldn't bear it if he no longer cared about me, but my question surprised him and seemed to render him speechless. Finally, when I thought I would cry from frustration, he put out his hand and touched my cheek lightly with the tips of his fingers. It was as much as I could hope for.

"Come to camp," he said finally. He took Thunder's rein and we walked on down the ridge to the rude camp they had set up. Three other men were there and they sat expectantly around a small smokeless fire as we approached. They all knew Red Cloud, of course, but Barred Owl had to introduce me.

Antelope I remembered as Barred Owl's younger brother. He took more after their mother than Barred Owl, and had a different look, more fleshy and rounded as opposed to Barred Owl's lean angularity. But he was younger than I, I recalled, and had not grown completely into the lanky stage of young men. He would no doubt become lean and hard in the next few years.

Rain the Mountains was from a different band and I did not remember him. He was what whites would call a cousin to Barred Owl, although that term was unknown to the Cheyenne. The son of Barred Owl's uncle, he had grown up in the band of his mother's people, as was the Cheyenne custom. Children belonged to their mother's band, young men only moving to another, their wife's, when they married.

The third man, Buffalo Robe, was also from another band, and not a relative to Barred Owl. He was a sharp-featured, intense man, the same age as Barred Owl, who apparently had joined the others on their renegade raids. He, as well as the others, recognized me as Painted Lance's daughter, and they all treated me with curt respect. While Barred Owl tied Thunder to their makeshift picket line, I took a seat near the fire and waited to find out what we would do next.

We didn't waste much time. After a quick evening meal of jerked buffalo meat and some discussion of which way to go, we set out again. I almost said something about the possibility of Jory's following us, but it seemed that Red Cloud had already thought of that, and he urged the others on. The four mature braves were ready to return to the great summer camp and voiced no argument about pressing on. I felt sorry for Thunder being pushed so hard, but it couldn't be helped.

As we rode farther westward in silence, I

allowed the knowledge and sensation of being home wash over me in joyous waves. I had done it! I had come back to my people, just as I had always sworn I would. Just seeing the hard, dark back of Barred Owl ahead of me and hearing the infrequent, quiet words of caution between the others sent ripples of happy wonder shivering down my spine. After seven miserable years, I had begun to wonder if I would ever accomplish it, and now I had! Nothing could dampen my ecstacy—not my less-than-joyous welcome from Barred Owl—not even the loss of Jory. I was home. I was where I belonged.

There was little time for conversation. We rode in quiet deliberation, alternating between a lope and a restful, strength-conserving walk. Buffalo Robe seemed to spearhead our drive and we normally took our direction from him. We kept to a westward course, without much variation, even after darkness fell.

At one point, just shortly after full dark but before the moon had climbed very high, Buffalo Robe led us down a half-dry creek bed and we wound around the watercourse's bends until we found a sheltered bluff. There he and Barred Owl took a stance before the rest of us, Barred Owl's hand on Thunder's bit to keep the horse quiet. We all waited, motionless and silent, for several minutes and I wondered briefly if my years in New York had dulled my senses so much that I alone heard nothing but the sighing of the prairie breezes, and if the others heard something I did not, distinctive and dangerous. Then, finally, I heard the peculiarly distant pounding of horses' hooves far away on hard prairie soil, and I knew a flash of fear. The others seemed unmoved; just still and watchful. I allowed myself to relax and tried to hone my senses on the sound. It was several horses—ten or twenty, I guessed, and not more than a half mile from us. The muted rumble of their hooves became louder as they neared, but the gait of the party was loping and easy, not the frantic pounding of a group giving chase. As the wave of sound rolled closer, I could distinguish separate hooffalls. I twined my fingers worriedly in Thunder's mane and he shrugged the taut skin over his withers in irritation. Mindful of the need for absolute silence, I unwound my fingers from the horsehair and sat stone-still, my breath lodged deep in my lungs. It was cavalry; I knew it was cavalry.

They continued on, past us, and the sound of their horses faded into the east.

Heading back to Leavenworth, I assumed gratefully. Where had they come from? Fort Kearney? I tried to recall Jory's quickly sketched map and knew Kearney was northwest of Leavenworth, on the Platte River. The overland stage went that way, but I knew we had skittered away from the well-traveled stage route. The soldiers, no doubt, did the same. I was thankful that they were too hasty or too confident to look for Indians. We could continue unhampered.

We rode for two or three hours after that, then

294

stopped in a sheltered bowl to make camp. I took it upon myself to do the woman's chores and broke out all the supplies I had crammed in my saddlebags. My companions eyed me over a smokeless fire as I made coffee, which they liked but seldom got, and happily accepted the bacon I cooked. Antelope slipped out with his bow and brought back a fat prairie chicken that we enjoyed as well. It was a good dinner for traveling as lightly as we were, and the men seemed satisfied as they sat around the small fire.

For a time they discusssed the way we would proceed the next day and I was content to simply sit and listen. It was a marvel to me hearing the tongue spoken so easily and naturally. I had been afraid I would be sketchy on some things, but the language flowed in and around me as if I had heard it every day of my life. Hearing my Indian name spoken again was like being found after wandering alone for seven years. And having Barred Owl so near excited all the senses of my body.

I watched him covetously as he spoke with the others. I could still see the slow cautiousness that had characterized him as a youth. Never headstrong, he had early won the approval of some of the older warriors because of his thoughtful, all-seeing thoroughness. The boy had not grown into an emotional man, ruled by feelings and blind to careful consideration. He was a deliberate reasoner, and would strive to see all aspects of a situation before he put himself or another of his blood in danger.

So now I watched him weigh the choices before us, ask the others for more information, and suggest possible advantages or drawbacks. I noted how the others answered him respectfully, listening carefully. He was what I had always known he would be—a leader of men, respected and looked up to. The promise I had seen in him years before was truth now.

But he was more than that. Seeing him now through the eyes of a twenty-year-old, I knew him as a masculine being, a sexual being, and his nearness excited me. I allowed myself the luxury of noting how large and expressive his hands were, and wondered how they might feel against my body. His chest was leanly muscled and hard, and I found myself stiffening at the thought of my breasts crushed against it, my nipples hardening at the touch. The smooth skin of his back rippled over the broad muscles there, and I imagined it was my hands flickering across his flesh instead of the muted firelight. At thirteen I had seen him only as a storybook husband, now I saw him as a man, alive and virile and arousing.

A decision was reached concerning our journey's next leg, and Barred Owl looked to me curiously. Caught dreaming, I smiled quickly and cast my eyes down. I had no idea if my desire shone in my eyes or not, but I could not trust myself to face him for a few seconds. Virginal maidens did not dream about warriors as I had for him. Knowledge of my thoughts would shock him;

I had to assume my rightful role.

"It is good that you came now," he said to me quietly. "The camp is good and all the bands are still on the plain."

I raised my eyes to him, subdued. "Tell me about the camp. About the hunting and the dances."

Barred Owl smiled slowly, his dark eyes exploring my eager face. "We killed many buffalo, and antelope as well. The dances are over, but they were good. The medicine arrows were renewed, and many young men swung to the pole."

I nodded, remembering. My years-old memories showed me the silent, smoke-shrouded ritual of renewal and the steamy, intense anguish of the Sun Dance. I flicked my eyes briefly to Barred Owl's chest and noted the slanting scars across the flesh of each breast. He had swung to the pole— years ago. While I was still imprisoned in New York.

"And my father?" I asked finally.

"Well," Barred Owl pronounced. "He is a Contrary now."

I started in surprise. "A Contrary?" My voice was a mixture of pride and dismay.

Barred Owl nodded. "After you were stolen away, he grieved for a very long time. Some say he became fearful, for your mother was the second wife taken from him, and you, his only child, were lost to him. He took up the Thunder Bow from Walks in Shade, and became fearless. He led a war party against the whites and counted first coup on two of them before the others killed them. And single-handed he has stolen horses from the Crow. He has been a Contrary now five summers and he is respected as one of the greatest."

"So he did not marry again?" I asked.

"No. Once he took up the Thunder Bow, he kept himself alone. He took it as a sign from the Thunder that he was meant to stay alone, after Dog Creek."

I nodded, knowing well that as a Contrary my father would live alone in a red tepee removed from the others, and that he would not socialize with the rest of the band. I had hoped to be able to live with him once I rejoined the others, but now I knew that would be impossible. I would have to arrange something else when I got to camp. Just what, I wasn't sure.

"Do the rest of the people know I am returning?" I asked tentatively.

"Yes," Barred Owl said, obviously pleased. "We had already returned to camp from our last raid when Red Cloud arrived, so we started back out right away. We decided also that Red Cloud has been away from the white man's town so long that they would be suspicious of him, so he will remain in camp with us now. When we return, it will be with two prizes."

I blushed happily at Barred Owl's slight praise. Seeing his eyes smile at me made my skin tingle, and I thought again of how it would be to be his wife. Since lying with Jory, I was well aware that love didn't end with a look or a kiss. For a fleeting moment I wondered if Jory had turned me into a cursed wanton, but I pushed the thought aside. It was not as if I felt such things for any man, and, after all, Barred Owl and I had been betrothed at one time. Was it so awful to desire the man I should have married?

"And you," I asked quietly, "have you married?"

Again, it was not a question for a Cheyenne maiden to ask a warrior, but I had to know. I could not even force myself to cast my eyes down timidly, for I wanted so desperately to hear the right answer. Because I was so bold, though, I saw the surprised question in Barred Owl's face. He was unused to such talk from a woman and was not pleased by it. After a moment of cautious silence, he answered me.

"Yes," he nodded. "Grass in the Wind is my wife."

I was immediately wounded by his answer, but schooled my features into stoic acceptance. Grass in the Wind was a sort of cousin to me, the daughter of my father's first wife's sister. She was the only "relative" I had in our little band, and I remembered her as a fragile child, willowy and graceful. A year or two younger than I, she had always seemed to possess a childlike beauty. I had not thought of her for many years, but suddenly I remembered that she had also been at Dog Creek.

"How did she survive the massacre?" I asked hesitantly.

Barred Owl's eyes clouded. "She almost did not. She was shot in the upper thigh and left for dead, but luckily the braves returned soon enough and took her to be healed. She is all right now."

Something in his tone sounded sour to me, and I searched his face for what it might be. His features were smooth and unmarked and unreadable. Whatever it was—and I was sure there was something—Barred Owl would not tell me. I had no choice but to let the matter drop, even though it pained me to have him shut me out. I tried a different subject.

"Do you have children?"

Then the smoothness of his face was lanced with a sudden, fleeting look of anger, and he turned away from me. "No," he said in a harsh whisper.

Then I understood.

───────────────Chapter Ten

BEFORE DAWN had brightened the eastern sky I heard the men rousing and I forced myself up. My body felt battered and bruised, as if I had been dragged behind Thunder all the day before instead of seated on him. I went upstream to wash in the cold creek that ran by camp but even the icy water could not ease my tiredness. Barred Owl must have noticed how awful I felt, for he helped me up on Thunder.

"We will ride easier today," he said. "But we must make sure you will not be followed."

"Yes," I agreed. "I understand. I hope no one is following. I left a note that I was leaving willingly, so the whites wouldn't worry." I wondered if

Red Cloud had said anything to Barred Owl about my asociation with Jory, but Barred Owl's face was impassive. I felt sure his concern was only cautionary.

We headed out just as the eastern horizon was paling and the misty dawn was clearing. Once on our way again, I didn't feel so bad, but whenever Thunder hit a prairie dog hole or jostled me, my body ached.

I had forgotten how expansive the prairie was. Although more or less flat, it was arranged in rolling swells so that we could not always see to the horizon. We were riding halfway between the Platte and the Arkansas so could not see either river, but small streams wound over our path occasionally and then disappeared behind us. It was an ever changing landscape for anyone who would look, but I was more interested in the western horizon.

We stopped in the heat of the day to eat a small portion. We didn't bother with a fire but ate jerky and some hard biscuits I had thrown into my bag, plus what was left of the prairie chicken. Buffalo Robe didn't even eat that, but scouted about on his horse around our camp until we mounted again. I wasn't sure if he was more worried about running into cavalry or enemy Indians but guessed it must have been the latter. We were quite a way from the stage line by now and didn't expect to see any whites about.

The rest of the day was uneventful; just riding, fording a stream and riding on. My soreness began to ebb away, either that or I was just too numb to notice it. I began to feel as if I were molded to Thunder and that we moved as one animal. It was going to be difficult for me to cross over from white to Indian again, but I was determined I would do it.

When we made camp for the night I realized I was running low on what I had brought to eat. Luckily I had more coffee and I still had some molasses, but everything else was gone. Antelope, Rain in the Mountains and Buffalo Robe took their bows and went off hunting on foot. At the last minute, Red Cloud ran after them, and Barred Owl and I were left alone by the fire.

"Your soreness is going?" he asked me politely. He sat a little way around the fire from me so I could study his face. Although he seemed unnecessarily solicitious, his eyes were gentle on me and it pleased me to have this chance to talk alone.

"Yes," I said, "it's better now."

"Good. We still have another day and a half before we reach camp, but then you will be able to rest."

I smiled gratefully. "That will be nice. It will be so good to be back with the people."

"You do not care for the white ways?" he asked.

"A very few," I said, "but not many. I do not like their crowded towns, or the many restrictions they have. There is so much a person should not do to be well thought of, and more that a woman is not allowed to do at all."

"We have restrictions also," he said.

"Yes, but they never seemed unreasonable to me, or difficult to understand. Perhaps it is because I was raised to the Cheyenne way first, but the white ways are too confining to me. I could never go back and live in the east again. I could not be happy there."

Barred Owl gestured to my outfit. "I have not seen white women dressed as you are."

"They don't," I said. "This was made for me by an Arapahoe friend. It was difficult to ride with white woman's clothes, so I had these made. They are much more practical."

He nodded in understanding but not, I could tell, in agreement. Cheyenne women traditionally wore soft leather dresses that came to mid-calf with moccasins underneath, and left leggings to the men. Barred Owl would have been more comfortable with me if I had dressed that way, but I had already decided I would keep my buckskins. Besides being practical, they reminded me of Angel—and Jory. Turning my back on the white society did not, to me, mean turning my back on good friends and happy memories.

"You have grown up in a pleasing way," Barred Owl said suddenly, his cool tone at odds with the way his eyes caressed my face. "You did not marry a white man?"

"No," I said, shaking my head demurely. "I found none that I wished to marry, for I could not tell them I was half Cheyenne. Most white men hold Indian women in great contempt, and half-breeds even more so. If I had wanted to marry, I would have been forced to lie about my blood and there was no man I would do that for."

Even as I spoke with the truthful ring of indignation in my voice, I thought of Jory. He alone had not thought me contemptible, and yet I could never have stayed with him and not yearned for my Cheyenne home. Marriage—to any man—had no place in my life until I was settled back among my people.

Barred Owl's face was thoughtful, and yet I felt he was pleased with my answer. Of that I was glad, at least.

"But what of Spotted Calf Woman?" I asked. "Does she still live?" My father's sister was the closest relative I could remember, although she had lived in another band. All this talk of marriage and belonging made me think more seriously of how I would live at the Cheyenne camp.

I nodded, grateful for that. "I had thought I might live with her, since I cannot live with my father. I will have no lodge of my own."

"I think Spotted Calf Woman would welcome her brother's child," he said carefully. "Or you could live with me and Grass in the Wind."

I watched him closely, looking for a sign of how he meant that. He could be just offering me a place to sleep or it could be much more. Since Grass in the Wind could get him no children and she was, for practical purposes, my sister, no one would blame Barred Owl for taking me as a second wife. It was not uncommon in Cheyenne bands—but I hadn't expected it from him. Whatever his reasons were, he seemed unwilling to explain any further, and I realized I would have to consider his proposal with no more qualification than that. It was not hard for me to decide.

"If Grass in the Wind would welcome me, I would be glad to live in your lodge," I answered politely. No matter what his reasons, living with him among my own band was preferable to living with Spotted Calf Woman. My heart pounded loudly in my ribcage at the thought of sharing a lodge with Barred Owl and being intimately close to him, yet I had no assurance from him that he would take me as his wife. I didn't care. I would be near him—and my father—and that was all that mattered to me.

"Good," he said shortly and nodded once to seal the agreement. We would have time later to analyze our roles. For now, our companionable silence bound us, even when the others returned with a freshly killed antelope for our dinner. I left Barred Owl by the fire and helped to prepare the meal.

For the next day and a half, our routine was much the same. We rode countless miles and clambered gratefully off our horses at each rest stop, sleeping the sleep of the dead when we dared. We had little time for social conversation, and yet it seemed that Barred Owl could always lope his horse near mine, or we could sit close by the fire. We had no more chances for private talks, but I felt his eyes on me sometimes, and I was content with that.

When we crested a prairie swell and I saw the great camp at last, I could have cried with happiness. My heart swelled with pride at the sight of so many Cheyenne amid their sun-bright tepees, the circle of the camp resting securely in a great bowl of ground. A lump of unshed tears rose in my throat and a thankfulness washed over me that I had feared to ever feel again. How good it was to be home!

We rode down the tide of prairie grass directly into the mouth of the horseshoe-shaped camp. Facing always east, it was as if the inanimate camp itself welcomed and embraced me. I sat tall on Thunder and tried to quell the powerful emotions that weakened and shook my body.

It all looked so familiar to me. The horseshoe ranged imperiously around me, the individual bands arranged along its arms according to custom just as they always had. The flaps of all the lodges opened to the east, so my view of the people was as direct as was their view of me and my companions. Before we had walked past the first band's lodges, we had a vanguard of children and curious adults surrounding us. They smiled and called to me happily.

As our crowd of well-wishers grew, my escort thinned. All but Barred Owl drifted off to their own lodges and families while Barred Owl and I pressed forward to our familiar place on the northern arm of the camp circle. The sea of upturned brown faces heartened me, but I was eager to see my band, to slip off Thunder and stand again among my own. I don't know if Barred Owl sensed my desire, but he led me slowly onward past our greeters until we arrived at my small band's location.

I was overcome with emotion. My throat closed painfully and my eyes swam with tears. Several small boys fought good-naturedly over who would take our horses to picket, but I slid off Thunder and walked past them, caring for nothing but the sight of the decorated lodges before me. The designs of earthen paint and quills leaped out at me, the abstractions of buffalo and horses and greater powers like a revelation to me. Given the chance, I would have gladly sunk down to the grass and cried my happiness into the earth.

But lonesome prayers were not for me yet. Scores of people pressed around me, calling my name in welcome surprise. They all knew me, knew I was coming, and yet it was difficult for me to recognize any of them. The girls I had known were women now, the children were teenagers, and I could not match faces to names. I was lost amid them, but not alone. My hands were grasped by others in a friendly fashion, and the sleeves of my buckskins were tugged playfully.

"Wait," I begged them in the face of their jostling and questioning. "I will talk to you all and tell you my story, but I don't know—I don't remember all of you—"

Barred Owl stepped close to me and waved the others away with a friendly ease.

"Later, my friends," he told them. "Later Gray

Feather will answer your questions. Now she is tired and needs to rest."

I pressed close to him gratefully and silently promised the departing people more of my time later. But for now, Barred Owl was right. I was exhausted.

It was then that I saw Grass in the Wind. She came forward quietly, her gentle face shining with joy. I knew she hadn't seen Barred Owl for at least a week, yet she and he only exchanged a quick, speaking glance, and if she noted how I clung to Barred Owl in my excitement, she made no show of it. Instead she came directly to me, her arms outstretched in genuine friendship.

"Gray Feather, my sister," she said softly. We hugged each other happily and I felt the tears pooling again.

"Grass in the Wind," I managed. "I am so happy to see you again. I am so happy to be here!"

Grass in the Wind laughed tremulously at my outburst and pulled me toward her lodge. Her smile lit up her face with a beauty I envied, and I unwillingly glanced back at Barred Owl. He nodded at the two of us with satisfaction, then strode across the camp. I could only follow after Grass in the Wind and hope that our friendship would survive.

"Come into our lodge," she insisted. "Have you eaten? You must be tired after so long a journey."

"Yes, I am," I replied gratefully. "But I'm not hungry. I'm too excited to be hungry!"

Grass in the Wind laughed at me again, and

preceded me into the lodge. I stepped inside and stopped to accustom my eyes to the cool dimness, then followed her around to the right, toward the back of the lodge. At least my Cheyenne manners had not deserted me. I knew without having to think that the owners' private area was to the left and no guest ever went that direction from the door. Instead Grass in the Wind pulled me down amid cushioning buffalo robes at the back and pressed a horn bowl of boiled meat into my hands.

"You must eat," she said. "It will give you strength."

"Oh, I couldn't," I told her. "Not yet. There is so much I want to know, so many questions I want to ask. How have you been? I hardly recognized anyone. Tell me who is here. Who else survived Dog Creek?"

My careless questions caught her off guard and I saw a shadow of pain flicker across her dark eyes and was instantly sorry. Undaunted, she smiled and took one of my hands in hers.

"Three of us were wounded but still lived. Quail Woman is here, married now to Wolf Shadow, and Leaves Falling Woman survived. Others escaped unhurt in the confusion—Yellow She-Bear and her son, Elk Robe; Willow, and Coral Sky Woman, and some others. We were all very lucky."

"Yes," I agreed. "Very lucky." I was glad to hear that there hadn't been the wholesale slaughter my mind seemed to remember, but no doubt my thirteen-year-old emotions had become embedded with the visions of death and dying. I was relieved to know my memories were not as accurate as I had thought.

"Tell me of the camp," I urged. "Barred Owl told me about my father. What of everyone else? I want to know everything."

Grass in the Wind laughed at my feverish questions, no doubt wondering when I had lost my Cheyenne patience and taken up the white man's ways. She mentioned names to me, telling who had married, who had children, who had died. With each name I tried to pluck a face from my memory, then add seven years of living to it. It was no use. I couldn't imagine those people any way but as I had last seen them.

"And you and Barred Owl," I finally asked in a conversational tone. "You two have been married some years?"

"Three summers," she admitted happily. Although her eyes sparkled at the mention of her husband and she answered me readily, I felt that she watched me more intently than she gave away. She knew I had been Barred Owl's choice of wife. Was she jealous? I thought not, for it was she who now held that place at his side, not I.

"And he is a respected warrior," I added without question.

"Yes." Grass in the Wind beamed. "He is of the Kit Fox Men, as his father was. I have even heard others say he may become its chief one day."

I shared her pride, but felt a niggling stab of dread at her boast. The Fox soldiers were the greatest of the soldier societies, the police force of the tribe, and she had every right to be proud of Barred Owl. But I shivered at the thought of his becoming a chief. That position was great and venerable—and normally culminated in death. A brave warrior would much rather die in glorious battle than shrink, aged and toothless, into a fleshless old man, but soldier chiefs were men prepared to die—willing to die in the flush of manhood. Again, my white self pressed forward and I let go a silent, fervent prayer that Barred Owl never become a Kit Fox chief.

Pushing aside my morbid thoughts, I asked her more questions. Had she joined a quilling society? What other young braves were now soldiers? Did she still have much work to do on skins and robes before camp broke up? She answered all my questions happily, finally passing me a pair of newly made moccasins that she was quilling, and while we talked, she reintroduced me to the art I had never been very good at. It felt good to sit beside her, however, and chat with hands busy. I knew instinctively that she would welcome me into her lodge even as a second wife to Barred Owl if it came to the that. She was sure and happy in her life; her place in the tribe was orderly and assured. She could afford to welcome me. With a bittersweet sadness I realized all I had lost when I had been wrenched away from my band. I knew inside that I would never have the calm sense of acceptance and belonging that she had.

Sometime in midafternoon, a polite cough sounded outside the lodge, as if someone cleared his throat. Grass in the Wind called admittance, and an aged man stepped inside. Following etiquette, he came around the right side of the tepee and took a seat near me.

"Dog Wolf," Grass in the Wind acknowledged.

Dog Wolf nodded a greeting. "There will be feasting tonight at the Lodge of Long Claws Curling, and storytelling. Long Claws Curling asks that Barred Owl's lodge come and join him in food and stories."

Grass in the Wind grinned at me knowingly. "Barred Owl's lodge will come," she said. "We are grateful for Long Claws Curling's invitation."

The old man seemed pleased, and passed a few more minutes with us in polite conversation, his eyes curious on me, then left. Grass in the Wind chuckled.

"Why do you laugh?" I asked suspiciously. "You said the hunt was good. Is that not a good time for a feast?"

"Oh, it is good," she agreed quickly. "But the storytelling will be much more interesting. I think everyone there will want to hear stories from you."

Then it dawned on me. Of course! The Cheyenne were tolerant, yet curious, and they would want to hear about the white man's world from one of their own. Too often a white trapper or cavalry man would make contact and talk of white ways, but never in a way that was easily understood. Too many things were left unsaid or, more often, unexplained. Any stories I told would have a

Cheyenne viewpoint.

"I understand," I sighed playfully. "I will have little feasting myself, then, until I tell my stories."

Grass in the Wind nodded, then sobered. "Do white men tell stories as we do? Do they enjoy such feasting and gathering?"

"Perhaps not in quite the same way, but they do feast and tell stories. I think the difference is that white men build upon their stories so as to appear better in the eyes of their people. They are not as truthful as the Cheyenne."

Grass in the Wind nodded. I hadn't, I realized, told her anything new. How many treaties—pens touched to paper—had been broken in the last years? How many white flags had been raised—white man's own symbol of peace—only to be shot down? Every kind of Indian knew the duplicity of whites. It was one of the major reasons the Cheyenne avoided them as much as possible.

"We will have a good night at Long Claws Curling's," Grass in the Wind pronounced. She smiled at me and I caught her eyes. We both laughed and resumed our quilling.

That night was good. By the time the three of us walked across the camp to the lodge of Long Claws Curling, I already felt embraced by the Cheyenne. I was at ease with my hosts and felt that they had accepted me totally. When we entered the already crowded lodge and edged back along the lodge skin behind the other guests, room was made for us close at the right side of Water Woman, Long

Claws's wife. Only a very honored guest would be seated to the left of Long Claws, so I had no illusions of that. It was enough that I sat on the close right.

The feasting was richer than I ever remembered. We had buffalo ribs and boiled tongue, tender young antelope and plump prairie chicken. At the beginning of the feast, Long Claws Curling set aside a little bit of each to the spirits, and a prayer was said; then we were free to eat. It seemed that every one of the twenty-odd people there pressed rich food upon me, and I had to caution myself to eat sparingly. My stomach was no longer used to the fatty, gamy meat, and I ate slowly while my system became reacquainted. Since I was still intoxicated by the nearness of my people, it wasn't difficult for me to forget the food in order to watch and listen.

The first story was called for when everyone had been satiated. Bearded Bull, an older man from Water Woman's band, had a story that was his own, meaning no one else could tell it unless given permission by Bearded Bull. It was apparently a favorite, as everyone but me became excited at the prospect. I rested my overworked stomach and listened closely.

"My father was Splintered Tree, of the Dog Soldiers, and was for many years their chief. He was great and fearless, and counted many coups on the Crow and the Ute. One summer, during the month when horses get fat, he led a raid against the Crow in order to get horses. He and six others went by night to a Crow camp and there they stole many horses, all the horses the Crow had at their picket line. They drove the horses back toward their homeland, running very fast, but the Crow mounted their war horses outside their lodges and came after. When my father realized they must fight or lose the horses, he called for his companions to stand against the Crow, and this they did. They struck with lances and axes, but the Crow were crazy with anger and would not be subdued. Finally it seemed that our Cheyenne would not win against them, and they turned to flee.

"My father then called upon the magic of his medicine and all the spirits, and brought out his dog rope. With the rawhide strap about his shoulder, he leaped from his horse and drove the pin into the ground, then called to his brothers to return and free him. So long as his dog rope remained pinned to the ground, he could not retreat, and he would surely die unless his companions returned to fight the Crow and pull out the pin that bound him."

I caught my breath. This was not the first story I had heard about a warrior using a dog rope, but it was nonetheless exciting. I had seen dog ropes—spans of rawhide six or eight feet long and a handspan wide with a shoulder loop on one end and a wooden pin at the other. They were carried only by the bravest of men, and highly decorated with paint or quills. Once a warrior committed himself to a fight by pinning himself to the ground on his dog rope, nothing could save him but the pulling out the pin by another Cheyenne. A man thus pinned would be rescued or died. There was no other way.

"The Cheyenne returned. My father fought valiantly on the ground, thrusting his lance again and again at the Crow upon their horses as they attacked him. One of the enemy sliced my father's shoulder with a lance, but still he fought. One split the lower bone of his arm with an axe, and he still fought them. His medicine was very great, and the Crow began to look worriedly upon him for he would not fall before them. My father made great noisy cries until even the Crow horses became fearful, and then his brothers descended upon the enemies and drove them back. One Crow was killed retreating, and the others fled back to their empty camp. My father's brother, Porcupine, finally pulled out the pin of the dog rope and set my father free. All seven of the Cheyenne returned home safely and each had many, many horses to give away."

I expelled my held breath, glad that Bearded Bull's story had a happy ending. While he told it, I had seen it all in my mind's eye, and I swelled with pride for my fierce, noble people. Was it any wonder the Cheyenne were known first and foremost as mighty warriors?

Then, suddenly, it was my turn. The people in the lodge clamored for my story and I tried to think of one that might compare to that of Bearded Bull. I was at a loss. I knew no stories of great bravery or magical happenings, nothing that

317

I knew to be unquestionably true, for truth was a necessity among the Cheyenne.

"I am embarrassed," I managed finally. "The ways of the white world do not make for stories such as Bearded Bull's. I know no man as brave as Splintered Tree, and no magic as strong as our medicine bags." The people whispered alarmingly, appalled that I had no stories of magic.

"But," I said, "instead of a story, I will tell you all that you ask of me. What questions do you have? I will answer them all."

Now this was more like it! They warmed to me immediately, asking about the great iron horse that snorted and squealed along its wood and iron paths, asking about the lodges in the great white camps, asking about clothes and industries and implements. I answered as meticulously as I could, describing the elaborate berths on the railroads, the grand trappings of the riverboats, the useless yet luxurious furnishings of homes in New York. My audience marveled over my description of a ballroom completely enclosed by mirrored walls, and they laughed behind their hands at the idea of a white woman wearing twenty petticoats beneath her skirt. I described fringed carriages and smoothly paved streets, five-story buildings and indoor plumbing. My Cheyenne devoured every word, like children fed candy, and demanded more. It was all I could do to keep up with their questions.

And somewhere during my recitation, I began to

feel Barred Owl's reluctant respect. Although seated next to him, my gaze seldom rested on him, so demanding was the rest of my audience, but I could feel his eyes on me as I described bicycles and cast-iron ovens and I felt more than saw his grudging admiration. Yes, I was different from the other Cheyenne, I was different from what I had been, but different was not necessarily worse. Ever since I had come face to face with Barred Owl days ago, I had confused him, surprised him —and not always pleasantly. Now I pleased him. He was enjoying my white man's fairy tales, and he was enjoying the fact that I, the new pied piper of stories, was of his lodge.

I felt very sure that my new friends would have kept me talking all night had I not finally pleaded for rest of my dry throat. Some were plainly disappointed, but the feast had been a success, the stories even more so, and no one complained loudly or for long. It was later than a gathering such as this normally lasted and once thanks and goodbyes were said, everyone began to fade through the night toward their own lodges.

Grass in the Wind was still smiling with excitement as we walked to our tepee. She, I had noticed, had been caught up in my wonderous tales, laughing or clapping her hands in childlike awe.

"The things you say are so amazing," she said finally. "It must be very wonderful to see all these things and know that they are true as you tell them."

"Yes," I said slowly, considering the fact that white man's industries had ceased to be amazing to me years ago. "But they are true."

"Oh, I believe you!" she said quickly. To be accused of lying was a grave dishonor; Grass in the Wind rushed to reassure me.

I laughed at her. "I know you do. And because you are my sister of my heart, I give my stories to you so that you may tell them, also."

Grass in the Wind clutched my hand in ecstatic thanks. "Oh, Gray Feather, I am so grateful! I will only tell exactly what you have said and I will use only your words. Your stories will stay as you have said them forever."

I was pleased that my gesture had brought so much joy to her, and I lifted contented eyes to Barred Owl. The look he met me with shook me. His dark eyes shone with gratitude and admiration and—what? Interest? Desire? I was afraid to guess. Disturbed by his eyes and the shiver that coursed up my spine, I dropped my eyes.

We came to our lodge and I felt the pleasant sensation retreat before a nervous fear.

"I think," Barred Owl said in a low voice, "this lodge will be happy with two women in it."

I froze before the doorway, tense and waiting. For a half second, Grass in the Wind was as still as I, but then, gracefully and without pretense, she came to me and hugged me.

"It is my belief that what Barred Owl says is true," she told me, looking deeply into my eyes.

"And mine also," I agreed, hugging her back. "I thank you for allowing me to make your home my own."

Inside, we went about the evening duties of banking our cook fire and arranging the buffalo robe beds on the south side of the lodge. Although we'd all come to agreement on my staying in the lodge, still no word had been said about my exact place, and I could not dismiss the gnawing nervousness I felt. Grass in the Wind chatted happily as she helped me spread the artfully tanned robes, her contentment both soothing and worrisome to me. What would happen now? Barred Owl sat complacently at the back of the lodge, leaning against a willow backrest, smoking patiently. If he noticed or disagreed with the fact that Grass in the Wind arranged a bed for me on his other side, he said nothing. My heart pounded against my ribs. When Grass in the Wind was finished, the three beds lay side by side, mine on one side, hers on the other—and Barred Owl's in between.

Was this how it was to be, then? When I agreed to live here, had I agreed to this convenient arrangement? I couldn't be jealous of Grass in the Wind, no matter my feelings for Barred Owl; she was too dear to me. And I had been raised to this possibility from birth. Polygamy was not novel to the Cheyenne, just infrequent. But seeing those beds like that gnawed at me. How easy for Barred Owl to come to me one night, to Grass in the Wind the next. We were both his women, both his responsibility, both his pleasure.

Immediately my reluctance gave way to guilty rebuke. What was the matter with me? This was a Cheyenne camp, not a New York brownstone. Whatever Barred Owl and Grass in the Wind did, they did genuinely, without second thoughts, without hesitation. Here I had traveled hundreds of miles, fleeing my civilized past to rejoin them, and I was questioning their ways. It was not for me to question! As a Cheyenne I would live as a Cheyenne must. Wasn't that why I had turned my back on my white heritage? Wasn't that what I wanted?

Diminished to a jumble of anxiety, I waited while Grass in the Wind made a final check of the banked fire, then began to slip out of her clothing. From the corner of my eye I saw Barred Owl doing the same. I turned away toward my bed and began to unlace my rawhide shirt, knowing as I did so that the two behind me were already slipping into their beds. As nervous as an inexperienced bride, I shed the last of my clothing and burrowed beneath my robe.

I shut my eyes tightly against the dimness of the lodge, preferring total darkness to the revealing shadows. Unsure of what might happen next, I clutched the edge of my robe in white-knuckled fingers. I was a coiled mass of emotions, hoping for solitude, praying for Barred Owl's desire, cursing the knowledge I had of physical love. As a proper young bride I could have rightfully employed a thong rope about my thighs and any

Cheyenne warrior would considerately grant me several days of grace before introducing me to sexual love, but I was not a bride and I had no rope. If Barred Owl turned to me, what would I do?

I loved him; at least I thought I did. After so many years, it was difficult to separate my adolescent feelings from my new, mature ones, but I did desire him. The image of his bare, firelit chest aroused me and I endowed his face and body with the gently fierce technique of Jory. I imagined Barred Owl's finely sculpted lips on my body, his mouth and hands smoothing and caressing as Jory's had done. I rememberd the way Jory's lips and tongue had teased my nipples into craving tumescence, and in my mind I set Barred Owl's head at my breast and imagined him causing the sweet tremors that racked my body. I thought it would not be difficult to accept Barred Owl in my arms and allow him to fullfill my shuddering desire.

I felt him shift in his bed, heard the soft drag of the buffalo robe as he moved. And he moved toward Grass in the Wind.

The postponement of my moment of truth did nothing to allay the frenzied emotions inside me. I tried not to listen, but in the confines of the lodge it was impossible not to hear the soft whisperings of the two lovers. Barred Owl's low, throaty murmurs came to me obliquely, answered by a contented mewing from Grass in the Wind. They communicated with soft sounds and unintelligible words, coming together in the pleasingly unhurried way of husband and wife. Barred Owl's time away from the camp must have sharpened his desire, for he seemed to forget all but his consuming passion for Grass in the Wind. When I felt the leathery whisper of the robe pull away from me and I saw Barred Owl rising above his wife, I turned away on my side and forced my eyes tightly shut.

I chided myself for the embarrassment I felt, knowing it was a product of my Victorian years in the east, and I could finally reason it away. But I could not reason away the throbbing ache of emptiness in my body, emptiness that Barred Owl could fill if he wanted to. Angrily I realized that I had never felt this way before the emotional seduction by Jory in the stable, and it was Jory's overpowering virility that had shown me what fullness was, and now introduced me to its opposite—emptiness. Frustrated and unsatisfied, I felt tears squeezing reluctantly from my closed eyes. I yearned for the completeness that only came from the merging with a partner in love, and I wondered if this emotional torment would attack me every time Barred Owl turned to Grass in the Wind instead of me.

The two bodies behind me were still. Luckily I had been too agonized by my own thoughts to listen closely to the shuddering sounds of completeness, and now the quickened breathing of Barred Owl slowed and smoothed to the more regular breathing of sleep. He would not come to me tonight. I was safe.

Safe?

I cried myself to sleep, my silent tears dropping down onto the softness of my bed.

Chapter Eleven

MY FIRST morning in the Cheyenne camp started early. The darkness had barely begun to gray dimly when I heard Grass in the Wind rousing, and I forced my aching body up off the robe bed. While I dressed, Grass in the Wind called forth the fire from the banked embers. By the time she had the fire blazing healthily, I was dressed and we took up bowls and left the lodge to get water for the morning. I remembered accurately how we must have fresh, or "live" water for the day. Water left standing all night was "dead" water, and not acceptable for drinking.

As we walked down to the small stream that girded the camp, Grass in the Wind smiled to me shyly.

"You slept well?" she asked.

"Fine," I lied. "It has been a long time since I slept beneath the weight of a buffalo robe."

"I am glad," Grass in the Wind said, and I winced at my own duplicity. I didn't mean to tell her untruths, but there was no way—and no need —to try to explain my aggravated emotions to her. I would only hurt her, and she would still not understand.

At the stream we encountered several other women and girls also getting water. Early as it was, there was good-natured talk and soft laughter, and I noticed more than one pair of welcoming eyes on me. If my acceptance in Barred Owl's lodge had proved traumatic, at least my acceptance in the tribe as a whole had gone smoothly. For that I was grateful.

By the time Grass in the Wind and I had filled our bowls and started back to the lodge, young men and boys were passing us in the opposite direction, heading down to the stream for their morning plunge into the chilly waters. The reminder of this daily cleansing brought to mind other, less pleasant memories of the whites' criticisms of the "dirty" savages. Even my grandparents had refused to believe that the Cheyenne bathed daily, summer or winter. They could not acknowledge an image of painted, uncivilized savages jumping into near freezing water simply for the sake of cleanliness.

Grass in the Wind supervised our early meal

preparation, and I was thankful for that. At thirteen I had just begun to be trained in the ways of women, but what little training had been instilled in me had been lost in the intervening seven years. By the time Barred Owl returned from the stream, Grass in the Wind had warm meat ready in bowls.

I had no doubt that my new family would be just as competent at planning and executing my entire day, but I had my own plans and decided to voice them early.

"Barred Owl," I began quietly, "where is my father's lodge?"

He stared at me calmly as he finished eating. He was not surprised at my question. I could see that.

"Behind and to the west," he answered finally. "I will show you."

"Are there other Contraries in our band?"

"No."

"Then I will find it," I said simply. "The red lodge of a Contrary will not be hard to see." He nodded curtly and I was afraid I had annoyed him by my independence. Quickly I rushed to soothe him. "Thank you for offering to guide me."

He grunted dispassionately and it was difficult for me to tell if I had succeeded in covering over my social blunder. I let a small sigh escape me. How long before I stopped being different?

Grass in the Wind was more accepting. After Barred Owl had left the lodge to see to more manly pursuits, she led me back down to the stream where we bathed in the yellow light of morning.

The water was chilly, but not cold, and I gladly immersed myself and scrubbed off the dirt and grime from my mad flight from Leavenworth. That seemed so far away now. Was it only days?

We both washed our hair and stood waist deep in the stream as the water ran off our bodies. Glancing covertly at Grass in the Wind, I ticked off our differences. She was half again as dark as I, and my body was banded with white where the sun had not touched for years. Her hair was as black, but longer than mine, and it shone blue black now that it was heavy with water. She was inches shorter than I, and of a more graceful and fragile build, her hips slender and her breasts small and high. Being unable to bear children, she would retain her own childlike form far longer than the child-blessed matrons of the tribe. I had never before compared myself to another woman, and Jory's praise had made me confident of my own curvaceous form, but next to Grass in the Wind I felt big and gangly. She was so perfectly exquisite that I felt a pang of unreasonable jealousy. No doubt Barred Owl was envied for having such a beautiful and good-tempered wife. Her only flaw was her inability to bear children.

Would that duty fall to me? I wondered.

Thrusting away the depressing thoughts, I rinsed my body a final time and rubbed myself dry with fragrant grasses. The slowly rising sun touched my hair with warmth and the lilting breeze lifted it from my shoulders and hastened its drying. While I dressed, Grass in the Wind pulled a bone comb through her hair, then handed it to me when I was ready for it.

I took meticulous care this morning. I wanted to look perfect for my father, regardless of the fact that I could not assume my familial place as his daughter. Even if I could not share his lodge or his life, I would make sure he could be proud of me.

"This is not as you say white women wear," Grass in the Wind noted, eyeing my clean new buckskins.

"No, it's not. This is clothing made for me by an Arapahoe friend, for my journey. I have found it far more practical than either the white woman's petticoats or our own long shift." I watched her closely as her eyes skimmed over the beaded seams and the manlike leggings.

"It is better for going horseback," she observed finally, her inherent humor surfacing. "Perhaps I will make myself something similar." She grinned broadly at her own joke. We both knew she would never wear leggings like mine; Barred Owl would not approve. We laughed.

"I think Barred Owl would throw us both away as sticks in a dance if my strangeness spread to you," I said easily. "It is better that Barred Owl's first wife remains solely as a Cheyenne. Then people should not pity him for two strange women in his lodge."

Grass in the Wind laughed happily, enjoying our joke. I was glad at least that we could talk teasingly of our differences—my differences. It was more the Cheyenne way to keep politely mute on points of deviation, but Grass in the Wind and I had already discovered a close, sisterly bond and we could converse about even the most glaring things. It was good to feel at ease with her this way.

"Now," I said, gathering up my dirty, discarded buckskins, "I must braid my hair and make ready to see my father. Would my sister have some otter skin strips that I might braid into my hair?"

She not only had some that she gave me guilelessly, but insisted on helping me braid my hair and even tied some small crystal beads into the black strands. I wondered idly how much had been traded for the tiny, cheap bits of glass, but passed it off as unimportant. If it pleased these women, why shouldn't they trade pelts and blankets for simple faceted beads? It was not my place to reveal how unworthy these things were to whites.

When at last we were done, I hunted through my saddlebags and found the small hand mirror I had brought with me. It amused me wryly that I had retained such a silly, vain habit, but I felt an insistent desire to check my appearance. Noting that Grass in the Wind had done my hair beautifully, I turned the mirror over to her.

"Oh!" she said suddenly at the flashing sight of herself. Her instant reaction was to push the mirror away, face down, but at my amused laugh she reconsidered.

"They say it steals your soul," she announced in an awed voice.

"It doesn't," I told her gently. "No more than your reflection in a calm pool steals your soul. It only shows what is there for you to see. Remember? I told you that the white men make walls of it in their lodges. There is no harm in it."

Unsure, yet maddeningly curious, Grass in the Wind retrieved the mirror and held it gingerly by the handle. When the flash of reflected light glared across her face, she caught her breath in a silent gasp.

"It is so clear!" she cried, reaching out a slender finger to touch the image. "It is magical! Like a twin!"

"It is just your image shown back to you. Whatever you do, your image will do also," I explained.

Grass in the Wind tested it. She put a finger to her cheek and I saw her eyes follow her reflection as it did the same. Her awestruck face broke into a huge, childlike grin.

"It is true!" she squealed. "It does all that I do!"

Laughing at my sister, I decided this was a good time to leave her and visit my father. She would be adequately entertained by the mirror, and I harbored no desire for sitting and watching her make faces into the glass for hours. Tossing her a quick goodbye, I slipped from the lodge.

It wasn't difficult to find my father's lodge. Once a man took up the Thunder Bow and became a Contrary he lived a very separate life from the ordinary members of the tribe. Still associated with our band, he lived nearby in a red tepee, set apart both by its noticeable distance and its color.

I approached with trepidation. Would he be glad to see me, or had he buried me in Dog Creek? I had never conversed with a Contrary before, only watched them at the Massaum, or "crazy" dance when they pantomimed their backward antics for the tribe. Suddenly I was terrified that I would blunder terribly and make some outrageous breach of conduct, and my father would send me away in disgust. I had traveled so far! I couldn't fail now.

At first I thought the darkened doorway of the imposing red lodge was empty and only revealing the dark interior of a deserted lodge, but as I neared I realized my mistake. The darkness was not emptiness; it was my father's broad, dark back. He sat before his lodge, backward, working at some industry. As a Contrary, he would do everything backward, from walking and talking to riding and sitting.

I took a quiet seat behind and to one side of him, my legs shaking too badly to hold me up. If he noticed that he had a visitor, he made no sign. He kept bent to his work on an obsidian arrowhead.

I coughed, a low announcing sound in my throat.

He ignored me.

"Father," I managed in a choked voice. "I am Gray Feather, your daughter. I have returned from the land of the white man."

His hands stilled, yet he did not raise his head to look at me. For a heartbeat my worst fears exploded painfully in my breast. Then he looked up and sent an impersonal glance over his shoulder.

"Go away," he said in a low voice. He rose and slipped inside his lodge.

My breath stopped in my throat as surely as if he had thrust a knife through my windpipe. I was crushed, my emotions broken into bits, my confidence shredded. How could he do this to me? He must have realized how far I had traveled to see him, how determined I had been to come back after so many years away! How could he just turn me away so bluntly? And a Contrary—

Then it dawned on me. A Contrary! A Contrary spoke backward! Whatever a normal person might say, a Contrary would say the opposite. I had to swallow to keep my heart down where it belonged, for it threatened to rise up and swell in my throat. Grateful tears pooled in my eyes and I dashed them hurriedly aside and followed my father inside his lodge.

Thankfully, I had been correct. He sat at the back of the lodge waiting for me, his face solemn and expressionless. I circled around the small fire on the right.

"Sit on my right," he said, and I immediately crossed behind him and sat on his left. I could have easily thrown my arms around him in joy, but it was important that I remain controlled.

"I feel pride that my father is so great a warrior," I said carefully, "but do not tell me how you have been." I worded my question cautiously, knowing that to ask a Contrary to come would make him go. I would have to phrase all my questions with such opposites.

Painted Lance turned and looked at me fully for the first time. His eyes were as black as night and still shone as brightly as I remembered, but the edges of his eyes were crinkled with years of sun and his face was more angular and hollow. He had always been tall and lean, but now, in his years, he was almost thin. His chest was still broad and the flat muscles there were hard and strong, but the sleek look of youth was gone. Quickly I calculated and decided he must be in his early fifties—not young for a great Cheyenne.

"Have you been well, Father?" I ventured finally.

"Well," he stated simply, his eyes still examining me. "As well as we can be with the whites pushing across the land. As well as a Contrary can be."

I realized immediately that he was talking straight to me, and I felt a surge of thanks. That he would abandon his Contrary ways for a quiet moment with me was worth all my trials.

"I am glad," I said, wanting to ignore the inherent bitterness in his first statement. "Barred Owl tells me the camp has been very good and many buffalo were killed."

"It is so," he affirmed.

"And the dances were good?"

"Yes."

I examined his face lovingly and wished I had

336

not missed them. "I wish I could have seen the Maussam dance," I said aloud. "I used to love the Maussam, when the Contraries acted so crazy. It was my favorite time."

My father looked pointedly away and I feared I had overstepped my fragile bounds. His face grew hard.

"Your mother never liked the dances," he said.

I drew in a ragged breath. "My mother is dead. She died of a lung sickness after we had been returned to the great white camp in the east. I lived in my grandparents' lodge there until I ran away to return here."

Painted Lance nodded silently, as if remembering some faraway thing. "She was sick the last few winters. She would not allow me to bring a shaman in to heal her."

I laid a halting hand on his arm. "I do not know if that would have helped. The sickness was very great. The white shamen in the east could not save her."

"And they have very great powers?" he asked.

"Yes," I nodded. "In some ways, greater than the shamen here. They have wonderful medicines that battle sickness. But hers was too great to be healed. She died shortly after we became settled in the east."

A gentle silence stretched between us, across the years. I wondered briefly if my father had come to love my mother for all their differences, or she him. I could remember days when we laughed in our lodge, or when my father laid a loving hand on my small head and my mother would smile. It would have pleased me to know that her savage capture had turned into passion, but I did not know how to voice my thoughts.

"You ran away from the white camp?" my father asked me gently, drawing me back to the present.

"I had to. My mother's people would not let me leave. They thought to keep me trapped there, hoping I would embrace the white man's ways. They did not want me to come back here."

My father looked admiringly on me. "It was a very brave thing to do as you did." he said.

I blushed at his open admiration and had to look down. "I—I had to do it. I could not live as they did."

A small, amused sound escaped from Painted Lance, and he laid his large, scarred hand over my smaller one. "You have grown into a worthy daughter of an aging Contrary. The blood of the Cheyenne flows undammed in your veins."

I glanced up, blinking through tears, and saw the restrained smile that threatened to turn my father's lips upward at the corners. His eyes were dark and smiling on me, and the effect they had was devastating. Without warning, I was sobbing uncontrollably and fell gratefully against my father's chest. Feeling his arms tighten around me only served to increase my turmoil, and I cried unashamedly. It was enough to transport me back over seven years, back to the time when all I knew were the proud lodges against blue skies and buffalo darkening the horizon.

I don't know how long I cried, but after some minutes I managed to pull myself together and regain some sort of calm. My father gave me up selflessly and he, too, pulled about him his mantle of control. We smiled weakly at each other.

"And you have counted many coups," I said to start again. "Barred Owl has told me of your bravery."

Painted Lance turned slightly away from me, as if I had said something distasteful. His lips twisted into a bitterness I had only seen a glimpse of before.

"It is good to die bravely against the Crow or the Black Feet," he stated evenly. "Better than to die of cold and starvation on the land with no buffalo."

"But there are many buffalo," I said earnestly, trying to recapture the optimism of our earlier discussion. "The hunt was good."

"Good, yes, this year. Next year it will not be good. The white man hunts the buffalo as well, and kills better than we do. He takes the thick skins and leaves the meat to the vultures and the coyotes. I have seen mountains of buffalo skins piled high upon the land, and no one eats the meat left behind. It is not good."

"Do our people live so close to the white men?" I asked hesitantly.

He shook his head. "Our people stay away as much as possible, but the white man comes in great numbers. He presses on us like the ripples of a stream, small but constant, and he pushes us before him like a twig that floats upon the water. He comes so slowly that some of our people claim there is no harm, and that he brings us good things —metals and guns and beads. But he infiltrates our land, like a coyote among the buffalo, becoming familiar, becoming accepted—waiting to kill. There will come a time when we have too many among us, and we will have no place to go."

My throat threatened to close again. When had my father lost his optimism and become this bitter, cynical man? When had he allowed that note of hopelessness to creep into his voice? I thought surely the future of the Cheyenne was not as black as he painted.

Then I thought back. How often in New York had I heard cries of Manifest Destiny, God's will and stewardship of the land? My grandparents had been diligent in screening social visitors as much as possible so as to shield me from the vocal radicals who cried for a clean sweep of the plains, but they could not screen every one. Some families were just too important to exclude, regardless of their frontier politics. I had made the mistake, once, of trying to argue knowledgeably with such a person and had been rewarded with the shocked looks of all our dinner guests and the memory of my grandparents staring at me as if they expected next to see me frothing at the mouth. After that, I allowed such talk to fly around me unanswered and I convinced myself that most of it was idle boasting. But now I wondered.

"The wagon routes of the whites are almost all south of us," I ventured. "Can we move up north, to the Powder River country, and be safe there?"

"For a time," he acquiesed. "But only for a time. Already the tide of white men pushes us farther north, farther east, until we clash continually with the Crow and Pawnee and Ute. Even our enemies have less area in which to hunt, and less game within that area. The white man's appetite is great. I believe he will not rest until he has taken all that we have."

As much as I wanted to argue with my father, I could not. He was right. I had seen those appetites firsthand, had seen the greed that drove men to acquire more than they needed, more than they could possibly use in a lifetime. In the back of my mind, I knew my father was right and the time would come when there would be no room for the Cheyenne.

"What will we do?" I asked the empty air.

"We will live as Cheyenne and die as Cheyenne. It will be a good day to die bravely, in battle, instead of like a starving dog."

I turned helpless eyes to my father. He was feeling his years. Gray threaded the stark black of his braids although he held his head proudly. He was on the edge of old age. I knew without asking that he would never live to see it.

I felt anger at the thought that my father would die and no one but a handful of Cheyenne would remember him. His stories might be told for a few years, then would fade to nothing. His red lodge would be burned, and his Thunder Bow with it. He had no other possessions except a few chipped bowls, and they were not even worth passing on.

"It is the way of the great spirits," he said suddenly in a soft, thoughtful voice. "When our people lived upon the great water to the north and east, many years ago, and walked about without horses to carry them, the buffalo were strong and numberless. Your grandfather, Elk Water, could recall the time when we had few horses and other tribes raided against us in our weakness. When we finally possessed as many horses as other tribes, we moved the whole of our people west, to the flat lands of the buffalo and there we became stronger than they. It was our turn to have the spirits behind us, and we have been strong against the buffalo. Now," he paused, "now a new strength comes, with spirits behind, and it is against us. We will not win."

With my silence, I agreed. In the celestial game of chance, we would lose and none would mourn our passing. It was an uneasy lesson in mortality that I might have chosen not to learn.

"You," Painted Lance said, "are of two worlds. You may leave the dying world for the living."

"No!" I cried in horror. "I am not of that world! I belong here, with you. If the Cheyenne must die then I will die with them."

"And who will remember us to the children that come after?" he asked softly. His eyes were turned sadly on me and a painful smile curled his mouth.

"Perhaps it will come that the only way to survive is by living in the white man's world. I do not know." He shook his head and stared absently into the fire.

"I have arrows to make," he said, and I knew my time with him that day was over. Sitting up on my knees, I faced him solemnly.

"Thank you, my father, for your wisdom. And your love. I have never been more proud to be called the daughter of Painted Lance than I am today. Goodbye."

"Hello," he said, and I moved out of his lodge.

Grass in the Wind was waiting for me when I returned, and I tried to thrust the uncomfortable thoughts from my mind so as not to spread my helplessness to her. She and several other women had planned to dig roots upon a nearby hillside, and waited patiently for me, root diggers in hand. I pushed my depressed thoughts aside—promising to think more of them later—and we started out.

Another group of women and girls had gone out earlier for wood, and on our way up the shrub-covered hillside we passed them. Several of the more supple young girls were up in the small trees, breaking off what branches they could, and the older women gathered wood from the ground. Other girls broke off limbs and twigs in order to make the wood stackable and arranged bundles for carrying. The vegetation on that slope was alive with laughing brown faces and contented conversation.

Root digging was familiar to me from the count-less times I had accompanied my mother on similar expeditions. Wielding a root digger Grass in the Wind gave me, I hunted for the particular leaves that meant edible roots and I dug indus-triously. The work was not hard, but physical enough to keep my mind occupied. Grass in the Wind and my other companions chatted loudly from nearby areas, keeping in constant touch in a companionable defense against surprise attacks. It was unlikely any marauding enemies would be about in the open Cheyenne plain, so we worked contentedly.

I wondered idly why we couldn't be allowed to live our simple, self-sufficient lives without inter-ference from others. It seemed so simply idealistic to live from day to day, hunting, digging roots and telling stories. Was there a reason our ways were being so methodically destroyed or just, as my father said, the chance driftings of spirit magic?

Little by little, we accumulated growing piles of roots. The turnips, bear-roots and other tubers were fat this year, and we crowed good-naturedly over our prizes. Some of the young girls that accompanied us separated the roots into small piles of five or six, then tied them in bundles, ready to carry home.

We had a good yield to show for our work, and gathered to parcel out the bundles and start back to camp. I remembered past summer days when one woman would challenge the rest in a contest over the roots, and a loud, excited competition would ensue. The most common game was that of throwing root diggers, the challenger throwing hers and the rest trying heatedly to hit her digger with a well-placed throw of their own. I had fond memories of those friendly competitions, but was just as glad no challenge was issued today. Somehow I didn't feel sportive and was quite sure my aim had been diminished awfully by my years in civilization.

Our expedition would not return wholly subdued, however. A small distance from the great ring of lodges several of our number began to wave baskets, signaling our return with a flutter of bright flags, and calling shrilly in mock war cries. Immediately the rest of us assembled in a line of defense, facing camp, arranging our bundles in front of us. I had been dawdling earlier, but now I scrambled for a place on the line and I dropped to my knees behind my roots. Already we could see men scurrying about the camp, making ready their attack.

They weren't long in coming. A score of young men rode out from the camp, all mounted on the sorriest, oldest horses they had been able to find. Each man rode hell-bent, armed only with flimsy shields of parfleche or willow twigs, screaming and calling their war chants. It would have been enough to scare the wits out of watching white men, yet we women quickly, confidently proceeded to gather up as many twigs and rocks and buffalo chips as we could, and waited expectantly for the charge.

This was the fun part. Great warriors with many coups leaped from their ugly steeds and charged us. We women began to hurl a barrage of odd bullets at the warriors, pelting them with sticks and dung as we aimed to put "out" any man who was struck. I saw several men get hit and withdraw, leaving the sport to those who could avoid being "killed." Meanwhile, other young men rode about us in a great whooping circle, their decrepit mounts blowing hard at the abuse.

I had forgotten the fun of this play battle and I devoted myself to it wholly. Unfortunately, my aim was worse than I had thought, and neither my sticks nor my rocks ever found a target. I cried in dismay as a brave lunged forward and captured my bundle, then spun off again in a whirl of laughter.

The battle did not last long. Four men "counted coup" on our root bundles, but seven "dead" men led their horses back in defeat. It had been a good match, enjoyable for all its brevity, and even though I had lost my roots, I crowed with the others over our success. Glorying in our triumph, we returned to camp.

Now the real work began. We divided the roots among us and went to our separate lodges for our individual labors. Some roots would be dried beneath the late summer sun, some pounded into paste with which to make pemmican, some boiled and mashed. Grass in the Wind guided me considerately in the things I had forgotten and we worked well together. I felt good about our day's accomplishments.

It wasn't long before we had guests dropping by, and soon we had a half dozen other women ensconced at our lodge door, all helping with our root preparation.

"We will be leaving soon," Red Grass Woman stated. "The Hairrope Band is going first. They will leave in two days. It will not be long before we go, too."

"What direction do they go?" another woman, unknown to me, asked.

"They say they will go south. They say our winter will be hard, after one so mild, and they have chosen not to go north."

"But white men are south," I said as calmly as I could. "More white men than last year."

All eyes turned expectantly to me and I was embarrassed by the sudden attention.

"The number of white men grows every year," Cow Elk said belligerently to me. "We can still fight them."

"For a time," I said, echoing my father's words, "but soon there will be too many to fight." I thought about all that my father had said to me, remembering his sad bitterness. "We should go north and get as far away from the whites as we can."

Cow Elk snorted disdainfully at my recommendation. Obviously not everyone thought I spoke truth. "The snow will be deep on the Powder River this year. The coats of the buffalo grow thick. We have no need to fear the white men."

Grass in the Wind glanced worriedly from me to Cow Elk and back. If she waited for me to say more, I disappointed her. Cow Elk was blind and unwilling to see; I would not waste words on her.

"The—stage lines," Grass in the Wind sounded out, "they are south, are they not? Where white men travel?"

I nodded, ignoring Cow Elk's barbed look. "Yes. And the white men build more forts and camps along the stage lines every year. Soon they will have an unbroken line of camps across the prairie. They will not like us to be close to that."

"They do not have to like us close!" Cow Elk snarled. "We have brave warriors who have counted many coups on the whites. We do not have to be afraid to fight them!"

"How many fighting men in your band, Cow Elk?" I asked quietly. "Fifteen? Twenty? The whites have ten times that many in a camp, and ten times that coming behind. Their great camps in the east have as many white men as stars in the sky or blades of grass on the prairie. How will we fight bravely when all our warriors are dead?"

I impaled her with my eyes, daring her to denounce my argument. Her kind of blind pride would lead the Cheyenne to destruction. The only way our people could survive was by being realistic. Myths of spirits and magic would not help us against the white tide.

"Bah," Cow Elk spat. "You are afraid, but I am not. I will tell my husband we should go to the south. You go north and live in lodge-high snow until the moon of red grass. I will be warm." She stood and walked pointedly away.

Our little circle was silent for a few minutes and I wondered, as I separated my roots, how my other friends felt. I could not ask. Whatever decision they made was up to only them.

Finally, Grass in the Wind broke the strained silence.

"Gray Feather," she asked tentatively, "do you believe we must avoid the whites?"

I sighed. "It would be best for us if we did," I said gently. "Whites care nothing for our ways or our people. All that they do, even if it is beneficial for us, they really do for themselves. They will never be friends to the Cheyenne that can be relied upon."

"Did they not take you in as one of their own and take care of you?" she asked.

"Oh, yes," I laughed bitterly, "but they suppressed everything about me that was Cheyenne. I could not talk, walk, or look Cheyenne. If other whites knew of my Indian blood, they would have hated me, perhaps even tried to harm me. That was why I left; I was not allowed to be myself."

The other women were thoughtful for a long time. We worked in silence, each grappling with the problem in our own way. I had decided for myself, however, that I would not say more. I had not returned to the Cheyenne to lead them, but only to find myself.

"I will tell my husband I wish to go north," said Walking Woman suddenly. Her voice was firm and her jaw was set. "I will not go south close among the whites, no matter what Cow Elk says."

"I also," said Rabbit Robe. "I will tell Wolf Moon we must go north, too."

"And I," said another.

"And I."

One by one, the remaining women all vowed to go north and I watched the quiet nods of assent ripple around the circle. Finally Grass in the Wind turned to me.

"We will tell Barred Owl the same," she told me. "He will listen to us. We will go north."

Amused, I finally agreed and then we were free to go back to our work, all of us of one mind.

When Barred Owl slipped silently into our lodge later that evening, Grass in the Wind and I had dinner prepared and full bowls warming by the fire for him. He seemed grateful for our thoughtfulness. I knew he had spent the day working on arrows and lance points, replenishing his supply before we broke camp. All the men were busy doing the sedentary work before our autumn journey.

I followed Grass in the Wind's lead and said nothing while we ate. The Cheyenne did not believe in broaching important subjects over dinner. But when Barred Owl turned his empty bowl upside down and leaned back against his backrest, dinner was over.

"Barred Owl," she began softly, "we talked today of where we would like to go for the snow months."

Barred Owl watched her indulgently.

"We want to go north."

"To the Powder River country," I added.

"Yes, the Powder River."

Barred Owl looked at us both curiously.

"The others are talking of spending the snow months on the south plains. The Hairrope Band is leaving soon."

"But white men are there," Grass in the Wind said. "Too many, and they are too close. We want to stay away from them."

I saw his eyes jump to me and I felt his assessing gaze. He knew somehow that I was behind this scheme, but I refused to take the lead. Grass in the Wind was doing fine.

"We all want to go north," she continued. "Walking Woman and Rabbit Robe and all the rest —all but Cow Elk. She is too stupid to understand the danger."

"So," Barred Owl said, relaxing once again. "You have all discussed this? You are all decided?"

I felt more than heard the amusement in his voice.

"Yes," Grass in the Wind said. "We all want to go north."

"Well," Barred Owl said slowly. "This must be discussed more. I will see if all the other husbands have had their minds made up for them."

Chuckling quietly, he left the lodge.

"We will go north," Grass in the Wind pronounced.

I knew she was probably right.

After years in the chauvinistic white society, I had come to recognize those telltale male looks that they turned on vocal women. Here, I knew, those looks did not mean the same thing. In New York, a decisive, outspoken woman was coddled and pampered, then finally wheedled out of her desire by indulgent, amused men who had "better ideas." Not so among the Cheyenne. Women here had as much input as men and were allowed to voice their opinions. Very often, the men concurred. That was the case that night, for when Barred Owl returned an hour later, all he said was, "We go north."

Grass in the Wind and I exchanged grateful glances then fell upon Barred Owl with questions.

"When will we leave?"

"How many bands go north?"

"Who will go south?"

He answered us as rapidly as he could, no doubt wishing for the quiet evenings when he had only one wife instead of two. We found out we would break camp in four days and that four other bands would either follow us or precede us. Several others had remained adamant about going south.

Grass in the Wind and I would have our work cut out for us in the next few days. There were robes and skins to finish, implements to be repaired, clothing to be made. Much of the work had been done during the summer, but now all last-minute preparations had to be made. When we took to our buffalo robe beds that night, it was with thoughts of all we had to do before we left.

I was already more than half asleep before I even wondered what Barred Owl was thinking.

In the morning we fetched water, fed Barred Owl and shooed him out of the lodge early. I was beginning to feel apprehensive, not knowing how well my needlepoint would hold up out here. What little sewing and quilling I had done at thirteen had been lost, I felt sure.

"Gray Feather," my sister said in a low tone, "I must move out."

I stared at her dumbly. "Move out? What are you talking about?"

"It is time I bleed. I must move out of Barred Owl's lodge quickly. Will you come with me to the women's lodge? We can work there."

"Yes, of course," I replied quickly. "What should we take?"

I had forgotten about times like this. Women were not allowed to live at home during this monthly cycle for fear their female magic might contaminate their male relatives. Grass in the Wind had to move into a separate lodge kept apart from all others for the duration of her cycle, and while bleeding she could not handle any weapon or men's articles, lest that man be wounded in battle. It was a testament to her concern for Barred Owl that she left his lodge immediately. She wanted nothing bad to happen to her husband.

So we took our work to the women's lodge. Other women joined us there, and we worked contentedly on robes and moccasins and parfleches.

Grass in the Wind was careful what she handled, but offered me whatever advice I needed in my work. Her isolation did nothing to daunt her considerate personality.

I was aghast at the amount of work we had to do. Grass in the Wind and I mended robes and cut leather for moccasins and winter capes. Other women worked on cradleboards and travois, or mended parfleches and made pemmican. There were hundreds of small jobs that needed seeing to and I was thankful Grass in the Wind did not have to be cloistered away from me. I never could have done all I needed to without her.

As the day passed, we saw more evidence of breaking camp. Another band, called the Eaters, were in the last stages of preparation, and their women were methodically packing and getting ready. I watched them briefly and felt a stir of excitement at the idea of traveling again. I was eager to see the Powder River.

Toward sundown, I was startled out of my preoccupation by Grass in the Wind.

"Barred Owl will expect his dinner soon," she reminded me gently.

My heart flip-flopped. Idiot that I was, I had forgotten that, with Grass in the Wind gone, all the wifely duties of the lodge fell to me. All of them. I was petrified.

"Yes," I mumbled inanely. "I had better go." I began to gather up our half-finished projects.

"Leave these," she chided me gently. "We will work on them tomorrow."

Deprived of my last excuse for delaying, I got up and walked to our lodge. I would have to stoke up the fire and cook the meal and see to Barred Owl and—Perspiration dotted my brow, cooling only slightly my worried body.

As soon as I reached the empty lodge, I threw myself into my domestic duties. I was grateful Barred Owl was not there to see me coaxing the fire back from embers, or the way my face reddened with my frantic blowing. I am sure he would have had second thoughts about taking me as a wife if he could have seen me fill a bowl with stewed meat, only to upend it messily on the edge of his robe. I cleaned up the mess as quickly as possible and it was only by accident that I was subdued and waiting when he entered the lodge.

"Where is Grass in the Wind?" he asked as he accepted his bowl from me.

"She will be at the women's lodge for a few days," I answered nervously. "She went there this morning."

Barred Owl nodded thoughtfully and relaxed against his backrest to eat. He seemed involved with his meal, yet I felt prickles of awareness, as if he watched me from the corner of his eye.

"We accomplished many things today," I rattled on. "Grass in the Wind has helped me regain my sewing, and Rabbit Robe is teaching me some small quilling." There was no reply from the stoic man at the back of the lodge. "I feel stupid when I think of all I don't remember how to do. Grass in the Wind has been so patient with me. I'm grateful

355

to her for so many things."

Barred Owl remained silent and when I could think of no more idle chatter, I lifted my eyes to his. He had finished his meal and set his empty bowl aside, and now sat watching me casually. In the firelit lodge his eyes seemed dark and feral.

"In three days we will leave?" I asked nervously. He nodded.

"I—I remember so little of the Powder River country. I know the snows are deep." I was floundering terribly. My disjointed sentences faded to silence.

Barred Owl shattered my train of thought. "I am tired," he said evenly.

"Oh." My eyes ran over the jumble of sleeping robes. They needed straightening. "Let me smooth the beds first; I should have done that sooner." Half numb, half screaming in panic, I straightened the robes into neat rectangles and plush bedding. I could feel Barred Owl behind me. Every sense of my body was attuned to him, whether I wished it to be or not.

"I will return shortly," Barred Owl said, and before I knew it he was slipping outside. I didn't know whether to curse or give thanks. He may have decided not to take me as his wife tonight, if he had ever considered it. Or he may have been giving me more time—a period of adjustment—before he came to my bed. I had no idea what he was thinking or what he wanted—or what I wanted, for that matter.

I spent as much time as I could on the arranging

of bedding, then had no other excuse to delay. Trembling with anxiety, I pulled off my clothes and slid beneath my robe. Only after I had hidden myself completely by the heavy hide did I remember that the fire had not been banked. Sitting up, I tried to keep the robe pulled up chastely to my chin with one hand while I prodded the coals into a pocket of ash for the night. I wasn't successful. Before I had covered the coals sufficiently, I heard the soft tread of moccasins outside. Blanching in panic, I sank back down on my bed and pulled my robe up around me as tightly as a nun's habit.

Barred Owl glided silently inside, his ghostly form only half illuminated by the poorly banked fire. His black eyes darted about the lodge and immediately took in my cowering position and the condition of the fire. In the wavering light, I almost thought I saw a smile flit across his face, but I couldn't be sure. He picked up a stick and finished covering over the glowing coals.

I averted my eyes as he stripped off the brief loin cloth and leggings, and felt more than heard him slip beneath his own robe. The small sounds of my own breathing and the gentle crackle of the fire were like thunderclaps to my ears. The air in the lodge was thick with expectation, almost cloying to my frenzied emotions. Again I was torn by my desires. What if he came to me? What if he didn't?

I didn't have too long to ponder the choices. I heard the whisper of leather against skin, then felt Barred Owl's presence close behind me. With my eyes squeezed tightly shut, the soft touch of his hand on my arm was enough to startle me and I jumped. Barred Owl appeared not to notice and lay quietly behind me, waiting.

My blood was pounding so furiously in my ears that I was afraid I would be deaf to anything he said. I turned toward him. In the darkness I could just make out the serious features of his face. He lay watching me, as if seeing me for the first time.

I could not seem to get a grip on my fear. My pulse raced and my breathing was fast and shallow. I wondered briefly if Barred Owl thought I were a foolish child, acting so terrified, and I wondered why it had been so different with Jory. I had not been afraid then. But I had had almost no warning of what our combustible collision would become, either. Now I knew what was forthcoming, and I had no idea how to act.

"Gray Feather," Barred Owl breathed, pulling me out of my desperate thoughts. He ran his hand lightly up my arm, as one might to soothe a child. The warm touch of his hand and his gentleness eased my mind, but not my body.

Finally determined that I would become Barred Owl's wife with honesty and grace, I reached out one hand and traced the angles of his face with my fingers. The tips of them found the slashing grooves beside his mouth, wandered up along the high cheekbones and smoothed the hard, sculptured brow. His face, the sight of which was so familiar to me, became equally familiar to my touch, and I began, finally, to relax.

"Little Gray Feather," he said softly, as if remembering the reckless, willful thirteen-year-old. I smiled tentatively at him. He pushed my robe off my shoulders and exposed the upper half of my body to his dark, smouldering gaze. Immediately I felt fear trembling through my body again.

Barred Owl propped himself up on one elbow and traced gentle fingers across my shoulders, my throat, and my breasts. I shivered at his touch, wanting yet afraid of taking. His fingertips glided slowly over the hollow of my throat where my blood pulsed, and around the swelling curves of my breasts. The teasing draw of his palm across my nipples pulled the buds into enflamed buttons that reached for his touch. I closed my eyes against the intent look on his face and my own trembling.

"Gray Feather," I heard close to my mouth, and then his lips came down on mine. He brushed his lips across the fullness of my own, softly, gently, while his hand continued the languid teasing of my body. I quaked beneath him, yet offered my mouth freely to his and hoped that he would take me quickly before I had time to question my hesitation.

His mouth came down full on mine, capturing it greedily and a rush of warmth spread through me. I slid my arms around his neck and stroked the corded muscles there, drawing him closer. His hand spanned my breast, cupping the swelling flesh against his palm and sending sparks of desire through me. I arched against him in the hope that I could enflame the feelings of desire enough to burn out the anxiety.

"You are very beautiful now, Gray Feather," he said against my mouth. One hand wandered through my loose hair as he pressed his lips against my cheeks and eyes. "I thought never to have you as my wife."

"Oh, please!" I cried, pulling him down to my mouth again. I felt his fleeting hesitation, but then it was crushed between us and I was aware only of the hard press of his chest against my breasts and the warm hand that slid down across my stomach.

My body shook uncontrollably with a dozen different emotions. I wanted Barred Owl terribly, but was so very afraid that I would displease him. He touched me gently on the sensitive inside of my thigh and I jumped violently within his arms.

That was when I felt him draw away from me. He pulled back slowly, sliding his hand back to the relative safety of my side. He raised himself off of me and stared down into my eyes.

"You are afraid, Gray Feather?" he asked in a low voice. I could not discern what emotion colored his voice.

"Yes," I admitted. I might have explained that the reason for my fear was not what he no doubt thought, but the words wouldn't come. Instead I cast my eyes down in shame and cursed my body for trembling still.

The soft touch of his fingers along my jawline brought me up to face him again.

"Do you not wish me as your husband?" he

asked.

I nodded miserably. "Yes, I wish it," I breathed. "Very much."

That seemed to please him, although he did little more than smile briefly. "If that is what you wish," he said kindly, "then it will be so."

He kissed me softly and traced his fingers across my cheek.

"Go to sleep, Gray Feather," he told me in a whisper. "Sleep and do not be afraid."

But long after he had turned away from me, I lay awake and wondered if he would still treat me kindly after he knew the truth.

Chapter Twelve

In the morning I performed all my wifely tasks quickly and quietly, preferring silence to Barred Owl's curious gaze. He did not seem angry or unhappy with me—just wondering. After he had taken his morning plunge in the cooling stream and eaten, he left me to my work.

I hurried to the lodge where Grass in the Wind stayed. She smiled happily to see me and immediately pressed me with the new moccasins that needed to be finished. I took the handiwork and bent to it with careful concentration.

"Our husband is well?" she asked me after several moments of silence.

I jerked my head up and looked at her guiltily.

"Yes," I managed weakly. "He is well." But I was not. I don't know what I felt worse over, the fact that Barred Owl had approached me or the fact that he had finally turned away.

Grass in the Wind smiled at my discomfort. "I think our husband is very lucky to have two wives such as we," she said. "I think he is envied by other men of the tribe."

"Yes," I agreed without conviction. But down inside I wondered how lucky Barred Owl was to have me—a misfit by any standards. The Cheyenne girl he had courted now brought stories and fears of the white man into camp and instigated disagreements among the tribe. The girl he thought to be a virgin was not—nor was she truthful or trusting. I could only pray for the strength to explain myself to him, and for his understanding. Maybe then he would feel as lucky as Grass in the Wind thought he was.

We worked diligently that day and finished all the mending and sewing of our winter clothing. Next was traveling aids, and between the two of us and several other women, we strapped together a new travois for the journey. Finally we had packs to sew and parfleches to mend. The day was not long enough to do it all, however, and we had some small projects set aside for the following morning. After that, we would be ready to leave.

When I made my way home to Barred Owl's lodge that evening, I determined to be honest with him. We could not travel to a new home with falsehoods between us. I could not fully become his wife—or a member of my own band—with the in-securities I had now. Somehow I would have to clear the way.

Barred Owl sat in front of our lodge hafting arrowheads to shafts and he greeted me quietly. After a moment of shy indecision, I slipped into the lodge to start cooking, then returned to sit beside him in the lowering sunlight.

"Your arrows are very fine," I said as I watched him attach a sheet metal head to a long, straight shaft. "I wish now that I had brought you more metal for your arrowheads."

Sheet metal was coveted for arrows and yet hard for the Cheyenne to come by. I recognized the flare of gratitude in Barred Owl's eyes.

"That would have been a very fine gift," he acknowledged. "I have enough for now, however."

I nodded, watching his hands work quickly and expertly. The sinew that bound the head to the shaft was strong and binding; this arrow would bring meat to our lodge—or kill to protect it.

I searched for a way to begin my catharsis to Barred Owl, but before I could find words, a troop of young boys ran laughing through the band in a hoop game. Their laughter and cheering voices filled the empty area between the lodges, causing adults in their labors to stop and watch the game. It was one I had seen often. They rolled a willow hoop ahead of them, each boy trying valiantly to spear the running hoop with a toy lance. The boys that missed were jeered good-naturedly, and the ones who succeeded were exalted with great cheers. The boys frolicked and ran like wild free things. The sight of them brought an unwitting smile to my face and I turned toward Barred Owl to share the happy moment with him.

He had been watching the boys as well, and I now saw the way his eyes lingered on the small ones. Was there sorrow there? If so, it disappeared quickly. Sensing my eyes on him, Barred Owl met my gaze and smiled briefly, and then I noticed his eyes train down my body—the body of his wife—to rest thoughtfully on my stomach.

He wants me to bear his children, I thought uncomfortably. I will be the mother of his sons, and give him what Grass in the Wind cannot. I can give him what he desires most.

Guilt assailed me again. How would Grass in the Wind fare after I had given birth? Would people still say how lucky Barred Owl was to have two pretty wives, or would they cluck sorrowfully over the woman who was barren? How would she feel, watching my children play about her lodge?

"Barred Owl," I said, my mind a jumble of discordant thoughts, "I must talk to you. I have many things I have to say to you, to explain."

Barred Owl gave me an understanding smile. "We will talk, Gray Feather, but later. Now I am hungry."

Cowardly, I gave in and preceded him inside the lodge to dish out our meal. We ate silently, with respect for our food, and then I cleared away the cooking things. Barred Owl leaned against his backrest and watched me companionably.

"We will leave on the day after tomorrow," he told me. "Have you much more work to do to prepare?"

I shook my head. "No. Grass in the Wind and I have completed most of it. We have only a few things left."

"Good," he pronounced.

I asked him the way that we would go, and he described the journey to me, bringing back distant memories of long treks across the plains. I was sure things would look very different to me this time, seen through half-white eyes.

"It is time for bed," Barred Owl said suddenly, jolting me out of my musings.

Nodding, I took up a stick and bent to the fire, prodding the coals back under the ashes. I was surprised to find Barred Owl close at my side. He took the stick from me gently.

"I will do this," he said. "You go."

Blushing shyness washed over me but I could not help but be pleased by his gentle thoughtfulness. I turned away to arrange the beds.

I don't know if I imagined it or not, but I thought I could feel Barred Owl's eyes on me as I slipped out of my buckskins. I imagined the banked firelight dancing across my bare back and wondered if he found me as pretty as Grass in the Wind. Thrusting aside the unsisterly thought, I slid under my buffalo robe and waited for Barred Owl.

He was not long in coming. The fire was a dim glow that barely gave shape to him in the darkness, but I could sense him as he approached and pulled his own robe up over his body. His warmth, just inches from my own bare arm, radiated over me.

"Do you wish to talk now, Gray Feather?" he asked me in a low voice.

I turned toward him in the darkness, my resolution of strength giving me purpose. In the shadows I could see the proud angles of his profile and the way his leanly muscled chest rose and fell with his breathing.

"Yes," I started, unsure how else to begin. "I—I want to tell you that I am not afraid of you, Barred Owl. I am not afraid to have you as husband. I am afraid of—of myself."

Now it was his turn to move toward me. "Yourself? I do not understand."

"I know," I whispered. "But I am different, I have always been different, first in the white man's world and now here. I feel as if two people war inside of me, just as the whites and Cheyenne war at each other over the plains. I am afraid that I will act differently with you than you would want, and that I will not please you. I am afraid you will reject me for my differences, the way everyone has always rejected me." All but one, I amended silently.

I felt Barred Owl's eyes on me in the darkness, felt their serious intensity. It was as if he weighed his words carefully.

"You speak as no Cheyenne woman does, that much is true," he admitted carefully. "But you are still a woman. You bend to your work without complaint and you are as a sister to Grass in the Wind. I have seen you look at me with curiosity, and I think it is not so different than the way any new wife regards her husband. And you say you want me to be your husband."

"I do!" I cried in a soft, desperate voice. "But I am still afraid! You don't know all about me. You don't know—"

"I think," he said, moving closer until his body pressed along the entire length of mine, "that we must get to know about each other in ways other than talking." He stroked my cheek with the back of his hand, his rough knuckles sliding across my smooth skin. "I think you will see that talking different is not so terrible, if we are alike in other ways."

I accepted his caress with a racing mind and speeding pulse. Maybe he was right. Maybe I was making more confusion out of my own thoughts than there actually existed. I fervently hoped so.

"Do not be afraid, Gray Feather," he soothed.

I closed my eyes as I felt his lips press gently on mine and twined my arms around his neck. I resolved to be trusting, both of him and myself. I would be myself. It was all I could be.

His lips brushed across the fullness of my own and the tip of his tongue traced the outline of my mouth in a gently erotic way. My body flushed with warmth that seeped throughout it, into all the small hidden places. When he nipped at my full lower lip with his teeth, he sent waves of more violent sensation through me. It was as if I had been holding my emotions in check for so long that now, when I released them, they flooded through me in a tidal wave of desire. I would be the woman I was meant to be, and I would be his wife.

His hand slid from my shoulder to my breast where he cupped the swelling flesh in his palm. The callused roughness of his hand excited my tender skin, and my nipples hardened in aching desire. I arched into his hand, thrusting the taut-ness of my breasts against him, crying silently for more. Now that I had made up my mind to give in to my womanly desires, I was almost feverishly driven.

Barred Owl's responses were slow and hesitant, as if he feared of hurting me. He stroked my pliant body with a knowing hand, yet used his fingers lightly on my body. His caresses were soft and considerate, meant no doubt to bring me carefully along the pathway of desire, but in my fevered state they only frustrated me. When the hard press of my breasts against his chest brought no relief to me, I untangled my hands from his neck and slid them down his back. His body was hard and corded, warm and silky against my palms. I gloried in the feel of him and freely explored the contours of his back. The hard ridge of his back-bone was strength to me; the soft indentation at the base of his spine was gentleness. My mind throbbed and my body pulsed with wanting. I wanted desperately to envelope him, to become one with him. I ached for the fulfillment of his body in mine.

Spurred by my seeking demands, he found my breast with his mouth and drew a gasp from me with the sucking insistence of his mouth. I arched into him, giving my breast up to the sensations his teeth and tongue elicited, my head falling back into the soft buffalo robes. Wild sounds came from my throat, small cries and savage groans. The pull of his mouth on my breast was heaven to me; the emptiness within me was hell.

The promise of fulfillment drove me to desperation. I explored him with my hands, cupping my fingers around his buttocks and stroking the soft inner places of his thighs. Somewhere in the back of my mind I remembered what had pleased Jory the most, and I ran a fingernail up his thigh to the place that sent a quiver through his body. I could feel the shock of my touch go through him. In response, he found the soft core of my own sex and touched me softly, the lightness of his fingers more a torture to me than a relief. My body pulsed with wanting.

"Please," I begged him, moving violently beneath him. "Please." I slid my hand around and found the hard truth of his desire and told him with silent strokes how badly I wanted him. I let my hand do all the things my body could not, caressing him, enveloping him, surrounding him with my flesh. I was on fire with a mad, driving need and strove to meld my body with his. A strangled scream of frustration died in my throat.

Finally he answered my demands, and he moved

over me in a way that was no longer gentle or considerate. Knowing that I was ready to accept him, he drove into me with a sharpness that forced a cry from me, and yet the pain of his entry was exactly what I wanted. His hands gripped my shoulders roughly and held me captive while he strove to fill me from within and I, in my madness, dug my fingernails into the soft flesh of his buttocks. I twined my legs around his body and arched into him, wishing desperately that I could transcend the bonds of flesh and meld with him completely, taking all of him inside me, using all of him to satisfy the awful craving that wracked me. My insane desire communicated itself to Barred Owl, and he impaled me with demanding thrusts that enflamed me even as they quenched my pains. He drove into me relentlessly, almost cruelly, pushing me past the point of caring, driving me into a mindless state of animal satisfaction that transcended human thought and became only feeling, pure, primitive sensation.

When I seemed to become human again, I realized the lodge was filled with the harsh, gasping sounds of our breathing. Our bodies were slick with perspiration and clashed against each other with the desperate drawing of air into our lungs. Barred Owl slipped down beside me and trailed a hand across my stomach.

I began to dread his silence. In the darkness, my fears returned to cloak me in uncertainty, and I wondered what he thought of me now. No virgin would act as I had acted. No woman came to her husband's bed for the first time and did what I did. I wished that he would say something, anything, to tell me he was not displeased with me.

Instead, he turned away from me and slept.

The final day before our leaving was a blur to me, images of working alongside Grass in the Wind while my mind whirled with unsaid thoughts. She spoke kindly to me, trying to keep me in the present as we made our final preparations, but it was no use. My mind was a storm of feelings, a maze of confusion.

Barred Owl had been no more than cool to me that morning, nor did I expect more. I felt sure he had his own decisions to make, his own impressions to form about his new wife. Grass in the Wind informed me that she could return among the rest of the band tomorrow, when we left. I felt sure Barred Owl would be pleased at that. He would have his normal wife back, and not have to placate the wild woman he had found in his bed last night.

The night before our leaving, Barred Owl and I lay silently upon our separate beds. I might have cried over the fact that my difference had made me an outcast once more, but somehow the tears would not come.

Being a small family, we had fewer preparations to make than most, and on the day we were to break camp, we did it quickly. Grass in the Wind and I took down the lodge, she reminding me of procedures I had forgotten, and we converted the lodge poles into travois behind the horses. Much as I disliked it, I had to hitch a travois to Thunder out of necessity. He didn't care for the strange contraption at all, and his eyes rolled wildly in their sockets. I realized he must have been broken to a harness at one time, however, because after snorting and crab-stepping for a moment, he settled down. I made sure he was tied securely until we were ready to leave, then climbed up on him and soothed him with my voice and hands. He still wasn't entirely complacent but he seemed better with me on him. Grass in the Wind rode a small dun mare, also towing a travois, and Barred Owl rode his big bay. Being a brave and wealthy man, he had several additional horses that pulled travois or were towed along with us, and with our band strung out in an irregular line, we started north.

It was hardly unusual for a Cheyenne woman to own a horse, since property often passed through the women down through a family, but seldom did a woman have a horse as tall or as striking as Thunder. Most of the ponies we rode or drove were small animals, whatever we could trade for or steal. I jockeyed Thunder in beside Grass in the Wind and accepted the glances at us with silence, hardening myself to the fact that I would never be able to merge quietly into the band I had traveled so far to find. I would always stick out; I would always be different.

I couldn't help but feel some excitement at the idea of traveling to the new territory, however. I saw this as a new beginning. Then I looked back and around at the collection of Indians, and even my feelings of optimism were curtailed. For days we would walk, some on horseback, more on foot, carrying everything we owned. For some reason it reminded me of poor immgrants I had seen in New York, all their possessions wrapped in newspaper or in torn carpetbags, searching for new opportunities. Seen with white eyes, we looked a very sorry lot.

The first day we covered ground effortlessly and reached the South Platte in the late afternoon. As settled as it had become, this fork of the river was cautious territory for us, and we crossed at some sandbars after skirting wide to the west. I hadn't seen any establishment at all, but I knew from our trail that either a fort or a settlement lay east, and a troupe of migrating Indians was open sport for whites. We crossed the Platte and trudged on until near dark, stopping in a prairie bowl where a shallow muddy creek pooled.

Grass in the Wind and I erected our lodge while Barred Owl and some of the other braves met to discuss and plan tomorrow's venture. I had kept an eye on my father throughout the day and I saw him put up his own small tepee at a distance from the main camp. Since that day I had visited him, we had not spoken, but it was comforting to me just to have him near. We looked on each other with mutual love and respect, which was all I could ask. It was more than I could share with anyone in the band.

We ate our evening meal in silence, the entire

small camp shrouded in cautious quiet. Our numbers were much fewer now, and our protection not as great. We could not afford great fires or loud voices. When we traveled in our small band this way, we were vulnerable. It seemed to me very sad to see my people reduced to this tiny group of watchful fugitives, and I began to think again of what my father had said about our future. Is this the way my children would be raised? Is this what their future would be, nomads forced to run and hide in the far reaches of our previous homeland? It was not a lifting thought to me to imagine my own children, sons and daughters with Barred Owl's dark, unreadable features, born and brought up amid the advancing threat of extinction. The idea of it settled in the pit of my stomach like bad meat, and I pushed my bowl away only half emptied.

Later, when the three of us had retired to our robe beds, I realized how silly my fears were. I had no guarantee that Barred Owl would ever again approach me in the night.

I had no guarantee that I would ever bear his children.

We crossed the North Platte the next day shortly before dark. Although the crossing was as uneventful as crossing the South Platte, what followed was not.

We had traveled a few miles from the river and were close to pitching camp when one of our scouts rode up on his pony and signaled for us to hide. With a few quick words and concise gestures

376

we were informed that soldiers—long knives—
were approaching from the southeast at a fairly
good clip. We cared not what fort they were from
or what leader they followed, only that they were
deadly to us. Luckily we had been traveling alongside a bluff cut by a stream that ran back into the
Platte, and we made for cover there.

The travois proved nothing but trouble once we
started down the bank, so the women on foot
quickly ran from one horse to another, slashing at
the leather thongs. Others pulled the heavily laden
travois among scrub and hid them, piling brush on
and around them until they were no longer visible.

The rest of us kicked the horses on down the
creek bed to where a gully widened off the bluff. It
was a small, narrow gully but would have to do.
We herded the horses into the end, barricading
them with our own bodies at the mouth of the
gully. There we waited.

It was a good twenty minutes before we heard
the hoofbeats, but the rhythm was that of the
rollicking canter the cavalry used to cover ground.
Wherever they were going, their intention was
clearly not to engage in battle, and although we
couldn't see them we knew they loped past our
braves at the lip of the bluff.

I tried to estimate how many there were, but my
instincts being diminished, I was not sure. I
thought perhaps twenty, but Grass in the Wind
said half again as many. We had just less than
twenty fighting men, so it would be best to let the
soldiers pass.

Unfortunately, it wasn't as simple as that. We learned later that a rider on the flank of the column had seen something, or at least pointed and gestured toward the bluff. At a signal from the leader, four men detached themselves from the rest and rode toward our men. Still hoping to go undetected, our braves remained still until the soldiers almost crested the bluff, then let fly four arrows.

Two soldiers fell immediately and one veered off with an arrow in his shoulder. The fourth cut back unscathed and called to his company. We had heard nothing until then, but we heard his call and knew we would not get by unnoticed.

Our men stayed low in the gully but crept toward their ponies and mounted without drawing fire. Meanwhile, the soldiers had disbanded, apparently undecided about how to go about routing the Indians, and our braves were able to burst from the gully in an explosion of hysterical yells and speeding horses. Having this much surprise and launching the offensive attack was good medicine and the Cheyenne circled and fired arrows with maddening speed. The cavalry had barely enough time to get off a few shots before several of their number had fallen, and after only a few long minutes of combat the soldiers scattered.

From our position in the gully we could see no fighting but we heard the sounds of the skirmish and waited anxiously. Grass in the Wind squeezed my hand until I thought it was numb and I hoped desperately that none of our men took a bullet. The sounds reminded me of my own band's massacre, but I was sure today would turn out differently. Still, I waited impatiently for a sign of how the battle went.

The only glimpse we saw was that of a single soldier that had managed to run up the edge of the bluff. He reined his horse in when he saw the gathered women and, with his horse spinning nervously, tried to gesture to his men what he had found. Before he could cry out, an arrow thudded into his back and he toppled into the gully, not far from where we stood. We dismissed him quickly and looked anxiously to the south.

The battle was over shortly. When our braves had scattered the soldiders and taken what souvenirs they wanted, scalps included, they brought us out of our cover. I was so glad to see Barred Owl alive and unscratched that I didn't care about anything else. Even the bloody scalp at his belt and the cavalry cap on his head didn't bother me. He bore his battle trophies proudly, for Cheyenne are realistic about their feats, a characteristic often interpreted as arrogance. Barred Owl had no need to be arrogant. Others would sing of his coups for many years and their songs would be accurate if not dramatic. This was just one feat of many for Barred Owl.

The final count was six cavalry dead and one Cheyenne. Luckily, he was a young brave who had not yet married. His parents cried loudly and made some mutilations in their mourning but at least he did not leave a wife and children with no provider. His death cast a shadow over the victory, but we had much to show for it. Other than the souvenirs, we had captured four horses and three rifles. That was good pickings for an encounter we hadn't even wanted.

As soon as we had assessed our gains and losses we retrieved our travois and strapped them to the horses so we could continue our journey. It would not do for us to camp too closely to the battle place, just in case reinforcements were sent. Even though the sun was already dipping below the horizon, we walked on for several more miles and didn't stop until well past full dark.

We pitched camp quickly and set small fires to cooking. Barred Owl had killed a rabbit earlier on the trail and Grass in the Wind gutted and skinned it expertly, then added it to the cooking pot. The smells made me realize how hungry I was and the chance to stop and relax brought out the tiredness in my body. I wouldn't be long for my buffalo robe.

Grass in the Wind and I didn't talk while the meat was cooking. She apparently had small things to keep her busy so I took the time to reflect. Although we had been victorious, the battle left me feeling odd. Those were white men that had been killed, possibly some of the soldiers I knew from Fort Leavenworth. I felt relief that Frank at least had not been one of them. I chastized myself for feeling pity for those men, but after all, I was half white and had never been particularly bloodthirsty.

When I had been among my band before, when I was a child, I had never thought about the enemy that was left bloody and mutilated on the plains. They were the enemy and that was sufficient. Now I saw differently. As eager as I had been to turn my back on white society, I had not meant to join in its destruction.

I was being foolish and I knew it. Indians and whites could not live together, they never would. Peace would come only after the domination of one by the other. And I knew who would be the winner.

Over dinner, Barred Owl gave us his account of the battle. He had counted coup on one soldier before passing again to plunge his knife into him. He had watched the young warrior, Arrow, fall to a bullet and he had seen Painted Lance kill three soldiers with his Thunder Bow. Since my father had not joined in the recounting after the battle, I had forgotten he had fought at all. Now I asked Barred Owl to tell me more about him.

He had fought bravely, as befitted a Contrary. With almost celestial inspiration he had charged in among the soldiers and killed one before they even knew he was there. He counted coup on three, then rode hell-bent away for a new attack. When Arrow fell, Painted Lance charged the killer and cut him down with his knife. Finally, he dropped another soldier as they scattered, had taken one scalp and then returned to the bluff to wait alone until our band traveled on. From now on this story would be part of the celebration at the big camp in summer. The bravery of our men would not be forgotten.

I was strangely unmoved. I murmured words of relief and congratulations to Barred Owl but I didn't feel it. How I wished I had never been taken from the Cheyenne, then I would never have anything to compare this life to. I would have been happy if I had stayed here, if I could have lived my life knowing no other way. Now I felt the old stirrings of restless discontent, the feelings of being a misfit. Like in New York.

That night Barred Owl dropped off to sleep without turning to either me or Grass in the Wind. I had wondered how she felt about the night before, but she acted no differently toward me. I knew my place in the lodge was confirmed and agreeable to all of us. Except perhaps me.

The next day we plodded on. Sitting atop Thunder, I barely saw the landscape as it slid by. My eyes were almost sightless as my brain raced.

I had been unhappy in New York, and I had striven to change my life. I had succeeded. Could I do it again? After all, I had never promised myself I would stay with my band once I found them. I had never known for sure. Now, it seemed, I knew.

Riding beside Grass in the Wind, I said nothing. I made my own plans and bided my time until that endless day was over. It seemed that the sun moved only inches each hour and the shadows hardly changed at all. Each step I took on Thunder was carrying me in the opposite direction I wanted to go.

When we finally broke for camp, I looked about through white eyes. These people were poor, put upon and rapidly losing all they owned. They had no present except traveling and fighting, being pushed from one desolate area to another. They had no future but the arid places the whites requisitioned for them, land no one else wanted because it was no good. I could no more stay with them than go back to Grandpere's and take my place on the china-blue brocade divan in the parlor.

Grass in the Wind saw to the cooking after we had erected the lodge. She apparently saw nothing unusual about my silence, and I watched her with new eyes. She was a friend, a sister to me, but still from another world. She would argue with me about leaving, but after one or two days, she wouldn't even miss me. Cheyenne do not dwell on past partings.

I tried to imagine how Barred Owl would react. He wouldn't try to stop me, I knew, but I hoped he wouldn't think me ungrateful or unhappy. I hoped I could make him understand that it was my failings, not his, that drove me away.

We ate quietly around the fire. Several times I tried to begin, but I found myself tongue-tied and unable to say the right words. Finally I finished my bowl of boiled meat and waited until the others were done.

Grass in the Wind and I cleaned up and put the bowls away. I made the menial task last as long as

I could, finding relief in the physical motion. The closer I came to saying what I had to, the more nervous I became.

"Barred Owl," I said finally. My voice surprised even me, it sounded so loud and firm. Both Barred Owl and Grass in the Wind looked expectantly to me.

"I must—say something to you," I began. They looked at me patiently, neither one asking what I wished to say or helping me at all. I wished they weren't quite so tolerant.

"I—I have to . . . I am grateful for the kindness and friendship you two have shown me. You have both been very good to me to accept me in your lodge. What I have to say is that I cannot stay. Tomorrow when we strike camp I will go south again. I can't go with you."

They sat quietly, their faces blank. For a moment I was afraid they hadn't understood, or else they were too angry to speak.

"My place is not here among the Cheyenne," I began again. "I wish it could be so. This is not my life, not like it is yours. I do not belong here."

"You belong wherever you want to be," Grass in the Wind said softly.

"I wish it could be so," I said again. "But I feel that I do not fit here. I am grateful to you for all you have done for me, but in the morning I will go my own way."

"I will go with you," Barred Owl said.

"No, I . . ."

He stopped me with a look. "I will take you

384

where you want to go. You cannot travel alone. When we have found where you must go, I will return to my camp. I can find my way across the prairie alone—you can't."

"I can't ask you to leave Grass in the Wind," I said. "I am grateful, but I have been too much trouble for you already."

"I will pack food for you both," Grass in the Wind said. It was as if she hadn't even heard me. "You can leave as soon as it is light."

Feeling relieved and miserable at the same time, I helped Grass in the Wind with our preparations. Barred Owl slipped out of the lodge and was gone for a long time, past the time when I finally settled into my bed.

The next morning I mounted Thunder without a travois behind. He seemed immediately more attentive, as if my excitement communicated itself to him. Barred Owl rode his bay, and after seeing that the band was ready to move, we waved goodby to Grass in the Wind and started south.

Every so often I turned on my horse and looked back at the rapidly disappearing group of people. Tears stood in my eyes so it was difficult to see faces, but even after I could no longer distinguish people, I still sniffed back the tears. One minute I was ready to burst into tears and the next I was wild with excitement. I vacillated between the high and low emotions until the band finally moved out of sight and I had no reason to look back.

The only thing I regretted was not being able to say goodbye to my father, but I knew I couldn't do it without crying shamelessly. It was important that I leave proudly, as befitted a Cheyenne, and my father would understand. If I had gained nothing else by my weeks with the people, I had seen him and knew he was alive and well—as well as any Indian could be.

We rode silently, going back over the miles and territory we had covered the day before. Again it seemed that the day dragged painfully, and every landmark I recognized only increased my restlessness. I was eager to be done with this part of the country, I wanted to be someplace else.

Barred Owl had never asked me where exactly I thought I wanted to go. I was sure he knew my life lay south, closer to the whites. He would not concern himself with my plans, nor did I expect him to. It was enough that I knew my mind.

As if he understood my urgency, we traveled far that day, crossing our camp of two nights ago shortly before dark and going on for a few more miles. We camped close to the bluffs where the cavalry battle had taken place, but with only two of us, we could make a small, obscure camp and no one would bother us. .

I prepared dinner and handed Barred Owl's to him. Sitting opposite each other across the smokeless fire, we ate silently. I kept my eyes down, wondering what he was thinking and if the feeling I had of being watched was from him.

"How do you need to go?" he asked finally. "Do

you wish to go back east, to the white village where you met Red Cloud?"

"No. I do not want to go to any large white village. The place I want to go is west, close to the beginning of the South Platte River. It is close to the base of the high mountains."

Barred Owl nodded. I wasn't sure if he knew the place I spoke of or if he was simply satisfied with my directions.

"Tomorrow we will turn west, then. We can cross that way and down the prairie toward your village. I think we will have two or three days' ride."

Although our relationship seemed somehow more cool than it was, I placed our beds close together near the fire. Barred Owl insisted I go ahead and sleep while he stood watch, but in the morning he was lying close beside her.

That day we talked considerably more. He pointed out things around us—small animals that hid from us or the dust kicked up by antelope miles away. Since we had veered away from the band's trail and were now in territory unfamiliar to me, I was more interested in the land around us. Sometime after noon I realized I could make out the dark hues and clouded tops of mountains on the western horizon.

That night we camped on the plain with hardly a tree in sight. Barred Owl decided against a fire since it could be seen from so far away, and we made a meal of the jerked meat and berries Grass in the Wind had prepared. The hobbled horses tore at the buffalo grass around us and made the only sound except for the wind.

I prepared our beds and expected to see Barred Owl sitting awake on the nearest swell of ground. I was surprised when I realized he had been watching me. His face and eyes were expressionless, telling me nothing, yet not denying anything. I went to sit beside him.

"There have been many times I have wished that day at Dog Creek had been different," I said. "If I had not been stolen away, we would have married and been happy, as we planned."

"No one knows which direction the wind takes," Barred Owl said.

"No. In a few minutes it can change, taking everything with it on a new path."

"I wish that your path will be a good one," he offered.

I looked at him and found his eyes on me, intent as I had not remembered them being. It was almost as if he strove to understand me, something I had never seen in his eyes before. Feeling suddenly that no words could ever explain our differences, I took his hand and led him over to our beds.

That night I made love to Barred Owl as Jory had taught me. I kissed and caressed his skin, letting my fingers trail over it lightly. When he would speak or take the initiative, I brushed it aside and gently led him through all the pleasantries I knew. I kissed him deeply, exploring his mouth and touching off the nerve endings that made him shudder. I pressed him down on his bed and used my hands and mouth on his body, touching and inflaming and teasing until he reached for me desperately. When he was so aroused that he took command and forced me back on the ground, I let him cover and possess me, finally letting my own passions rise to meet his. The pleasurable sensations were enough to bring us both to a shuddering climax. Then we lay still in each other's arms.

"You said you did not marry," Barred Owl said finally. I knew what he meant.

"No, I didn't. And I may never marry."

"It is not a disgrace among the whites for a woman not to marry?"

"It is not well thought of," I admitted. "But it is still done on occasion." I thought about it for a moment. "I do not think I will ever live by anyone's rules but my own. I can't bend to what another thinks is right. I have to find my own way."

Barred Owl had no answer for that, as I was sure he wouldn't. I had chosen the path I would follow and he would respect that. He held me close to him until I fell asleep.

We traveled another day heading southwest, and the mountains grew larger on the horizon. That afternoon a raging thunderstorm massed above us and we took cover on the opposite side of a low butte. The lightning flashed and crackled around us, the thunder crashing loudly and almost spooking the horses beyond control, but we managed to wait until the dark clouds passed over us. Soaked to the skin, we rode only a few more miles that day before pitching camp. The storm had cost us hours on the trail.

The next day we rode more intently than we had before. Every hour or so I was tempted to ask Barred Owl how far we were from the white town, but I refrained. We began to pass through low foothills and mounded buttes, and in the distance I could see snow-covered crests of mountains. I knew we were getting close.

Shortly before dark I made out the wandering line of cottonwoods that marked a river or stream. I meandered some miles to the south of us, crossing the plains, then dipping southward along the low hills.

"We are near," Barred Owl said suddenly. So that was the South Platte, and Denver was built somewhere on that southern leg. I had trouble keeping the excitement from showing on my face and rather than have it sound in my voice, I remained still.

As dark came on, we slowed and rode carefully in single file, Thunder following the tracks of the bay. Occasionally I could see small lights blazing in the distance, probably from the windows of isolated ranches. Barred Owl chose our way carefully and we never rode close to any houses. Two Indians riding stealthily this close to Denver would not be welcomed with open arms.

I was intent on the ground in front of us, watching how the bay went around the low hills and gullys when Barred Owl pulled rein. I kicked Thunder up beside him and looked south. There, not more than two miles below us, were the lights of the white man's town. Sprawled across the rolling hills and growing outward from either side of the Platte was Denver. And somewhere in that jumble of humanity, I hoped, was Jory.

We camped in the bowl of the hills with no fire that night. I was nervous and lightheaded and I had to concentrate on preparing dinner and attending to Barred Owl. I was sure he saw my excitement, but he gave no sign.

"You will be happy here, in the white man's camp?" he asked finally.

I gazed at him and suddenly felt very sad that I could not stay with him. The love I had felt for him at thirteen could have matured and grown into a lifetime relationship if it had been left to us, but as it was, my love had shrunk into only respect and hopefulness. I still loved him, but not the way a wife should love a husband. That kind of love I felt for only one man.

"I may not stay here in this camp," I said, "But I know I will be happy. I will find my own way from here."

Barred Owl nodded. He seemed as regretful as I that things had not worked out the way we planned, but his own life was purposeful and ordered. Once back among the Cheyenne, he would resume where he had left off that day Red Cloud rode into camp, telling of the return of Painted Lance's daughter. It wouldn't be long before he ceased to think of me.

We made love again that night, desperately, as if the sadness we felt could be eradicated by the intensity of our motions. When I felt tears coming to my eyes, I forced them back with a more violent display of biting or scratching, holding Barred Owl to me as if my life depended on our union, spending every bit of strength I had in our last coming together. But when it was over I still cried, and Barred Owl held me in his arms and let my tears run unchecked down his chest.

At first light we rose and made ready for our separate journeys. I was extremely nervous, but I felt it was more for entering white society than for leaving Barred Owl. He was very quiet as he threw on his bow and arrows and strapped on a parfleche. When we had both mounted, he guided his horse up next to Thunder so our legs brushed.

"You will be all right, Gray Feather?" he asked.

"Yes, I'll be fine. I thank you for bringing me, and I am grateful to you and Grass in the Wind. I wish you many good days on the Powder River."

He watched me as I spoke and when I thought he would say something he only nodded. Suddenly he kicked his horse and had walked past me, north, leaving me standing alone facing Denver. I patted Thunder's neck and then we started down toward the city.

It took me almost an hour of easy riding to reach Denver. I passed countless ranches and farms, and in the early morning there were already men and women out tending their stock and they all eyed me curiously. I wore my hair loose and with my buckskins there was no mistaking me for anything but an Indian. They watched me carefully as I rode by.

When I guided Thunder down the city streets I already knew what I should look for. I passed the mining office, the churches, the stables and the general stores. At a cross street I looked down and saw the saloons and turned that way. They were strangely quiet, for the all-night poker games were over and the day trade hadn't quite started yet. The few traders on the street watched me curiously, but stranger things had been seen on the Denver streets.

There were several saloons, so I just picked the first one. When I walked in, the few patrons there eyed me strangely. The bartender's eyebrows raised quizzically, then returned to their normal place. I asked him if he had a big mountain man staying there. He looked me over boldly as I stood waiting, then finally said no. I went to the next place.

They had trappers renting rooms there, but none named Donnelly. The bartender there apparently thought me unworthy of his attention and dismissed me curtly, but luckily a man at a small table heard my request.

"It be the big Irishman you're looking for?" he asked.

"Yes, that's him. Do you know where I can find him?"

"If it be the same one, he's at the Lodestone, on down the street. It's a big place on the other side."

I rode directly to the Lodestone.

I should have known Jory would pick the least desirable place in town to stay. Being a loner as he was, he would want to stay out of sight and discourage visitors. The Lodestone was just the place to do both. Although big, it was dingy looking and the one girl I saw inside looked haggard and unkempt. I put her out of my mind and went to the bartender.

"Do you have a man named Donnelly staying here—a big red-haired man?" I asked. By this time, knowing I was so close, I was so excited that my speech came in a torrent.

The bartender looked at me funny but I was too single-minded to care. "We don't allow no women in here," he said finally.

"But is he here?" I asked.

"We don't 'low no Indians, neither," he added in a contemptuous voice.

"All right," I said, "I'll leave, but I have to know if he's here or not. Is he renting a room from you?"

He took his time wiping the counter before he answered. "Yeah, he's here."

"What room is he in?" I asked.

"Now, I told you, we don't allow no Indians and no females in here," he began angrily.

"Just tell me what room and I'll leave. I promise."

He glared at me, his mustache twitching. "Room two," he said sulkily. "Now git."

"All right, I'm going," I said. I turned to go, then spun around and ran up the stairs as fast as I could go. I heard the bartender shout for me to stop but I had already gained the landing before he had come around the bar. I hurried down the hall, having to look closely at the doors to see numbers in the dim light. By the time I found the door that said two I heard the barkeep stomping up the stairs after me.

I tried the door but it was locked.

"Jory!" I yelled, pounding on the door. "Jory, let me in!" The bartender was at the top of the stairs and heading for me. "Jory, please!" I said.

I almost fell inside when he pulled the door open. I ran past him, barely noticing that he held his gun, but when the bartender reached the room, the gun was all he saw.

"Now look here," he began hotly. "I told her weren't no women and sure as hell no Indians allowed in here. Now she's got to go."

"She's all right," Jory said levelly. "She's with me."

"I don't care who she's with, she's not staying here."

Jory cocked his gun. "She stays."

The bartender glared at us both, then at the gun. "I'll give you both about twenty minutes to get out of here, then I'm calling the law. You want your squaw staying with you, you go someplace else."

"Fine," Jory said. He closed the door and locked it again.

"I'm sorry," I said to him while he put his gun

away. "I didn't mean to get you thrown out, but I didn't know any other way to see you. I had to find you before you left for the mountains."

"You are the goddamnedest woman I ever met," he said, sitting on the bed. For the first time I realized I had woken him, and he had only just pulled his pants on to open the door. The bed was torn apart and the room was a mess.

"Now where in hell have you been for the last month?" he demanded.

"Oh, Jory, I'm sorry I couldn't tell you when I left, but I had to do it that way. Red Cloud took me to my people and I found my father and all the people I hadn't seen for so long."

"Including the man who probably already married someone else?" he asked.

"Yes," I said quickly, "including him. But I couldn't stay with him. That's not my way anymore, and I only realized it a few days ago. I asked him to bring me to Denver so I could find you. I'm sorry I left, Jory, and I'm sorry I couldn't tell you."

"You're sure sorry for a lot of things, aren't you?" he asked.

"I'm only sorry for the things that took me away from you. Now that I've found you I don't plan on being sorry for anything again." I went to him and knelt before him on the floor. "Take me with you to the mountains."

"Get up off the floor," he said angrily. He pulled me up beside him. "The only time I ever want to see you on the floor is if I'm there with you. And if you ever take off like that again and I have to spend a week trying to track you . . ."

"You followed me?" I asked incredulously.

"I tried. I followed you until what little supplies I had ran out. When I got back to Leavenworth I decided that if that was what you wanted, I'd have to let you go, but I didn't like it. So I'm warning you, if you ever take off like that again . . ."

"I won't. I promise."

"You'd better not. If I wasn't so damn glad to see you, I'd like to tan your backside."

"Are you glad to see me, Jory?" I asked.

"You're a goddamned crazy woman."

"Tell me you're glad to see me."

"I'll do more than tell you." He pushed me back on the bed and stood up to take his pants off.

"But, Jory, the bartender said we have to be out of here in twenty minutes."

"He can wait. We're leaving for the Rockies today and it'll be a long time before we have a regular bed to sleep in. We're going to take full advantage of it."

"I love you, Jory," I said when he came to me.

"You crazy halfbreed," he said against my neck. "I guess I love you, too."